Falling for Flynt
Bad Boys Book Three

Christine Young

Published by Rogue Phoenix Press, LLP
Copyright © 20202

ISBN: 978-1-62420-552-1

Credits
Cover Artist: Designs by Ms G
Editor: Sherry Derr-Wille

Chapter One

September 1826
Glasgow Scotland

Flynt MacTavish dismounted, handing the reins to the stable hand. He'd just spent the last few hours bored to tears with the beautiful Melessand. When he asked her to go riding with him, he never believed the time spent would be gossiping about the latest fashion and just how beautiful she was.

He looked at the dark sky. Riding home this late had not been prudent, but he needed to expend some energy and weigh the pros and cons of the lovely Melessand while he considered spending the rest of his life with her. Bloody hell, why did he suddenly decide he needed an heir. His sister Bliss with his best friend, Broc, had two boys and Chelsea, another sister and her husband, Cam, had a son. Two of the bad boys had met their demise at the hands of his sisters. So why did he want to follow them to his death? This courting thing was taking its toll on him.

A crisp breeze hit Flynt in the face when he strode outside the stable; a breath of fresh air, a much-needed one. Autumn was upon them. Leaves cluttered the ground, making swishing noises as he walked through them. A full moon appeared in the almost cloudless sky. He could be riding to see his mistress instead of going home to an empty bed.

For a moment, he thought about Beatrice, his second choice for a wife and to be the mother of his heir. She didn't prove much more interesting than Melessand. At least she didn't spend hour upon hour expecting compliments, but she had very little to say if anything. While he enjoyed silence at times, with Beatrice the silence was absolute and overpowering as well.

He sighed heavily, wondering why this had to be so complicated and uninspiring. Just a year ago he had no intentions of marrying anytime soon, enjoying his life at the fullest. His friends, the bad boys, started dropping like flies, to his sisters no less and they seemed to be in marital bliss.

Ah, he thought about Hope. Hope came to him quite unexpectedly. The sister of one of his friends, one of the bad boys, she was fragile yet beautiful and unassuming. Her memory of her past life was nearly nonexistent. Much of what she seemed to know was instinct, not memory. Hope was unlike any woman he'd ever known. Her friendship was priceless and he'd do most anything to keep it, including staying away from her.

As he strode up the front porch steps, he noticed a light shining in the parlor. Hope must still be up. He would enjoy talking to her while having a nightcap as he wondered if she'd waited up for him. Conversation with Hope always proved delightful, sometimes so spontaneous her words could leave him roaring with laughter or stealing his breath. She never failed to surprise him.

"Hello," he said as he stepped into the parlor after leaving his jacket and hat by the front door. "You're up late."

She sat up, pushing a few strands of flyaway red hair from her eyes. "Hello, I must have fallen asleep. And no, I didn't wait up for you. I was reading and the time got away from me." She showed him the book.

Her clothes were wrinkled and out of place while her face was slightly flushed. He thought she'd never looked more perfect, beautiful. In the light of the candle he could see a spattering of freckles across her nose and cheeks. He was, he thought, bored with perfection. The Melessands of the world be damned.

"Didn't mean to wake you." He grinned, striding to the sideboard and pouring himself a brandy.

He turned to speak to Hope, holding up a glass, "Would you like anything?"

She made an attempt to smooth her gown into place and rearrange her luscious red hair, pushing back the delightful tendrils that had come lose from the matronly chignon she wore. "Whatever you're having, I suppose."

"Did you wait up for me?" he finally asked again, curious as he brought her a full glass before sitting down beside her. "I know you said you didn't, but I'm not sure I believe you."

"I guess I did. I've something to tell you. Talk about." She looked at the brandy, swirling it around.

"You've piqued my interest." He watched her closely, picking up her hand in his as he smoothed a thumb across her wrist, delighted by the tiny shiver in response. "What is it you want to tell me?"

"How was your outing today with Miss Melessand? I do hope it was an enjoyable adventure." She avoided his question, which spurred his curiosity even more.

"So, it's to be this way, is it?" He laughed, appreciating her antics even though she appeared to be serious. "Take your time. I'm not in a hurry tonight. In fact, I'm wide awake and will relish some time spent in the company of an intelligent woman."

"Melessand is very beautiful, arguably the most beautiful woman in this part of Scotland." She smiled sweetly at him. "I'm intelligent. Thank you. I suppose those are words that should make a woman pleased."

Truly he thought Hope to be more beautiful, not in the classic way of great beauties but inside and out. "To hear the lady tell it, she is the most beautiful in all of Scotland and England, perhaps the world."

"That lovely?" She sipped, grimacing slightly when with the heat of the liquor as she swallowed.

He roared with laughter. "Her face, yes. Nothing else that comes to mind, however."

"Are you going to marry her?" she asked bluntly.

Rubbing his chin, he thought for a few seconds. "Not any time soon, if ever." No, he was never going to tie the knot with that woman. His life would be over as soon as he said the words, I do.

"You do need an heir," she reminded him. "I suppose you should think more seriously about that. Is Beatrice a better choice for you? She isn't as sweetly, sickening beautiful, but she is adequate. I suppose she would do in a pinch."

Do in a pinch, that was hardly good enough. He didn't want a life mate who would work in a pinch. "Yes, but I've just begun to look."

He scrubbed his hands through his hair, frustrated, irritated as well as thoroughly annoyed with this process. Instead of courting, he could spend his time in a more productive manner. Anything would be more fruitful. A lifetime with either of these two ladies, he realized, was not tenable.

"Neither Melessand or Beatrice will do for you?" She plucked at her skirts, not meeting his gaze. "I wonder why you're being so picky?"

He rose, agitated, pacing. "I don't have any other possibilities." Certainly not the sister of his best friend even though said friend seduced his sister and finally married her just before she gave birth to his twins.

"There are no other women who appeal to you?" Her head tilted slightly as if contemplating what she said.

"Not in these parts," he told her, understanding the lie even as he spoke the words.

When he turned his attention back to her, the look in Hope's eyes was sad. "That's too bad. Perhaps you should try your luck in Edinburgh. I've heard the women there are bonny lasses."

"Enough about me and my prospects. What about you? Do you have possibilities?"

He was suddenly concerned some of this strange conversation with her revolved around her, realizing the last thing he wanted was for her to see someone.

"You don't have to limit yourself to those two women." She smiled, setting her finished brandy glass on an end table.

He shouldn't let her put this off much longer, but at the moment he was enjoying the conversation. "They are both twits." Needing something to do, he picked up her empty glass. "More?"

He lifted an eyebrow studying her but didn't wait. He strode to the sidebar and the bottle of brandy.

She didn't answer, just nodded a wistful look now on her face. Then, "Please. I suppose another glass or two wouldn't hurt."

"Perhaps I will take a trip to Edinburgh for just that purpose. You could come with me. I've heard the earl of Sanford is planning a ball. There will be debutants there and gentleman as well searching for a woman to wed. Maybe one of those new young ladies will be more palatable to me." He handed her the refilled glass. "What do you think? Would you like to travel with me?"

She lifted her shoulders in a delicate move he appreciated. "You will do what you want, I believe. And no, the gossip would never end if I visited Edinburgh with you."

He laughed again. "You know me well. Yes, I do believe I should consider the ball in Edinburgh. Nothing better for me to do than to put myself at the scrutiny of young debutants searching for a husband. I've been bored these last few months and the trip might prove interesting. Would be more interesting with you as my guest though."

"When you put it that way," she spoke softly, tilting her head to one side. "I wonder what a man like you must go through to find that perfect woman to fill his life and give him an heir. Seems a bit beastly to me."

"No more beastly than a woman searching for a husband of wealth who can give her baubles and gowns, as many as she wants." He rubbed his chin thoughtfully. "I would have to be careful with her pin money, wouldn't I? A woman who wanted nothing more than what I could give her would be worse than if I was a wastrel."

"Would you be heavy handed?" she queried. "Knowing you, if you loved her you would most likely give her anything she asked for."

"Within reason. Love..." He paused a moment in thought, "Don't know what that is. I do believe it's a feeling, some emotion that would make a man weak and vulnerable. Don't like those thoughts at all."

"What is it? Your perfect manly self would never be weak," she said, watching him it seemed for a reaction to her statement.

No, he would never consider himself weak and neither would he fall in love. That was not for him. "I would have to keep the upper hand in a relationship. Love is not for me." Changing the subject, "We still haven't spoken about you. What was it you want to talk to me about?"

Her eyes closed as she waved a hand in front of her face. "I'm exhausted. Perhaps we could speak of it tomorrow."

"Too much brandy," he murmured huskily, even while he poured her more, unsure if the alcohol would loosen her tongue or put her to sleep.

She sat up straight, her back stiff, amber eyes flashing. "Then why do you keep giving me more?"

"Hmm..." His grin was knowing and pure male. "That's a good question. I don't know except I do enjoy you when you are more relaxed, not intoxicated, just sleepy-eyed and stress-free. Sometimes your back is just too stiff. You seem to hold everything inside yourself."

He sat down next to her again. Her hand in his, he pressed gentle circles on her wrist, enjoying the way her eyes grew wide and seemed to shine with what he knew to be desire.

What would it be like to experience her raw passion? She had learned so many ways in the harem she grew up in to please a man. At least that's what she'd told him. Perhaps it would be nice to experience those sweet things she knew but kept to herself.

She swallowed, looking away from him but not withdrawing her hand from his. "I'm going to move out."

The earth seemed to stop for an instant. "You're what?"

He felt blindsided by her sudden statement. He'd never imagined when he walked into the parlor, she would shock him this way. When she said she needed to talk, he'd thought it would be something frivolous like buying more rose bushes, which of course he would say yes to.

Moistening her lips then tucking the bottom one beneath her teeth, "I'm moving out," she repeated quickly as if she was trying to convince herself. "There is nothing here for me. I feel as if my life has no meaning and that it is passing me by. I, too, would like to find someone I can share my life with."

"You can do that and still live here. Why?" he asked abruptly, his heart racing.

He didn't want her to go anywhere. She was a constant in his home as well as his life. Bloody hell, but she was an intricate part of his life, a meaningful part he didn't think he could do without.

She met his gaze now, seeming to make her point. "I just told you. Just as you want an heir, a family, a wife, I need to move on and find some of those things for myself. When you wed, I'll be in the way and underfoot. I don't want that for myself or you."

"I don't understand." She was a servant, a trusted one but a servant nonetheless. "Why would you be in the way?"

"I would feel out of place. That's all." She didn't meet his gaze as she smoothed her skirt.

"Blessed hell, I don't see why. You're a servant."

"Nothing more," she finished for him, a small tear sliding from her eye which she turned from him and quickly brushed it away with the back of her hand. "Not really a servant. I work for you only because I don't want to be in my brother's way or underfoot in his household."

Anger built inside him, his fists tightening. "You know that's not true. You're more than someone who works for me. You're important to me."

"Do I? Whatever have you done or said to make me feel as if I was more than a servant to you?"

"I don't understand."

"You don't. Needless to say, I don't believe you. If you ever took the time to listen, you would comprehend everything I'm telling you." Her back stiffened again. "I'm moving out."

"Where will you go? My ex mistresses' townhouse is available." He knew the moment he uttered the words, it was wrong of him. She would never accept a proposition of the nature he just offered.

"I will give you the benefit of the doubt. Not for a second do I believe you meant that the way it sounded. You would never ask me to be your mistress. I also don't think I have to tell you, I'll never become your mistress, just as I risked my life to leave the harem for that same reason. I won't be the pawn of any man."

Trying to tamp down the rising anger and the pain in his gut, he tried to unclench his fists at his sides, "Where will you go then?" Yet he understood she had options.

Her brother, Broc, would provide for her. His sister, Chelsea, would do the same if she asked. Arie, the sultan who followed her to Glasgow, would make sure she lived in comfort.

"My brother has offered me his ex's home. However, unlike your offer, the good people of Glasgow won't believe me to be my brother's good horizontal." She seemed beside herself with emotions, anger rising with the force of each word.

She was cross now and perhaps annoyed as well. He read it in the lines around her eyes as well as the pursing of her lips.

"My apologies." He bowed deeply. "Guess I don't want to see you leave. I enjoy your company too much. You are a breath of fresh air in this crazy world I've found myself in."

"Life goes on. It makes no difference in the scheme of things if we have good conversation or not. There is nothing here for me and like you, I'd like a family, husband and children."

A sudden wave of jealousy swamped him. If he'd been standing, the sensation would have sent him to his knees. He'd do anything in his power to stop that from happening, but that was all wrong too. He forced a calm to settle inside, something he truly didn't feel. "Do you have someone in mind? A suitor who would be appropriate for a husband."

She plucked at her skirts again. "I do but I haven't met him yet."

Her voice was so soft and small he needed to bend over to hear her. "Does this person have a name and does he know how you feel?"

Her face slightly flushed as she blinked and stared at him, "He does and no. I'm not sure I know as of yet."

"And..." It seemed to Flynt she was forcing him to drag the information from her. She didn't want to give him any knowledge he didn't ask directly for.

"Angus," she told him then with a bit more volume, "Angus Kinross. He works with Cam at the university."

"How did you meet him?" He tapped a finger on his chin. "You've barely been anywhere." He didn't like this idea of Hope being courted by a male. Well, the devil, who else would court her?

She shrugged, looking away from him, seemingly unwilling to meet his gaze. "As I said earlier, but you don't listen, I haven't yet."

He knew once again his friends, the bad boys, were interfering in his life. He was happy though, she had still to meet this man who was taking her away from him. "How do you know you'll like him?"

She smiled then, "Cam says he's ever so nice and gentle as well.

He called him a gentle giant. He as big as Thor, or as big as the Norse God was rumored to be."

"That must be nice," Flynt murmured, wishing he had a better hold on this conversation while he planned to pay Cam a visit tomorrow in order to find out exactly who this Angus Kinross was and what he did to deserve to court Hope. "Cam should keep to his own business," he blurted.

"Why would you say that? He's just trying to help me." Hope sounded defensive, her frown lines deepening with each of his questions. "Broc told him I was moving out and why. Seems you should keep to your business. This really doesn't concern you. You have no hold on me. I am, after all, your servant."

Yes, he should but he always thought Hope would be part of his life forever. His voice hoarse and heavy with unspoken emotions, "Want to see you safe and happy, that's all."

"That sounds better." She smoothed her skirts again, her fingers winding into the fabric negating the previous gesture.

He would give just about anything to know what she was feeling, thinking, other than nervous. "When are you going to meet this guy? How did you say Cam knows him?"

"You haven't been listening to anything I've said. This guy is Angus and he's a mathematician at the university. Top of his field; he does these amazing calculations for Cam and his astronomy. You know, they chart the stars and the galaxies, things like that."

"What the devil do you mean?"

"I'm not sure. Cam said something about charting the distances to stars and planets. Think I heard the words solar systems. It's all somewhat over my head since I cannot even add a few numbers. Would like to learn though."

"A real paragon of virtue," Flynt said sarcastically, an intelligent man. He wondered if he was just smart or wise in the ways of the world. If they wed, would he know how to give her a woman's pleasure?

"You don't have to act that way." She stared at him, his lips actually.

"Back to my first question. When are you going to see this

mathematician?" Flynt couldn't tamp down the jealousy. Didn't want to in any case.

"This weekend, don't know if I should tell you anything else." She yawned, slumping a bit in the chair. "I am tired. We should put off the rest of this discussion until tomorrow."

"There is more?" He sat down beside her again, wishing he dared kiss her.

She was staring at his mouth, and he had the distinct impression she wanted him to kiss her, no, was subconsciously begging him.

"He is taking me to a competition, caber tossing I believe was what Cam said. He's a contestant. It's a highland celebration and there will be lots of things beside the caber toss, like dancing and all kinds of food."

Flynt was nodding his head, thinking of all the things to do. "I suppose he's the best too."

"That's what Cam told me. He almost always wins." She yawned again, moistening her lips and seeming to suggest other things.

"Suppose he's wearing a kilt also." The thought sent another jealous bolt knifing through him.

"That I wouldn't know, but I can only assume. What does one wear to toss a caber?" She yawned again, closing her eyes. "Should probably go to bed before I'm forced to sleep here on the sofa."

"I wouldn't allow that." Smiling, he watched her as she tried to stand, pushing from the couch only to find herself back in the same position as she was before.

"Can I help?" He extended a hand as an offering before he swept her into his arms and to her bedroom.

She nodded her approval, "Perhaps I drank too much."

"Perhaps you did," he agreed, wondering just how he was going to keep himself from kissing her, tossing her on her bed, making love to her, in the process ruining her for Angus Kinross. With Hope in his arms, Flynt carried her to her bedroom.

Sitting on Hope's bed and holding her so close, he felt one with the world. This feeling inside him was right, so what was he going to do about it?

She sighed softly, opening her eyes now. One soft fingertip stroked his jawline. "Kiss me, Flynt."

"Kiss you?" He chuckled, "You're smashed."

"No really, I want you to kiss me. Need to have something to compare." Her tongue darted out to moisten her lips, her gaze resting on his mouth.

She must not realize how provocative that simple gesture was. When he stepped into his parlor a few hours ago, he had no idea the evening would end this way. He wasn't going to turn down an invitation such as this one, even though she was half asleep and had clearly drunk too much.

"If you insist, I never turn down a lady," he whispered so close to her lips he was sure she would feel his breath.

"I do," she closed her eyes, waiting. "Insist."

"Open your eyes, sweet lassie." His lips found hers, touched, explored before his tongue delved inside, finding the soft inside of her upper lip then the edge of her teeth. She was sweet and hot. Her softness intrigued him as well as her willingness to allow him inside. Her tiny sounds of pleasure sent him over the edge. All he could think of was discovering more of her, all of her. That discovery would have to wait for another time. He liked his women willing but also of clear mind when he pleased them with his sexual expertise. He wondered if Angus could claim that thought.

It seemed she relaxed in his arms. She was asleep, soundly asleep. She would never remember the kiss and would have naught for comparisons sake. He laughed at himself as well as his thoughts of making love to her. Even with her strange and erotic upbringing, she was by far too innocent for the likes of him.

What to do now?

She wouldn't sleep well, not if she went to bed wearing her clothes and her corset. He could undress her, perhaps without looking at her. No, don't get too far ahead of yourself, old chap. No way in hell could he do that when presented with such a golden opportunity.

With Hope totally uncooperative, Flynt managed to remove her dress and corset, leaving her with only her chemise to cover her. He looked at her then, her soft feminine curves. Groaning, he pushed more carnal thoughts from his head.

He couldn't help himself. He continued looking, dreaming about her as well. She was slim, her breasts perfect, seeming to invite him to taste. Nope. Walk away before you do something you'll forever regret. Pulling the covers over her, she woke.

"Flynt?" The question in her voice stopped him as she sat up, her covering slipping to her waist.

"Yes." He sat beside her, wishing he had permission to touch and explore, to curl up beside her.

"Stay with me tonight." Her hands rested against his chest, imploring him to heed her request.

"You wouldn't like it when you woke up," he argued to no avail. "There would be regrets and recriminations on your part.

"I don't like to be alone. You're here with me now." She closed her eyes for a second. "Please don't go away. I've been so lonely. Sometimes I want to cry."

Cry? So lonely? "You won't like it in the morning," he told her again, knowing he was too close to accepting her proposition.

"I don't care." Her voice was soft, her breathing shallow.

He could see the pulse point at her neck, which was beating rapidly.

Blessed hell, but she wanted him. It wouldn't hurt he told himself. Her invitation was not the one he would have preferred right now. Nonetheless, how could he refuse? "Very well."

He strode to the other side of the bed, ridding himself of his shirt and sitting on the bed to remove his boots. Prudence told him he should leave his buckskins on despite his preference to sleep naked.

She watched him, staring at him while he settled in next to her. Pulling a quilt from the end of the bed over him, he wrapped her in his arms. "Go to sleep now. I'm here and I won't leave until morning."

This was heaven and he was a saint for his gentlemanly behavior. In the morning he could give himself a pat on the back. In the morning, she would be shocked to find him in her bed. He could effectively get rid of Angus by regaling him about her and their escapades.

He was a cad, yet...

The raging thought held too many beautiful possibilities

~ * ~

"Bloody eyes," Hope murmured as she opened blurry eyes to discover a pounding head and a man's arms enfolding her. The sweet kisses, she paused in thought. It had to be Flynt but why was he in her bed? The feel of his mouth against the back of her neck then down her backbone sent a myriad of shivers along her spine as it did everywhere else.

She wore next to nothing, she realized as she ran her hands along his strong arms. Turning in his embrace and discovering him naked, sleeping with her didn't seem prudent. This was exactly what she'd been trying to avoid for years. Why her mother helped her escape the harem and the fate that waited for her if she stayed. What to do now?

With his lips he caressed her ear, tickling the lobe before gently worrying it with his teeth. Her body heated, reacted as she unconsciously pushed against him in response. She wanted more. Yet...

"No." She pushed away, sitting up her sheet held tightly to her breasts. "Flynt, stop. What are you doing in bed with me?"

When she finally turned and looked at him, he grinned at her, a charming very Flynt grin. "Why?" he asked, his voice husky with what she could only assume was desire. "After last night and what we did together, I would think you'd be more than willing to do those wonderful things again. You are wonderful, you know. Besides, you invited me into your bed. Don't you remember?"

"I did not. What did we do last night?"

Her breaths were rapid little pants, which she tried desperately to slow but to no avail. She clung to the sheet, her grip tight, not wanting to let the meager covering go. Her modesty had been important to her, but he must have seen all of her, touched and explored her. She groaned, thinking of all the possible consequences.

"You don't remember? Well, you did have a bit too much to drink and while I'd never taken advantage of a woman in an inebriated state, you did beg me. I recall your sweet please clearly. So, I thought to myself. What to do? I couldn't very well let you down. After all you begged me to make love to you."

She wanted to cosh him over the head with something hard, but all she could find was her pillow. "I did nothing of the sort. I didn't beg for you. I wouldn't. I've never wanted such a thing for myself."

He smiled again, gazing at her lips for a second. "I'm sorry you don't remember. Perhaps we could try again tonight or right now for that matter. It is a disappointment to me when a woman doesn't remember the pleasure I gave to them."

"Stop it." Her hands on her face, she felt the rush of heat to her cheeks. Quickly, she reached for the sheet, which had fallen. "Don't say another word." She pointed at him, her hands shaking. "I think I would know if we did that. If you did that."

"Did what?" His grin widened.

"You know."

Now his grin seemed to reach nearly from ear to ear, his perfect white teeth showing. The silence unnerved her more than his accusations.

"Go away." She pushed the sheet away from her then looked at herself and the view she presented to him. Her body had been his to see yet he still wore his buckskins and while his shirt was unfastened, it hung loosely from his shoulders. His chest was well muscled, his body so hard and fascinating, intriguing. Her fingers itched to caress, explore, and discover every hard inch of him.

"Cook sent coffee and pastries," he finally spoke. "Are you as hungry as I am?" He stared at her breasts as if he wished to devour them.

"Cook knows you spent the night? Stop looking at me like that." She swallowed hard, thinking, trying to defuse the gossip before the rumors found their way to Glasgow.

"Like how?"

"As if you want to devour me."

"Oh, can't help it. It's true." Changing the topic back to the cook. "All she knows is that I brought you breakfast. Told her you had a headache and she claims her coffee will cure everything that ails a person. She also sent a bit of laudanum if you wish it. I would advise against it though. Heard it could be addicting."

"My stomach is churning." She inhaled deeply, terrified of asking her next question. "I'm not a virgin anymore?"

"I wouldn't say that."

His voice took on a different tone. One she couldn't define. When she looked at him, she couldn't stop the tears from flowing. This was not how she planned her life.

He sat beside her, pulling her into his arms, running his hands along her nearly naked back. "I'm sorry. That was not well done of me. I got caught up in the moment and wanted to tease you. We didn't do anything last night. Had I taken your virginity, there would be blood as well as my seed on you as well as the sheets. Forgive me for being so blunt but..."

She remembered the women in the harem after sex. What he said was true. She coshed him on the head with her pillow. "I'll never forgive you for that." She hit him again and again until he roared with laughter, falling back onto the bed.

"Telling the truth? I give up. I surrender. Promise to lie to you just so you won't hit me."

"Don't you laugh at me." She hit him again then again, putting all her efforts behind each blow.

Grinning still, he tackled her, rolling on the bed with her, laughing, holding her hands over her head. She stared at his mouth, couldn't help herself.

He was resting on top of her, bracing himself with his forearms. "You shouldn't do that. It's foolhardy of you."

"What?" She felt his length against her, his sex hard against her belly. He'd spread her legs and he was lying between them. She gulped air.

"Stare at my mouth." His eyes blazed with raw passion and desire and a hunger she'd never seen blazing in his eyes before. Letting go of her hands, he traced her eyebrows then along her jawline. "I'm hard pressed to resist you. You enthrall me, never bore me and you're definitely not a twit."

From what her mother told her about men, he hungered for her.

She saw the passion in his eyes and couldn't help the sigh. "Your mouth, it's beautiful and soft, so different from the rest of you."

"You know your lips are asking me to kiss them."

Hearing his words sent a wave of desire rippling through her. "That's impossible." She tried to be strong. "My mouth wouldn't ask that."

He chuckled. "Little liar, nothing is impossible."

With his teeth he gently tugged at her bottom lip, pulling the soft flesh into his mouth, running his tongue across it, soothing the tiny nip.

Her fingers beneath the fabric of his open shirt, she clung to him, reveling in the way he felt against her hands. She yearned for more than she should, more than she had any right to ask for. Tell him no. She couldn't, in any case she didn't want to lose this magical moment with him. These few seconds might well be the last for her.

His breath whispered against hers, "Open for me, sweet lassie. Open your mouth so I can reach inside. I need to taste you."

Unable to resist the temptation he offered, she did as he bade, felt the pressure of his lips as they closed over hers, gasped as his tongue slid inside caressing hers. He explored and she responded. Primal hunger filled her, touched her soul. She loved him. Loved him desperately yet he didn't reciprocate. All he wanted was sex with her. She understood what drove him. Still, she couldn't refuse.

His hands settled on her waist then rose, enticing, caressing over her slightly veiled body, the chemise she wore would never protect her from the raw desire he enticed. Heat raced through her, the inferno building with each mysterious stroke of his fingers. The fantasy he wove around her would vanish as soon as he left. Then her world would crash down around her and bring her shame.

His lips found hers again and again. She moaned, unable to stop herself. Running her hands down his torso, she basked in the feelings encompassing her. She should stop him now. *Stop.* Now before it was too late and she really did lose her virginity.

Her body arched against his as his lips found a nipple. "Flynt..."

"Sweet, sweet lassie, you taste so wonderful." He paused in his attentions to her, smoothing her hair away from her face, gazing down at her. "I should stop. You should tell me to go away."

"I can't." She sighed into his mouth as it once again closed over hers.

It was true. Sometime in the last minutes, she lost the will to turn him away. It seemed he didn't want to stop either. If this would be her undoing, she would have no regrets.

She held on to him, pulling him closer, never wanting to let him go. Against her belly she felt his hard arousal pulsing against her. She arched, searching for something, for some fulfillment she didn't understand.

"Sweet lassie." His hands roamed the length of her leg. "I want to kiss you everywhere. It's just kisses," he whispered. "Kisses never hurt anything. Innocent kisses." Again, his lips closed over a veiled nipple as he pulled it deep into his mouth.

She was mindless now, quivering, needing him and knowing his kisses were not innocent. "Flynt," she sighed again. "What you do to me..."

Suddenly he left her, pulled away by an unforeseeable force. "Get off my sister." She heard the words, tried to register them in her head. *Broc?*

Sounds of knuckles hitting flesh, grunts then a moment of silence while hard breathing followed. She sat up, once again holding the sheet against her, shocked to see her brother standing over Flynt, his hands fisted at his sides.

Siting on the floor, Flynt rubbed his chin, "Guess I deserved that." He was staring at her though, still smiling. "Suppose I should leave now."

"Not so fast." Broc stepped between him and the door, looking from Hope to Flynt. "What are your intentions? I'm not going to make the same mistakes you did."

"Ironic, don't you think," Flynt said. "You get to make love to my sister, leave town never caring to find out if your seed took root and now you want to hold me accountable for something I haven't done yet."

"Only because I got here before you could take what you wanted. Did you ask her for her hand? Did you commit to her in any way?" Broc gritted out, the lines in his face still pressed together in fury.

"I wasn't going to take what I wanted," he spoke, shrugging nonchalantly.

"Get out, both of you." The men turned to Hope. "Get out now and Flynt, don't come back. Broc you can wait for me downstairs. This has been the most horrendous night and morning. Both of you, you've mortified me to the tips of my toes." She couldn't stop the tears from filling her eyes and falling down her cheeks.

"I promise you, Hope, I will come back. We've things to talk about, and I'm not going to leave them unsaid." Flynt grabbed his boots, heading out the door. Before the door closed, he stopped to look at her one more time.

"Go to the devil." She didn't want to see either man. Embarrassment heated her, rushed through her. Covering herself with the sheet, she hid from them, holding her breath until she heard the door close and both men's booted steps heading away from her room and down the stairs.

Trying to calm herself, her shaking nerves as well as come to terms with what she'd just allowed Flynt, she was shocked to hear the door open. A very soft feminine voice followed. "I've your bath water, Miss Hope. Master Flynt ordered it. May we come in?"

Still beneath the sheet, "Yes," her voice wavered as she still felt nearly spineless from the encounter with Flynt. None of this should have happened. She knew better. Thank her lucky stars Broc came by.

What did her brother want?

Well, she supposed she'd find out soon enough. She didn't understand men, didn't think she ever would. Now, she meant to take her time and make them stew downstairs for as long as possible, hoping they would have something better to do with their morning and leave.

"Your bath is ready, Hope." The maid left the room.

Once again Hope waited to hear the door close behind the woman.

Warily she sat up, still clutching the sheet against her. They were gone, thank God, but Broc would expect her to explain herself to him. Well, her brother could wait in hell. After all she was an adult woman and the only person she needed to explain herself to was her.

Now she began to understand Bliss' feelings a bit better. Bliss gave her brother all of herself and he'd run away, afraid to commit to her. Blessed hell, Bliss had twins just seconds after they were married. What kind of man did that to the woman he loved?

What possessed her to offer herself up as a virgin sacrifice to Flynt when she knew better, had counseled other women against doing just this sort of thing. She was smarter than that, but she suddenly realized this sex thing had nothing to do with intelligence.

Slipping into the hot water, she tried to rid her mind of the morning events. She found the feat impossible even while she closed her eyes. Shutting her eyes made it all worse. With her eyes closed, she imagined every heated caress, the evocative ways he stroked and kissed her, nothing innocent about his kisses and where he placed those kisses. He was a man who knew what he was doing.

A bad boy.

With a heavy sigh she sat up, washing all of her, retouching every place Flynt caressed. "I'm going to forget about Flynt, a man I can never have. Angus, a gentle giant, he sounded just right for her. She hoped his kisses would be as nice as Flynt's. If no, he would just have to do."

She supposed Broc was here to see how she was doing, maybe tell her a bit about Angus. She stiffened suddenly, water sloshing over the rim of the tub. What if Angus was here, right now, waiting downstairs with Broc to meet her? Good God, he wouldn't do that to her, would he?

Angus would know she had been with Flynt when Flynt walked through the parlor to leave. No, you silly ninny, Broc would never tell him and Flynt would never leave his home unless that was what he wanted.

Flynt might tell everything. This had all started because Flynt didn't think Angus was the right man for her. He wouldn't say the words outright, but he might imply by subtle innuendos that he just came from her bed.

He wouldn't dare.

He would.

Well, she still meant to take her time getting ready to meet her fate. Whatever that was. Letting the water sluice from her as she stood, she reached for the bath towel that had been set out for her.

Let them stew.

An hour later, unable to find anything else to do, she walked down the steps to find her brother sitting with Angus, visiting and seeming to enjoy each other's company.

He was handsome, in a medieval sort of way. When the two stood, Angus, she assumed the man was Angus, towered over her brother by almost a head and her brother was a tall man. His shirt tightened around his shoulders when he reached forward to place her hand in his. He brought her hand to his lips, gently kissing the back. "Hope."

"Angus?"

Against her skin, his red beard was soft and when he smiled at her, his green eyes twinkling, the expression was tender. "I'm very pleased to meet you, Hope. May I call you Hope?"

Beside herself with worry, she didn't know how to react to this man who seemed so sincere. He would realize soon she didn't reciprocate that tenderness, "Of course." At least the first question was easy.

She sat down, smoothing her skirts wondering, "Why are the two of you here? It's a long ways to come without good reason. I doubt if it was just to meet me."

"It was," Broc smiled at her "Cam thought you should get to know Angus before Saturday's outing, and I wanted to accompany you to your new home in Glasgow. Angus thought he would help out." Broc's voice was tight with emotions she was sure he didn't want to show.

"Flynt would have seen me to the house. Neither of you needed to come here." *And humiliate me.* The words were out before she could take them back. "Where is Flynt?"

"He left," Broc bit out, clearly still displeased with what he saw earlier.

"For town? For a ride? This is his home, why should he leave?" she asked, knowing she was ruffling her brother with each inquiry.

"Didn't ask and don't care," Broc said with a masculine shrug and an air of indifference. "Well then, perhaps we should be on our way. Is Angus coming with us also? I've packed a couple of valises and a trunk. They are upstairs and they are quite heavy. You should go get them."

Angus stood, shifting from one foot to the other, "Lass, do you still want to go with me tomorrow? You seem a bit restrained. After Flynt left..."

"My apologies," she murmured, lowering her lashes for a second, then, "My brother showing up here today without a note, anything to let me know he intended to surprise me not only with himself but with you has left me a bit on edge. I don't appreciate surprises such as this. It seems my morning has been filled with the unexpected."

"I would not have taken such liberties, rest assured, if Broc and Cam had not made sure to tell me multiple times that my presence would not be an imposition. Were they wrong?"

She felt the flush of color rise to her face. "It's not an imposition. Truly, I was looking forward to getting to meet you, of learning about you more thoroughly and intimately but not with an audience." She shot her brother an angry glare.

"You are not going to be intimate with Angus," Broc said, his voice harsh.

She noticed a flush rise on the part of his face the beard didn't cover. "Why don't you get my bags?" she asked Broc. "Angus and I could use a few moments."

"Of course," Broc said, reluctantly rising from his seat, his glare furious.

"I can certainly help," Angus started to stand.

Broc looked at his sister then Angus. "No, Hope does have a point. The two of you should have an opportunity to speak without big brother hovering. Perhaps the two of you can find something in common to share."

She watched her brother's back as he strode upstairs. "Take your time," she called after him.

"You're a bonny lass," Angus told her when she returned her attention to him. "One I would like to get to know."

"Thank you. Cam tells me you are a mathematician. Goodness, it's all I can do to add and subtract a few numbers. I would love to have your skills."

"I could teach you," he offered, a grin showing beneath the beard.

She waved her hand smiling. "You would probably just confuse me. You see, my education was not in numbers and letters. I was taught other things." Other things, such as how to seduce a man and how not to be seduced by one. She had not learned the second lesson at all, Flynt being proof of that fact.

"What did you learn? History perhaps, maybe literature."

Pursuing another answer was not what she expected. She smiled then knowing she couldn't tell him the truth. Flynt, she could be honest with him, because he knew most of her history if not all.

"I don't want to shock you. I would have thought Cam told you that I grew up in a harem. My mother was captured and made a concubine of a wealthy Turkish sultan. My education has been unorthodox at best."

"'Tis nothing to be ashamed of. One cannot control their past and the life they were born into. It's what you do after the fact that counts."

Goodness, but he was just too nice. "You don't care that I've learned a lot of things our society would scorn." He needed to know the truth before they invested too much time together and she wanted to know how much of her past he could accept.

"No, but you've piqued my curiosity." He smiled at her, sitting down on the sofa beside her. "Tell me whatever you feel comfortable sharing."

"Perhaps another time, if there is another time. I take it you're not one of the bad boys." She started another line of questioning, eager to leave her past behind at least for the time being.

"Bad boy?" He lifted an eyebrow. "Don't know what you speak of. I've spent my entire life trying to be good."

He had. "Didn't think you were one, but you're not boring like most who I've met who are not."

"Was there a compliment in there somewhere?" He laughed outright and she liked the sound of it.

She shrugged her shoulders flirtatiously. "I have a way of saying what is on my mind. I suppose a compliment did exist in the words. Tell me about your family and later I'll speak more of my life before I escaped and found my way here. You should know some things about me so you can make a decision."

His eyes grew wide as she thought they would yet his smile

remained. "I'm guessing, compared to your story mine will inevitably bore the tears from your eyes."

"Try me. Do you have siblings? I've one, Broc, and he can be overbearing as you just witnessed."

"I've seven siblings, four sisters and three brothers. Guess one could say we grew up poor even though my parents made sure we wanted for nothing, at least until they passed away."

"In a sense, at least until I came to Scotland, I had more siblings than you. In the harem there was always someone to play with as there was always a new baby. We are all half brothers and sisters. My mother only had me. I was never quite sure why until I was older."

He watched her with what seemed like avid curiosity. "I always excelled in school, numbers more precisely. Being crofters, the likely hood of attending the university was nonexistent."

"How did you get so lucky, assuming that's what you wanted?" She was curious now, intrigued by this man who worked his way to a better life.

"More than anything. The man overseeing the crofters and the crops noticed my capabilities and brought me to the attention of the lord who owned the land. One good thing led to another and I found myself studying to become a mathematician. It was the best thing that ever happened to me, and now I'm hoping you will take that place."

She swallowed hard, deciding she had to give this man a chance and forget about Flynt who obviously wanted her for only one thing. "You'll have to show me where you work."

"A tour would be in order. We can speak of a time after the competition. Perhaps on Sunday after, the students wouldn't be there."

"What do they do at games besides the caber toss?" She was interested in the highland games. "I've never been to anything like this. In some ways I'm a foreigner in the land I should have grown up in."

"Ah, so many things: dancing, piping, the toss and the hammer throw. I do both of those."

"It's time," Broc let the bags fall to the floor with a crash. "I'll send someone to get the trunk."

Her hand flew to her chest, surprised by the jarring noise. "You don't need to be rude."

"You should have let me get the bags. They look heavy," Angus said, rising to give assistance.

A slight flush rose to her brother's cheeks. "Nothing I couldn't handle. Did the two of you get enough private time?"

"Not nearly enough for me. We'll talk again on Saturday. We do have the ride into town to further discuss what we would like to do, perhaps the direction of our relationship." Angus picked up one of the bags before offering Hope an arm.

"I must tell you nothing happened upstairs with Flynt," Hope blurted as the stepped onto the porch.

~ * ~

Cam paced the parlor in Glasgow, his heart thundering in his chest. He just set something in motion he wasn't proud of but would have to live with. He stopped his pacing to watch his wife.

Chelsea sat in a chair, studying him while shaking her head. She was knitting something, booties or a baby blanket. He could never be sure until she finished. He was always amazed, the yarn coupled with the needles ever turned into anything substantial or recognizable.

"Cam, please sit down and talk to me. You're making me nervous and you're about to wear a hole in the carpet."

She set her work aside to listen to him, her gaze pointedly riveted on him.

He knew she wasn't going to let this go and perhaps it was for the best. "I set something in motion I now regret and it's too late to take it back. Even though I understood how Flynt felt about Hope, I did it anyway. Thought to put a spur on his behind, but I'm afraid it might have backfired."

He watched her inhale a deep breath of air, her breasts rising then falling as she exhaled. "Very well then, tell me what this is all about." She closed her eyes, sighing softly, a sound that was very endearing to Cam. "What does Flynt feel where Hope is concerned? I didn't realize there was anything between them. If there is something there, they both have managed to hide their feelings."

Cam strode behind his wife, his hands on her shoulders before bending to whisper into her ear. "He is as enamored of Hope as I am of you. He just won't admit to his feelings. I believe she reciprocates those emotions, but Hope on the other hand is hell bent not to be his mistress, which of course makes complete sense."

He felt the shiver his whisper created, thinking to take his wife to bed and forego this conversation, one that would inevitably result in an argument if he didn't do something to waylay it.

She turned then, pointing across the room. "Stop it. You brought this up, so until we are finished, you need to sit in that chair. I need to understand more than these abstract notions you have about the two of them."

"You do have a point, but your lovely ears, and neck, and well...your soft lips. I get side tracked way too easily. You have to do your part and stop enticing me."

He wondered why he didn't bring up this problem with Hope and Flynt after he bedded his wife. Too late now though, he would have to do her bidding. He left her side, striding across the room and taking a seat. He grinned at her.

"Cam, what makes you think my brother is in love with Hope? He's courting two women at the moment."

"Ah, yes," Cam stood again but prudently retook his seat across the room. Uncharacteristically placing his hands in his lap, "Have you ever noticed the way he stares at her? He's smitten, I tell you."

"So you say. What about Melessand and Beatrice? Has he no feelings for either of them? He has certainly put enough time into courting them." She picked up her knitting and the needles seemed to fly.

He drew in a long deep breath, concerned now that Chelsea wouldn't understand or agree with him. "Melessand is a twit. There is no other way to describe the woman, and Beatrice is a total bore. Lovely as she may be, she cannot keep her nose out of books. She is a true bluestocking. He could not possibly fall in love with either, and if he wed either one, he'd regret it the day after, perhaps even sooner."

She paused in her knitting "Let me get this straight. Flynt is in love with Hope but doesn't know it, and the two women he's courting, neither one is good enough for him. Am I right? What is wrong with reading? Beatrice must be very intelligent."

"That's it in a nutshell." He knew when he mentioned the books, he would be in trouble with his wife, and he didn't know how to explain himself.

"So, moving on, what is it you did that you now have regrets about?" She smiled at him. "This tale could prove to be very interesting."

"I told Broc about a man I know, a professor at the university, a mathematician. He's single and I thought it would be fun for Hope to meet someone, have a choice, you understand, and perhaps make Flynt a wee bit jealous."

"You also thought this man's attentions where Hope is concerned would prompt Flynt to make a commitment of some sort. You assumed Flynt would be jealous." She was staring at his mouth.

"Yes. Angus is a very nice man. Yes, I hoped Flynt would be jealous. You have an extraordinary way of reading my poor man's brain." He wanted to laugh at the emotions sweeping across Chelsea's beautiful face.

"So, he would be good for Hope if she liked him."

"If she liked him," Cam agreed.

"Yes."

"If you keep that up, I'll toss your skirts right here in the parlor." He rose, striding toward his wife.

"Not in the parlor and the middle of the day." She set the needles down again. With a laugh she picked up her skirts, racing up the steps.

He roared with laughter, knowing he would catch her before the bedroom. Perhaps he would lift her skirts and make love to her in the hallway. The bed would do for a second round.

Chapter Two

The morning was shrouded in mist. Flynt was hopeful the clouds would burn off and the sun would end up shining throughout the day. It galled him that Kinross won most of the competitions he entered. Caber toss. What civilized Scotsman still participated in such an ancient sport in these modern times? No need to scale walls or span rivers with logs anymore. What was even worse was that Hope seemed interested in the man, reported by Broc to him, just to irritate and annoy. The thought Hope liked that huge man, left a damper on his day. He would have to find a way to dissuade her.

Flynt picked up Beatrice at noon sharp before heading to the games. This time her silence was heaven sent. He didn't have anything to say to this strange woman who would rather read than participate in anything else, including conversation. Not that he didn't like an intelligent woman, but she carried it too far. On the way to the games, she plucked uneasily at her skirts and sighed what seemed to be every minute.

Both of them were clueless as to what to say to each other. Small talk obviously was not her strong suit, and he had no reason to speak to her about what was on his mind, Angus and Hope. She wouldn't understand he didn't want to be with her today but longed for Hope's company.

What on earth was going on and why did Cam do this to him and ruining the day? It seemed to him his world had been wrested from him and was slowly toppling. Was it revenge on Broc's part? He could only guess but it wasn't he who abandoned Bliss. It was Broc and as far as he was concerned there was still a lot of answering to be done where his sister was concerned. He didn't care if Bliss and Broc loved each other or that Bliss forgave her husband. He was a long way from forgiveness where Broc was concerned.

Unfortunately for him, Bliss didn't agree with him and neither did Grams. He remembered his last talk with his grandmother, and she pointedly ordered him to cease and desist from a confrontation. Broc was his brother-in-law now. He needed for family unity to forget what passed between the man and his sister.

"Here we are."

He stopped the carriage, smiling and trying to make this day a bit easier for Beatrice. Nothing would make this palatable unless he left with Hope. He didn't see how that could possibly happen.

"Are you angry with me?" Beatrice asked, placing her hand in his when he attempted to help her down. "I'd like to know what I've done wrong. Perhaps you would care to enlighten me."

"What? No, of course not, and you've done nothing wrong. I'm not angry just preoccupied." He wondered where this inquiry originated. "Why?"

"You haven't said a word to me. Most of the way here you looked distracted. I certainly don't want to be here with you if you don't like me."

She let him hold her by the waist so she would land on both feet and not hurt herself.

"Really? I didn't think you cared about small talk. You've always been so quiet."

He looked a bit closer at this lady who seemed to have more facets about her than he previously thought.

Beatrice was a small woman, with slender curves. Her breasts were tiny, barely visible beneath the fabric of her gown. She rarely wore anything that would reveal or tempt a man. Today she chose a pale blue gown, which did accentuate her light blue eyes, her blond hair tied severely in a knot behind her head. He didn't understand how he singled her out for a possible wife. Perhaps it was her complete indifference to everything or that she was the total opposite to Melessand.

"I've something important on my mind and didn't believe you'd be interested," he told her. His excuse sounded insincere even to him and he doubted if she would accept it.

"I enjoy talking with you even though I don't say very much. Your opinion means something to me."

She walked beside him, her steps small but she did interest him in an unusual way, just not as much as Hope.

"Tell me why you agreed to let me court you." He'd wondered about that several times.

A soft color rose to her cheeks. "Father." She paused, turning to look at him. "He wants me to wed even though I've not really found anyone interested in me. You're the first to overlook the fact I'd rather read than go on outings. Horses and I don't get along and I've been surprised you didn't want to ride somewhere."

He felt taken aback by her honest words. "I didn't realize..."

"Of course not, your mind has been elsewhere. Do you still want to take me to these games or would you rather take me home?"

She plucked at her skirts, watching him, the look in her eyes guarded.

He offered her his arm, an idea taking root in his head. Well, if he was honest with himself, as soon as he heard where Hope was headed today, he had an ulterior motive in bringing Beatrice here. "Let's enjoy the day together and agree that we're not suited for each other. We can be friends."

"Friends would be nice," she agreed with a halfhearted smile. "I do like you and your company as well."

"Friends it is then."

The sound of pipes, slow and drawn out assailed them, bringing a wistful smile to her face. "I believe we should follow the music. Mayhap we'll see something interesting," she said as she placed her tiny hand on his arm.

"You're right of course. We should eat something too, anything you like. I'm sure there will be an array of food offered."

The path was lined with trees, their leaves changing colors while rustling in the soft breeze that even now was chasing the mist from the ground. The day was perfect. If only he was with the right woman.

"Why is it you really want to be here? Just as this event is out of character for me, it seems to be the same for you."

"Again, you're astute. I need to keep tabs on someone. Her name is Hope and she's involved with a man I don't know. I fear for her safety."

Well, that wasn't the entire truth, but Beatrice didn't need to know that.

"That seems extreme for a bad boy, overt concern for a lady you're not involved with."

When he looked at her a bit of shock whirled though him. His fists tightened. "You've heard about that."

"I'm not naïve or stupid although I do disregard most gossip. You and your friends are well known in Glasgow for your assumed exploits."

"It is more chatter than truth," he muttered, taken aback by her revelation about his younger days.

Since Broc abandoned them a couple of years ago, nothing had been the same. In truth they'd never really been bad boys, but they enjoyed the title. While each had a mistress, and two of them still did, they never took advantage of women, never exploited anyone. He'd dismissed his own when he decided to court two ladies.

"Men like to be considered bad, naughty, perhaps. In the scope of things, the good people of Glasgow might have embellished your exploits more than necessary."

She smiled at him and he realized she would make some man happy, just not him.

He wanted to ignore her comment, pointing toward a colorful display of clan tartans, "We're here. What do you want to do first?"

"Why don't we find Hope and the man who brought her here. I assume you'll be restless until you see her for yourself. What is his name? Did you tell me already?" Beatrice asked.

"Angus Kinross, and no, I don't believe I've told you."

"Who is this Angus Kinross and why does he have you shaking in your boots?" she asked seemingly interested in the man. "Since you are interested in Hope perhaps this man might be more suited to me. Does he like to read?"

"A mathematician at the university who might indeed be interested in a bluestocking such as yourself." He noticed the play of emotions across her face and appreciating the fact she seemed to be thinking the same way. Then quickly, "Not that the label should be used."

"I do appreciate a learned man," then turning to him, "not that you are not," she hesitated, "learned but you have interests different from mine. We definitely would never suit. A long-term relationship would just not work for us. We are already bored with each other."

She picked up her step, seeming interested in meeting this man.

"I completely understand. I'm not on the level of the university professors, except for possibly Cam. He doesn't like the attention though. Would rather be thought of as a bad boy than a genius. So, we have always gotten along just fine."

"Do you think Angus is a genius?" she asked, her eyes shimmering with the possible disclosure. "I would like a man who could talk to me of important things, things that matter in this life and not just trivia."

"Quite possibly," he laughed. "That intrigues you? This genius status?"

"Oh yes, I doubt if the conversations would ever be boring." She smiled again then added, "Not that conversation with you is boring."

He roared with laughter. "You needn't worry about my feelings. I find you quite endearing but boring also. Neither of us knows yet if Angus would be more interested in you than Hope. Let's make finding out our mission for the day. What do you say? If all goes well, we'll leave with the proper person."

Her head fell then she looked at him, clearly disappointed. "He probably won't be interested. I'm so plain. Everything about me is uninteresting."

Flynt squeezed her hand, "No worries. I will do everything in my power to make sure Hope finds me more appealing. Beatrice, you are a beautiful woman. Unfortunately, you don't do the things other women do to enhance your good qualities."

"Thank you, you are a very sweet man. I'm saying that I haven't even met him but I've hopes."

"Flynt? I didn't expect to see you here."

"Hope, how nice to see you." He wrapped an arm around Hope pulling her close before winking at Beatrice. "Where is Angus?"

Inadvertently, Hope leaned into him before pointing, "He's on the field, over there. See..."

"Ah, the caber toss," Flynt said, a bit sarcastically. Then he turned to Beatrice, watching her closely for a reaction. "He's the big man wearing the Kinross tartan. What do you think? Isn't he a braw Scotsman?"

"I'm afraid he doesn't really appear scholarly. He is all brawn and raw muscle. Are you sure he is a mathematician?" she asked, her tone and manner skeptical.

Hope walked away, looking from Flynt to the woman he was with. Standing in front of Beatrice, "You are interested in Angus. I find that thought-provoking. What part do you play in this, Flynt?"

"Just a conversation I had with the young lady on the way to the games, nothing more. We'll leave you to congratulate your man when he wins. Come along, Beatrice. Let's get some haggis and something to drink. What do you think?"

"What?" She stumbled a bit, but he steadied her. "What are you doing? I thought I was going to meet him."

"Making sure Hope is jealous. I know she wants me, just hasn't come to terms with her feelings yet. She is out with Angus because her brother is insisting she find someone besides me, which I find quite ironic given our history."

"I don't think..." Beatrice began, her voice wobbling while gazing over her shoulder at Angus.

He interrupted her, touching her chin with a fingertip, insisting she focus on him. "You are going to have to trust me in this and have a bit more confidence in yourself. I've much more experience in affaires of the heart. After we eat, we can meet them together. I'm sure you will know immediately whether or not you are interested in your young man."

"I..."

"Yes, and if you follow my lead, I will make sure things go as we've calculated. Now, we must plan for tomorrow. That is very important. I want to make sure Hope and Angus make this decision on their own. According to Hope, Angus plans on a picnic as well as a tour of the science and mathematics building on Sunday. We will be there of course to convince them in some way the tour should be with you."

"This is so dishonest. I'm not sure I can go along with this premeditated scenario."

"You can if Angus is the man you want to court you."

Beatrice sighed, staring at her shoes, back to Flynt, then reluctantly, "Very well."

At the food cart, he paid for haggis and coffee for both of them before finding a place to sit and watch the games. The sun finally appeared as the day grew increasingly warm. Beatrice drew out her fan, methodically wafting cool air on her face.

"May we join you?" Angus asked as he pulled out a chair for Hope.

"By all means," Flynt grinned, watching as Angus sat across from Beatrice, his gaze riveted on her mouth then her eyes then back to her mouth. His plans would come to fruition sooner than later, he suspected.

"I see you won the competition," Beatrice said as she fiddled with the food in front of her. "Did you toss that log the farthest then?"

"The caber. Yes, as a matter of fact I did, but that isn't all we are judged on," he laughed as he squeezed Hope's hand.

"They are judged on their finesse," Hope answered for Angus. "In short he had or has the best form." She let her gaze settle on his broad shoulders. "And he looks the best in a kilt."

"Yes, he does," Beatrice mumbled, agreeing with Hope before turning red as she realized what she'd just said.

Angus laughed, seeming to feel no discomfort from the women's scrutiny. "I do enjoy wearing a kilt. There is so much freedom. Makes me wonder what life was really like one hundred years ago."

"Beatrice has told me the same thing, haven't you darling? You adore it when I wear a kilt," Flynt prompted, slanting her an amused grin. "You love my man's body. Don't you, sweetheart?"

For a moment she looked shocked at his proclamation then she smiled her eyes alight with humor, "Of course, you are so manly."

"We should go for a stroll and leave these two lovebirds to themselves. I'm sure they would like some private time to pursue whatever lovebirds pursue."

He treasured the scowl on Hope's face. She knew what he was doing and he was sure she wanted to toss something at him.

"Lovebirds?" Angus seemed puzzled. "We have only just met, but yes, we've a lot to talk about."

"I would think you and Beatrice are closer to being called lovebirds than Angus and myself. Are you wanting to steal a kiss in some secluded corner?" Hope asked sweetly, her gaze focused on him and he was sure his mouth then her gaze drifted lower to his crotch.

He choked.

He recalled their kisses a few days ago and he'd give nothing more than to pursue that in some secluded corner with her, but he was a patient man. He would pursue her when he was good and ready and not a moment before.

"Oh, we are and her kisses are sweeter than candy." Flynt gently touched Beatrice's lips with a fingertip.

Inwardly he grinned when Hope's scowl grew deeper. This was going just as he hoped.

Fortunately, Beatrice played along by smiling. "I..." she moistened her lips, "Shall we go for that walk?"

He wanted to hug her, delighted she was playing the game to perfection. "Are you through with your haggis? You must eat enough. Keep up your strength you know. For what I've planned you will need to be strong."

Ah, he saw that Hope knew what he was doing. Whether or not she appreciated his efforts was unclear at the moment, yet he understood she was with Angus only because of her brother.

"Yes, Beatrice, you must eat enough. I've heard from my brother that Flynt's appetites are huge, especially where women are concerned. He's insatiable you understand."

Angus slanted her a strange look then clearing his throat, "Should women speak of such things?"

"I, well, I don't know what is proper and what is not. I grew up with women and they spoke their minds to each other. It's important that we appreciate men and what they want from us sexually. Don't you think?" She smiled sweetly at Angus.

Both Beatrice and Angus colored at her words. "Hope, you embarrassed my little sugar plum. You should really watch what you say. Unlike you she is an innocent in every way."

At his words, Hope blushed and for a moment he thought he'd overstepped. He would apologize and undo all that he'd accomplished today.

"Your statement doesn't merit a response." She stood, knocking over her chair, her food uneaten. "Angus, would you like to go for that walk you promised me? I need to get away from this heathen."

"We'll meet you back here in an hour or so. Perhaps we can do something together," Angus said, seemingly oblivious as to what transpired between them. The two walked away hand in hand but with Angus looking over his shoulder at Beatrice.

Flynt sat back, his hands clasped in front of him, savoring the moment, his grin wide. Beatrice's silence confirmed the fact that she was confused, mayhap even frustrated. She was sure to say something in a few seconds. Still he reveled in the silence as well as the pure male satisfaction that was twisting through him. He would have Hope in his arms soon.

"What have you done?"

Sure enough, she questioned his motives as well as his expertise. "We can't make this too easy. The two of them must come to the same conclusion at the same time or they will forever think we manipulated them."

"We both know you are manipulating them."

"We won't tell them that. Now, if you've finished eating, we should take that walk in the opposite direction. We wouldn't want them to notice we are not taking advantage of the private time. Perhaps we should discuss our next step."

"Perhaps we should," she agreed as she stood, smoothing her skirt in the process. "You have more plans? It would be nice to know what shocking thing you will do next so I can prepare myself and not appear dazed. I don't think Hope believed anything you said."

"Hope is wise and worldly in these kinds of things. It's difficult to surprise her. She knows me. Perhaps Angus believed something."

"Because she grew up in a harem? I'd like to know more about that."

"Aren't there any books on harems? Never mind, they would probably be filled with fiction, pure fantasy nothing that would even begin to hint of reality."

"I've not seen any and most likely you're right about anything that is written as being untrue."

"You would have to ask Hope if she wanted to talk about her past life. While most of her previous life is known by her friends and family, it's not my place to divulge her secrets."

It was so true, he thought. Her life was in the past and now that he'd made his decision to wed Hope, she was not going to say nay when he asked. She had to be convinced simply because she was actually terrified of men and their base needs. She grew up seeing women go to a man with no choice or say as to whether they would be in their bed. For a long time, Hope thought that would be her fate as well. He grinned though. She proved the other night she was no longer averse to his advances.

"What do you know about Angus, other than he's a professor?" Beatrice asked as they strolled down the path.

"Not much." He allowed her to take his arm as they headed away from the games and into the surrounding park. "I know he's a friend of Cam's. I know that he's probably as innocent as you are in the ways of men and women. According to Cam, he's spent the last several years of his life studying and researching. You don't have to be afraid of him taking advantage of you."

"How do you know all this? Because Cam says so?" It seemed she didn't believe him credible.

"It's just an assumption on my part and my friend. Broc would have never suggested this relationship if he believed for one second the man was anything like us, the bad boys."

He grinned, realizing soon he would no longer be able to add that title to his name.

"From what you've told me, Cam was the one who gave Broc his name," she said. "Explain it."

"I can't. My guess is that there is some kind of game in this. Cam is a jokester at times."

"I believe we walked in the wrong direction." Beatrice pointed to Hope and Angus.

"We'll have to get creative then. Pretend you want this." Flynt pulled her into his arms.

"Flynt..."

For a second, he looked into her eyes. "Don't believe I've kissed you before. You're going to have to make them think this is something you want just as much as I do."

With that said, his lips molded across Beatrice's, his hands around her waist, drawing her close.

He heard the tiny gasp of surprise but also recognized the softening of her body against his. She responded by clutching his shoulders. If he was right, she enjoyed his kiss. Maybe he could teach her something about kisses that she could share with Angus when the time was right.

He pulled away from her slightly, his face still so close he felt her breath against his cheek. "When I kiss you again open for me. It's something Angus will want you to do."

"But..."

"Trust me."

"You're always asking me to do that," she whispered then his mouth was on hers again.

She did open for him, his tongue running along her lips before gliding inside. The startled gasped gave him reason to smile as he thought, once a bad boy always a bad boy. He wondered if Angus had ever given a girl his tongue, ever explored her body or touched her intimately. Once Angus realized Beatrice was the woman for him, he'd have to make sure the man knew how to pleasure a woman.

Angus clearing his throat behind him gave Flynt good reason to end the kiss but not before he made sure both Angus and Hope would see his hand on her breast. Beatrice had not protested the intimacy, but he also understood the innocent woman was so far out of her depth of knowledge he could have probably tossed her skirts and taken her where they stood. There would have been no protest.

"Really, Flynt, can't you wait until you get her to your house and your bedroom?" Hope asked, her voice clearly sounding agitated to him.

He hid his smile of success from her.

"It seems you don't know how to keep your hands to yourself."

"Jealous?" he asked with a wicked grin. "Angus, you really need to take care of Hope's needs. Have you kissed her yet?"

All he could think of was the one kiss they shared the other day and his urgent need to repeat the process.

Angus looked away then to Hope, "Did you want me to kiss you lass?"

Hope's back stiffened. "Not with all the onlookers. No, when you kiss me, I'd like it to be just me and you, somewhere private."

"Good, because I don't want to share you with the world or anyone else," he said but his narrowed gaze remained on Beatrice.

Flynt couldn't stop grinning all his plans were proceeding as planned. "That's what makes all this so exciting. Who knows just who will walk by and see me kissing my little sugar plum?" He placed a chaste kiss on her nose. She is so much more excited in these circumstances. Why, I could have made love to her here if I wanted."

"I would never let you do that," Beatrice protested, hitting him on the arm.

"Shall we see who is right?"

This time he placed a long slow kiss on her lips, his hand once again resting on her breast before he pulled away. Strange how he was not moved by the kiss, didn't want to pursue more from her, even though he teased her with that very thing.

After he pulled away, Beatrice's eyes were slightly glazed. She ran her tongue along her lips. "I don't want you to do that again, at least not here."

"You enjoyed my kiss, right?"

"We need to leave," Hope said, turning her back on him.

Beatrice nodded, unable for a moment to speak. Then, "Very much so but it wasn't right."

"You never told me no. I would have stopped if you said the word." His voice was a soft whisper of emotion.

He smiled, agreeing with her and wishing Hope had been in his arms. His experience allowed him to remain detached and he cursed himself for putting Beatrice in that position.

"I won't do it again. Come let's make plans to meet tomorrow at the university. I will stop by Hope's townhouse tonight and make sure she tells me her intentions then I'll send you a message. If we're lucky we won't have to wait until tonight. I'm still hoping to leave here with her."

"Do you think they are kissing too?" She touched her lips with a fingertip.

"They better not be," he growled, searching the park for a sign of the pair. Finding them sitting on a grassy knoll, he once more extended an arm for Beatrice. "We should pay them another visit."

"You don't know what kind of man Angus is. What if he is kissing her? What if he doesn't want anything to do with me?" she asked, clearly nervous at the prospect.

"As I said before, you need to have more confidence in yourself."

She lowered her gaze, once again staring at her shoes.

"In any case, together we'll make sure Angus only kisses you."

~ * ~

Her heart in her throat, Hope sat beside Angus, watching as Flynt and Beatrice strolled towards them. She wanted to cosh him over the head, knowing he teased without restraint.

Angus seemed oblivious to all that had been going on. He was talking now about his job and the young adults he was molding into mathematicians. She wished he'd stop and kiss her. Making Flynt jealous was at the forefront of her head but she was running out of time.

"When do you want your first lesson?" Angus asked, his smile genuine as he waited for her to answer.

"What?" Hope pushed hair from her face. "What did you say? I guess I wasn't listening."

"I thought you wanted to learn how to add and subtract for starters and perhaps something a little bit harder after that."

She blinked a few times, trying to bring her attention back to

Angus. The feat was devilishly hard, given the fact Flynt stopped and was kissing Beatrice again. How dare he and right in front of her. "Yes, I do want to learn." *Would you please kiss me?*

The man was oblivious to everything she tried. She'd been flirting shamelessly for several minutes now to no avail. "Should we start right now?"

She pulled her gaze from Flynt. *If I have to*, she sighed. "What do I need to do?"

She slanted him a smile, moistening her lips before leaning into him all the while staring at his lips. Damn, but it worked with Flynt. "I'm not completely lacking in skills."

He pulled back, a curious look in his eyes. "Let's start with the simplest calculation and go from there. On second thought what do you already know?"

"Well." She sent her gaze in Flynt's direction again. While she really wanted to learn more, this was not that time. She just couldn't find a way to concentrate. "I can add and subtract. Nothing big, no large numbers or complicated, but I can do numbers under one hundred."

"So, you know say twenty plus twenty-five," he prompted.

"I'll have to think about it for a minute." She sucked her bottom lip into her mouth, her concentration nonexistent. After a few seconds and the sound of Angus impatiently clearing his throat, she finally said. "Forty-five, I suppose. Was that right? Can we do this some other time? I'm not in the mood."

"What would you like to do then?" He seemed confused.

"Kiss me." She leaned into him, hoping he would come through for her. Now, before Flynt reached this spot.

Angus' eyes widened then, leaning forward...

"Ah, are we interrupting something," Flynt asked, scowling, his arms crossed in front of him, frown lines across his forehead deepening.

Angus jumped back, startled by Flynt's words. "No, nothing at all." Angus stood. "Suppose I should be getting you home."

"You don't need to do that. I'm going right by her townhouse on the way to mine. Why don't you take Beatrice instead?" Flynt smoothly handed Beatrice over to Angus.

Angus wiped his hands on his britches. "I could do that if Beatrice doesn't object." He looked relived and Hope almost laughed that Beatrice's position with Flynt was so tenuous. For herself Hope wasn't about to fall into Flynt's plans so easily and without making the point to the man that she wasn't going to allow him to manipulate her.

"Yes," Beatrice said, "yes, I'd like you to take me home. Perhaps we could discuss the Fourier Series or Argand's paper on how complex numbers could be represented on geometric diagrams." She smoothed her skirts, smiling at him.

His brows drew together as if he doubted what he just heard. "I'd like that. I've never met a woman who understood or even heard of any of those concepts. It will be a delightful endeavor."

As if remembering, "Hope, I will pick you up tomorrow at noon to give you a tour of the mathematics and science building."

Hope nodded, wishing Flynt would suddenly step in and tell Angus she wasn't going. He didn't.

Instead he held out his arm. "How was your day with the caber tosser?"

"You can't really mean to ask." She felt the sudden deflating of her ego. "He is not my type, and I would just as soon go somewhere with you tomorrow rather than suffer a tour. Angus and I are not suited. I have no idea what my brother and Cam could have possibly been thinking."

"An afternoon with me could certainly be arranged, but I would hate to disappoint the man when he seemed so enamored of you."

"He is not enamored of me. In fact, if I were to put it bluntly, except when he was tossing the caber, he was bored nearly to tears as I was with him. He is too academic for me."

"Beatrice is perfect for Angus, don't you think?"

"I wouldn't know."

She was in the middle of a huge pout and didn't want to answer any of Flynt's questions.

"Would you like to go home or perhaps visit the observatory? Cam gave me a key and showed me how to focus the telescope so we could look at the stars or the moon if you prefer."

"What else do you plan? I won't let you coax me to be improper with you even if it is a romantic environment."

She stared straight ahead, understanding if she looked at him, she would give into whatever he intended. She was stronger than that, smarter than that. Especially when she understood his man's needs. She wouldn't give in to hers.

He stopped and with a finger under her chin, he turned her face so she had no choice. One look into his eyes had her melting inside. It wasn't fair. If she thought about it, she could imagine his lips caressing hers. A kiss from Angus would not have left her wanting more. She knew it as certainly as she knew she would be in Flynt's bed sooner than later.

"The observatory it is." He placed his hand on her back, striding to the carriage. "I did enjoy Beatrice today, but I'd much rather spend the evening with you. Did you have a good time with Angus?"

"I saw you kiss her more than once," she accused, wishing she'd kept her mouth shut, understanding how envious she would sound and he wouldn't wait a minute to point that fact out.

"Jealous?" He chuckled, his hand moving up then down her back sending little shivers along her spine.

"Never." She stiffened her back, seeing the carriage waiting for them and wondering what Flynt had in mind for the evening besides the observatory. He wasn't wasting any time sending her sexual messages.

He bent close to her, whispering close to her ear, "It's not dark yet. Would you like to stop somewhere and get a bite to eat?"

That sounded innocent and it would delay the inevitable. She inhaled a deep breath calling on her woman's control, power she needed to parry his advances. Advances she knew would be forthcoming before the evening's end.

"We should eat."

"Some wine too?"

"We could forego the wine." She needed all her faculties to be attuned to his seduction ploys.

"Afraid of me?" he asked, his hand settling on her neck, stroking slowly. "I thought you were a bricky lass."

His gesture sent shivers throughout. "Very afraid. Perhaps terrified would be a better description of how I'm feeling."

"Of what?" His lips followed the path of his fingers.

"If you must know, of losing my virginity." She felt his hand tighten slightly, heard the slight hitch in his breaths.

"Maybe in the near future, but not tonight, my sweet lassie. I recognize your hesitancy and would never take anything you weren't more than willing to give."

"You could have had it the other day when you were in my bed," she admitted reluctantly, giving him power over her she didn't want him to have.

"Seduction, yes..."

"Seduction, you're an expert and while I've certain it is knowledge most virgins don't have..."

"You would succumb to me if I pursued you." He finished the sentence for her. "I will make love to you when the time is right, not a moment before."

"When you were kissing me, I couldn't think." It was the truth, she felt everything, every expert touch, felt and felt but she never thought of anything but the alarming sensations snaking through her.

"You will feel that way again tonight. I promise you though, I won't go the way of your brother and take your virginity before..."

"Before you wed me?" Blessed hell, she didn't know where that question came from. Flynt wasn't about to marry her.

"Perhaps or perhaps not. I will know when to make you a well-pleasured woman. When that happens, you will beg for me."

"Arrogant." She wanted to counter with some quick word that would put him in his place, but she could think of nothing.

He helped her into the carriage and while she tried to sit on the opposite side, he wouldn't allow it, following her.

"That doesn't make me less afraid."

"It wasn't meant to. Come, sit on my lap and I can begin to persuade you to enjoy more than kisses. I want you to feel so much pleasure with me you won't look to find it from any other man, especially not Angus."

Her heart raced and she could hardly inhale a breath of air. "Flynt really, can't this wait?" she asked, pushing away from him.

"It could, but neither of us wants to wait. Am I right?"

He touched the tip of her ear with his tongue then worried the tiny lobe with his teeth.

She gasped a shaky breath, "No, nothing could be farther from the truth. Waiting would be for the best, put it off, don't do anything rash."

"Why does your body tell me something different?" He nibbled kisses down the length of her neck, sipping as he went. "Even now, if I wanted to touch you intimately, you would be slick with your cream."

"Please," her voice quivered, shook even while she fought the feelings surging through her. What did he mean by slick with my cream? Something she'd have to ask Bliss or Chelsea.

"You don't have to beg. I want to explore every inch of you, but I do mean to take my time. A kiss before dinner and I'll be a satisfied man."

"Promise."

She knew her body needed him, cried out for him to pursue this until there was nothing more to chase. She felt strange and hot, just as she had when he kissed and touched her the other day.

"Whatever you ask, or want." He hesitated a soft chuckle pulsing around her. "Maybe not anything. If you ask me to take you right here in this carriage, I'd have to tell you no."

"You don't want that?" She believed he would cajole and tease until she gave into him.

"Not in the carriage, not our first time. There is a bit of romance in this man. I would not take your innocence so casually. Everything should be perfect for you, us, our first time."

Her hands rested on his chest, her eyes wide and her body responding to every word, each caress of his experienced fingers. Even while he spoke of waiting and romance, his fingers danced on her body. "I don't..." she closed her eyes, trying to remember what she was about to say.

"You don't what?" His hand cupped her breast, traced the line of her bodice before dipping slightly to explore the valley between. "I want to touch your nipples, suck them into my mouth. Would you like that, Hope? You need to experience a little bit more of love making each time we have the chance."

"Flynt, let me think. Blessed eyes, but you don't give me a chance to breathe."

She was making no sense whatsoever.

He stopped then, letting his hands fall from her. "I wouldn't want you starved for air." He grinned at her, his hands now at his sides. "I do want to taste every splendidly remarkable inch of you. Remember, kissing is just kissing. Even Grams says kisses are fine."

"You're enjoying this." She grabbed as much air as she could. "Your mouth on different parts of me is not the same as a kiss on my lips. Is it?"

Truly she didn't understand how kisses could be the same anywhere on her body. His words just weren't true.

"Of course, I wouldn't kiss you if I didn't enjoy it. Wouldn't touch your breast if it didn't make me feel pleasure. Don't you like this, what we are doing here? I know I do."

Sometime when she wasn't thinking, he'd pushed her sleeves from her shoulders and her breasts were bared to his eyes. His lips closed over one nipple, sucking, biting, licking and seducing. She gasped again and again as he continued the discovery of her. Her fingers wove into his hair, tugging him closer, needed him more than she would have ever believed. She arched her back, pushing herself closer.

"I like it too much."

When he pulled away, she rested her head on his shoulder, her hand around his wrist as if she meant to stop him. In any case, she could not, in fact didn't want to stop the sweet torment he was inflicting.

"Ah, my sweet lassie, one cannot like something too much. I'm glad to hear you appreciate my proficiency. Do you think Angus is pleasuring Beatrice?"

"Probably not." She closed her eyes, relieved he was giving her a moment to recover and catch her breath as well as some common sense. "Probably talking nonsense about some mathematical theory."

The carriage drew to a stop. He kissed her lips, a hard-fast kiss before pulling her bodice and sleeves to their proper place. "No one else is going to see you naked, feast their eyes on you. Only me. It is my manly duty to make sure of that."

"What are we doing?"

If she told herself the truth, she was incoherent, mindless and a heated mess, a woman who would allow him to do anything with her he wanted. She never thought to be under a man's power so thoroughly she would lose herself.

"Stopping to eat before continuing on to the observatory to look at stars and perhaps share a bit more of each other. Would you like to share more of yourself with me?" He hopped from the carriage before turning to help her down and acting as if he didn't expect an answer.

His hands on her waist then down to settle on her rear and bring her closer to him, increased the inferno rushing through her. "I don't know if I can eat anything. You've..."

"Do you feel that?" he queried smiling at her. "That's how much I want you, but I'm giving you time."

She nodded a yes without answering, unsure of what to say.

"You can say it. Yes, say I feel your rod, your sex, or any another word you want to describe me, my cock. You feel me against your belly and I want you to think of how it might feel when I'm deep inside you."

"It will hurt," she blurted without thinking but realized she truly didn't care if it hurt. She also knew that when he made love to her, she would feel the most wonderful pleasure.

"Only the first time. I don't want you to think about any pain I might cause. At least not for the remainder of the evening. Now, what would you like to eat? Some oysters perhaps. I remember Broc, or was it Cam, who fed his new wife oysters before they were married."

"It was Chelsea who ate them. She didn't have any idea about their so-called magical powers but I do. The aphrodisiac they possess is mild compared to others I've known."

"You have knowledge of other aphrodisiacs?" he asked, sounding too curious by far. "Is that something harem women learn?"

"I do know of them, have been asked to mix them before. They are cruel if used in the wrong manner or with too much intensity. Some men use them to exact revenge on unwilling concubines. However, a tiny dose can make a woman willing and compliant to a man's needs even if she would rather say no."

He paused then, their banter stopping for a few minutes. "I understand. Concubines can't say no." His voice was solemn. "I promise you I will never do anything like that. You can always say no to me."

"Arie understands them, the aphrodisiacs."

She thought on Arie, the man her father sent to bring her home. She was meant for him, yet he was a half-brother and he didn't want her. He followed only to make sure she arrived safely. Somewhere along the way he lost track of her and that was when she found Flynt's sisters in the tiny cottage on the MacTavish estate.

"Of course he does, and has he used them on women just as the other men? Arie has changed though. I doubt if he would ever be so cruel again," Flynt said.

"It is inbred in Arie. If he thought the use of aphrodisiacs would suit his purpose, he would use them. If Alison, his new conquest, continues to tell him no, he will most likely use one on her."

The thought made her shudder. Once before she left, she was given an aphrodisiac. She would never forget the horrific night she had. "Can we change the subject?"

"Of course, what would you like to talk about? The way your beautiful nipples hardened for me when I kiss them." His gaze shifted to her bodice.

She squirmed under the heat of his gaze. "No, I want to know what your intentions are. What are you planning for tonight, for the observatory? I'm not someone you can just take advantage of."

"I don't want to take advantage of you, sweet lassie. I want to make you happy. Pleasure you but only if that's what you want also. What would it take to make you happy?"

She sat down at the table, wondering at his question. What would it take to make her happy? "I am happy. Are you?"

"With you in my arms, yes, I'm a very happy man now that I realize that it is you I should be courting not Melessand or Beatrice." He sat across from her.

Her elbows on the table, she rested her chin on her hands. "Doesn't it take more for a person to be happy? I would think you should trust in the woman you are with. Shouldn't she be someone you can confide in too?"

His brows drew together as if he was thinking about her words. "I suppose so. What do you want me to confide?"

She tossed her napkin at him. "How would I know? That's what you are supposed to tell me, something straight from your heart and sincere as well."

He leaned back, crossing his arms in front of him, his grin stretching seemingly from one ear to the other. "A woman shouldn't have to worry about a man's problems. I keep them to myself."

"So, I'm to be coddled. If something was wrong in your life you wouldn't tell me, and conversely if something was good you wouldn't tell me either."

"If that makes you happy." He leaned forward, placing her napkin back in its proper place.

"I don't want to be coddled. I want to be a part of your life. Need to know what you do each day and how you feel about things." She wondered at that.

Flynt didn't seem to work so she assumed his money had been earned, invested and saved in previous generations. Many families were like that. Indeed, her own family was the same, but Broc continued to work.

"You lived in my home for nearly two years and you don't know? I'm surprised. I would think you would be able to recite all my flaws backwards and forwards." Now he held her hand in his.

"Why? You don't ever go to work that I could tell."

"I do play a lot but the family has crofters, land that needs to be tended to. My overseer is very competent and brings to my attentions issues that need to be addressed before they become serious problems. I do keep track of the books though and visit my tenants when it's convenient."

"Broc goes to the shipyard every day, but I'm not sure if he owns it or just ships. Perhaps I should ask him." She did want to know everything. Flynt had a way of dismissing things she thought important as unimportant.

"So." He drummed fingers on the table. "I've told you something about myself that you didn't know. Now it's your turn."

They served them the dishes they had ordered earlier. Hope looked at the chicken in cream of curry sauce skeptically, pushing the pieces around on her plate. She still wasn't sure she wanted or needed to eat.

"I wouldn't know. It seems you know everything about me. There hasn't been a single detail left out of my life." She lifted her shoulders slightly, wondering. "You will have to ask me something."

"If you were granted one wish, what would it be?" His grin looked smug as if he knew what her answer would be.

Perhaps he did know what she would ask for, perhaps he didn't have a clue. On the other hand, he could be baiting her again. It seemed he took great joy in teasing her.

"I'd like to go on that tour of the mathematics and science building with Angus tomorrow." She smiled demurely all the while staring at his lips as she moistened her own. Two could play at this game.

"This sharing business won't work if you aren't honest, lassie." His voice was gruff, irritated. "Lies won't improve our relationship."

She understood her answer annoyed him, wasn't at all what he wanted to hear. "Are you irritated that I didn't tell you I wanted you to kiss me and take other liberties with my woman's body?"

One eyebrow rose a fraction in a perfect arch, "Somewhat disappointed, you caught me off guard. Of course, I'd like you to tell me that you're enamored of all my manly parts. I want to know when a kiss would be acceptable to you. Would it be alright with you if I leaned across the table and stole a kiss."

"That would not be a wish. So, it would not be the truth." She sipped the wine then watched him over the rim, waiting to see what new direction he would send this conversation.

"Since you didn't answer my only question honestly, I'll ask again. What would be your one wish?"

She inhaled a long slow breath, suddenly wishing she hadn't started this. "Honestly, if I could have one wish, I would want my mother to come here or at least I'd like to be able to see her, talk to her. I don't even know if she is alive."

"If I could grant that wish to you, I would. I think that would be my one wish," he told her with sincerity. "Arie would know. I'm sure he would tell you if something happened to your mother."

Her heart melted for this man. "You would give up a wish for me?"

If he wanted her in his bed this moment, she would oblige. She'd always fancied herself in love with him, but now she knew the truth and understood this sacrifice he made for her.

"If seeing your mother would make you happy, I'd give up that wish. What's in a wish anyway?" He shrugged his broad shoulders. "A person makes their wishes come true. I will speak to Arie. There might be a way to do this for you."

"Thank you, but I doubt even Arie could accomplish that feat. If the sultan died, seeing her might be possible, but that would be the only way."

"I would have to draw the line at killing Arie's father who is also yours, but I will still talk to him about the matter. I think I still have one more question."

"What is it?" She was curious now.

"I'm going to wait until after we look at the stars. You might be even more amenable by then. Should we take a bottle of wine with us?"

"I get to ask a question. No more wine."

She smiled at him, hoping he would give heed to more inquiries.

"I like this but I should exact some type of price if one is caught in a lie. You lied, you know. I believe you owe me a kiss."

"You just think I lied. There is no proof. It was my first thought that just popped from my head."

"No." He leaned forward again. "I know you lied. You were bored to tears today and you accepted my invitation to bring you home almost before I gave it. Indeed, I thought you were about to ask me if I would whisk you away and put some light and sunshine into the drab day you were not enjoying."

She stiffened not wanting to admit to the lie, but he was right. "When I lied, there were no terms so you can't hold me to that one mistruth. I won't make the mistake of stretching the truth again. What do

I get if you lie to me?" She shouldn't have said that.

"Whatever you want. My man's body is yours to do with as you please."

"Well. I'm not going to kiss you if you lie. I don't know what I would ask but it's not for a kiss." She should always think before she spoke, especially around Flynt MacTavish.

"Why?" He was grinning because he knew her reasons.

"You would lie every time. You know that and I know that. So, don't pretend something different."

"You think I want your kisses that badly?"

She turned her back on him, crossing her arms in front of her while heat spread to her face. "You certainly act like it."

"You're right and you know I want more than kisses. So, what price would you ask of me if I lie?"

"That's just it. I don't know." She was frustrated and angry with him as well. "Can't we just tell the truth without a price to pay if we don't?"

"I can, can you?"

"Fair enough, I started it by lying about Angus. Are apologies accepted?"

"Need a kiss from you first then I'll decide." He seemed to pursue this without hesitation. "You did lie."

She meant to ignore him, just as he ignored her on so many levels. Then asked again, "Are apologies accepted?"

"With a kiss," he told her again, persisting in his desires.

"All right, I give up, a kiss if that's what you want. Just when do you plan on claiming it?"

"Believe I'll keep you guessing. Have you finished your chicken? Doesn't look like you ate much." He rose, striding around the table.

"You know I have." Her body quivered, shaking with desire, passion, terror of what would inevitably happen, could happen this very evening if she didn't find some measure of control regarding Flynt and his bad boy tactics.

"Shall we go look at stars? The sky has darkened enough."

A few minutes later they were in his well sprung carriage. She didn't want to look at him, and this time he didn't insist she sit on his lap.

"Are you waiting to see if I'll kiss you now? If I do, it won't be the kiss for the lie. It will just be a kiss I'm sharing with you."

"It's not fair to keep me waiting and wondering?" She wanted to get it over with.

"Ah, sweet lassie, I plan on kissing you more than once in the next few hours. You will just have to be patient for the one you will get because you lied to me. I know how much you enjoy the pleasure I give you when are lips are molded so sweetly together."

"I will look forward to the wait as well as the anticipation."

~ * ~

Grams, Catherine Creighton, sat in the Wallace townhouse, tapping her fingers on the arm of the chair. "I'm truly concerned for Hope."

"She is enamored of Flynt who seems bent on only one thing, conceiving an heir," Bliss said. "My husband has not done his due diligence in taking care of his sister. He has sought revenge against Flynt for the part he played in our shaky courtship."

"It seems Broc would have learned that a man like himself, and Flynt as well, cannot be manipulated," Chelsea said as she poured tea for everyone. "I'm tired of their machinations at our expense, and I truly hope Lacie and Daryl don't find men who like to play games such as these."

"To be honest here, it was Cam who came up with the idea. I've met Angus Kinross and he deserves better than to be set up in this way, never mind the fact that Hope could be hurt."

Grams listened to the girls, intent on hearing everything they had to say. When she spoke with Flynt, and she intended to do just that on the morrow, she wanted to have all the facts straight.

"Where is Hope staying?" Grams asked. "I've heard she moved out of the MacTavish home and her things were brought to the city. I certainly hope she has the good sense not to let Flynt give her his mistress' old home to stay in. The rumors will run rampant, and it would be devilishly hard to repair the damage. The label could well be permanent."

"No, Broc would never allow such a thing for his sister," Bliss said as she added milk and honey to her tea. "He would haul her out of there before she could take a breath of air."

"He would go along with the ploy to keep his little sister away from his longtime friend," Chelsea said, hands on her hips sighing softly then, "He could make things so difficult..."

"This was not well done of either man," Catherine interrupted. "They need lessons in manners and how to treat a woman. I'll set Flynt straight if it is the last thing I do. He has more grace than that."

Grams reached for a ginger cookie, "Hope is an innocent young woman even though or despite her sordid background."

Perhaps she should speak to Hope first and give her a little insight into the ways of men. At least Hope would listen.

"I know what you're thinking, Grams," Bliss said laughing as she reached for a cookie. "Hope has always been the level headed one, and she has given all of us advice about men."

"What is it that you are thinking?" she asked, curious that her granddaughters could read her mind so easily.

"That you want to give her the same woman to girl talk you gave to us," Chelsea said, smiling. "I'm not sure the little speech changed the way we acted around our men, but it did give me something to think about when he was kissing me."

"Trust me, your words of wisdom didn't sink into my head nor did they do any good," Bliss said. "When I was in Broc's arms, I forgot every word. No, you need to put the fear of God into Flynt."

"Fear of God in Flynt?" One silver eyebrow rose hesitantly before Grams continued with a wry smile. "I would guess that feat would be nearly impossible if not impossible, but I will give it a try.

"Do you think Hope liked Angus?" Grams asked, thinking it might be a good thing if she did. "If they had fun together, this conversation might be entirely irrelevant."

"No, probably not. They are far too different. Angus is a genius and not only does he excel in mathematics, but he reads treatises and other things that leave me bored to tears. Hope can't read nor does she excel with numbers. I'm afraid they are drastically unsuited for each other,"

Chelsea said with a tiny huff before she bit into her cookie. "They would have nothing in common to talk about."

"Flynt is a very competent man in all those areas," Catherine said. "So, why is he more suited to Hope than Angus?"

"Flynt is a bad boy and a lady's man. He appreciates women and knows them well," Chelsea said thoughtfully. "I doubt if Angus has ever kissed a girl let alone given one pleasure. My guess is that he's a virgin."

"Really? That shy and unworldly," Bliss paused, thinking, "Didn't know any men now days were shy or virgins."

"True, but even though Flynt is very smart, he doesn't make that an integral part of his life. According to Cam, Angus lives and breathes to learn new things. He spends hours at the university pouring over mathematical theories," Chelsea said. "And just for the record, I chastised Cam for his part in this. He was doing it just to make Flynt jealous, and he had no concern for Angus."

"Men just don't learn," Bliss said with a soft sigh.

"No, they don't learn and they don't listen either nor do they play fair. They never understand women are stronger and smarter than they are," Grams said, feeling a bit bemused at her grandchildren and their attempts to find love.

"I've told the same to Cam and he had the audacity to prove he was stronger and faster but he didn't understand anything I was talking about. He thought it all physical strength, but it's more emotional and pound for pound I do think women are the strongest of the sexes. Can you imagine if a man had to give birth? Why, it would be the end of the human species. They would cry and whimper about the pain they were in throughout the entire birthing."

The loud banging on the front door sent a chill down Catherine's spine. Fear reverberated through the door. She felt the unspoken terror emanating from the other side. "Who could that be?"

"I'll check, any of the men would probably walk inside," Chelsea rose, opening the door. "Arie, what are you doing here?"

"Is Hope inside?"

Arie strode through the door, seeming to check out everyone sitting in the room as well as every corner in the room. "Flynt?" His hands clenched at his sides, "Where is she?"

"We don't know," Chelsea said as she was shaking her head. "Hope went to the games with Angus, but no one believes she would be with him this long. We're thinking Flynt intervened because he did know where Angus was taking her."

"That leaves Flynt and his whereabouts," Arie's dark brows drew together. "With Hope which can only be a good thing. He'll protect her."

"Nope, he was out with another lady, Beatrice someone but we all hoped Angus would find Flynt's date to his liking and Flynt would finally realize that Hope has had his heart for years. Men are so difficult when it comes to love and denying their feelings."

"So where would they be, given that scenario is true?" Arie's fervent demands didn't go unnoticed by Catherine.

"What is going on and why the urgency?" Catherine spoke up. "We need to understand what this is all about."

"The man who would have been given Hope when I refused might be coming here. At least that is the news from my last ship. He wants Hope. For as long as I can remember, he's coveted my half-sister. Now that he's discovered she is here in Glasgow, her life is in danger. I have to put a stop to this before he kidnaps her and takes her away. If Hope ends up in his harem, there is very little anyone can do to get her out."

"Cam gave Flynt the keys to the observatory. I'm sure he would have taken Hope there or Beatrice if he is still with her. Depends on what happened at the games," Chelsea said, sensing the danger.

"Have you checked Flynt's home?" Catherine asked.

Arie waved a hand in the air, "He wasn't there but suppose he could be now. Looked at the townhouse first but didn't ride out to the estate. From what all of you are saying, he is most likely at home or the observatory."

Arie's man spoke up, "I'll go back to Flynt's home, you go to the observatory then I'll meet you."

"Whatever you do, if Hope arrives here, don't let her leave." Arie turned on a heel, striding from the room.

Catherine inhaled a sharp breath. "Best we get ourselves over to Flynt's home. If I know my grandson, if anything happens to Hope, he will bring her to his house.

Chapter Three

"Will you take me home now?" Hope asked, her smile vanishing. "Every bone in my body is exhausted."

"We should go to the observatory tonight. We might not get another chance," Flynt said, helping her into the waiting carriage, concern for her marring what he planned for this evening.

He didn't want to take her home though. Needed to keep her with him as long as he could. "You can take a nap on my shoulder, and I promise you I won't try to steal any kisses while you are asleep. Even though I would like to do just that."

He was anxious, this day had been busy but she shouldn't be so tired. Although their banter might be enough to exhaust the most robust, he'd actually enjoyed every moment of their verbal exchanges.

"Very well," she said, sounding reluctant. "I'll try. For you I'll try to stay awake, except for the short nap that is."

"I'd like that. Don't want to take you home at all." When he sat down beside her, wrapping his arm around her as he drew her close, he wished with all his heart she still lived with him, "What makes you so exhausted?"

"Do you really need to ask? I have been off kilter since I saw you this afternoon with Beatrice." She pushed away, staring at him, her amber eyes shining with emotions he couldn't decipher, but he hoped were passion. "I never know what you're going to do or say. I'm still waiting for the kiss, which you say will be given when you feel like it. You could make things a lot simpler."

"Perhaps now would be a good time." He gently traced her eyebrow. "A kiss before you take a short nap."

"No, no, the nap sounds good, the kiss later. If you kiss me now, I won't sleep. Think I'll just close my eyes."

A kiss to say goodnight sounded more appealing than ever. He'd like to kiss her in the morning when she woke up too.

He squeezed her shoulder. "Go to sleep then. You'll enjoy the stars even more if you get some rest. I want you wide awake and alert. Cam said there would be a stargazing quiz afterwards just to make sure we are really looking at the stars and not doing something else."

"No quizzes," she murmured as she closed her eyes.

Flynt knew the moment she fell asleep. Her body relaxed completely, and he understood just how much he loved holding her, watching her sleep. At this moment, there were no sexual innuendos, no flirting or sexual play between them. This moment was poignant. He understood why she was so tired. She'd matched him word for word in their conversations. While he tried, he'd not bested her by any means.

He meant to ask her to marry him as soon as possible. It would be prudent though to court her a week or two before he got down on one knee. She was so resilient and strong yet fragile too. He understood her heart would not be given to him lightly and without thought. He would have to convince her he was suitable and deserving of her love.

Introducing her to the pleasures of lovemaking they could create together was something he would pursue in the coming weeks. He knew he must proceed cautiously. The first time they made love would not terrify her, he determined. She would have to experience everything that could exist between the two of them, a man and a woman, before they consummated their relationship. Only then she could fully become his wife and enjoy the pleasure without the pain.

For the remainder of the time, he rested his head against the seat, closing his eyes and enjoying the night sounds and scents as well as the clatter of the carriage wheels against the cobblestone. She was his and always would be. Nothing would stand in his way.

The carriage slowly drew to a stop, the horse's hooves rattling on the cobblestone. He gazed at her, tracing the line of her eyebrow before placing a gentle kiss on her cheek. "It's time to wake up and look at the stars."

She curled into him, her hand on his chest. Good God but he enjoyed the sensations of her soft curves pressed against him. She was so unlike any other woman he'd ever known. He didn't want the moment to end but the evening was growing late and he did want to show her the stars, share some kisses and perhaps something to drink when he took her home.

"Hope, open up your beautiful eyes. Look at me." He stroked her neck and across her collarbone.

She sighed, arching her back and pressing into him even more. He wondered if it would be like this in the mornings after a night of pleasure. He wanted to wake her every morning for the rest of his life.

"The evening is growing late and I promised to have you home before dawn."

He laughed, thinking no chaperone would agree to something so outrageous, especially Grams. But Grams didn't have a say in his life. He would do what he wanted as long as Hope was willing.

She pushed away, her eyes sleepy and gorgeous. "Before dawn... What are we going to do until then?"

Not wanting to weave stories he said, "Think I'll have that kiss now." His lips found hers, molded over hers, his tongue sweeping inside.

She responded, her lips opening for him. He enjoyed the way her innocence affected him. Even when she touched his mouth with her tongue, the caress was hesitant and gentle, untried. Her kisses moved him in ways he never experienced before. He groaned then, wishing they were in a more private place where they could be more intimate. He wanted to take this one step farther but decided to wait until he brought her home.

"Flynt," she sighed softly. "I do love it when you kiss me. Maybe I should have exacted a kiss from you every time you lied to me." She touched his face with her hand.

"Maybe you should have but then," he paused, brushing silken tendrils of hair from her face. "As you said though, if that were the case, I would never tell you the truth. If you would kiss me every time I lied, what incentive would I have to speak honestly?"

"Perhaps your pride as a man." She seemed to challenge him.

"Yes." He grinned lopsidedly, appreciating this conversation.

"My manly pride. We'll have to see how this develops."

He helped her from the carriage and to the observatory. Before they entered the building, he turned her so she could look out over the city and the myriad of stars dotting the night sky.

"Everything is so beautiful," she spoke softly, leaning into him.

He pointed, "Cam tells me that bright light near the horizon is not a star at all. It's a planet. Don't remember its name though." He laughed then, "Suppose I'll fail his stargazing quiz. How can you tell the difference? Believe he told me the stars twinkle and the planets do not. If you see something flying across the sky, it would have to be something from another world."

It seemed Hope was waking up, her smile reached deep into his heart. She punched him, "Liar. There is nothing from another world we'll see flying across the night sky."

"Does that mean I get a kiss?" His eyebrows rose in speculation as well as anticipation.

"No, not this time."

"Why?"

"Because Cam might have told you that very story. I wouldn't put him past some tall tale such as beings from somewhere else, and I would also expect you to repeat said story."

"He didn't though." His lips brushed her ear, teased it with his tongue. Then, "Come, let's see what I remember about the telescope. It's a complicated machine, not sure if this poor man's brain can figure it out. We're looking for the North Star and from there we can find some constellations, a grouping of stars," he told her as he unlocked the door. "Have you heard of any constellations?"

"No to constellations but I've always enjoyed looking at the night skies and the stars as well."

Inside it was dark, nearly pitch black. Flynt could see very little so he kept one arm around Hope.

"Are there any lights?" she whispered, her voice a soft sound in the night.

"Gas lights, I believe." Letting her go for a moment, he searched the wall near the door, successfully.

"It's cold." She was rubbing her arms, seeming to force a smile. "Didn't expect it to get so chilly so fast. It is fall though and the days are getting shorter."

"Let's warm you up then," He shrugged out of his jacket, wrapping it around her shoulders. "Better?"

"Yes," she was shaking her head. "It smells like you."

He groaned, wondering if she could have planned to say something so evocative. For the first time since this morning, his body shook with need for her. It seemed he lost control. That had never happened to him before. The entire day and until this moment he'd been able to moderate his feelings. Well, mostly... "Good, don't want you to freeze." He tried to think of anything but the words she'd just said. He wondered if his bed would smell like her after they slept together.

Blessed hell, he told himself to get his unruly body in check.

Stepping to the telescope, he adjusted the eyepiece. "There you go. If you look through this, you can see the moon." He was relieved there was a slight diversion.

"Don't see anything. It's hard..." She paused looking at him. "Is there some trick to seeing through this? I'm not really tall enough, I can't."

"Here." He set a stool where she'd been standing. "Is that better?" he asked after she tried again. Fear for her falling, he held her, his arm around her waist.

"Yes." She peered at the night sky. "What are all the dark spots?"

"Craters I believe. Think that's what Cam said." She stepped down and he found the planet.

They continued from there, finishing everything Cam told him they could see, given his meager knowledge about the heavens. The lesson had been short, and he knew they had time for some intimacy. He was looking forward to holding her again, kissing her and perhaps something more.

"Well, well, well, seems you took advantage of my offer. Did you see everything I told you about?" Cam stood in the doorway, his smile reaching his ears. "See I didn't interrupt anything. So, the two of you will have to find some other place for the intimacies I know you've planned with Hope."

"Not surprised you showed up. Expected you earlier," Flynt said dryly. "Don't you have anything better to do than to torment me? A wife perhaps to pleasure."

"Torment?" Cam stepped into the room, laughing and clearly pleased with himself. "I set the two of you up. You'd still be dangling Beatrice and Melessand on your matrimonial quest and your need for an heir if I didn't step in and help this relationship along."

"I'll give you that. Neither Beatrice nor Melessand would do for me. They don't suit. Yes, I will admit that Angus and Beatrice work much better than I ever would. You have anyone you can pair with the beautiful Melessand. She will most likely knock at my door soon wondering where I've been."

"No, afraid not but I'll think about it. The girl needs someone who can overlook her perfect self and make sure she learns how to treat others. She is really quite conceited about herself," Cam said.

"So, what are you doing here?" Flynt asked, wishing the man would disappear as quickly as he appeared. "You've never quite answered that question."

"Chaperone duty. Your grams wouldn't want you to be alone with this beautiful woman. You need someone to make sure you don't toss her skirts here in this observatory."

He looked at Hope. "Sorry for my use of words, but I am one of the bad boys."

"I'm not about to take advantage of her and you know it." Flynt's anger was rising with each passing moment. "She is important to me."

He shrugged, striding to the telescope. "Don't know anything of the sort. Did you show Hope any stars. No, I see that you haven't. Or were you planning on looking at them outside?"

"Everything you mentioned to me. You're right we were just getting ready to step outside and find the constellations."

"I'll help."

"That's what I was afraid of," Flynt muttered, pulling Hope close and stepping outside with her.

"Ah, let me see. Can you see that bright star?" he pointed into the darkness. "The brightest one is the North Star. Sailors use it to chart their course."

It seemed chaos erupted then. Arie, waving his hands and yelling, raced toward them. Flynt couldn't tell what he was saying, but he was followed by three of his men. He reached them, "Inside, now. Both of you. Hurry!"

Confused, he hesitated. "Bloody eyes, what are you talking about."

"Get inside. I'll explain later."

Turning to Cam. "Do you have a gun?"

"No." Cam appeared just as confused as he was while Arie tried to push all of them inside. His movements were frantic and left Flynt to wonder what the devil was happening. The man must have gone daft, cobwebs in the belfry.

They finished with the telescope and Cam locked the door behind them. He was now fumbling with the key when a shot rang out, ricocheting against the building.

Another shot then another reverberated in the evening stillness. Men yelled, cursing as blows were heard. Seconds seemed to turn into minutes as the fighting continued. Finally, they were inside, the door closed and locked behind them.

"What is it?" Flynt asked, breathing hard, desperate to know why people were shooting at them. "Why?"

"I did not foresee any of this. My men will take care of those who wish you harm. He wants you dead and Hope in his harem. Once they learn that will never be allowed, they will sail home. I will use my considerable influence to make it happen. For now though, we must be patient and let my men take care of this moment."

"Me? Who?" Flynt asked. "Don't know..." he swallowed hard. "Don't know anyone who would want to kill me."

"Hope." They all looked at Hope who was slumped against the wall, holding her arm.

"Light the lanterns," Flynt said, kneeling beside her.

Blood flowed down her arm. His gut tightened, as his heart raced. A cold sweat broke over him. Running a finger around his collar he tried for a calm he didn't possess.

"You've been shot." He looked to Arie then Cam. "We have to get her home and to a doctor."

She closed her eyes, her breaths short and shallow. "I suppose the bullet was meant for you and hit me instead," she said, seeming to question this.

"Probably true. Musa wouldn't want you dead."

"He found me? No, no, no..."

Flynt looked to Arie for answers. "This one sultan pursued her since she came of age. He told our father he would have her no matter. In part that is why Hope ran away when I didn't want to marry her. She feared this man. It's also why our father allowed her to leave."

"Don't want to be in his harem. How, Arie? How did you discover he was here looking for me? How did he find me?"

"None of that matters now. We have to see to her wound." Flynt's gut churned, fear for Hope paramount.

Slowly, he pulled down her sleeve, needing to see the damage. He was relieved to learn the bullet was not embedded in her shoulder. Yet it did substantial damage. She would need stitching and immediate care to make sure there would be no infection.

"Can't do that until it settles down outside," Arie said. "My man, Victor, will let me know when it's safe. We have to stay here. Just glad I got to you two before he did. Nearly impossible to get a woman out of a harem."

"Be advised you are not taking her to your townhouse," Cam spoke quietly. "As you well ken, it isn't proper."

"Fuck proper. My place is the closest. When we get there, you can bring every chaperone you know of, anyone who wants to sit in my house while I tend to Hope. If you think for one moment, I would take advantage of any woman with a bullet wound, you're crazed and you don't know me."

"Just thinking about Hope's reputation and the gossip that will spread throughout the city as soon as a few people hear about the tiny indiscretion."

"Gossip doesn't matter. I intend to wed her as soon as she'll agree."

Sweat ran down his forehead, dripping onto the floor. He was terrified for her. It seemed the pain got the better of her. She was unconscious now. Thank God but he knew she would wake up soon and she would feel the pain again. He wanted to take this all away.

"Very well, we'll travel to your townhouse as soon as all the fighting has finished outside, assuming Arie's men have the upper hand," Cam said.

"They do, I'm sure of it. They are well trained and my men will not let them get away. He will die today. Scottish authorities be damned."

They waited for confirmation of Arie's statement. He held Hope close, praying throughout. How had this evening turned so drastically? Cam paced the small confines of the room, impatient also to know what was going on outside.

"Sorry, Flynt. I tried to get to you sooner. Didn't know where you were or who you were with, Beatrice or Hope. This was not supposed to happen."

"No, it wasn't." Flynt tore one of her petticoats to bind the wound. There was so much blood, too much for his taste. This needed to be taken care of. "The damn bullet was meant for me. What the hell would have happened if she'd been with Angus?"

"How is she?" Cam stood over him, his concern written on his face.

"Not good. Have to stop the bleeding and the infection that is soon to set in if nothing is done. We have to get her out of here. I fear for her."

In his arms, she groaned, the pain evident. "Flynt..."

"It won't be much longer," Arie ran his hands through his hair. "Don't like this, don't like it at all. Need to know what is happening out there."

"All of us want to know. Should I poke my head outside and see," Cam asked.

"Only if you want to get a bullet through your brain," Arie told him succinctly. "Yet I'm tempted to do the same. While I have every confidence in my crew, there is always the off chance they won't succeed."

"Well then, do you have a plan if something has gone wrong?" Cam asked, staring at the door then back to him. "We can hardly stay here forever."

"We're going to have to take that chance soon."

Flynt knew time mattered here. Taking care of Hope couldn't be put off much longer.

Arie was nodding his head even while he strode toward the door. "I'll look. Not going to wait another second."

"It's safe," The voice through the door gave him hope. "You can all come out now."

This time the serious expression on Arie's face told him the truth before Arie could speak. "That's not my man."

More gunshots rang out. They heard. "Stay put, Arie. Don't let anyone inside."

Flynt's fear for Hope escalated, his hands shaking so hard he stuffed them in his pockets. He held her close, rocking her and murmuring nonsense to her. The bleakness in her eyes terrified him. More seconds past turning to minutes. All was quiet once more.

"We have to take the chance to leave," Flynt said, clearly impatient, his mind on only one thing, Hope's life.

Arie seemed to finally agree with him as he was nodding his head, hand on the door. "Let me go first."

Crouching low, Arie slipped through a tiny opening in the door while Cam closed it behind him. "I know you're worried, but leaving before it's prudent will not help."

"I understand," Flynt said, wondering what happened to turn everything in his world so upside down. This evening was not supposed to turn out like this. Earlier only romance and seduction were in his mind, now all those thoughts vanished to those of survival.

"Do you?" Cam questioned, kneeling beside the pair. "You have to stay calm even though I know it's not easy. Sorry all this has happened."

Calmness was anything but easy it was damn near impossible. If he hadn't insisted on the visit to the observatory, Hope would be safely ensconced in her bed at home, not suffering from a bullet wound. Before leaving her to her bed, he would have initiated her on one more aspect of lovemaking.

"This is not your fault," Cam seemed to read his mind. "You did not shoot her. No matter how hard you try to make this about you, it is not."

"You're wrong on that score," Flynt mumbled, his words making an impact. "I made sure we came here. If not for that..."

"They were following you. They would have tried to kill you wherever you went. You don't know but they might have succeeded. The two of you are lucky in that you had the shelter of the observatory and Arie's knowledge."

"It's not your fault," Hope whispered, "And really it doesn't hurt all that much, just a little soreness."

"Liar. When you are mended, I will claim my kiss for that falsehood."

He pulled her closer, hugging her to reassure. She was shivering now, even with his jacket covering her.

"This one doesn't count. I was trying to make you feel better," she sighed, leaning into him.

"Absolutely counts. You should never tell me a bullet wound doesn't hurt to make me feel better about something I've done to you. That statement translates to two kisses." He placed a gentle kiss on her forehead. "This one is just a peck so it doesn't count. Hope you remember this lesson because I will claim all my kisses as soon as you are feeling better."

"Perhaps I would like that, a kiss. You could do it now." She smiled at him, touching his face with a fingertip. "I need you and want you. You know that though, don't you?"

"You sure?" He wanted nothing more than to take her into his arms and place kisses over every inch of her face then her body.

She nodded, moistening her lips. "I didn't lie. The wound feels numb so..."

"It doesn't hurt," he finished for her.

She stared at his mouth before touching his lips. "I could have died today. I want you, Flynt."

He bent low, so close to her, he could feel each breath as she slowly exhaled. "I would make sure, tell me if I hurt you."

His mouth closed over hers. He kissed her softly, not as he usually kissed her deep and long. She moaned into his mouth, opening for him. He didn't know if it was pain from the gunshot or passion.

Then he pulled away, "I'll save a better kiss for when we are alone. I forgot Cam is just three feet away from us."

Cam was standing, his back to them as Arie slipped inside with more news. "My men have everything under control for the time being. I can promise you though, that your would-be kidnapper will not give up this easily. Now he is regrouping and figuring out a new strategy. I will do everything in my power to dissuade him. As I promised, if he doesn't agree to leave, he will die."

"Is my carriage still there?" Flynt asked, lifting Hope from the floor as he waited to leave while trying to ignore Arie's words. As far as he was concerned, he never wanted to see this observatory again.

"Ready and waiting."

They strode into the night, still wary of any danger that might not have been subdued.

"Where are we going?" Hope asked.

"To my home."

With a pointed look to Cam, "There will be no discussion about this."

~ * ~

"I won't argue. I promise," Hope said, realizing she truly didn't care. All she wanted was a warm comfortable place to lie down and sleep. She needed to close her eyes and let the rest of the world float into oblivion. Before they left for the observatory, she'd been exhausted. Now she was beyond that point.

It seemed with every bump and clatter of the carriage, her arm throbbed with more blood pounding into the wound. Indeed, she lied to Flynt but the falsehood was for a very good reason. She smiled, thinking of the kiss and the promise for their future.

She closed her eyes, soaking up Flynt's warmth as well as his strength.

"We are almost there." He ran his hand along her good arm, soothing her. "I don't want you to worry about anything. You won't end up in that man's harem. I promise you."

The danger and the fear so prevalent in her mind, she laughed softly, wising it would all go away. "You've made a lot of promises to me. In this case I actually trust Arie more to make sure that doesn't happen."

"I will keep them all." He placed a gentle kiss on her forehead.

"I don't doubt that fact. All I wish for right now is for this to be over. Can you make all this end?"

"To know your arm will mend and there will be no infection. The wound has not been cleaned or stitched. From my brief look at the injury, I will have to clean it as well as stitch it and that will hurt. It won't be over very soon."

"The sooner we take care of this, the better I will feel. I can take pain."

She wanted to reassure him but she didn't have the words. He internalized everything that happened in the last few hours, blaming himself.

"We are home," he whispered to her as Cam climbed from the carriage before offering help to them.

Reluctantly, Flynt handed her over to Cam then jumped from the vehicle, taking her into his arms again.

"I'll see to the horses and the carriage," Cam said, setting off in the direction of the stables.

Flynt strode up the porch then into his townhouse, calling for his valet and assistant. The man appeared as if he'd been waiting for them.

"Get me some water and soap, a bottle of whiskey also. Something to stitch her bullet hole."

Setting her on the couch, he stepped back for a moment, raking his hands through his hair while he waited for the items to be brought to him. "How are you feeling?"

"As if I've been shot in the arm." She tried to smile for him, wishing all this to end so she could go to sleep.

"Here you are." Grams appeared at his side. "When we heard the news, we came to your home. I knew you would stay by her side and you wouldn't want her anywhere but here."

"Thank you, Grams. Considering everything that is going on right now, this is for the best. I wouldn't feel safe. Arie has men surrounding the house. Still we both know there are ways a desperate man can find to get what he wants."

"You must take care," she said, leaving the room and disappearing down the hallway. "Send for me if you need anything. I'll stay here tonight and tomorrow, perhaps longer. We'll see."

"Now," Flynt sat down beside her. "I want you to drink this. It will help with the pain."

"Whiskey?" She grimaced just thinking about drinking the potent stuff made her nauseous.

"Will help with the pain. Drink up."

He crossed his arms in front of him, a stern look on his face.

She grimaced as she swallowed the whiskey, gulped a second time before handing the bottle back to him. "It burns."

"The whiskey will also burn your arm but it will keep any possible infections at bay." He slowly unwound the bandage, looking at it carefully. Touching it, he reassured himself the ball did not remain in her arm. "This is going to hurt. Would you like something to bite down on? No that's not a question." He turned to Grams who had returned and seeming to be hovering over her. "Would you get me a leather strap? There is one in the master bedroom near the wash basin."

She nodded, hurrying out of the room and returned a few seconds later, "Here."

"Put this between your teeth and bite down hard."

Really, she thought this was unnecessary. Yet when he poured the whiskey on her arm, she jumped, nearly crying out. She had not realized.

"Now I'm going to clean and stitch the wound. It's going to hurt too. Are you alright?" He waited, seeming to need a reply.

"More than the whiskey?"

He inhaled a long deep breath of air, his brows dating together.

"Perhaps you should lie down."

She heard the reservation in his voice, almost fear. "If you think it's best."

Suddenly Cam stood beside him. "Would you like me to do it? It's not personal that way."

"No."

"You ready with that leather strap?" he asked, watching her closely.

"Not really but if it needs to be done." She couldn't keep from staring at the needle that was going to bite into her skin. "How many." She licked her lips feeling her heart pound. "Stitches?"

"About ten, I'm sorry." His eyes darkened while his brows drew together. "I'll try to be as gentle as possible."

Hope understood he was worried about her. "Get on with it then." She was resigned to the pain.

"Cam, will you hold her arm still."

"It would be better if I was unconscious."

She watched as the needle grew closer. With the first impression, the pain excruciating, she fainted.

Flynt paused, looking to Cam, "It's better this way. Hopefully she will not wake up until after I finish."

Hope groaned. The searing pain in her arm would not vanish. She heard herself crying out but he didn't stop. She cursed him, heard him curse her back. Her arms pushed at the covers while she tried to kick them away.

"Hope." His hands were on his arms. "You will be alright but you have to hold still."

Something cold was pressed against her forehead. She was so hot, burning from the inside out. "Flynt."

"Hush, you've a fever. It is coming down now. We had to wait too long to get all the tiny pieces of fabric out of the wound before we were able to stitch it."

He used a rag to spread coolness across her arms and chest. She tried to press into it, but there was his voice again, this time so soothing and so gentle, telling her to lie still, that he would see to it that she felt better.

"Trust me," he said, "trust me."

She did. He would make sure everything was better. It was like him.

"I don't understand." She tried to sit but was too weak.

When she opened her eyes, it was dark in the room except for the light from one candle. She squinted her eyes but nothing would come into focus.

"Rest, that's what you need. A bit of infection set in and your body is fighting it. I will keep you cool until your body does it for you. Now, you need to drink some water. Water is good for everything." Flynt sat beside her, talking to her, soothing her with the calmness of his words.

"You look tired." She touched his face, trying to smile. "There are bags underneath your eyes, dark circles as well." The exhaustion filled her again.

"How I feel makes no difference," he said.

"In that you lie so you owe me a kiss," she murmured yet the world appeared to spin slowly around her and it seemed she might have fallen back to sleep.

The dreams were so real she couldn't be sure though.

She was awake again and he was talking to her. "We'll save the kiss for later when I can make you scream with pleasure. Now we're going to get you into another nightgown. It will make you more comfortable. Grams brought several for you."

She felt the cool air touch her skin. She vaguely understood that someone was taking off the sweaty nightgown, and she was thankful for it. She realized that someone was Flynt. She felt the wet cloth wipe over her breasts and ribs then down her legs. The cooling didn't go deep enough. She was still so very hot, deeper inside, and the wonderful cold of the cloth didn't reach the inferno burning within her. She tried to arch her back to bring the cloth closer to her skin.

It was Flynt seeing her, touching her, how strange that she didn't care. She was naked and he was looking at her, caressing her. The thought seemed natural and right. Even though her eyes were open, she watched as if from a distance. She needed to tell him thank you. She tried but her mouth was so dry she could barely swallow.

His hands were on her arms, pushing her down. She must have tried to sit again.

He was quietly saying now, that beautiful man, "Hush, sweet lassie, I know it burns. I had a very bad fever once, I felt as if there were flames on the inside, where nothing could reach, and I was burning form the inside out. Everything will be better soon."

"Yes," was all she could say.

"I'll keep doing this until that burning is gone. I promise you. Soon you will be cool and back to normal. We can carry on where we left off."

She smiled at him even though his face was blurry. "You are always promising something, aren't you? I'm so glad you're here."

"Yes, I'm staying by your side until you can hurl insults at me and tell me no, until you can claim that kiss I owe you."

It seemed she needed to make him understand. She tried to lift her hand to touch his face, to gain his attention, and her voice was raw and hoarse. "You must take care. If he wants you dead, nothing Arie can do will stop him. I don't want you hurt for my sake. I'm nothing to you, really. Just a woman whose caused you nothing but problems."

She could see Flynt's dark brows draw together. It seemed to her that he did a lot of that lately. Either he didn't understand what she was trying to tell him or he wasn't going to heed her warning.

"What the devil are you talking about? If Arie doesn't take care of that man, I will. He could hang for what he's done here, to you. He's a foreigner on Scottish soil, and he'll answer for his attempt at murder. He could be in prison as we speak or on his way home. He won't cause us any more problems."

He didn't know that for sure.

Closing her eyes again, weary from all the exertion her thoughts brought on, he was still rubbing her with the damp cloth until she was finally cool to the touch. Methodically from her face to her toes he stroked her. When he turned her onto her stomach, she moaned softly, then sprawled boneless on the sheets.

He covered her. "You will be cold for a while. I also know the burning will return. I know you will handle it and keep handling it until you are normal and healthy again. The infection should not have been as bad as it was." He inhaled a long deep breath. "If you will survive, I will know by the morning."

She heard his voice, soft and melodic as he hummed. Daylight slanted in through the window. She had slept and she felt so much better. "I don't burn any longer. You helped me last night or has it been longer?"

Truly, she didn't know what day it was. While it seemed like it was just last night she was shot, she somehow understood more days than she could remember had passed.

"What day is it?"

"Two days after I owed you that kiss. Three days after everyone decided for us that we should wed as soon as you are well."

"People decided that for us."

"I had my say in that decision."

"You haven't asked me."

"Are you well now?"

"Why is it that everyone is making decisions for us that we should be making ourselves?" She didn't like this not at all. "Why would they come to this untenable plan?"

"Ach, sweet lassie, you don't want to marry me. I'm hurt." He clasped his hands over his heart.

"You didn't answer my questions," she shot back, feeling stronger, almost as strong as before that horrible night at the observatory.

"Which one do you want me to answer first?" He was smiling, seemingly extraordinarily pleased with himself.

"Why aren't we making these decisions, to start?" She watched his eyes narrow then he looked away for a second. "It seems as if the people involved should decide whether or not they want to get married."

"I'm in complete agreement. I need to marry you so this sultan, Musa, who is after you won't want you. It's really pretty simple. If I take your virginity, you won't be good enough for that man."

"You said he was in jail."

"Probably in jail," he corrected her. "Arie will do his best to keep him there and if he can't, there are other ways to get rid of him although the task won't be as easy as the men who hurt Chelsea.

Her breath caught in her throat. "I hate men," she murmured.

She watched him and it seemed he was taken aback by her sudden statement as well as the vehemence, not sure quite what to say. He winked at her, deciding to take a lighter track. "I thought you would be pleased at the thought of the wonderful night of lovemaking that would follow our wedding."

"I would be if it was something you wanted, but you don't. I won't have you committing yourself to me when it's the last thing on your mind." She was adamant and meant to stand by that decision.

"Well." He pulled up a chair. Sitting and stretching his legs in front of him, "I was planning on marrying you, just not tomorrow. Although, the closer tomorrow gets the more I believe it's just perfect."

"Did you not think to ask me?" Whether he liked the fact or not, she did have a say in this, her life, marriage, exactly how she spent her future and with who. "A man needs to ask."

"Will you marry me?" He grinned, sitting forward, no longer relaxed and looking smug. "It is the first thing I want, not the last."

"Too little too late." She was feeling stronger by the second. She breathed deeply searching for even more strength. "A little romance should accompany a proposal, don't you think?"

He crawled onto the bed, pulling her into his arms. "I can tell you're feeling better. I like my feisty sweet lassie. We don't have to wed. I can take your virginity now or you could give it to me with the proper persuasion. A little encouragement is always fun. We could do it this instant and all would be fine just like I promised."

He was right. She knew it. He knew it and he could probably do that very thing right now if he wanted and she would never say no to him. "I hate it when you're so arrogant."

"No, I'm just confident in my manly prowess and I'm also right. You know it. I know it. So, what are we waiting for?" He laughed then, kissing his way up her neck until he placed gentle nibbling kisses on her ear, his teeth worrying the sensitive lobe. "I would prefer you became my wife rather than my mistress. If we made love right now, you could conceive my heir this very day. I would have no more work to do."

She knew he felt her sudden response to the kiss as well as his words. She couldn't help the tiny sounds of desire that always accompanied the way his lips and teeth moved on her. Pushing on his shoulders, she managed a weak and desperate, "Stop. I'm not about to become your mistress and I'm not going to let you sweet-talk me into the wrong decision right now." Brave and courageous words from a woman who couldn't say no to this man, didn't want to anyway.

He pulled away, heeding her adamant request. "I'm going to allow the no for today. I'm waiting for after the wedding to make you mine. You must get back your strength before we pursue this farther. However, you wanted me, admit it." He ran his finger across her lips, grinning from one ear to the other as a man well pleased.

"Of course, I didn't. You surprised me that was all."

"Liar. That's another kiss. Not that I'm going to need them after we are married. I plan on squandering several days in this very bed with you, teaching you about the ways of love."

"I haven't said yes."

She felt as if she was drowning in a cesspool of words and sentiments she didn't understand. He couldn't possibly want to marry her, could he? She needed to stand on principle but... Blessed hell if she did that, she would never marry this man who she loved.

"I'm a patient man. You have until tomorrow morning to say the word yes, but you should know Grams and your sisters as well have been caught at the dressmakers designing a wedding dress for you. They've spoken to Daryl about the wedding cake although I believe they decided on a bunch of tiny cakes instead of one big one. There are the flowers. What do you like best?"

"What?" She felt her eyes cross then tried to sit up, clinging to the covers.

"It's all true. Arie has given his input as well, saying he knows you better than anyone, even me. Which I disputed but he does have a strong argument because he's known you longer. Together they will come up with something very beautiful for our special day."

"Flynt, you're rushing all of this. I'm not ready. You can't just wake me up after three days of sleep and tell me we're getting married.

It's not right or fair. I won't have it." She desperately needed to stand up for herself or he'd run roughshod over her for the rest of their lives.

"Life isn't fair. You just have to make the best of it." His grin widened if that was possible.

"Really."

He pulled a ring from his pocket. "Will you marry me?" He was on one knee and it might have been romantic in a different setting, if she wasn't lying on her bed, gunshot wound to her arm, wearing a sweaty nightgown.

She let a long breath of air out, staring at the ring. "You're incorrigible. When did you get this bauble?"

He was holding her hand now, not waiting for an answer, he slowly slid the ring on her finger and she didn't understand how he did it but even that simple gesture heated her through to the core. "Grams sat with you yesterday for a short time. I was planning this the day of the games. I knew then you were perfect for me. We will make perfect little heirs together."

"To beget your heirs?" she asked sarcastically. "There is more to a marriage than babies. I won't do this." She tried to take the ring from her finger but it was surprisingly tight. It wouldn't budge.

"Yes, to beget my heir, to pleasure me in bed and vice versa, to talk to everyday for the rest of our lives. I enjoy your company and you keep me guessing at times as to what you will say or do next. It looks fine on your finger. Do you like it?"

"Yes, it's very pretty. I've never had anything this beautiful." She was still tugging at the ring but it was stuck right where it was and Flynt seemed to be ignoring her distress, carrying on as if nothing was wrong.

"Good, then you've agreed to marry me? You won't take the ring off, will you?" he asked and this time his voice sounded hopeful not his usual confidence as he watched her tugging at it.

"Don't think I could if I wanted to so I suppose so, as there is no other choice." She blurted, understanding she should not have said such a thing.

"Should I be hurt? I like to think of myself as a good catch. Perhaps one of the best in Scotland."

"You are."

She was so tired. Closing her eyes, she let everything he told her settle into her head which was now pounding. She didn't know if it was because she was tired or because of the conversation they just had. Somehow, he always managed to exhaust her.

"Would you like some water?" he asked, tenderly smoothing her hair away from her face. "Food perhaps?"

"Yes, that would be very nice." She heard him rise, walk to the pitcher, the sound of water running into the glass then his footsteps back.

"You should probably sit and open your eyes as well," he chuckled, his laughter sounding like music to her. "Don't want to spill this down your front. I'd have to change your nightgown again if that were to happen. Not that I'm complaining, but you might not want to be naked in front of me while your entirely aware of me staring at your beautiful white breast and..."

She opened her eyes when she felt him sit on the bed, remembering though the fog of her dreams how he cooled her when she was so hot, she could barely breathe. "Okay."

He helped her sit, her back against the headboard. "You should probably prepare yourself for your sisters and grandmother. They've been downstairs for the last hour waiting to see you. They have a million questions to ask as I'm sure you understand. They will want to know how all of this, the wedding, came about so suddenly. I hope you have answers that will appease all of them."

"I don't want to see anyone. Can I have a bath and something to eat?" She would feel better after that.

"They are not about to give you a choice. Wedding plans will be the reason to see you, but I've ordered a bath and breakfast as well. You must get all your strength back. I'll let them know they can talk to you in a couple of hours. The best thing would be for them all to go home and come back after lunch. What do you think? Will that work for you?"

"Suppose it will have to work." She plucked at the bed covers, not looking at him. She had a family now, a real family and everything, the good as well as the bad that came with it.

"There is your bath right now and food as well. That way you can choose what to do first." He strode to the door. "Thank you," he said, then turning to her, "The bath water and food, just as I promised."

"I feel as if I'm in heaven," she said, staring at the steamy water as it was emptied into the tub.

"Good I want you to say that every day for the rest of your life. My plan is to make your life a heaven on earth. Now, do you need some help? I'm more than willing and I promise I won't take advantage."

She didn't want to say yes, but, "Yes, please. I guess you helped me the last three days. You saw all of me..."

"And I will see all of you tomorrow and the next day and the next for the rest of our lives. You've made me a happy man, perhaps the happiest in all of Scotland, no, perhaps the world. You need not be shy with me now."

"It's just that I wasn't aware of you looking at me with no clothes on or touching me for that matter." Her fingers wound into the fabric of her nightgown.

"If you think you can manage by yourself, I'll leave." He appeared reluctant although the grin never faded. "What if I just sit in the chair over there with my back to you. I'll have a cup of coffee while you bathe."

"Promise you won't look?"

"Even though I'd like nothing better than to wash your back and your front as well, I'll behave myself. If you ask for my help, I'll be there."

Slowly, she nodded, "You never behave yourself. It's out of character but I suppose I will have to trust your word this time."

"Good." He helped her from the bed, walking with her to the tub. "If you sit on the chair, it will be easier for you to take the gown off."

She didn't know if she could get into the tub. Walking here, she'd been unsteady on her feet. She sucked in a huge gulp of air as if that would give her strength.

"I'll just be over here." He pointed to the chair, walking sideways in that direction. "If you need me, just say the word."

She watched as he sat down, turning his back to her while he put strawberry jam on a piece of bread and poured a cup of coffee. Maybe she should have eaten first. With wobbling fingers, she unbuttoned the gown, slipping it from her shoulders. She was reminded of the fact he put her into the gown, recalled his hands stroking her with the cool cloth. She gulped another breath of air. The sudden stream of air into her lungs did nothing to steady her shaking legs.

The bath looked a mile away. Two footsteps and she could brace herself on the rim then put one foot after the other into the tub. She didn't think she could do that. Wasn't sure at all that she wouldn't fall into the water if she tried by herself.

"Flynt..." She was looking over her shoulder at him.

As promised, he kept his back to her.

"Hope?" Still, he didn't turn. "Do you need something?"

"I don't think I can do it, get into the bath without help." She was sure he was grinning.

"Are you asking me to put you into the steaming and very soothing hot water? I promised you I wouldn't look at you, but I'm not sure I can keep my promise if you need my help."

"Please Flynt, I don't care about the bloody promise." She very nearly yelled at him. "I just want my bath. If you help, I'll close my eyes."

He was standing beside her then, laughing, "You'll close your eyes? How will that help? I'm looking at you now."

"With my eyes closed I won't see you looking at me. Now, will you help me into the bath?" She was impatient and indignant.

"I'll have to help you out too."

"I know." She felt defeated and vulnerable. She did not want to admit she wasn't strong enough to get into a bath but she wasn't.

Suddenly she was swept into his arms. Shocked, she opened her eyes to see the water in front of her as he slowly lowered her into the tub.

~ * ~

Catherine and all of Flynt's sisters gathered at the dressmakers. The morning hours were ticking away and Catherine wanted to have the gowns ready by noon. She looked at her watch then impatiently looked again. The wedding would take place at one o'clock sharp. Her nerves on edge and her heart pounding, she wanted this to be perfect. This was taking too long. Neither Chelsea or Bliss had proper weddings. Hope's wedding was the first one she could help plan and she so wanted it right.

The seamstress brought out the ice blue wedding gown she had ordered the day before for Hope which would look perfect with her red hair. Catherine paid extra to have the gowns finished on time, and the seamstresses must have worked overnight to have all the dresses finished.

"It's beautiful, Grams," Lacie, the youngest sister said, smiling. "Mine is beautiful too. I can't wait to wear it. Who are the groomsmen?"

"The bad boys, I assume," Bliss said. "Broc is the best man as well he should be in this situation."

"In any case, if it is Leslie you're hoping to see, this dress will cover you unlike most of your gowns now," Chelsea said laughing. "You really need to get the big brother to give you enough money to fashion more dresses that will hide your growing assets."

"I don't want to ask Flynt for more money. I had one fashioned last week. It will have to do until I can save up for another one."

"You can't go around with your breasts falling out of your gowns," Bliss said, "It just won't do. If you won't say something to him, I will."

"Yes, well, I know you'll do what you want," Lacie waved a hand in the air. "When I ask Flynt for money, it feels like begging and I don't like to do that."

"Now girls, let's get this wrapped up here. We've got to make it to the bakery as well as the florist to make sure everything is delivered on time. We've only a little more than an hour to accomplish all this.

"We have to help Hope dress for the ceremony," Daryl said. "The cakes are finished and on their way, so we don't have to go to the bakery."

"What is cook preparing for the reception?"

"Lots of appetizers. There will be more than enough food to eat, I'm sure." Catherine said. "I'm pleased my grandson has found such a wonderful woman to marry. There were a few weeks I was afraid he would pick Melessand. Not sure if we could have tolerated her for the duration. That would have been a horrible choice, and he would have regretted it for the rest of his life."

"Or Beatrice for that matter," Chelsea said, grinning. "He wanted an heir so badly he was willing to settle for any willing woman."

She turned to Daryl and Lacie. "Whatever the two of you do, don't settle for anything less than your true love. You will know him when you meet him."

Grams smiled then watching the two girls. "I do think these two know who they want."

"Is that true?" Bliss asked. "Who are they?"

Daryl blushed and looking away, she said, rather than answering the inquiry, "Isn't this fabric beautiful. Perhaps I'll ask Flynt for enough money to have a dress fashioned from it."

"Don't change the subject." Chelsea set the fabric back on the stack. "You've money from your bakery, so you don't have to ask for more from Flynt. Who is the man whose captured your heart? Tell us all even though I'm sure we've all guessed the truth."

Daryl shrugged, looking to her younger sister as if asking for help. "He barely even knows I exist. I would never tell for fear one of you would say something but one day maybe things will change between us. I do know he cares a little, but he also believes I'm a little girl who doesn't know what goes on between a man and a woman."

"Well, I don't mind saying something," Lacie said, "Ever since that night when the bad boys were playing cards, I've known I'm going to marry Leslie Stewart. That is if I can grow up fast enough."

"No," Grams said. "He's a dangerous man. You can't set your sights on that man."

"Dangerous? How so?" Lacie asked, looking clearly puzzled.

"Well, not in the way you are thinking right now. From all the rumors abounding around town he's a spy. He's been involved with the Scottish government and the English as well. He has skills. Well he can do things with his hands and feet that no one else can. I've heard they are lethal weapons. He has enemies, numerous enemies and he's been involved with that Montgomerie fellow who kidnapped Broc to make sure he knew that his sister was in Glasgow."

"Well, what would he be doing now?" Lacie asked, seemingly more intrigued by this man she should have nothing to do with.

"Just understand that he is dangerous, lethal even and people who are involved with him are automatically in danger."

"Couldn't be more dangerous than getting shot," Lacie said, folding her hands in her lap a self-satisfied expression on her face.

Chapter Four

Flynt paced the third-floor room where the wedding was set to take place, every nerve stretched to its breaking point. He looked to the door then pounded the floor some more. What if she didn't show up? What if she changed her mind? He could not stop the questions of doubt from rushing through his head. This was not how he imagined the courtship and the wedding. He would have liked it to be more romantic, but he couldn't do anything to change that now.

Hope's life was in danger.

Grams stood in the center of the room and he had no idea when she stepped through the doors. She smiled at him, her hands clasped in front of her. "She is almost ready and more beautiful than I've ever seen her. You are nervous and rightly so, but she is the right woman for you. You couldn't have chosen anyone better suited to you. By the way, you look grand in the kilt, the MacTavish dress tartan along with your velvet jacket. She will fall in love all over again when she sees you. Your knees are nice too."

"Thank you for that. I'm just afraid she'll change her mind." He waved his hand around the room. "Even though Musa has been reported as leaving, Arie's men stand guard at every door. What kind of wedding is this? I can't keep my wife safe and she takes a bullet meant for me. This is a damning situation, one that is untenable, but it doesn't seem there is anything I can do to change the situation."

He swore under his breath. Giving Hope everything she wanted and making sure she was happy his only objective.

"All will be fine. I wish your mother and father could be here today to witness the marriage." Grams held his hand in hers, patting the back of them. "You'll see. In a few more minutes, she'll be standing by your side saying the vows that will bind you together for life."

"How can you be sure?" His voice shook, all his usual control vanishing. "She's had plenty of time to leave."

"The girls will make sure she doesn't panic and do something she will come to regret," Grams said, still smiling, still trying her best to reassure him.

"I don't understand how you can be so very positive. I won't rest easy until as you say, she's saying I do and the minister confirms that we are wed."

"Well, you haven't seen the bride today. We made sure you were out of the room before she woke. Thank you for that. It's bad luck, you know, to see the bride on the wedding day before she walks down the aisle. And," she paused, "all her gifts are in order; something borrowed, something blue and something new."

"I see," he said, rocking on his heels, the first smile of the day, but he really didn't understand what the gifts had to do with anything. He would be thrilled when this was over. "So, all of the traditions have been executed, poor choice of words, and that means we will have good luck. I can only assume. It's all nonsense to this man's poor brain."

"I hope you do see. Have you had anything to relax those nerves that are even now taking over your body? You should not keep second-guessing this event. Hope will not flee. Besides isn't that what your best man is for? To make sure your soon-to-be wife doesn't leave?"

"You noticed," he said dryly. "I've never been this nervous, felt this type of anxiety. It's not just about the shooting. It revolves around the commitment I'm about to make. My best man would probably help her leave."

"Of course, he wouldn't. Well, in my mind, it's about time you realized your feelings for her. She is a wonderful woman, and we've all known she was in love with you since the first day she came into your life."

"I never noticed?"

He didn't like to believe he was that ignorant of other people's feelings. He always liked her, thought she was the most beautiful woman he'd ever seen, but she was Broc's sister. So, he'd used that as an excuse not to pursue her or believe he could court her let alone win her hand in marriage.

"You weren't interested in changing your life, making a pledge. You had your mistress to satisfy your sexual needs. What more does a man need?" she asked with a slight shrug and another smile, clearly enjoying this conversation. "I do hope Cook has prepared some ginger cookies for the reception or perhaps Daryl made ginger cakes."

"You know me too well. It's disconcerting that everyone else saw what was right in front of my face but I did not. Yet, now we are here and I'm going to be a husband and a father. Soon, I hope. Thank you for talking to me. I do feel somewhat better, a little more optimistic about today."

"Ah, make sure Hope understands you want her for herself, not for the fact she can give you an heir. What if she is unable to bare children? Have you thought of that?" she asked.

"No, I haven't." He rubbed his chin, wondering what the answer to that was. "I'm not going to worry. You yourself just told me everything would be fine. We have everything in order so nothing can go wrong. No bad luck today."

"Did Broc decide he would be your best man?" Grams changed the subject. "I guess you mentioned that before. My, I'm getting forgetful in my old age."

"Let's get that wine. Broc is my best man with little to no coercion. I suppose he wants to see her wed rather than live as my mistress. We are no longer at odds. Haven't been since he wed Bliss."

"What about Angus?" It seemed she wanted to push the conversation. "Angus seemed to be interested in Hope."

"Doesn't mean either Broc or Angus are beyond a practical joke or two. Angus was interested in Hope until he met Beatrice."

Between Broc and Cam the joke worked in his favor. When he saw Hope with Angus, he realized how he felt about her. If not for that, he'd probably still be trying to decide between the bluestocking Beatrice and the incomparable Melessand.

"Well, for the family's sake I'm glad all differences have been mended. It's best to get along," Gram said. "I see your best man and my husband. It must be time to for the wedding to begin."

He tipped the glass, drinking the wine before setting the crystal aside. Grams made sure all the best stemware and silver were set on the tables. Striding to the front of the room at the altar, he took his place with Broc, his best man, the minister next to them. They had been close since they could walk. Had run all over the countryside together. Broc and Bliss had twins now, a little boy and a girl. They would be grown before anyone could blink.

He would have an heir soon and they would also play together. He closed his eyes, breathing deeply, content.

Pipes began to play, slow and melodic. Bliss walked down the aisle, one child on each side holding her hand. One of the boys dropped flower petals while another held the pillow with the ring.

His happiness reached all the way inside, to the depth of his soul. He was filled with joy. In all his wildest imaginations he'd never thought this would happen for him. Only a week ago, he'd thought he'd be marrying either Melessand or Beatrice. He shuddered at the thought. How could he have possibly been so stupid when the woman of his dreams was living in the same house with him?

Bliss stopped on the opposite side while Broc reached out his hand to one of his sons and the other boy stayed by Bliss. Chelsea followed with Cam then Daryl with Donal then Lacie with Leslie, two of the other bad boys.

His breath caught in his throat when he saw Hope standing in the doorway, Grams husband, Nial, at her side. Grams must have given her the sash. She wore the MacTavish dress tartan pinned with a broach. Her hair was swept on top of her head and covered with a veil. A bouquet of white and blue flowers in her hand, she seemed hesitant and probably just as jittery as he was.

The pipes changed to a different song as they began their walk down the aisle. His gaze riveted on his bride, he couldn't keep the smile from his face or the happiness from his heart. Now that the moment was at hand, he was no longer nervous but eager. Yes, eager to start their lives together. Cam had offered them his beach home for a honeymoon, and he graciously accepted. After the ceremony they would make the thirty-minute or so drive to the ocean.

Nial handed her to him as he held her hand in his. She gave her bouquet to Bliss. They stood, hand in hand, gazing into each other's eyes. *I love you.*

He suddenly realized he needed to tell her how he felt.

The wedding continued. "Do you have anything you want to say to Hope?" the minister asked.

"Yes." He slowly kissed the back of her hand feeling tenderness as well as protectiveness well up inside. She was his. "Hope," he began, "you came unexpectedly into my life almost two years ago. You were different from all the women I knew and that was a good thing. For the longest time you couldn't remember where you came from or who you were so we called you Hope. Your amber eyes called to me as if you were a part of my soul, but I didn't realize it then. You disconcerted me with the way you spoke freely of things no women did." He paused then hoping to say the right words.

He squeezed her hand then continued. "Until you told me you were moving to your brother's townhouse, I didn't realize what you meant to me or how you touched my heart. Seeing you at the games with another man brought the point crashing down on me. After that I knew I never wanted you to leave my side. You made me the happiest man alive when you agreed to be my wife."

The minister turned to Hope. "Do you have anything you would like to tell Flynt?"

She nodded a few times. Moistening her lips and inhaling a shaky breath she began, "Unlike you, I knew the moment I saw you. You were looking at me with concern coupled with tenderness. I didn't understand but somehow I knew I wanted to be with you for the rest of my life. In the harem no one cared about each other. They just survived. I never really thought of marriage because I didn't know if I was good enough for a landed gentleman. As my memory slowly returned, I was sure you would never want me. I'd seen things no gentle woman should have seen, heard talk also. I said outrageous things before I stopped to think."

Hope looked to the floor for a few seconds as if gathering her thoughts. "I was terrified when you decided you wanted an heir and started looking at other women. I was sure I would lose you. When you brought Melessand home all my fears were magnified. She was so beautiful. That day, the day of the games, it seems like a lifetime ago. So much happened to me, to us and I found I was falling for you even more than I could have ever imagined. Flynt, I do want to spend the rest of my life with you as your wife." She smiled at him then.

The rest of the ceremony passed, the rings exchanged and I dos said. Then, "You may kiss your bride."

Before he kissed her, he whispered, "This one doesn't count for a lie." His lips found hers He didn't want to stop. By his standards it was a chaste, quick kiss but when he drew away, his lips still close to hers, they were met with a round of applause.

The minister announced them as Mr. and Mrs. Flynt MacTavish. He held her hand as they walked down the aisle while their friends and family watched. The pipes played again. He'd never been more pleased.

"I like you in a kilt, Mr. MacTavish," she whispered, her eyes alight with joy. "What do you wear beneath it?"

He roared with laughter, "Your audacity astounds me. What do you think I wear? Ach, sweet lassie, you'll have to wait to discover the truth until we arc in thc carriage on the way to the ocean."

She stopped, turning to him, "The ocean?"

He pressed a quick kiss to her forehead, "Yes, Cam has offered us his beach house for the week, and Arie has famously said he would supply all the security we needed to keep us alive."

He'd wanted and needed a special place for them to go. This would be heaven. A week with her all alone.

It seemed she mulled that over in her head for a while. "Suppose I should thank him."

"You should dance with your husband. Thank the man later." He pulled her into his arms then danced around the room until she was breathless and pleading for him to stop.

She laughed, seeming to have a pleasant time. "I need more stamina to keep up with you. I will have to practice."

"Practice only with me," he told her, stealing a quick kiss. "We need some wine and a bite to eat. I'm famished. I don't know about you, but I haven't eaten anything since last night."

"Neither have I." She lifted her shoulders a bit, along with a sideways glance. "I was too nervous. My stomach was in knots. Still not a lot better."

"Now some of the nerves have been vanquished I hope."

He held her close, his hand at her waist. This was not enough and he would have to wait during what seemed like an endless carriage ride. Perhaps he should spirit her downstairs to the master bedroom and consummate the marriage so she would have no more qualms for the rest of the night.

No doubt the guests would miss them and one of the bad boys would come looking for them. He couldn't risk embarrassing Hope. No, he would have to wait and exercise the control he needed, the control he prided himself having. He groaned, realizing just how difficult that would be.

Control was overrated.

With food and wine in hand, Flynt led her to one of the small tables on the balcony overlooking the city. The sun was still high in the sky and the day was cloudless. He reminded himself he would have to bring her here in the evening so she could see the lights of Glasgow.

"When did you plan on leaving? I'll have to pack, and everything I own is at Broc's townhouse," she asked as she sipped her wine.

"Grams and the girls took care of everything. You've a valise crammed full of things you might need and in the carriage waiting for our departure. As to leaving, we'll do that as soon as we can. If you need something they forgot to pack, there is a village close by. We can buy anything you want."

She was staring at his mouth and he wanted to laugh. She was seducing him with a look. This habit of hers was endearing yet provocative as hell. She had this way of making him forget all his good intentions. Now he planned to begin their lovemaking in the carriage on the way to the ocean.

"Alright then, I want to leave now."

He bent close, "Drink your champagne, eat all the food on the plate and I'll consider leaving as soon as we feed each other a bite of cake. We don't want everyone to think we're in a hurry to consummate this relationship."

"You mean that?" She pursed her lips together then moistened them with her tiny pink tongue. "Will you kiss me now?"

He leaned across the table, a brief kiss was all he would give her, "Just enough for you to want more."

She sat back, a look of perplexity on her beautiful face, amber eyes shining, "You're a tease."

"So are you. Shall we dance again?" He rose, holding his hand out to her, thinking then he was the luckiest man alive.

"I'd rather feed you your piece of cake then leave." With a bit of reluctance, she accepted his hand though.

"How about a compromise, my sweet lassie. We will dance our way to the table and Grams will make sure everyone is watching, the cake and our departure following."

"See the two of you found a place to be alone," Broc, holding Bliss' hand stepped in front of them. "I suppose congratulations are in order. You did the deed. Only two more bad boys to go."

Flynt patted Broc on the shoulder, "At least I didn't rush the wedding night. I'm sure you can appreciate that since Hope is your sister. My wife is not giving birth as the wedding vows were being said."

"I do grasp the importance of that. Bliss was insatiable though when it came to our lovemaking. She always wanted this man's body so desperately. There was no way I could tell her no. Refusal was just not in the cards as much as I tried." He laughed when she punched him on the shoulder.

"You seduced me, you cad. I had no idea what you were doing until I couldn't tell you to stop."

"You never wanted to tell me stop," Broc laughed, seemingly pleased with himself as well as his wife. "You were constantly begging for more."

Bliss punched him again to his seeming delight.

Cam and Chelsea joined them. "Congratulations, Flynt, I'm happy for you, even though this was a bit rushed," Chelsea said, giving him a hug and a quick kiss on the cheek. "I'm glad you finally figured out your feelings for Hope."

"Thank you for the offer of the beach house. It was the least you could do considering your other endeavors," Flynt said. "We're going to leave soon, and Hope is eager to begin our lives together."

"Perhaps you will have an amazing thunder storm. Make sure you sit on the porch swing and watch the ocean. It's very romantic," Chelsea said, her eyes alight as she reminisced.

"Don't forget the roof top possibilities either. If it's not raining, you'll find them quite amenable," Cam said, staring at Chelsea as if he wanted to devour her, as if he recalled their honeymoon.

"We should do the cake thing," Hope said, tugging on his hand. "He's right. I am eager to leave. I want to be alone with Flynt."

"She wants some very bonny lessons in lovemaking. That's what she is trying to say," Flynt laughed, as he watched the slow and very endearing rise of color to Hope's cheeks.

"I know I shouldn't be embarrassed. I've heard and seen so many things a young woman shouldn't. The harem women spoke of everything, even the size of the men's—"

Flynt quickly covered her mouth with his hand. Then leaning in close, with a whisper, "You probably shouldn't say anything more."

"But I've never seen..." She seemed to be babbling now, her nerves getting the better of her suddenly.

"You will tonight, I promise you. Now."

Giving her a wink, he turned to the others who seemed to be enjoying Hope's words more than he thought they should. He wanted those reflections all to himself, sharing wasn't in his plans. "We will give each other a bite of cake then everyone will toss rice our way and after that they won't see us for a week."

"Where are your other sisters? I'd like to say good bye to them first." Hope turned in a circle.

Flynt searched the room too, "There is Lacie with Leslie. They seemed to be enjoying themselves."

"Do you think that is wise? He's much older than Lacie," Chelsea stepped into the conversation. "Should we make sure they have a chaperone?"

Flynt wasn't sure if his sister was teasing or concerned for the youngest sibling. "Grams will take care of it if they become serious. Don't think it will be a problem today though. Heard he's off to Edinburgh then somewhere else under the direction of the crown. Works for someone by the name of Montgomerie."

"Drake Montgomerie is the man who found Hope for us and protected her before Arie arrived here," Chelsea said.

"Leslie works for him?" Flynt asked, curious as to why he'd never heard any of this.

"Never mind that, Lacie is leaning into him, to hear every word. I do believe she'd like a lot more than he is offering at the moment."

"I for one am just glad the bodice of the dress fits and she is not popping out of it right in front of Leslie. That would be horrid for her," Chelsea said, straining to see her younger sister. "You must see to it that she gets some dresses that fit her. If she is interested in a young man, she has to have something decent to wear."

Flynt really looked at Lacie. "She is quite endowed, isn't she? Never noticed before. When we return, I'll send her to the dressmakers or you can take her, Chelsea. Just have the seamstress put it in on my tab. Now to the cakes."

Daryl was waiting for them expectantly, Donal by her side. Another surprise for Flynt who didn't realize his sisters were growing up so fast. Good Lord, two were wed and the other two seemed absorbed with men he'd rather they were not attracted to. They were bad boys after all. They were, however, better than Angus and that other man, what was his name, who wanted to court Bliss, or was it Chelsea? He couldn't remember any of it, had put it in the back of his head. It seemed he was finally coming to his senses.

"About time," Daryl said as they approached the reception table. She was tapping her toe, but what had Flynt worried was the possessive hand Donal placed on his sister's back.

He slanted Donal a frown but the man, his friend, grinned back at him, seeming to understand exactly what he was thinking. "Nice to see you happily wed," Donal said, slapping him on the back.

"There is a basket for the two of you. I packed it with the best foods and it's waiting in the carriage. You will have plenty of food and drink while you travel." Daryl smiled prettily then looked at Donal as if for approval.

Flynt groaned, understanding he still had two sisters to worry about, and it appeared as if they were more interested in bad boys than they should be. Grams had no idea how to handle these men. She was too lenient by far and both men would take advantage if they were given free reign.

He didn't have time to worry now.

Daryl handed him one of the little cakes. "Break off a piece with icing on it."

He did then held it to Hope's lips, making sure the tiniest amount of icing stayed there. He grinned, leaning forward and tasting the frosting. "You taste better than this sweet confection your sister made."

"My turn?" she asked, looking pleased. "I didn't want you to smear it all over my face. Thank you."

She did the same to Flynt. He nearly groaned out loud when her tongue moved across his lips. "I do believe it's time to leave. My poor body cannot take any more of this delicious torment. I must have the tiniest bit of relief."

"A toast first." Broc held up a glass of champagne while Bliss made sure both Flynt and Hope had one of their own.

"Is this necessary?" Flynt was impatient to leave and needed no more interference from his friends. They would intentionally put the departure off as long as possible just to torment them.

"It is. Now." He held up the glass. "This is to the happiness of the sister I never knew existed and to a man I've called friend for as long as I can remember. They will do well together, and I wish them all the happiness in the world. I do believe it is time for them to leave though. Flynt has that impatient look in his eyes I've often felt myself."

"Here, here." The others chanted while they gathered the tiny bags of rice the sisters made and rushed to line the stairway to the first floor.

Running down the stairs and ducking to avoid as much rice as possible, Flynt and Hope finally reached the ground floor. He swept her into his arms, carrying her to the carriage.

Once inside, he leaned on the cushions behind him, his arms resting on the back of the seat, gazing at her and wondering just how far he should take things while they traveled. "You are my wife," he said pleased with himself and the fact.

"And you are my husband." She smiled back at him then lowering her lashes for a moment. "That means I can do anything I want to you or with you. I want to see all of you, like you promised a little while ago"

"Come here." He patted his lap as the carriage began to roll. "I am going to have those kisses you promised me. Then a few more for good measure."

"What about the ones you promised me?" she countered.

He couldn't wait. Pulling her to him, she was sitting on him, staring at his mouth again. You are beyond a doubt the most provocative woman I've ever known. His lips settled on hers, parting hers with his tongue, reaching deep inside. She matched him, responded with fervent honesty and enchanting need. Raw savage desire ripped through him. He reminded himself he wasn't going to consummate this marriage in the carriage.

His hands rested on either side of her head, kissing her and kissing her again. He couldn't get enough of her. His lips found their way along her neck then to her ear where he whispered, "You are so beautiful."

She ran her fingers through his hair, "No, you are beautiful."

Drawing slightly away, "Men aren't beautiful, but I appreciate the compliment more than you know."

His lips explored again, discovering places he'd seen but never touched evocatively or to seduce. Along the line of her corsage, he kissed and nibbled, delighted to hear the tiny sounds of pleasure he created in her. He wanted to feel her arch against him, feel her need.

The sleeves of her dress were barely there, hardly anything at all. With little effort he slid the fabric down her arms until her breasts were bared to his view. "So stunning, I can barely breathe." His voice turned husky, deep and raw, vibrating with pleasure.

Her gasp of surprise gave him cause to look into her eyes and smile pleased with her response. "Are you alright?"

She moistened her lips. "I want you to touch me, I think. Kiss me everywhere," she said. "I'm not afraid, if that's what you are asking. It was such a shock, the knowledge you were staring at me, at my breasts. Something I knew about but forgot I suppose."

"Good, that's good," he murmured as he kissed her nipple, drew it into his mouth, knew joy when she arched drawing him closer with her hands. He touched and teased, created a fire within himself that he knew burned inside her also. She needed him as much as he needed her.

In the back of her throat a soft moan rippled out.

"We should stop for a moment. Have something to eat. I want you to get used to me looking at you, touching you. You taste so damn sweet though I can barely resist."

"I need to taste you too," she said, gazing at his mouth again, "I'm only hungry for you."

He groaned then, pulling the bodice up to cover her breasts. This much of Hope wasn't enough of Hope, but if he continued on this vein, her skirts would be tossed and he'd be deep inside her before the trip ended.

~ * ~

"Are we here?" Hope asked, looking out the window at the ocean. "It's so beautiful." Except for the minutes they spent drinking the wine and eating, Flynt had explored just about every inch of her.

"We are." He sat back, a self-satisfied smile on his handsome face, his arms spread across the back seat. "What are you feeling?"

"Nervous but eager. Even though you're not touching me, I still burn for you. There is an inferno deep inside me that yearns to be quenched. I need you in the most elemental ways. Is there no end to these feelings?" She didn't know what else to tell him.

"Yes," he smiled. "In a few minutes you, well, I will give you your woman's pleasure and you will also pleasure me at the same time. You must be patient. Lord knows I'm having a devilishly hard time doing the same, but we are very nearly there."

"Flynt, I want to get this over with." She saw the stunned look on his face and immediately regretted the words. "I'm sorry what I said displeases you, but it is the truth. You've teased me so much it seems I'm hot and needing something I don't know what it is."

He didn't seem to be able to form the words that would help her understand. "We should take a tour of the house. I want to see this rooftop view Cam and Chelsea spoke of. After that we'll figure out how best to get the lovemaking over with. I warn you I'm more inclined to take my time with your pleasure."

She stared at her clasped hands, trying to steady her rattled nerves and pounding pulse. "I don't understand why."

"In a few hours maybe less, you will understand completely. Now," he stepped from the carriage, "we will see what this place has to offer. Cam guarantees me it is amazing, wonderful, spectacular. No other place compares in ambiance. Servants have seen to the house so everything will be ready for us." He paused for a moment. "May I?" he asked, holding out his arms. "While I've been here on one occasion, I've never been to the rooftop."

Nodding, she allowed him to carry her onto the porch before setting her on the swing Chelsea spoke of. He sat down beside her, his arm behind her resting on the back of the swing. "Now, I'd like to kiss you in every even remotely romantic place this house has to offer us."

"You've used up all your kisses."

She couldn't stop from looking at his mouth. Whenever he mentioned kisses, that was where her thoughts traveled, where she was forced to look. She moistened her lips, waiting.

"Do I need to lie to you to get a kiss?" he chuckled softly. "I'll do whatever is necessary. I'm ready and very willing. At the moment, however, I can't think of anything to lie about."

"Maybe I should kiss you."

She smiled at the expression in his eyes, passion that seemed to shimmer. She really liked the way they sparkled, but his mouth was soft and moist when she touched it with her lips.

He didn't respond and she understood this was her kiss to give and he would wait for her. "Open for me," she whispered, running her tongue along her mouth, but she didn't wait for him to do her bidding. She kissed her way to his ear, ran her tongue around the lobe, biting gently, enjoying the masculine groan of pleasure her exploration caused. This was what she wanted, what she needed to do to him. She wanted to give him as much pleasure as he gave her.

"You are getting too good at this," he said as her lips found his once more and her tongue delved inside, touching, tasting the wine, exploring.

It was a heady sensation this giving of kisses, this control she'd always expected from him. Something she would enjoy and hold as special for the nights to come. She pulled away. "I believe you are an excellent teacher. Should we take a look inside the house or go to the rooftop?"

"The rooftop, when you're ready for me to make love to you, I want to be in the master chamber or perhaps this bed Cam spoke of. All our foreplay will be in the spaces before. That is if I can wait that long."

"It's almost sunset. You should grab that bottle of wine we left in the carriage before we go up the steps."

"Cam told me he keeps wine on the rooftop. There are lots of things up there as long as the weather is good. Perhaps our first time should be with the view of the ocean and the setting sun."

She felt shy suddenly, anticipating this moment with wonder and eagerness. She was afraid of the pain and she hoped he would be gentle. She also knew from the women of the harem the first time could be agonizing or not so much. She hoped in her case the moment would be all about pleasure.

"We could do that if that's what you want."

She touched his face, memorizing the contours the angles and planes.

Munroe, his valet and confidant appeared on the porch. "The house is ready for you, Sir. Arie has men everywhere. He assured me they would not be seen and they would not invade your privacy as long as you remained in the house and on the grounds."

"If we want to go for a ride?" Flynt asked.

"They must be informed. Just because you are wed doesn't mean whoever wants you dead will quit trying," Munroe said pleasantly. "After all, we don't want to lose you, especially on your honeymoon."

"Very well. I don't want to be lost either. We will be on the roof for a while. I don't want to be interrupted unless it's a matter of life or death."

"As you wish." Munroe nodded before leaving.

Flynt stood, holding out his hand. She accepted and they walked around the house to the stairs leading to the top of the house. Heat rose to her cheeks as they strode past the covered bed, all sorts of pillows adorning it.

"We should have our first time right there." Flynt looked toward the bed, his eyes clearly filled with passion and seeming to realize how private and romantic the spot was. Cam had been right about everything. This place was magical.

Her body heated more with the feelings sifting through her head. She didn't have to close her eyes to imagine his mouth on her, his fingers caressing her intimately. He'd done all those things on the way here. She felt hot and wet, almost as much as before they arrived.

His arms brushed across her breast then he pulled her close as they walked. He draped his arm over her shoulder, his hand resting on her breast, his fingers teasing the hardened nipple just below the fabric. She shuddered, leaning into him. Blessed hell but this was a beautiful torment but would he ever finish what he kept starting?

"You're enjoying tormenting me, aren't you? If you must know it is tantamount to torture," she said, knowing he would tell her yes.

"Did you know my rod is bruised from pushing against my buckskins? I would love to be naked with you. Deep inside your warmth and the tortured moments for both of us would be over."

"I want that too, but I'm also afraid, afraid of the unknown. That's why I want to do this and be done with the fear. After that you can take your time, tease and torment, tantalize to your heart's desire and I won't complain."

"I suppose I must have teased you too much in the carriage, but I still believe with all my heart it is necessary." His voice wavered a moment when he spoke. "This is a huge responsibility for me."

She bristled at his words. "Then you should just make love to me as if I'm one of your mistresses. Why should anything be different? Why should I be such a huge responsibility?" This was strange to her, unnerving as well and why, she didn't understand but she felt a surge of exasperation.

"My mistress was not a virgin and when I made love to her, she'd had another lover before me. This is entirely different, and I don't want to hurt you more than necessary." He sounded angry to her, frustrated or annoyed possibly.

She was suddenly surer of herself than ever before. He needed to know what she felt. "I think you've overthought this and we've over talked it. We are making more of this initiation into lovemaking than we should."

"Perhaps you're right. I've been too concerned about you, your first time and all." They stopped at the railing overlooking the ocean. "The sun is about to dip below the horizon. You should make a wish."

"Why? I've never heard of such a thing."

He laughed then, "Neither have I. Nothing wrong with wishing is there? I know what I'm going to wish for."

He was acting strange and she didn't understand, but he was surprisingly relaxed after the conversation. "I will make a wish then."

Opening the box that held the wine, he pulled out a bottle of Bordeaux and two crystal glasses. "Cam makes everything very nice. Only the best for him, I suppose."

"Cam brought Chelsea here for their honeymoon also. We didn't know they were married," she mused, thinking about the outrage surrounding their elopement. She laughed then, "Cam tried so hard to be the perfect gentleman. Probably something like you are doing now. He didn't want to frighten her and if you protested, he was going to make sure he'd done everything in a gentlemanly manner. To my knowledge he didn't lay a hand on her until they were wed. Just kisses. He did react poorly when Arie made him jealous though."

"Think we have time for one kiss before making those wishes." His lips found hers. He kissed her long and deep, filling her with longing, her body responding urgently to his explorations as she pressed against him. He kissed her face, her neck along her bodice. She ran her hands through his hair. It was soft, silken to her touch. She pulled his shirt from the waistband and slipped her hands beneath to caress him.

The stubble of his beard across her breasts gave her reason to shiver in response. His mouth was on hers again. The heated glide of his tongue over and into her mouth scattered her thoughts. She tried to think about the wish, but all her attention was focused on his lips. They were vividly alive, hot where his tongue was touching and cool where it passed on and soft, perhaps the only soft part of him.

Her arms tightened around Flynt until she was pressed hard against him. He helped by arching her back, pressing more kisses along her neck and just above her breasts.

Her breath came in brokenly, opening her mouth. His tongue dipped beneath her upper lip, gliding, probing, circling. His teeth caught her lower lip. He tugged gently. She heard the ragged sound and opened her lips wider. She knew his tongue was hot inside her mouth. The taste of his kiss was sweet beyond bearing.

When he drew away from her. "It's time to make that wish." Still he held her close, offering her the wine left in her glass.

Slowly the sun settled beneath the waves, the vivid colors spreading across the horizon. She caught her breath when his lips were once more pressing against her neck. Without words he led her to the bed, the pillows, the covers. He guided her to the spot where she would truly become his.

She sat on the bed, her hands in her lap, waiting expectantly for something she'd been anticipating since she first met him.

"You should finish your wine," he said as he drank his and set the glass on the table beside the bed. While she drank the last of hers, he left her side and returned with the bottle.

"I don't want anymore," she told him.

"What is it you do want?" He smiled that all knowing smile of his, the one that always touched her heart.

"I want you, all of you, to see you naked and your..." She looked at him wondering if it was alright to say the word now? She didn't wait. "I want to see your rod. I want to stop playing games and make love. I need you Flynt. I know getting it over with are the wrong words to use but Flynt... Please."

He sat against the headboard. Drawing her between his legs he pulled off his shirt. "I understand and will do my best for you. You have to trust my judgment in this" His kisses were gentle, and hot so sweet she wanted more and more.

"I've never seen you without your shirt," she said, trying to turn in his arms, "and now I still can't."

He laughed, pulling the sleeves of her gown down her arms as he'd done in the carriage. "I'm going to touch your breasts and, in a few minutes, I'm going to take them into my mouth. Will you like that?"

"Yes."

She swallowed hard as his fingers touched her, tugged on the nipples, rolled them. She felt his breathing as well as the hair on his chest. "I want to see you," she whispered. "Let me turn around and look." She could see his face when he leaned close and spoke to her.

"In time." His voice was husky and his eyes were a smoldering silver blue beneath his nearly closed lashes.

While he kissed her and fondled one breast his other hand drew her skirt to her hips. The sensation of his hands on her legs, left her breathless and in need of something she couldn't define. He ran his fingers along the inside of her thigh then higher, higher still. She stiffened and he stopped for a moment. She heard his deep rumbling chuckle before he continued on in the same manner.

"You groaned," she told him. "Do you like this as much as I do? Do you like to touch me?"

"More probably but I'm glad to know I'm not hurting or embarrassing you and you are receiving pleasure."

"I didn't say you weren't embarrassing me. Your hand where it is now... I didn't know exactly that you would touch me there."

The feelings cascading through her were delicious. So was the taste of Flynt, the textures of beard stubble, lips, tongue and teeth caressing her skin.

"Your body has softened, begging me. Are you slick with need, the honey flowing? Let me touch you intimately."

"More intimately than this?" she questioned even though she

knew better.

Sometime in the last few seconds he drew her underclothes off. They lay on the floor below the bed. His hand rested on her belly, his fingers on her mound and he wanted to touch her sweet feminine folds, more than this.

"Open for me my sweet, sweet lassie, spread your legs just as you open your mouth to give me better access," he whispered close to her ear, his teeth grazing the lobe, his tongue swirling inside. He turned her head and merged his mouth with hers. The sensations were slow and tender, hot and so overwhelming passionate, she cried out.

Suddenly, her dress lay beside her underwear. She wore only her chemise. He settled his hands lower until he touched her more personally just as he said. She was hot, wet and she couldn't help herself, didn't want to in any case. Her hips moved seeming to implore him to explore further. A sensitive spot seemed to captivate his fingers, and it appeared he knew just what to do. She was losing control, melting into him, for him.

He teased, excited her and she was helpless in his arms. An inferno swept through her and the enchantment was overwhelming. "Flynt..." she moaned softly, her voice barely a thin whisper in the darkening night. "Flynt...please..."

"Please you, of course I will. Do you like this, lassie? You know you don't have to beg. I'll give you exactly what you want." he said, his voice so deep and raw she didn't recognize it. "You're just about there. Relax and let your body respond."

Then she was. She spun out of control and tremors of sweetly painful pleasure swept through her. She cried out his name again and again. Unable to think, all she could do was feel the hot sweetness, the delicious tempest. She didn't want this to ever end. Yet slowly she calmed, her breathing not as ragged as before, her pulse not as fast and hard.

She closed her eyes and for the longest time, it seemed she lost the ability to move. She turned in his arms. He allowed it, her hand resting on his chest. "You, you still have most of your clothes on. I don't like it."

"I know. Do you want to take them off me?" He grinned wide, his eyes sparkling with raw desire as the blue deepened. "There is still more."

"Perhaps we should have wine and a bite to eat." She procrastinated. "You still haven't really made love to me, have you?"

He rose then, slipping his buckskins and boots off. She saw him, really saw him. Her breath caught. Her gaze was no longer riveted on his mouth but his sex.

"Your eyes look to be popping out of your head."

He laughed as he poured more wine, obviously comfortable in his nakedness.

"They are," she swallowed hard, unable to remove her gaze.

He didn't seem concerned about his nakedness. That surprised her. He was experienced, had at least one lover, probably more.

He brought the wine, "Something to relax you more." He drank deeply then waited for her to follow suit.

She looked at him over the rim of the glass, studying him, wondering even more about the events to come. She wanted to touch his sex, see what his rod felt like. Tracing her finger along the rim of her glass, she wondered just how he would fit, but she didn't mean to ask him because he undoubtedly would have an answer or he would lie. He might even laugh and she didn't think it funny.

"Relaxed would be good," she mumbled, her mind still on his size and the fact he meant to put it inside her.

He heard her and laughed. "Now who has more clothes on. Lassie? I've touched every part of you. Don't' you think it's time I saw you clearly and with no fabric of any sort concealing you?"

She looked at herself, covered only in her thin chemise then, "Why you can see most all of me as it is. This," she plucked at the fabric, "doesn't leave much to the imagination, you know."

"It's nice. I'm going to have to purchase some see through lingerie for you. What you have on is very provocative but nothing compared to you wearing nothing, nothing at all. Take it off."

She plucked at the fabric again then unable to meet his gaze. "I don't want to. Really I don't."

"I will help." He stood beside her. "Now, you can either stand and let me pull it over your head or..."

"You would rip it from me?"

Her body gave a tiny shudder of fear or excitement. She truly wasn't sure of anything right now let alone her feelings.

"No, I can think of other ways. The simplest would be the best though." He grinned at her again, his hands resting on narrow hips. "Not meaning to rush you but...you wanted to get this over with. Your words not mine."

His thoughts she knew would leave her blushing. She stood then and slowly pulled the sheer garment over her head. Before she could let go of the fabric, she was on her back on the bed with Flynt hovering, his big body above her, eyes shimmering with raw desire.

"Now, it is finally time."

He braced himself above her on his forearms. Somehow when he put her on the bed he came down between her legs. He was kissing her again, doing all those delightful tantalizing things to her. The magic and the enchantment grew.

And she wanted it, longed for it with all her heart. Never wanted him to stop.

She closed her eyes, needing to feel everything passing between them as he kissed his way down the length of her body. He rose above her then. She was compelled to wonder.

"Open your eyes, I want to see you." He slipped a finger inside her then two, moving them slowly as she arched to meet him.

She gasped once again startled by the intimate touch. "Flynt," she breathed deeply still in awe of the moment.

"You are every small and tight but I will fit. I touched your maidenhead. This will hurt. I was hoping it was broken just a little or perhaps not there at all."

"I wouldn't be a virgin. You wanted that, didn't you?" Once again, he'd shocked her, surprised her with his statement. Men wanted to wed virgins, didn't they?

"Women who were untried, naïve in the ways of lovers, of lovemaking. I just didn't want to cause you pain. Now, I want to taste you," he lowered his mouth to her. Savored her intimately, his tongue creating an erotic dance within.

She gasped again as he continued, but she lost all thought process, the sweet heat was unbearable. She was moving against him, building and building to that pinnacle of pleasure she reached only a few minutes ago.

"That's it, sweet lassie. Keep your eyes open. You're almost there. I'm going to come inside you this time. No, don't tense up, relax, let me do everything and you will know the sweetest agony turned to bliss."

She tried to do as he requested. Knew he was right as she felt the enchanting spasms begin once more then he was inside her, his rod pulsing, hot, deep then deeper still. She cried out, the searing pain enveloping her, felt a tear slide down her cheek. She pounded on his chest, beating on him. He didn't move for seconds and seconds.

Then, "Sweet, sweet lassie, I'm so very sorry. While I knew it would hurt. I didn't want this for you. Never again though."

He was kissing her, kissing her everywhere. The sensations were building inside her once more and she wanted him to never stop. "It's alright," she whispered. "There is no more pain, only pleasure as you told me."

"I know, I can feel your response, the way you're answering me with your sweetness," He was moving inside her, harder and deeper until it seemed they cried out together.

She lay beneath him now, his huge body covering her but not all of his weight pressed down upon her. His body was sweat sheened as was hers. "I don't think I can move, can barely breathe," she whispered.

"I'm sorry," he said again. "It won't ever hurt you, now that I've made you mine. Never..." Slowly he moved off her body then walked to an end table where a basin of water and a cloth had been set. "Don't be afraid."

He was looking at her again and she followed the direction of his gaze. There was blood... She stared at him, alarmed. Yet she remembered the stories the women told, recalled the blood on their first time with the sultan.

"Your virgin's blood and my seed, what didn't go deep inside you to make an heir for me and a child for you. I'll wash you." He opened her thighs and gently cleaned the remnants of her initiation to love.

Heat flooded her cheeks and she closed her eyes, mortified by all he did and said. She inhaled then did the same again, knowing she would have to get used to baring everything to him.

"No need to be embarrassed," he told her smiling. "This is what married people do. All is so very natural and normal."

She moistened dry lips, "I'm trying not to be." Then she whispered, "I don't think I can sit here in front of you stark naked. I don't feel comfortable or relaxed, just vulnerable."

"I've robes if you want but in time you will get used to it. Do you like to look at me, lassie?"

She couldn't lie to him, so nodding her head, "Yes you are quite handsome, beautiful too, so different from me. I've never really thought about a man's body and the differences, only that men are usually so much bigger."

He handed her a robe then put his on, clearly looking pleased after her answer. "Go ahead, I dare say you won't have it on much of this night. We should walk downstairs before the rain starts."

She had not noticed the clouds or the wind for that matter. She'd been aware of nothing or no one but Flynt, "Rain," she murmured.

"I'll send Munroe to retrieve our feast. Let's get out of here before we are drenched to the bone."

With that said, the sky opened and rain sluiced from the sky.

Broc paced the townhouse, Flynt's home, appalled at the news. He would have to send a message to him and interrupt the honeymoon "So, one of the crofter's cottages has been set on fire, his field as well?"

"Yes, sir, arson sir. Left a message. Said Flynt would die. Didn't have any use for a man of his nature. Don't think this has anything to do with that sultan fellow who shot Hope."

"What nature is that?" Broc asked with little patience.

He roughed his hands through his hair, wishing he wouldn't have to interrupt the honeymoon to bring Flynt this news. A matter of life and death, did this fit that category? To Flynt it would. Did this have anything to do with the man who coveted Hope? He was of a mind to agree with the man who delivered the message."

"He will want to see this first hand," Catherine said, one hand on Brock's arm as if steadying herself. "His crofters as well as the land are important to him and his livelihood."

"What nature?" Broc repeated, his voice harsh.

"That's the thing. The messenger was a little vague. Didn't really say what it was just that he didn't like the way Flynt acted. Said he seemed all high and mighty, he did, and had no right to behave that way."

"Well." The man fidgeted with his hat, slapping his leg. "The first thing they set afire was the cottage. The family ran out. The men were on horseback you see and they corralled them. Wouldn't let them leave to try to put the flames out. When nothing was left, they set the field on fire. Those people won't get crops this year. They'll starve."

"MacTavish won't let that happen," Broc said. "Do you know if there were any other homes set on fire?"

"No, no, sir, I don't. I saw the flames and ran to help. I got on my horse and rode straight here. Knew MacTavish was celebrating his wedding night somewhere. Didn't want to waste any time."

"Good then, go home to your folks. If anything else happens, come straight here. Catherine will listen to any messages you might bring. You can give her the news and she'll report back to me."

Leslie appeared in front of them, "What has happened, the two of you look too somber by far? I saw the man and thought you might need some help."

"Seems there has been a fire, home and a field burnt. Flynt and Hope might be in danger from a second source." Broc told him.

"Arie's men are there. He should know but do we have to inform Flynt? It's his wedding night. Seems telling Arie might be good enough."

"No, but I don't think he would forgive us if we didn't tell him. These are his people after all," Broc said. "He can always go back to the beach house when this matter is taken care of."

"At least he should be able to make the decision. If he chooses to stay at the house, it will be his decision not ours," Leslie said.

"We could use your help as well as Donal's. I'll ride to the beach house. Should be there by morning and give Flynt the bad news." Cam said. "The rest of you should go to the crofter's home, what is left of it, and assess the damage. You can stay there and wait for me. Flynt and I won't be much longer since it is on the way to the ocean."

"Do you ken if it's the man who wanted Hope?" Donal asked. "Arie has a way of making people pay. He's quite handy at it."

Donal's words brought a smile to Cam. He remembered the men Arie stripped naked and left in the town square then when they didn't get the message that Chelsea was off limits. When the man and his partner persisted, he kidnapped them before he sold them as slaves. The Turkish had a different way of finding vengeance, and perhaps at times it fit the crime to perfection since the men wanted to sell Chelsea to the highest bidder.

"Yes," he agreed. "Arie has a way of settling scores. Last I heard the sultan was on his way home. This isn't his doing."

"Whoever this person is..." Cam let the sentence hang waiting for the rest to write their story.

Chapter Five

Hope was warm and soft, her back against his chest, his leg sprawled lazily over hers. This was true bliss, and he wanted to hold on to this moment forever. She pushed back against him, her sweetly rounded derrière touching him, arousing him further.

He placed tender kisses down her spine, hoping to wake her. The day was wasting away, not that it mattered. They could spend all day in bed if that was what she wanted. The night had been splendid; today would prove to be just as amazing. The promise of tranquility loomed in front of them.

She moaned softly then sighed her contentment. He cupped a breast in his hand, touched the nipple, rolling it between his fingers. Then he was inside her and he knew the instant she woke. She stiffened slightly, surprised before she pushed against him again.

"How are you?" he whispered near her ear, gently pulling on the lobe with his lips and teeth.

"You want to do this again?" she said in question. "Seems that's all we've been doing for the entire night."

"Don't you?" He waited for her to answer. When she did, he touched her intimately until he felt her, response. "That's it. Come for me."

"I didn't know you could..." she said when they were finally sated.

"From behind?" he laughed, loving the way she accepted everything he did. "There are other ways too. Maybe later today we can explore more ways to appreciate each other."

"Why not now?" She rolled over, the covers slipping to her waist while he feasted on her beauty, caressing her gently.

Her silken hair cascaded over her shoulders, one lock curling delightfully around a breast, the nipple poking through, begging for attention, his attention. He brought the strand to his cheek, eliciting another tiny gasp of surprise when the back of his hand touched a soft rosy peak.

"Insatiable, little lassie. You ken I've got to rest after last night and this morning. I canna keep pleasuring you."

"Nay, that is not me. I need to sleep. You kept me up most of the night with your lovemaking," she told him petulantly.

"We should go for a ride and enjoy the sunshine after last night's drenching. The air will be crisp and clean. The sun will feel good. We can find a private grassy knoll where we can make love or perhaps a secluded place on the beach."

She looked at him. The only word he could think of to describe the expression was askance then, "We should eat. It seems there is always food for us then we get sidetracked and forget to put something in our stomachs," she told him indignantly. "I for one could eat just about anything right now. I want a cup of hot tea first though." She paused in thought. "A bath next."

"I will see what our cook has prepared for this morning. First another kiss before I leave for downstairs."

"If you kiss me again, we won't be getting our breakfast anytime soon and you act as if it is a real chore to retrieve breakfast."

"That's not what I want to be hearing. No kisses, lassie? I need a bonny kiss or I'll surely die of longing."

The pounding on the door stopped him.

"Flynt? Flynt are you and the missus in there? Have to talk."

"Monroe, this better be important." Flynt rose from the bed, pulling on his pants even while he turned to Hope. "Pull the covers up, lassie. Don't want anyone but me looking at your sweet charms."

Broc burst into the room, "Sorry, but this can't wait. Didn't mean to interrupt the two of you the morning after but..."

"Get on with it," Flynt waved a hand in the air, impatient with his friend. "You've already interrupted so you might as well tell us what has you beating down our door on our honeymoon."

"Thought you should know one of your crofter's home and field was burned last night. Don't know who did it but the crime was arson. Luckily no one was hurt," Broc continued. "Knew you'd want to check this out."

"Was it the sultan, Musa?"

"Don't think so. I've already spoken with Arie. That man's ship sailed when Arie made his point with him the other day. When you leave to check this all out, he'll make sure Hope is protected."

She sat up, covers to her neck. "I'm not staying here if Flynt goes. I don't want to be rambling around in the house by myself, afraid for him or terrified someone might be looking for me."

"You're staying," Flynt said but was taken aback by the look in her eyes.

She was clearly not pleased with his statement.

"I'd be safer with you and you wanted to go for a ride anyway. This could all work out for the best."

She smiled, lifting her shoulders slightly as if she realized she'd won this round when he softened his features.

"Alright then. I'll grab you that cup of tea and you find your riding habit. Hopefully, one was packed. The bath will have to wait until we return."

He finished dressing and left with Broc. Arie sat downstairs. "Didn't want to be the one to barge in on the two of you, so I sent Munroe and Broc. Now, shall we go and see what all the dither is about? Fix it then you can get on with your post nuptial plans."

"We're waiting for Hope." Flynt grumbled as he looked up the stairway for her. "She gave a good argument and is getting dressed as we speak."

"I see," Arie said, grinning now and looking up the steps as if she'd appear right now. He returned his attention to Flynt. "Believe you have an enemy. One you don't know is one who is harder to fight than the one you do know. Take care with your precious wife."

"I'm pretty sure I know who it is, a man whose father lost a sizeable amount of land to my father. He's coveted this piece of property all his life. His father was a wastrel and gambler. The man is fortunate he didn't lose everything. My father took pity on him and only accepted half of what he won in the game of cards. Whose land and home was burned?"

"David McClintock's," Broc said.

"Makes sense, that field is adjacent to his. He must hope with this year's profits up in smoke the man will leave." Flynt turned his attention to the stairs, smiling as Hope hurried toward them with flushed cheeks, one hand on her bosom. She made an enticing picture.

"Did I take too long?" she asked breathless, her hair swept on top of her head, stray locks falling in wild disarray around her face.

"Probably not long enough. Let me check to make sure all your buttons are fastened before you leave the house. You certainly didn't spend any time on your hair," he told her as he tried to pin the chignon into place.

"Here is your tea," Arie handed her a cup while Flynt perused her riding habit. "I believe you have time for a sip or two, nothing to eat until later."

"Only if Flynt lets me go," she said indignantly, smoothing her skirts. "Everything important is fastened and I'd like a bite of something."

Arie laughed. "You wanted to come along. Perhaps there is a chunk of bread I can get you. You can eat it on the way to the stables."

~ * ~

Except for the bad news and the threat to his land, the day was perfect for a ride. As he expected the drenching rain from last night cleaned the air. If the sun continued to shine, the ground would dry. On the way home they could find that grassy knoll for a little private time.

He watched her ride, her long red hair falling lose from all its pins, streaming out behind her and catching the rays of the sun until it seemed on fire. The sight was glorious, intoxicating. She rode well and astride as his sisters did. He smiled. The only thing that would make this better was if they were alone.

She slowed and let him ride beside her. "What are you going to do? Shouldn't you have a strategy of some sort?"

"You're right of course. Plans are always nice but if what Broc told me is correct, all we know is that there is no proof pointing to that man. I can hardly set the constables on the alleged perpetrator unless there is good reason."

"I see, but you do know Arie would take care of him. He has this way of exacting revenge without facing any consequences."

"I've thought on that. It has serious possibilities and allowing Arie to have his fun would rid me of the escalating difficulties as well as the cost of replacing all he burned."

"He could make an example out of them like he did those other men. No one likes to be stripped naked in the town square for everyone to ogle. Although they didn't understand the length of what Arie would do if family or friends continued to be threatened."

"This is true," Flynt smiled wondering just when Hope became so blood thirsty. "I'll reconsider but would have to discuss it with Arie before I let him have free reign."

"It's the way of things where I used to live," she told him almost as if she understood his thoughts. "Laws exist, but if one takes what isn't theirs, they must pay the consequences when caught."

"Arie does this quite well."

She nodded her agreement. "His father taught him, and his father before that and so on. Arie has had lots of practice in meting out justice."

"You've never told me how your mother became part of Arie's father's harem."

He had wondered but just never asked. Before it seemed too personal, but now that she was his wife, he felt perhaps he should know.

"Their ship was attacked by Arie's father. Broc's father was murdered and his mother was taken as a slave. Broc was left with only his grandmother and a nanny to take care of him." She tilted her head slightly, staring at him for a few seconds. "Arie's father liked mother a lot and asked for her most every night. She danced for him. He would laugh at her awkwardness, but then he'd pull her aside and make love to her. I wonder if he made love as well as you."

Her last statement gave him reason to pause and inwardly puff up his chest. Not all men were gentle. Her mother would not have been a virgin but... "Then you were born," he said, trying to ignore her comment.

"For a long time, he stopped asking for her. Mother told me his first wife had grown jealous of her. I remember one day she asked for an audience with him. I had just turned seventeen, older than most girls when they were sold or told they would remain in the harem where they grew up. I think that is when they made plans for my escape."

"So, if he was willing to let you go, why did you have to escape?" That was a perplexity he needed an answer to.

"Because... He would lose strength and power over the others if he allowed a woman from his harem to leave freely. That just never happens. Their plan was an elaborate ruse. The only thing that went wrong was the carriage accident which left me with amnesia."

"Arie had to figure out how to help you remember. What I don't get is why Arie has stayed here in Scotland."

"The sultan likes it here and he has a woman. I think he's fallen in love with her, but he'll never admit to it. He bought her and he hasn't let her go. Taking her home would mean she would become a concubine, not his wife. I'm sure she would be conflicted. As for now, he tells us she can come and go as she pleases but that's not entirely true. My half-brother is a very possessive man and he would believe that what he says is gospel, no room for her to make decisions for herself."

He recognized some of what she was saying to be true about himself, and he wasn't at all sure he liked that side of him. "We're here but we need to continue this. I'm still curious about this man you call friend and half-brother." His gaze roamed over the men and women gathered here as he tried to assess the situation.

They drew to a stop. The others had arrived ahead of them. Cam stepped forward to greet them with David by his side.

"David gave me a description of the man who tossed the first torch," Cam said, reaching out his hand in greeting.

Flynt directed his attention to him, shaking his hand. "Well?"

"The pretty boy who owns the land next to mine. He's been snooping around. Thin features and brownish hair, he has and dark brown eyes. Looks like he should have been born a girl. He's not very tall, but he likes to puff out his chest as if he owns the world."

"Would you be willing to swear it to a constable?" Flynt asked.

"I believe Leslie is bringing one here. Just had to wait for morning. Should be arriving sometime soon."

"I would be swearing the fact. Lost all my crops and your share as well. Going to starve this winter if I don't have anything to sell."

"You're on MacTavish land," Flynt said with a wave of his hand. "No one is going to let you starve. We can get field land planted with some winter crops and come spring you'll be fine. Until then I'll personally supply whatever you need."

"What about my home? It rained last night, and my wife and kids had to sleep in the barn. Not sure why the man didn't burn that too."

"I'll take care of everything," Flynt roughed his hands through his hair, and with a huge sigh watched as Hope dismounted. He'd told her to stay put. He supposed she wasn't ever going to follow his directions. Now there was too much to take care of for him to follow her. Arie watched her, strode after her, sending him a nod and a grin.

Catching up to Hope, Arie took her arm in his then spoke to her. Flynt wondered what the Turk was saying to her. He hoped it would be similar to the words he would use, a conservative order she would understand and follow. It seemed though, Hope needed to agree with the command in order for her to so what was asked. She should understand it wasn't prudent for her, a female, to wander far from him in a situation such as this one.

In a rush to finish the business at hand and before returning to his honeymoon, he spoke to everyone, listening carefully. Leslie arrived with the constable and David was giving his statement. The man would be punished but by who was the only remaining question.

Cam stood by his side, "You should go home now. This is your honeymoon after all. We can take care of everything else. Arie and his men will go with you. Now that we know who is responsible, we can apprehend him. Don't know if he is the one who shot, Hope but we'll also check that out."

"I should get Hope out of here before she wanders off with someone else." She just wanted to help but this wasn't the time or the place. His heart nearly stopped when a shot rang out.

Pandemonium escalated in the small area where they were

standing. When he looked for Hope, she stood seemingly frozen to the spot. He was sure she was recalling the past shooting. Remaining a target was not prudent at all.

"Get down!" he yelled, waving his hands, but she didn't hear. He raced to her, heart in his throat, terrified for her, his heart pounding harder than he thought possible.

She was directing people to the barn, oblivious of the danger to herself. Waving them by her when she should have been running to safety. What the bloody hell was she doing now?

Another shot.

Leslie and Donal on horseback raced toward the area where the shots were fired. He sprinted to Hope, picking her up in his arms and heading for the barn. It quieted then. It seemed whoever was shooting at them left when they were about to be confronted by two mounted men.

He wanted to shake her, at least enough for her to have enough good sense to stay out of harm's way if this ever happened again.

"What are you doing?" she gasped, sounding outraged that he was rescuing her from peril. "Put me down."

"I'm saving your precious hide," he yelled at her, still furious she risked her life. "What do you ken I'm doing?" He did put her down, still holding her close, his heart thundering in his chest.

"I dinna need saving."

She was screaming at him, hitting him on the shoulders. If the situation had not been so serious, he would have laughed. Her tiny fists barely made an impact on his thick hide.

"You're a wee mite of a girl. You cannot take on a man and probably very few women as well. I don't want to lose you the day after we wed. Shots were fired and you did not take heed. You didn't run for cover as you should have done."

He was breathing hard, his nerves in turmoil, ready to shatter into a million pieces.

"I was just helping out your people. You shouldn't be angry with me for doing such a fine thing."

"So, how should I feel?" he asked, wishing he could press home the point but wanting to take her in his arms and kiss her senseless. Mixed emotions were making him stupid.

"You should be thanking me. Your wife should help not shy away and run from trouble. Our people need us." Hope stood her ground despite his words.

A crease appeared between her eyes and her hands were fisted by her sides.

"All you say is true and in a normal situation I would be thanking you. Not today. We are going home with your half-brother and his men. To finish what we started during our honeymoon."

"What..." She stopped, hands now on her tiny waist.

"Leslie, Cam, Broc and Donal are more than capable of seeing this situation through to its end. David has already given his statement. The constables are here. I would not be surprised if the man responsible for this is in custody by this afternoon. In any case if he's not, it would mean he's left the area and perhaps the country. If he is not found one way or the other, Arie will take matters into his more than capable hands."

"I see." She stared at his mouth.

Shaking his head at her, desperate for control, "You're doing that on purpose to distract me." He tried to stifle the groan of desire pummeling through him.

"Doing what?" She lifted her shoulders slightly, a smile on her serene face. The gesture was flirtatious and he knew her intent.

She was not only arousing him but she was also diverting his attention from his reprimand. "I'm not going to explain anything you already ken." Arie held the reins of the horses, grinning at him an all-knowing smug expression on his face. The man overheard and was enjoying himself. "Shall we?" Flynt grabbed the reins.

He then gave her a foot up before mounting his horse. "Stay close."

Once more he wondered if she would follow his directions.

The ride back was slow and solemn. She seemed to be brooding. The sun, which broke through the clouds this morning, was now covered by them just as his mood seemed to be darkening. Flynt kept his thoughts to himself as did Hope. They would have to talk though, tonight. He just didn't know what he was going to say to her or how.

As they closed the distance to the beach house, the wind picked up, leaves and dirt swirling in circles. She rode near the edge of the rocks and once again his heart nearly stopped. "Hope," he called out to her, but she ignored him or didn't hear him. For arguments sake, he decided he would pretend the latter.

Arie rode beside him. "She has a mind of her own that one. You will never get used to it because she will keep you forever on the watch, but..."

Flynt let out a long slow breath of air. "I wouldn't have it any other way. She is perfect for me just the way she is." He realized just how true that was despite his overpowering need to keep her out of harm's way.

Arie let out a roar of laughter. "You need to learn that some women don't want a man to protect them, just love them. Hope and your sisters as well are that way. I can only pray the woman who I marry next will be that way too."

"You would know this how? All your concubines in your harem? You plan on wedding more women?"

Flynt wanted a fight. Didn't want to fight with Hope so Arie was the most convenient.

"Don't have a harem although I do have three wives, but I learned this from your sisters. They are just as Hope is, independent enough to expect their man will let them think for themselves and make decisions even without your support. I suspect she rode to the edge just to set your nerves on edge. Did it work?"

He gritted his teeth together, unwilling to admit to Arie he might be right. "Better than she could have thought possible."

"When you go to throttle her, you'll make love to her instead."

Arie was still laughing and that irritated Flynt even more than his words. He rode to meet Hope, not wanting to listen to the sultan any longer. "Did you mean to scare me half to death? If you did, the ploy worked."

She stared at his mouth, her amber eyes shimmering with raw passion. He watched and groaned as she moistened her lips and now, he couldn't remove his gaze from her mouth and the tiny pink tongue he loved to taste and play with.

"You're doing that on purpose," he said, his body pulsing with desire, "Just to make me forget the lecture I planned with you in mind."

"Of course not and I don't need or want a lecture. I want you and I'm thinking about the way you look naked and how your..."

They were riding abreast, so he pulled her from her horse, settling her on his lap. His lips found hers and she pushed her tongue into his mouth. When he could finally breathe, "Bloody eyes, woman, you have no idea."

But she did. She knew just what to do to make him hard and hopelessly her pawn. He would have to figure out how to ignore her ploys. He was the man after all and she should do as he said. Somehow, he just didn't think that was ever going to happen. For him it was a magical fantasy that he actually didn't want to come true.

"Flynt..." She lightly touched her finger to his lips.

"What?" It was almost a growl.

He'd urged the horse faster, eager to find his way to the master chamber or the rooftop, he couldn't decide. The weather didn't seem to be on their side though.

"I think I'm going to fall off. Can you put me back on mine?"

"No."

He reigned in the horse, realizing she was right. They were in front of the house. He set her on the first step of the porch, then turning to Arie who still followed them, "Can you see to the horses?"

"What, you can't wait another minute or two?" he asked, laughing.

"No." Flynt swept her into his arms.

Seconds later they were on the bed, clothes almost torn off.

"I love you," Hope murmured.

He stopped, frozen in the moment. He stopped kissing her to look at her and reply, "It is just lust."

Much later, Hope lay in his arms, running her fingers along his chest to his belly, teasing him with thoughts of more pleasure. "I've decided you are right, Flynt. It's lust I feel. I lust for you day and night. Does that sound better? I don't want to get it wrong. You are the man, you know." She touched one of his nipples with her tongue. Looking up, smiling at him, staring at his lips. "We don't make love. We make lust."

He didn't like what she just said at all. He was not making lust with her. He desperately needed a diversion. "Blessed hell, woman, we have to have food."

He kissed her quickly on the mouth, understanding full well if he did anything more, they wouldn't ring for dinner then it would be time for breakfast. He could waste away making love to his wife.

"I thought you'd never feed me. I do need food to keep up with your manly prowess."

She still lay in his arms, her hands coming ever closer to his hard, pulsing rod.

He stopped her. "I'm serious about food. Not that I don't want you to touch me. It seems I've no control over myself when you do that."

"Do what? She smiled at him again, staring at his lips while she swished her tongue across hers.

"You bloody well know." He rose, striding to the bell cord that would signal for a servant. Slipping on his pants, he waited at the door.

Munroe was there before he could have imagined. "Thought you'd be wanting a tray of food, sooner than later. Cook left it in the warming oven before retiring for the night. The two of you have any idea what time it is?"

"I'm sure you'll tell me, but I don't really care."

Flynt accepted the tray, which was piled high with food as well as two bottles of wine. He didn't dare look at the bed or at Hope who had somehow in the short two days become at ease with her nudity. As soon as Munroe left, she let the covers pool around her hips, leaving almost nothing to his imagination. When he closed his eyes, the image of her completely naked was seared in his head.

If he looked, he wouldn't eat.

If he looked, she wouldn't eat.

Blessed hell.

~ * ~

"Do you think Flynt will like the breakfast we made him?" Hope asked Cook who had all but tolerated her this morning.

The mess she made was total, the kitchen covered in flour. What few eggs they cooked were only edible now because she didn't drop them on the floor when she tried to crack them.

Earlier this morning when she woke, Flynt was gone, vanished. She assumed to see to business and find out what happened after they left the McClintock's parcel of land. He would have wanted to talk to Leslie and the others. With nothing to do she dressed and walked downstairs.

For a few minutes, she sat on the porch swing and stared at the ocean. Growing bored with that she began to wander the house, looking for someone to talk to. She found Cook who told her Flynt would be back in another hour or so. The woman was busy but she somehow convinced Cook to let her work alongside her.

Together they put together a breakfast of haggis and scrambled eggs with some fresh baked bread Cook made earlier in the morning. She asked Cook to teach her how to bake bread, but the disaster she created on the kitchen floor left Cook swearing.

"Now, I'm sure your man will be loving every bite and appreciating that you went to all that trouble just to make it for him. I on the other hand will be left with cleaning up the floor." She raised her hands in the air as Hope began to speak, "No, and you won't be helpin' me clean today either."

"You're afraid I'll make an even worse mess," Hope grimaced.

"That I am, lass, now you go on and sit outside for a bit. Your man will be home sooner than you can blink. Make sure you eat the meal before you let him take you back upstairs and that big bed of his. Seems that's all he's got on his mind nowadays. I've thrown out more food it seems than I've made."

Hope grinned, thinking it might be her that lures him to that big bed before they eat. She wasn't that hungry since she'd been nibbling on everything as they cooked so she could wait.

"We're going to eat down here and you're going to stay until we're done," Hope told Cook matter-of-factly. "It's the only way we'll eat."

"Well, for heaven's sakes why?" she asked drying her hands on the dishcloth that had been hung near the sink. "Nothin' like having too many people in a room. You're goin' to be gazin' into his eyes and thinkin' romantic thoughts. If I stayed it wouldn't do at all, no, just wouldn't do to have a third person watchin' the two of you makin' eyes at each other."

She did a tiny shrug of her shoulders wondering what Cook would think when she told him about her husband and what he said to her. With thoughts as well as second thoughts swirling in her head she gave up and with a long sigh then began, "He's in lust with me and can't seem to keep his hands off, even to eat. So, you are right. We better stay downstairs until we eat everything."

"Now, lassie, I'm sure that his feelings for you are more than lust. By the way your husband has been looking at you I can tell, he's in love. His body might be tellin' you now that it's just lust, he's a feelin' but there are more emotions involved and lust might not be the only sensation he feels."

"No," Hope sipped the strong hot coffee Cook made, just the way Flynt liked it. She was shaking her head knowing full well what Flynt admitted to her. "No, he told me I didn't love him but I lusted for him. Personally, I would have thought the feelings were a bit more but he is the man after all and I trust his judgment. Lust it is," she said with emphasis. "I will tell him I lust for him."

Cook was shaking her finger at her. "Your man is just confused and won't admit love exists until it bites him in the arse. It's a man thing you know. My late husband was the same way, but he didn't put it quite so boldly. After a year or so he admitted he loved me. Thank God I might just have coshed him over the head with my rolling pin if he kept on that way."

"So, you think Flynt is in love with me. I told him I lusted for him just to see his reaction, and he actually looked angry with me. Why do you suppose?" She was hoping Cook would shed some light on this.

"That's easy. Because the man wants you to love him even though he won't admit to lovin' you."

"I see," she said not really sure that she did.

"Do you now? Do believe you should just keep on agreeing with him because he's a man. Perhaps there is something to being too agreeable. He might get so angry it will knock some sense into the stubborn man. They want you to accept everything they say as gospel when they tell you somethin' foolish. They get angry because they didn't realize how stupid they were until they hear it said back to them. Men folk."

"I like to agree with him when he doesn't want me to."

Her hesitant laugh surprised her as well as Cook. It was true. She knew when he spouted nonsense just to make her to do something, he could chastise her for later. Yet at times his words seemed sincere although ridiculous.

Cook was waving a spatula in the air and grinning delightedly, "You just keep doin' what you've been doin'. It seems to be workin' for you and your man. He's wound tight around your little finger, and I do believe he would swim the Irish Sea for you if you asked."

"There you are." Flynt appeared out of nowhere, stepping into the kitchen, his broad shoulders filling the doorway.

She'd been so caught up with her conversation with Cook she didn't hear the door or his boot steps. She hoped he heard little to none of their conversation.

"Where have you been?" She sounded accusatory and she didn't like the tone of her words. She waved a hand in the air. "Not that I care. Suppose you could be with your ex-mistress. Since what we share is just lust, I shouldn't be jealous. Did you lust for your mistress too?"

He appeared shocked, frown lines creasing his brows as it seemed he tried to make sense of her words. Watching him, color flooded his face so she decided to divert and stare at his mouth. She touched her tongue to the coffee in her mug before sliding it around the rim. His eyes seemed to darken and change color as she continued to encourage.

Then, "You make an erotic picture. Actually, I did want to see her. Needed to tell her how wonderful you've been for me. She needs someone to take care of her now that I'm not available fulltime. So, I'm helping her find a man who will please her and," he paused thoughtfully, "lust for her."

Not available fulltime? Inside she raged. Provoking him might not have been that great of an idea. Still, she didn't want to fold and let him know how disturbed she was by his words that would give him the upper hand in this little skirmish of wits and words.

"Perhaps you should make an appointment with her. You can make sure it's only lust we have for each other." She knew she was taking this too far, but she didn't seem to be able to help herself.

Cook frowned at her and Hope felt the heat of her gaze and understood Cook was trying to tell her the same as she was thinking. "The two of you hungry? Hope helped cook the breakfast for you, Flynt."

"She did? Well, that was nice of her. When did you learn how to cook?" His eyes narrowed as he smiled at her. "To the best of my recollection, Hope never stepped foot in a kitchen before today."

Instead of staring at his lips, her gaze dropped to below his waist. "I didn't. Cook did most and I made this mess." She pointed to the kitchen floor. "Cook is giving me way too much credit. We have to eat before you go see your mistress. Cook said we have to eat everything or she'll be very displeased. We wouldn't want to make her angry, now would we?"

"I'm not going to see anyone but you. There are some things you need to be set straight on before we can do much more."

"Can you lecture me while we eat?" She looked into his eyes then, surprised to see them smoldering, the passion simmering.

"Now, in the bedroom." He stepped toward her.

She didn't move but she wanted to stand and run which would do her no good at all because he ran faster than she did. He would catch her before she got through the door.

"No, we have to eat."

"We can eat afterwards." He stood in front of her now.

The time to run had passed. "We've barely eaten in the last few days. Don't you think we should replenish our strength? Cook says we have to eat this or she'll be very unhappy with us." Beneath the table her hands were clasped tightly on her lap, her eyes cast downward.

"If that is what you want." He pulled out a chair and sat down.

Cook poured him a cup of coffee before setting two plates in front of them. "There is more in the warming oven. May I go now?"

It seemed the woman didn't want to be in Flynt's vicinity any more than she did.

"What? Don't want to witness what's going to follow our meal?" Flynt asked, a lopsided grin slowly forming on his too handsome and arrogant visage.

"I'll be back soon enough to fix your dinner and clean the floor. Now, don't you be hurtin' this wee lass of yours. You got to be careful, you're such a big brute of a man."

"Not going to hurt my wee lassie, just make sure she kens a few things about a man and a woman. What's expected between them."

"Like I said, you treat her right and she'll give you the world as well as everything you've ever wanted."

"To be honest, she already has." Flynt looked at her then, his gaze squarely on her bosom.

Suddenly realizing where he was staring, she inhaled a sharp breath of air before covering herself with her hand and watching his lopsided grin widen to a full and complete smile in seeming pleasure. Understanding he was playing her game she straitened, and when she removed her hand she tugged on the bodice, her breasts now nearly spilling free.

His brows drew together, his voice husky. "You might be sorry you just did that."

Cook backed from the room, "It's too hot in here for me. The two of you need to eat, but I can tell it's not going to happen anytime soon."

"No, well, I'm going to eat."

She wanted to make Flynt pay for turning the tables on her. She picked up a piece of bacon and chewed it slowly, trying to figure out where she should stare this time. His crotch had been a great idea but now that he sat down, she couldn't see it. Lips it was.

"I'll be happy to join you."

This was not what she expected. She could barely breathe while her heart raced. While she meant to arouse and entice Flynt, she'd managed to do the same to herself. Closing her eyes for a moment, it seemed she could feel him caressing her, touching and sightseeing everywhere. Her imagination was wreaking havoc with her body.

"What are you thinking?" he asked, his fork half way to his mouth.

"That the food is very good and I'm glad I didn't really cook it."

She set the fork on the plate, unable to eat another bite, her body so aroused she could barely think. She had been left mindless by this play between them.

"Liar."

Startled she looked up and with a rush of air. "No."

"Liar again."

"What am I thinking?"

She meant to make him accountable. He would have to know her thoughts exactly. What she told him was actually true although not everything.

"There is a lot of lust in the air." He sat back, his legs crossed in front of him. "You are ready for me, I've not a doubt in my mind. Your honey pot I'm sure is overflowing."

"Don't know what you're talking about." She picked up her fork, set it down again then tried the coffee.

"Three lies." He ate his eggs, his gaze fixed on her mouth then her bodice again.

She realized then that between her pulling it down and squirming on the chair he could see not only the valley between but pink around the nipples. She started this and she wasn't about to run away before it was finished to her satisfaction. She wasn't frightened of him, no she wanted him desperately, never stopped wanting him.

"What do you want me to tell you? That you could toss my skirts and take me right here on the kitchen table?" She inhaled a swift shallow breath of air, wishing she had not set an idea into his head.

He stood, his chair toppling to the floor behind him. "That's exactly what I was thinking." He hauled her over his shoulder. "Munroe!"

"Sir." The man was in the kitchen in less than a few seconds.

"See that no one comes into the dining room."

"Put me down." She was pummeling his back, squirming precariously on his shoulder.

"That's exactly what I'm planning on doing. Going to put you on the dining room table and have lust with you," he growled at her.

He tossed his words then her words back to her. As he strode into the dining room, he hummed a lively tune, seemingly pleased with himself and this notion she put into his head.

"No, what if someone comes in? What if..." Her voice quavered but he was so right. She wanted him now and when they finished, she would want him again, need him desperately. She wondered if these feeling for him would ever end.

"Yes." He gently set her on the table after he brushed the linens aside. He spread her legs wrapping them around his back. His gaze was riveted on her, set on her heaving bosom.

"Really?" she asked while she was leaning on her elbows watching him unfasten his pants. "You really mean to do this here, like this?"

"Really."

He was deep inside her. She was climaxing almost as quickly. Mindlessly it seemed she was crying out his name. The intensity of the moment overwhelmed her.

"No, don't close your eyes, sweet Lassie. I want to see the lust shining in them."

"You can't."

"Of course, I can."

She opened them and was rewarded with the expression on his face as he lost his seed in her body. She fell back, sweat sheened and breathless. Unable to breathe, she closed her eyes, feeling him withdraw from her.

"Lust is amazing." He fastened his buckskins. Helping her to a sitting position. "Shall we finish breakfast?"

The question was rhetorical and she was sure he had no intention of allowing her to decide. They would now finish the meal that was still sitting on the kitchen table. She was sure it would be because this lust thing had taken less than five minutes. No one would have cleared the dishes.

"I'm sure you're not asking me so I suppose we will do whatever is your whim."

Her pout was meant to forge some emotion, but when he laughed, she knew his merriment was not what she wanted.

"I like that, a submissive wife. When did that happen? No, wait," he paused, staring down at her legs and her woman's mound still uncovered. "You will learn that to be submissive is to make us both happy. Now, would you like me to cover you and cease staring at you, at your beautiful lady parts?" His grin stretched from one ear to the other.

She didn't want to answer him. Instead, she glared at him as she wondered how this situation suddenly got out of her control.

"Hmm...so you want me again? I'm exhausted and famished for food. You will have to wait for round two until I've put something in my belly. Pleasuring you is such difficult work and so very exhausting."

She wished she had a lamp or something hard so she could cosh him over the head with it. Unmoving she waited for him to make the next move. She wasn't about to admit defeat yet.

"I see, you're trying to figure out what I'm going to do next. Well, since I didn't even kiss you once, I've still three kisses you owe me or was it five? Again, I'm not going to collect until we have both eaten our fill."

"I'm not hungry. Think I'll take a walk on the rocks." She smiled when his grin changed to a frown.

"You're not to go out on those rocks."

"Another ultimatum? One I don't plan on abiding."

The play of expressions on his face nearly caused her to smile. Slowly, she was learning how to crack his stoic and demanding façade.

"I won't let you. It's too dangerous."

"How are you going to stop me?"

She understood the only way he could keep her from doing what she wanted and when she wanted was to lock her behind a closed door or never leave her side.

"I'll think of something," he muttered, leaving her half naked on the table and striding quickly to the kitchen.

Well, he might have won the first round of verbal exchanges, but she won the last. She smoothed her skirts over her legs then hopped from the table. Instead of following him into the kitchen, she walked to the porch intent on continuing to the rocks.

A stiff breeze blew from the west with a slight mist of rain. The temperature was unusually cool for this time of year so she grabbed a blanket and wrapped it around her. The thought of walking the short distance to the rocks crossed her mind again, but she sat on the porch swing instead, staring at the mist crashing skyward. The scent of salt spray in the air.

Her hands shook as she brought them to her face to push wayward strands behind her ears. She didn't remember Flynt undoing any of the pins in her hair but somehow a few came lose. Usually the moment they started kissing the hair pins flew. This time had been different, and she wasn't sure she liked it although he gave her soul shattering pleasure.

He had not kissed her, he reminded her before he left for the kitchen to finish his food. That fact made the intimacy so different. It was fast and furious, not slow and leisurely as normal. She half expected him to follow her to make sure she didn't go to the rock's edge. The concern had been verbal only. A few minutes later she heard the kitchen door open then bang shut. He left without saying goodbye. He must be angry with her. She could only guess.

What to do now?

Pushing the moisture that was welling up inside her throat and her eyes to the back of her mind, she wiped the few drops that escaped away with the back of her hand. If she wanted to live with Flynt on equal footing, she needed to be stronger than this. She needed a stiffer backbone, because he was going to test her every moment she stepped out of line or what he perceived to be the boundary he set.

"See you took my order seriously." He sat down beside her, one dark brow arched perfectly upward.

He startled her and the gasp of air rushing from her lungs put a tiny smile on his lips. "I didn't know you were there. Thought you left again. You're angry with me."

"Didn't mean to scare you. Had to speak with Arie for a moment. I'm not angry. I'm in lust as you put it."

"Speaking to Arie bout what?" She didn't want to admit to being too curious but she was.

His gaze was hard and she thought calculating. "About you." With that said he turned away for a second, closing himself off to her. "Think there's a storm coming." He pulled her into his arms, his breathing against her slow and even, his big body warm.

A storm coming, was he referring to their relationship or the weather? "Why would you be talking to Arie about me?"

The two reminded her of a bunch of gossiping women, and she didn't want to think what they told each other.

His hands at her waist, he pulled her closer. "Because he knows you better than any living soul. I want to make you happy, and I was just asking how to go about doing that."

"Ah, words of wisdom from Arie. What did he tell you?" She held her breath waiting for the answer.

"He told me to let you have your way from time to time, but only if having your way would not kill you. You see that's the problem. Every time you are away from me, I fear for your safety even if the fear is ridiculous. It's more about me and my terror of losing you than it is you."

"Standing near the rocks edge would not kill me. You are overprotective. I'm not a child." His fingers on her waist tightened.

"No, you're definitely not a child." One hand cupped her breast, his thumb grazing the tight bud. "A huge wave could sweep you away and you would never be able to fight the battering of water against the rocks."

"You are being ridiculous. Don't, just don't make me want you right now even though you know you can."

She tried to squirm away from him, but he wouldn't allow her the distance.

"You can seduce me in a heartbeat. Is there any difference? All you have to do is stare at my mouth or my covered man parts and I'm under your spell. I lose all ability to think of anything but burying myself deep inside you."

"I don't know," she sighed softly, wishing for the lighthearted banter they usually had.

She was suddenly tired of this argument that wasn't going anywhere. She just didn't care anymore.

"Perhaps I should try to keep my hands to myself. Would that make you happier than you are now?"

It seemed even while he talked about keeping his hands to himself, they roamed over her.

"I would not be happier, but Flynt I'm not unhappy." *No, I'm madly in love with my husband and he considers the feeling nothing but lust.*

"Shall we walk to the rocks together?" He rose, holding out his hand. "That way I can keep my eyes on you as well as the waves churning below."

She accepted and his hand felt large and warm, holding hers. Yet she could not let it go, "Why is it safe to walk to the rocks edge with you and not alone?"

"I knew you would ask and I don't have a verbal answer for you. The sensations are all in my gut and the instincts that have kept me alive through a few precarious incidents. I've learned to trust those instincts, and I would like you to trust them also. Can you do that?"

"Can't make any promises except that I'll try."

They walked the short distance. Ocean spray misted the air. Beneath their feet waves churned, battering the rocks. He pointed downward.

"One misstep..."

She understood what he tried to tell her and shuddered. "One misstep, an accident but one there would be no turning back from."

"Aye, lassie, and that's the truth of it. I dinna mean to belittle you, only protect you from accidental harm."

"Sometimes I feel as if you are just ordering me about for its own sake. A few reasons as to why might be in order." She would meet him part way in this.

"When there is time for reasons, I'll grant you the particulars. There are times however I cannot take a moment to tell you why."

"As of yesterday, when you told me to stay put?" she questioned, realizing the truth of his words.

"A few moments later there were shots fired and there you were out in the open a target for whoever was shooting. Someone might have wanted you dead to exact their revenge when they couldn't kill me as easily. The sight stopped my heart from beating. You ken? If you had been hurt again..."

~ * ~

Leslie sipped the fine French brandy Drake Montgomerie offered while he waited for the news he sought. Drake made an unusual visit to Glasgow at his request and he'd been surprised.

Drake arrived with the tide that morning, his wife Ella by his side, telling him it was a much needed vacation. They left the children in the capable hands of their grandmother, The Duchess, telling her she must make them mind, knowing full well Charlotte would give them anything they asked for and most likely more. They understood that whatever happened at The Duchess' home stayed at The Duchess' home.

"Want some advice and information on a man named Sean McGinnis. Whatever you have at your disposal would be helpful. I need to piece some facts together to send on to a friend. McGinnis wants my friend dead, his wife or both and I don't intend to allow that to happen."

"Would have been able to bring you quite a bit of material on the man if you'd included that with your letter asking me to come. He has not spent the last few years idly, of that I know. The McGinnis name is notorious and from what I understand, Flynt's father won a sizable amount of land from his father, resulting in a suicide because the man was unable to cope with the loss."

"I understand your need for more information about this specific situation, but I couldn't risk putting anything in writing. Had to trust to your memory and since I know first hand how good yours is, I made the choice. Everything you say is true. I suppose the man is looking to get the land back at whatever the cost."

"Lacie MacTavish has arrived." His butler of many years announced.

Leslie smiled. He hoped she would come, and he understood because her brother was occupied with his honeymoon there would be no one to prevent her from doing just as she pleased. He smiled content at the outcome. Within an hour or so he would have Lacie all to himself.

My God she was lovely. Her long blond hair was lifted high and held with two combs, a few strands framing her face. He met her in the hallway, picking up her slender hand in his. He kissed the back. "Enchanted."

She moistened her lips, seeming unsure as to what to say. As she shifted from one foot to the other, "Thank you."

While Lacie was a young woman of incomparable beauty and had grown up in a privileged environment, she was lacking in many social skills. Her brother had not seen to that part of her education. She had been allowed to run wild over the countryside and do pretty much just what she wanted. Yet he was compelled to explore the possibilities of a private and personal relationship with her. Her brother now was busy with his new wife, and her grandmother granted her far too much leniency when it came to men. Had done the same with all the MacTavish girls.

He vowed that he would never take unholy advantage of, her but he'd also vowed he would never marry a virgin. What he did not promise himself was that he would never deflower the girl he hoped to wed, thus keeping the latter vow.

Lacie would be his.

How and when was still the question. If he had his way, the sooner the better, but time was fleeting. He was leaving for Edinburgh in a day or two, and he needed to find some way to bind her to him. The enticement of sexual favors to an untried woman was the quickest and most effected way he could think of.

As with Flynt he wasn't getting any younger and he needed an heir. Another Duke of Southcliff was necessary. His younger brother certainly did not want the job or the title. He was having far too much fun as the second son, the bastard count now reaching four children under his care. Next time he saw Link there would most likely be more.

He held her hand in his, "I'm so glad you could clear your schedule and take time for me. This is Drake Montgomerie, the Duke of Richmond, an acquaintance from London and his lovely wife Ella. They have come to help with the problem your brother is having with Sean McGinnis."

"Why am I here?"

She stared at him with the most beautiful summer sky blue eyes he'd ever seen. If he didn't keep his emotions under control, he would fall under her spell and not have a wit of common sense left in his man's body. "For now, to keep me company. When my guests have left, I'll explain a bit more."

Lacie wore a gown he'd seen her in nearly a year ago. Now it barely covered her bosom. He tried to look away but couldn't. She enchanted him.

Ella rose, "Lacie? May I call you Lacie? Why don't you come with me? I believe it is necessary or my husband's eyes will pop right out of his head even though he doesn't mean to. My own breasts are quite ample for his pleasure."

Lacie looked to Leslie as if confused and needing some sign she should go with this woman she just met and who was now spouting seeming nonsense words. He nodded, realizing Ella must have noticed the problem the same time he did.

He turned his attention back to Drake. "Your lady friend is beautiful, but I noticed you'll be alone with her when we leave. Do you think that is wise? She seems awfully young."

Leslie shrugged, sipping the brandy he just poured for himself, "Shall we have another drink while we wait for the ladies. I doubt if they'll be long, and I've been told dinner is served."

"No." Drake rubbed his chin, looking in the direction Ella and Lacie disappeared. "Since we all noticed Lacie's slight clothing snafu, I suppose they will return in seconds. I certainly won't dwell on something you seem uneager to speak of."

Leslie didn't want to discuss his soon to be wife's amazing bosom with anyone. However, he didn't see much of a choice. Her bosom had been popping out of her gowns for a while now. As a young woman, she'd been coltishly thin and he'd often wondered if she'd develop hips and breasts. There was no doubt in his mind now. He chuckled to himself and was gifted with a bemused smile from Drake.

"Ah, there they are." Leslie said, relieved Ella found a small piece of lace to tuck into the corsage of Lacie's gown. "Looking lovelier than ever."

He offered his arm to Lacie to escort her into the dining area. The time seemed to pass with easy conversation. When he gazed at Lacie, he couldn't help but wish the modesty piece would vanish. He liked being able to see into the valley between her breasts and watch the exposed half-moons rise and fall with each breath. Once Ella and Drake left, that feat could be easily accomplished.

Drake lectured him on the fact there was no chaperone then seemed to remind himself of his well-known escapades with Ella before they were wed.

As they left, Drake gave a piece of advice. "I only hope you do the right thing where Lacie is concerned. She is a lovely woman and deserves the best. Don't take advantage of her unless you plan to marry her."

"What Lacie and I do is of no concern of yours. Whatever happens, I'm sure I'll act no better or worse than you did with your beautiful wife."

Drake nodded, "I suppose I deserve that. Good luck with your endeavors wherever they lead. Come along, Ella."

Ella hugged Lacie, whispering something before the duke and duchess left. When the door closed behind them, Leslie lounged against it, watching her, his gaze resting on her bosom.

"Do you like me, lass?" He slowly pushed away from the door and walked toward her.

"What kind of question is that?" She appeared baffled as she stepped back, nearly tripping over the slight rise of the rug.

"The question is simple enough. Do you like me?" He held his breath, waiting as he watched, a myriad of emotions sweep across her face. Not daring to come any closer, he waited.

She inhaled long and deep, her bosom nearly pushing the modesty piece Ella had given her from its protective spot. "I have been enamored of you since the first time I saw you playing cards and sipping whiskey with my brothers. I was only fifteen then."

"I wanted to hear that. Let's go into the parlor and discuss our, er, possible relationship a bit farther."

Once again, he offered her his arm, enjoying the warmth of her hand. He placed his over hers. There was so much more he could do, but he didn't want her to panic any more than she already had.

"I dinna ken we have a relationship."

He smiled down at her. "I ken we will." Then, "A brandy for you or would you like tea?"

"Brandy would be fine."

She sat on a sofa where he directed her, gaze focused on the floor.

When he returned to her, he held two brandies in hand, giving her one. "Drink up."

He needed her relaxed and by the way she inadvertently plucked at her skirts and wound her fingers together, he knew she was far from at ease. She downed the contents in one gulp before holding out her glass silently asking for more.

He'd brought the bottle with him, hoping she would open up to him and to do that she would need more than one drink.

"You've had brandy before, I see."

Her sweet smile and innocent nod melted his jaded heart. He'd been with women before, women who only wanted the title and wealth that came with his name. Lacie always seemed different. She was still young, time enough to make sure she understood a relationship was more than what one could get but what one could give.

"My sisters and I used to drink Flynt's brandy when he was away from the house. We saw you, the bad boys drinking it and thought what was enjoyable for them could also be enjoyable for us. We didn't see how men could be so different they could drink spirits and women had to drink tea. Tea is bitter." This time she sipped, her fingers relaxing. "This burns on the way down, nothing like tea."

Chuckling softly, he sat down beside her, wondering about everything that she did since she wanted to emulate the bad boys. Perhaps she wasn't so naïve after all.

"I don't like this. No, I much prefer the dress without the modesty piece. At least when I'm the only person in the vicinity to enjoy the view."

"I don't know what you mean."

When she looked at him her eyes looked blank and confused.

She gasped then when he divested her of the scrap of lace, her hand replacing the fabric. He gently removed it.

"That is much better. I like the way the curve of your breasts tells me they will nicely fill my hands."

He was sure her eyes crossed and it almost brought a smile to his lips. He held it back, unwilling to frighten or confuse her further.

"Ella told me you might say something like that. Are you intending to seduce me tonight? I must tell you no. Ella instructed me to allow nothing but kisses. She told me The Duchess, her aunt, always said kisses are alright but don't allow anything else."

"Ah, my precious little imp, I do intend to persuade you to my way of thinking but not tonight and if that's what you want, I will only kiss you, nothing more. No, tonight I want to discover what you have and haven't done with men. Not that it really matters to me but still, a man likes to know."

"You make no sense, no sense whatsoever. I've done nothing with men, except that kiss so long ago..." She broke off looking at him, lowering her lashes.

He was liking her unfeigned innocence. Let's see what else she doesn't know. "It will in time. Have you ever been kissed by a man?"

"Not a man, no. Just you." As if embarrassed, she stared at her hands that were clasped tightly in her lap.

"I'm not a man?"

"I didn't mean...you're confusing me."

"A lad then?" He meant to pursue the question.

She looked up, seemingly startled. "Should you be askin' this? Don't see where it's any of your business."

He placed her hand in his, brought it to his lips and turning it over kissed the palm. "Do you want to tell me?"

He felt the shiver of pleasure as her eyes widened. She seemed to think over the question. "His name was Seamus and we were fourteen, I believe. Didn't want him to kiss me though. Told him no. He didn't listen."

"He did it anyway. That was not well done of him. If you ever tell me no, I won't kiss you."

"Are you askin'?" Her voice shook.

This came about sooner than he planned but why not? "I would like to kiss you, then kiss you again and again. I've the feeling that once I start kissing you, I won't want to stop." He brought her hands to his lips, kissed the back before turning them over. "Ach, but you've tiny hands."

His lips caressed the palm while his thumbs created lazy circles on her wrists. He was delighted when she shivered with sexual pleasure and her eyes closed for a moment.

"Just because yours are big doesn't mean mine are tiny."

He laughed, sensing her unworldliness and was heartily glad. "Did you like the kiss? Be honest now or I won't know if I can trust you."

Her blue eyes sparkled, shimmered with desire and passion he'd just created if he didn't miss his guess. "It was nice, I think. Your mouth on my hand made me feel things, different kind of disconcerting things. I've never imagined anything like this. So, I suppose I like it."

"Can you be more specific?" He kissed her again this time grazing her flesh with his teeth."

A tiny sound squeaked from her lips. "No, I dinna think I can."

"I want to kiss your lips. Remember, Ella told you kisses were fine. Do you trust your new friend?" This time he didn't wait for an answer. Decided not to chance a no from her.

His hands on either side of her head, he brought his lips to hers, swept her mouth with his tongue then waited for a response.

She seemed frozen and he was afraid she didn't want the touch. To his grateful surprise, her fingers rose to his shoulders, not to push away but to pull him closer. This was what he wanted from her, needed. He longed for a passionate woman.

In his arms she was soft and willing. Once more he brushed her lips with his tongue. With hers she touched him tentatively, oh so sweetly. He nearly lost control at her unknowing caress. He drew away, looking at her closed eyes.

"You need to open your eyes as well as your mouth. Touch me with your sweet tongue if you'd like. Remember when I kissed you in the stable a couple of years ago? I was sure you liked it then."

Her eyes were wide open now as was her mouth. Her lips were moist from the kiss they just shared. When he looked down, her breasts were nearly bared to his view. Good God, why didn't Flynt dress his little sister appropriately? Forget her lack of clothing, tonight he meant to kiss more than her lips.

He bent close, whispering so he knew she felt his breath against her. And he smiled at her, patiently waiting.

She looked at him, questioning. Ran her tongue across her mouth in anticipation.

"You kiss me this time." His voice was soft and gentle, hoping to give her the encouragement she needed.

"Me, kiss you?"

"Yes. Just like I taught you."

"Alright." She placed both hands on either side of his face. "Like this?"

He nodded once and she pulled him toward her. His hands ran through her hair, silken and hot to his touch. The pins came lose, strands falling down her back. She touched him tentatively with her tongue. Unable to restrain himself farther he opened, sucking her tongue into his mouth and exploring hers. He couldn't stop, couldn't pull away and the kiss went on for the longest time. Her fingers wound into his shirt pulling herself against him, her tiny little mews filled him with pleasure.

She created a sweet hot tempest deep inside, and he wanted to hold on to this moment for the months ahead that he would be in Edinburgh away from her. Her untried sexual advances aroused him far more than those of his mistress, ex-mistress.

Unable to restrain himself, reacting not thinking, he found her breast. With the smallest tug his hand found silken flesh and a hard-tight bud beneath. Resistance was impossible. He drew away, waiting for a no, then began to kiss, lick and tease his way to her bared breasts. While he fondled one with his fingers, his lips found another.

"Wh...what are you doing?" Her words held a hint of panic.

He looked up, grinning, "Kissing. You told me Ella said it was alright to kiss. Did you change your mind, sweet imp? You don't want to kiss anymore?"

He knew he confused her but she would have to figure this out on her own. Giving her help certainly was not part of his plans.

"No, I like your kisses. It's just that..." She licked her lips, her fingers pushing on his head almost as if she tugged him closer.

"I have your permission then?"

"Yes, oh..." she sighed, "I feel..."

He paused watching her, "What is it you feel?"

"So hot. I feel as if I'm catching on fire and damp, in places," she paused, her eyes darkening. "Why would that happen?"

He couldn't answer, but he continued kissing her, playing with her breast and the hard tips with his fingers and tongue. Tempted to explore her all the way to the feminine petals of her sex and discover just how wet she was, he stopped himself. That would have to wait for the next time. He had to control himself now.

"There." Pulling her dress to cover her bosom, "You pleased me. Did I please you?"

"You're stopping." She appeared distraught. "Do you want to stop? I don't."

"We said only kissing, but truly I would like to know if I pleased you."

He looked one last time at her amazing breasts and finished covering them.

"So much I didn't want you to stop. Why?"

"Why what?"

He knew what she was asking but wanted to hear from her and he wondered if she could manage them through her embarrassment.

"Why stop when we both enjoyed it."

"Well," he paused, tracing the top of her bodice with a fingertip, wishing he didn't have the control to cease this beautiful seduction, "because if we kept this up, you would no longer be chaste, no longer a virgin."

"You don't want me."

He thought for a moment that she might cry and he didn't want that. "I quit now because I do want you and I promise you that someday I won't end this before we both want it to be finished."

"I'm not understanding."

"I need to get you home before I do something you'll regret in the morning." He pulled her close, molding his lips to hers. With a swift, harsh breath of air. "It seems I canna help myself."

"Perhaps I don't want you to."

"Will you wait for me lass?"

Chapter Six

Mist and clouds hung over the MacTavish land. The one-week honeymoon seemed to flash by in record speed. They were home. Now Flynt had to see to the issues at hand.

"Leslie called in a favor from Drake Montgomerie," Broc said as they looked over the land. "He was worried about you and the rest of the family. Spies, you know, they've a way of finding out about things people want to remain hidden.

"I've heard and it seemed he elicited favors from my little sister too." Flynt didn't bother to hide the newly found antagonism to his longtime friend. "He had no right and to vow her to silence as well."

"Doubt if there was a vow of silence. If what I heard is true, Lacie confided in Bliss. I ken your suspicions, but this isn't the problem to face at the moment. Drake told me there was allegedly some kind of treasure on the land your father won from McGinnis' father.

"Treasure, that's interesting, my father mentioned nothing of that sort." Flynt wondered at the rumor, which could have started with Sean McGinnis.

"Of course, he didn't. He wouldn't have known anything about such nonsense. It's just one more reason for Sean to resent you and claim the land so he can search out this so-called wealth. Your father winning that land is the best thing that happened to those crofters."

"When you mention treasure, it makes me think of pirates," Flynt laughed, his mind splintering into a million different directions. "Huge chest filled with Spanish doubloons. Of course, McGinnis treasure would have nothing in common with doubloons. What do you suppose it could be?"

"Probably something that might have been hidden years before during some of the more turbulent times in our history. Suppose a few important documents of some type. Rest assured it's most likely gossip, nothing that would be true," Broc said. "Although I've heard that McGinnis has been hunting out hollow trees and digging in various places."

"A waste of time, if you ask me," Flynt said as he tried to get his rambling thoughts from Leslie and what he might have done with his sister. Two weeks had passed since that night, but Lacie remained mute save for a few comments to his sister according to Broc. All she told him was that Ella said kisses were fine and that was all they did.

"Hardly, if there is truly something out there."

"If there is a treasure on MacTavish land, it is mine. Not that I really care, though. If it wasn't for the principle of the incidents, I'd let him have whatever he finds."

"You should care though. It would be part of your heritage and your children as well. By the way, how are your attempts at siring an heir," Broc laughed.

Flynt was pretty sure Hope carried his child, but it was really too soon to make an announcement of any kind. After all, only two weeks had passed. Instead of answering, he listened to the hoof beats as they rode down the trail and the sounds of the birds. Leaves rustled on the trees, shimmering silver and gray in the muted light of the day.

"Glad we didn't stay in the city." Flynt kicked his horse to a faster pace, smiling. He enjoyed a good ride, relished the wind on his face. A ray of sunshine would make the day better. He'd been glad when Hope agreed she'd rather live in the country. A trip into the city a few times a year would be nice, but that was all either of them needed.

"Bliss took Lacie to the seamstress for a few new gowns. Leslie said he would be quite happy to pay for them. In fact, he planned on doing just that, but understood you would most likely refuse him," Broc said.

His gut churned as he listened to Hope's brother. "At this point in time, Leslie had no right and the gesture, as nice as it looks on the outside, would be totally inappropriate as the entire city would say. What is wrong with Lacie's gowns and why is the duke paying for them?"

Brock let his chuckle rumble out while shaking his head, seeming to punctuate his astonishment at Flynt's words. "You haven't taken a moment to look at your sister lately. If you had, you would be thanking Leslie for undertaking to remedy a problem which you should be rectifying, the fact that the man has ulterior motives aside."

"The problem would be..." At the moment he was clueless and would much rather get to the bottom of the rumored treasure.

"Her bosom."

"Don't think it's appropriate you and Leslie are talking about Lacie in that manner." Yet he couldn't stop himself from asking more questions. "What is it about her bosom?"

"Probably you're right about the appropriateness, but are you really that obtuse? Perhaps you should ask your sister, or take a closer look at her. I'm sure Hope could explain the problem to you if you still don't understand." Look over there. He was pointing to a hollowed-out tree, lose dirt piled high as if someone had been digging there.

Spurring their horses toward the tree, he felt a moment of exhilaration and was pleased to get the topic of his sister's bosom out of the way. They dismounted, walking quickly to the fresh dirt. "Do you think they found anything?"

"No, I doubt if there is any kind of treasure anywhere. Don't have a clue what it could be," Broc laughed. "What I want to know is where the man is hiding. He should have been caught within the day and that was two weeks ago."

"Someone is hiding him. Find the traitor and we'll find McGinnis," Flynt said. "Do you recall if he had siblings who might benefit from this?"

Brock ruffed a hand through his hair, thinking, and "No other family that I can recall, but none of us were close with them He seemed a bit strange to me even when we were kids. I could never quite put a reason to the thought."

"He's too pretty in my mind. Should have been a girl," Flynt muttered, his mind still more focused on what had not been said about his sister and her bosom.

"Perhaps therein lays the truth," Broc said as he sat on his haunches, examining the hole that had been made as well as the pile of dirt. "Nothing here now. Doubt if there ever was."

"There is nothing here," Flynt muttered, agreeing with his friend, "just a heap of dirt and nothing that would tell us if anything had been discovered."

"Do you want to keep riding?"

"Need to see to my sister. As you said, I'm sure Hope will shed some light on this situation when I ask. I want to take care of it before Lacie's reputation is left in shambles, no thanks to the duke." No, he didn't trust Leslie. Well, he did trust him with his life but not his sister's virtue.

Blessed hell, but his feelings were mixed. What more could he want for his youngest sibling? Leslie was a wealthy duke. If his intentions were pure, his sister would have an amazing marriage and life. With Bliss and Chelsea, all he could see was their deflowering, not a marriage that any father would want for their daughter. Problem was, he was not a father but a brother who knew the rakes his sisters associated with very well and assumed only the worst about the men as well as never giving his sisters credit for taking care of themselves. Ah, but that was the crux of the matter. The men could seduce, would seduce if given a chance. His sisters were or had been innocent.

He mounted and not waiting for Broc yet knowing he was behind him, he set off for home, eager to see his wife and his sister as well. At the stable, he handed the reigns to the stable boy.

"Going on home," Broc told him. "You take care of your sister. Let me know how it all turns out."

"I understand. Leslie will."

He needed to see first-hand what all the to do was about Lacie's bosom. Taking off his riding gloves and slapping them on his leg, he strode to the house and up the steps determined to solve the little issue of his sister's dresses.

Hope slanted him a flirtatious grin when he walked into the parlor. "Good afternoon, and how was your day?"

"Is Lacie home?"

He bent to give Hope a quick kiss before pouring a cup of tea. He sat across from his wife. He didn't dare sit next to her. They, as usual, would end up in bed together, and he didn't have the time this morning. Making love with his wife would have to wait for evening.

She nodded, seeming to understand the distance. "She was here, but she left for town about ten minutes ago saying she had an appointment with the dressmaker that couldn't be missed."

He tried to look relaxed but knew Hope would see through the ploy. "What is this business about the dressmaker and who made the appointment?"

"Well." Hope set her teacup on an end table, her perfectly shaped lips thinning. "I believe I might have mentioned this earlier, but there was so much going on two weeks ago it might have slipped my mind or yours."

"And," he tried to be patient but it seemed Hope wanted to drag this out.

"Lacie is growing up and her gowns cannot keep up with her ever enlarging bosom. She is quite well endowed for a young woman who has never had a child. The one gown she purchased a few months ago with her own money I might add, no longer fits, the buttons refuse to remain closed. At the moment, she has the dress she wore at our wedding, but it is far too fancy for everyday wear."

"Why hasn't she asked me for the money? Heaven knows I don't want her running around showing off her breasts. Why the hell is Leslie involved in all this?" Somehow, sometime he'd lost touch with his little world.

"I can't answer your question. Suppose you might have to ask your sister. Perhaps it is pride. As to Leslie, I can only assume he is interested in her and doesn't want the rest of Glasgow's male population ogling her bosom." Hope picked up her cup sipping again. "This really needs some lemon but we don't have any. I'll have to ask Cook to put it on her shopping list."

"Maybe you can tell me why Leslie has an interest in purchasing her clothing." He already knew the answer, but he wanted to know if anyone else would believe the same.

"I thought I just did but if you need more, it seems he had Lacie over to dinner a few weeks ago. I believe it was when the Montgomerie's were in town. I heard Ella gave her some sage advice."

"I heard a little about that from Broc."

Hope cleared her throat, seeming to try her best not to stare at his lips, which made him grin and think of tossing her skirts, a much more enjoyable venture than setting his sister's wardrobe to rights.

"It seems Ella gave her a modesty piece to wear because she was showing way too much cleavage. As I heard tell, she was almost popping out."

"Good for the Duchess," he mumbled, yet he was relieved there was someone who could give advice to the little sister he'd all but ignored the last few years. "What about Daryl? Does she have the same problem?"

"Rest assured she does not. Yet, because of her successful bakery, she has money to purchase things for herself without bothering you for money. It seems neither of your youngest siblings enjoy asking you for anything. If you must know, Donal is pursuing Daryl, but she has told him she will not marry anyone ever. They are both in need of chaperones, but not for a moment do I think either man will take advantage of your sisters."

"Not without marrying them, they won't."

"No, I suppose not. All of you are really quite the same. You like to think of yourselves as rakes and notorious lovers." She grinned, focusing her attention on his mouth. "You really are the sweetest of men where women are concerned. Now in Broc's defense, Bliss was not honest with him when they met."

"I would hardly call any of us sweet," he muttered, not wanting that thought to circulate among his peers. "But thank you for the compliment, nonetheless."

"You're welcome." She smiled. "So, what do you plan on doing? If I'm right, this appointment at the dressmakers is one Leslie made when he discovered no one was buying Lacie new gowns, ones that would cover her bosom. In Leslie's defense, he did wait two weeks for something to be done about it. You should give him credit for that fact." Hope seemed to be reminding him.

"I think I need to go into town. Would you like to come and

oversee the creating of the new clothing for Lacie? If I had my way, all her dresses would cover her to her chin, but that might be a little overbearing."

"Of course I'll go with you, and I'm glad to see you are beginning to come to your senses where your sisters are concerned."

"As far as I can figure out, Leslie has no business paying for Lacie's anything's. How long will it take you to get ready?" he queried.

"I'm ready right now," she smiled prettily.

"How..."

"Expected as much since you'd been out riding with Broc. If you didn't intend to ask me, I planned on going into town by myself." She held up her hands as if she could ward off the upcoming lecture. "I'm sure there is nothing dangerous about a ride to town alone and in one of your carriages. Is there?"

It seemed she was making an attempt to listen to his concerns, "McGinnis is still free and capable of anything. I would prefer your trips were with me as well as at least two of my men. He has, to date, made two attempts on our lives. So no, I would consider it a dangerous trip."

"I'm glad you are planning the little journey with me. Should we make a night of it and stay in town? We could go out to eat or see a play."

"I'd rather go out to eat then retire to our home for a leisurely evening with you. We could play cards or...we could." He winked at her, leaving the rest of the thought up to her.

"You want me to arouse all your manly parts, you," she murmured, lowering her lashes. Then, "I dinna ken if I know how to do smoothing so bold and outrageous. What would you think of me?"

He roared with laughter, thoroughly enjoying his wife, "I'm sure you can figure it out if you put your agile mind to it. All that needs to be done is to act natural, but my sweet lassie, if you've forgotten all I taught you, then I'll have to do the difficult task by myself."

She shot him another flirtatious glance but didn't choose to pursue the conversation. Instead, "What else did you discover talking to Broc?"

"I see, then you're lookin' to change the subject. McGinnis believes there to be buried treasure belonging to him on the land his father lost. Broc and I looked for a little while but discovered nothing that could have passed for a place to hide a treasure."

"It's a ruse," Hope said, "I've heard about things like that. The dastardly man is simply searching for some way to discredit your title to the land. We both know it won't work."

"The carriage is ready, sir," Munroe stood at the door to the parlor. "Would you like me to accompany you or stay here?"

"Yes, you can drive if you wish, or ride alongside. I want two more men to accompany us, and all should be prepared for a fight if it comes to that."

He felt his wife's glare but didn't care. He smiled at her then offered a hand of assistance.

"Come, we should enjoy the day. The clouds have been blown away, and the radiant sunshine is warming the ground even as we speak."

"Perhaps we should ride."

The glare he challenged her words with should be enough for her to understand riding horses to town was not going to be acceptable. The downturn of her mouth told him she understood but also that she was displeased. He would make the disappointment up to her tonight.

"I trust this no is coming from your gut." Her tone was petulant and for the moment unforgiving. "It would be so nice to ride at least part of the way."

"It is, although rational thought is telling me nothing will happen in broad daylight." He held her hand in his as they left the house. "The carriage will be more comfortable for the duration. At the dressmakers if you wish you can pick out a few new gowns of your own."

"You know I don't need anything. What is it you want?"

She batted her lashes at him before dropping her gaze to his lips and moistening her own.

He chuckled light heartedly. "You know exactly what I want, and I don't need to bribe you with new clothing to get it. I only thought you might appreciate something new." He helped her into the carriage, emphasizing his words by letting his hand rest on her bottom.

"You are anything but devious, I'll give you that. Subtleness flew out the window with you a long time ago." Sitting inside the carriage she turned to him.

"But you'd have it no other way."

She stared at his mouth as he stepped into the vehicle. "I wouldn't be in lust with a man who left me guessing."

"I'm not falling for that ploy."

He now stared at her bosom.

"What ploy?"

He pulled her onto his lap, his mouth molding over her lips, his hand up her skirts. When he drew away for a second, "The trip will seem like only a minute while I have my wicked way with you."

He was right. The time spent making love in the carriage made the trip feel as if it went by quickly. The vehicle pulled to a stop.

Inside the dressmakers, Lacie was absentmindedly gazing at fashion plates.

"There you are. Do you know what you want?" Hope asked as she waltzed into the room, grinning brightly.

"I just don't feel right about this. Leslie has ordered so many gowns for me. I've never had this many before," Lacie was shaking her head. "I can't accept them. It wouldn't be right."

"Flynt will make everything right. He will pay for them. If and when Leslie becomes your husband, he can then by you whatever pleases him."

"I had no idea your situation had become so dire. You should have said something," Flynt said. "I will always take care of my sisters. After all I do have the damn groats to pay for them."

Lacie didn't answer. She was now absentmindedly picking up bolts of cloth then setting them down. A wan smile creased her lips. "I've no idea what to pick out, or what would look good on me."

"First, we'll start by trying a few things on. It appears Leslie has sent some directives as to color choices as well as patterns. Let me see if I agree."

"If he doesn't pay for them, he has no say," Lacie said, still seeming detached from the goings on around her.

"That's exactly right." Hope shuffled through the choices Leslie made, methodically nodding her head from time to time. "The man does have marvelous fashion sense, and it appears he knows what will look good on you. Since you have no idea what you want and despite the fact Flynt will pay for this not Leslie, I think we'll go along with his choices."

"There is so much here. How could I possibly need all of this?" Lacie asked, waving her hands around the room.

"As Flynt's sister you do not. As a debutant or as a duchess you will need this and more."

"She is right of course," Flynt stepped into the conversation. "I believe you should have a season. One you've refused for the last two years and I've not had the good sense to gainsay you."

"I don't want a season."

"If I'm paying for this, you bloody well will have one."

Flynt felt as if all he did these days was argue with his wife about this or that. He didn't intend to argue with his sister.

"I'm too young for a season," she murmured. "I promise you if you make me attend balls and recitals, I'll sit at the back of the room and make sure everyone there knows it is the last place I want to be."

"You won't make her go. Why she is most nearly promised to the Duke of Southcliff," Hope said. "Surely that is enough reason to have these gowns made."

"I've neither seen or heard a proposal from that man. Until I do, we will consider this idea preposterous." Flynt casually leaned against a table filled with bolts of cloth, feeling smug.

"One would think I'd have a choice in this. No one has asked me anything," Lacie said, holding up a dark blue day gown. "Now, is this one of the dresses I should try?"

"It is one the duke picked out especially for you. Had this and two others sent from Edinburgh with you in mind. Well, he used his hands to show my sister the proper sizing," the seamstress said. "Now he told me the bust might have to be adjusted, but he'd had the measurements in his head so the seamstress there could make the changes," the dressmaker continued, seemingly oblivious to the conversation taking place around her.

Flynt nearly choked at her words. Turning to Lacie, he started to mutter but one look from Hope brought the onslaught of words to a rather sudden and abrupt halt. For this evening's sake with his wife, he would keep his thoughts to himself.

"Don't you dare," Hope said to Flynt, tilting her head as she eyed him apprehensively.

"We can discuss this later." He looked at Lacie who remained silent as well as a bit belligerent.

"Now, dear, go try these on. When you are dressed, come out and show us. We will," Hope looked to Flynt, "decide if your brother should purchase the gown."

"It's been paid for already." The dressmaker cut in abruptly. "The duke feared Lacie would try to pay for them or leave them here. I can't accept your money in addition to what has already been paid."

"Come along, Lacie." Hope pointed to the dressing room. "We'll let your brother and the dressmaker hash this out while you try on the dresses."

The two women vanished into the dressing room while Flynt was left to discuss this. "It's really quite simple. Put the money on the duke's account then I will pay for the dresses. My sister is not his mistress and never will be. You will keep any gossip surrounding Lacie to yourself and if you hear any, you will squash it immediately. Am I understood?"

"Oh, my, everything is understood perfectly. He shops here quite often so putting the money on his account is quite easy to do. I'm not sure how he is going to feel about it though. He did give me express orders and reminded me to keep her measurements in my files. He told me he would commission some lingerie soon."

Relieved, Flynt sucked in a deep breath. "If his intentions are right and good for my sister, he will not want gossip about his soon to be betrothed floating around the town." Then the dressmakers last words hit home. "Lingerie?"

"No, no, I'm sure he won't. I wouldn't want him to think I was spreading gossip either. Perhaps I over spoke and the lingerie was meant for his mistress. Oh my, he hasn't purchased anything for anyone in nearly a year. Oh my." She was wringing her hands.

Hope stepped outside the fitting room first. "What do you think?" she pointed in Lacie's direction. "It's beautiful, yes?"

The sight of his sister dressed so elegantly brought a brotherly smile to his face. The bosom fit to perfection, and Flynt was brought back to the reality that Leslie saw as well as held his sister's breasts in his hands. He wanted to throttle the man for taking liberties. He wanted to throttle Lacie for allowing it.

Only kissing, damn it all to hell. To know the shape and size to that kind of perfection, he would have had to see them touch them, kiss them. "The bounder."

Both Hope and Lacie turned to stare at him. He shrugged. "The two of you finish up here. Going to take a walk and see to other business. I'll leave the carriage as well as Munroe. Go to the townhouse when you're done. I'll meet you there."

He had to get away before he said or did something that would embarrass his sister as well as his wife. Stuffing his hands in his pockets, his mind everywhere but where it should be, he wandered.

"Blessed hell!"

Two men surprised him from behind. The knife slashed through his thigh, his head pounded with some kind of blunt object. Now he was alone on the street blood pooling on the ground. His head throbbed. His mind whirled in a haze of shapeless figures and wordless sounds.

~ * ~

Laughing, while thoroughly enjoying the moment, Hope left the dress shop with the sisters who somehow had heard about the shopping and joined them. "Flynt definitely put a damper on the shopping this afternoon."

"He was too preoccupied with what Leslie did or didn't do with Lacie," Daryl laughed. "At least he need not worry about me. I'm not going to get married, ever. Don't see why I would need to."

"Even if Donal asks?" Bliss asked, seeming surprised with the revelation. "He spends a lot of time staring at you. It still won't stop him from kissing and other things."

"Never, and I mean never," Daryl confirmed, ginning. "I'm going to be independent and self-sufficient for my entire life. A woman doesn't have to be leg-shackled to be happy."

"What about children?" Hope asked, wondering what had caused Daryl to become so jaded about men and marriage, "You do want to have a family, don't you?"

"I only need a man to sire my children, not to help take care of them or pay for them," Daryl pointed out with a smug grin.

"By the way Donal has been looking at you, I'm sure he'll have something negative to say about that notion of yours. It's a bit too progressive for most men these days," Chelsea said, smoothing her skirts.

"Are you ladies hungry?" Munroe stepped into the parlor, a smile on his face and seeming more than eager to please. "Cook has assembled a bit of food, and I'm more than willing to bring it all to the parlor rather than the dining room."

"Famished," Hope said, wishing Flynt was here so she could stare at him. It was everything he deserved after the way he treated Lacie earlier in the day. His words and thoughts were not good, not good at all. He treated her as if she was a brainless child.

"Do we have any wine?" Bliss asked, "We should celebrate Lacie's new wardrobe. What do you think, Lacie, should we?"

"I don't know, seems like we have better things to celebrate than covering my bubbies."

The long forthcoming sigh left Hope wondering what was really bothering the youngest sister who was usually the most optimistic and enthusiastic sister.

"So, Daryl has decided to disappoint Donal by not marrying him. What is it that has you in the seeming depths of despair, Lacie?" Chelsea asked, apparently needing to get to the bottom of Lacie's long face.

Lacie looked up, a wan smile to present them. "Perhaps that is what I should do too. I don't want to be any man's pawn. Not that Leslie has asked, but maybe I should say no if he does."

"You are hardly in a position to opt out of marriage," Bliss chastised. "You have no means to take care of yourself. You can't stay under Flynt's roof forever nor do I imagine you want to."

"I'm sure he wouldn't mind," Lacie said. "Most likely he wouldn't even notice."

"Leslie might take exception. After all, it was obvious to anyone who has eyes a minimal fashion sense he planned on dressing you as his duchess until Flynt stepped in and paid for the gowns as well as the underclothing," Bliss reminded her. "The underclothing which I'm sure Leslie meant for only his eyes."

Lacie sat down, her hands in her lap, gazing at the floor and appearing uninterested in responding. Then, "Enough about me. I'm quite tired of this conversation. It's all been speculation. There has been no words forthcoming from Leslie that he wants to wed me. So far all he has done is tease and torment me."

"You're right of course," Daryl said, touching her sister's hand in reassurance. "No reason to speculate, at least not when he is on the other side of Scotland doing lord knows what. It seems he comes and goes as he pleases with no thoughts of informing anyone as to when he is coming home. In any case, you are still too young to wed."

"I wonder where Flynt has gone. He should have been finished by now with whatever business he might have needed to do," Hope said, beginning to feel a bit of apprehension where her husband was concerned.

She didn't like this at all. Her gut was telling her something was wrong. Before tonight she'd never really believed in her husband's gut instincts.

"Here is the wine." Munroe appeared in the door holding up a couple of bottles and the needed glasses. "May I pour?"

"Yes," Hope said, trying to see as far as the front door. "Perhaps you can shed some light on the whereabouts of my wayward husband. It's not like him to be so late for dinner."

Munroe cleared his throat, shifting from one foot to the other. "Can't do that. He told me he had unfinished business to attend to. His head didn't seem to be on all that straight though. Told me also to stay with the ladies no matter what."

He finished pouring the wine and handed it out to the ladies.

"Could you see if you can track the man down? I'd appreciate the help." Hope smiled at him but unlike her husband, the smile didn't sway him.

"Can't do that. Your husband told me not to let you out of my sight, not for an instant. I don't mean to disobey. Your husband is probably taking a long ride somewhere. It's what he does to clear his head."

"His life could be in danger," Hope persisted, understanding the man couldn't be swayed. He took orders from Flynt not her. "You have to think of something."

"Very well, if I think long and hard. If one of Flynt's sisters would be so kind as to write a note, you could have the stable boy or Cook's boy take the messages to Donal, Broc and Cam. Tell them it's urgent and they'll be over here as soon as they receive the missive, if not before," Chelsea said.

"That is something I can do. Glad you didn't ask me to send one of the men guarding the house, but I'm sure the boys can be missed and they would like to earn a few extra coins for their troubles," Munroe looked from one lady to the next.

Chelsea set about writing the notes after retrieving the paper and pen. A few minutes later all three notes were written and Munroe delivered them with a promise of coin to the messengers and a side note to hurry.

"Now all we have to do is wait for the men to arrive," Bliss said. They were most likely waiting for the proper time to stop by and retrieve their wives. "Broc learned a long time ago I would rather hire a carriage myself than wait for him to figure out when to pick me up. Although the twins usually dictate his actions."

"See, that's what I want for myself. That very same independence," Daryl said, crossing her arms in front of her. "My shop is doing fine and I might even make a bit of spending money soon."

"But you are up at the crack of dawn every morning. You've not had any time to relax since you opened it," Lacie reminded her thoughtfully. "Your bookkeeping is atrocious. It took me all day to decipher the scratching's you made. Even then, you couldn't account for where this thing or that thing came from or how much you spent on the items. You don't even write down the profits."

"If I could figure all those numbers out, I might be able to pay you to help me with the accounting. I know how astute you are with figures," Daryl said with a long drawn out sigh.

"I daresay my books are also a mess, but I refuse Broc access. I know what I can spend and I don't come anywhere near that quota because he still gives me pin money despite the fact I tell him I don't want his money. If I could show him what my expenses are compared to what I make, he might have more confidence in my business. He knows I can sell paintings, but that is about as far as he can trust what I do. Perhaps you could help us both out," Bliss said turning to her sister. "I'll pay your salary until we get everything smoothed out where Daryl is concerned. What do you say?"

"Yes, yes I'd like that. That's what I've told Donal about my business. He can't seem to wrap his head around a woman who is just as smart and capable as he is. He wants me to need him and I don't. I can't marry a man like that. I need to be equal in his eyes and right now I'm not."

"From what I've seen, he doesn't seem to be listening to you," Lacie laughed. "Just like none of your husbands have listened to the three of you. The good thing for all of you is that we've had no one to gainsay our wishes. I'm sure what they are attracted to is our independent thought, but it also terrifies them."

"It's their manly ego that doesn't allow for that," Bliss said, squinting into her drink as if something might be floating in it. Looking up she must have decided nothing was there. "Broc came around somewhat to my way of thinking as I'm sure Donal will succumb to your wishes given time as will Leslie if you decide to become our accountant. It will take some compromise."

"At the moment I intend to stand my ground until he knows I mean what I'm telling him. The other night he had the audacity to be in my bed when I closed the bakery. He never asked or gave me reason to believe he would be there."

Hope's eyes grew wide. "What did you do? You didn't let him stay, did you?"

"Of course not, I kicked him out after I let him kiss me. He did deserve something for his efforts," Daryl said, smiling as if she remembered something pleasant.

Perhaps Flynt should concern himself more with Daryl than Lacie.

Donal was present in Glasgow and in Daryl's bed at times while Leslie, while his intentions were more obvious, was in Edinburgh and as far as she could tell they had not as yet slept together.

Once more Munroe stood in the doorway, "Donal is here." Munroe stepped aside.

"I got the message to come at once. I was at the bakery, so it wasn't far. What is the urgency?" His gaze rested on Daryl as if he searched her for something wrong.

"There is nothing about me to trouble yourself with," Daryl seemed to chastise the poor man who had only her best interest at heart. "I am just fine. Nothing you need to worry your handsome self about."

"We are missing Flynt. We all think it is unlike him to miss dinner, so we would like the men, when they all arrive, to search out his favorite haunts," Hope said. "Unless you would agree to let us do it."

Donal ignored the last statement. "And where might that be? Nowadays his favorite place seems to be in his bed with his wife. Where I would like to be when the time comes." Once again, his gaze was focused on Daryl, his eyes simmering.

"I believe he won't give up without a fight," Bliss laughed as he watched the silent exchange between the pair.

"I take it you were waiting for me in my bed again," Daryl said, but she didn't sound angry just a bit breathless as if anticipating his kisses.

The grin on Donal's face was pure male, and his eyes seemed to smolder with raw passion. "Ach, lass, I was not there but waiting for you downstairs in the bakery as appropriate for a man who intends to court a lass. Was told you were busy but would return soon. I see you told your sisters about me being in your bed. Perhaps they can help sway you to marry me. Maybe I should become a bit more persistent."

"Be serious," Hope said. "Where is it that all of you used to meet? Was it the Bridge End Tavern? The Hole in the Wall?"

"We liked both those places well enough. Can't say any of us has done much carousing over the last two years. What with Broc and Cam married and now Flynt our business takes over most of our time."

"That doesn't sound promising. Does he have an office he visits in Glasgow?"

Hope was suddenly much more terrified than she'd been seconds ago. All thoughts flew to McGinnis and Flynt's instincts to keep her safe. When he left the dressmakers, he left Munroe and both of his men with them, not even thinking about his safety. He'd also been distracted by thoughts of Leslie and his sister.

"Not that I know of. Our conversations rarely revolved around business, if you get my drift. Most of the time..." He ran a finger around his collar. "Most of the time we talked about women."

"Your honesty in some circles might be refreshing," Bliss pointed out, "but here, none of us cares to learn about your conquests or our husbands'. If you can think of anything, feel free to blurt it out. For now, please feel free to help yourself to the brandy or the food sitting on the tray while we all wait for the others to receive their messages and find their way here."

"Wouldn't mind something to eat and drink," Donal said before helping himself then sitting beside Daryl.

"Who is going to close up your shop? It's about time to do so. If you like, I'll stop by and make sure everything is done."

He held her hand in his before bringing it to his lips and placing a chaste kiss on the back, leaving Daryl blushing and turning her head away.

"Thank you, believe I'd like that." She bent close to whisper, "I don't want to find you in my bed when I return."

"No, you won't find me in your bed but at your side. I don't intend to let you get home all by yourself."

Hope heard the whispered exchange and silently applauded both Daryl as well as Donal. While Daryl hoped to be independent, there were things a woman needed a man for such as late walks or carriage rides home was one of them.

"The viscount is here," Munroe announced.

"Cam," Chelsea set her wine on the nearby end table before rushing into his arms. "I'm so happy you got the message. Flynt is missing and in light of the past troubles, we're afraid for him."

"Missing, you say. What troubles do you think he might have gotten himself into?" He wrapped an arm around Chelsea, walking with her to the sofa where she'd been sitting.

"Would you like a brandy?" she asked, pouring him one before he had the time to answer.

"You are reading my mind again, I see." He accepted the drink and picked up a few morsels from the tray of food.

"Suppose I know you better than most, and at times even you," Chelsea smiled affectionately at her husband.

"Do you know of any places we might find him? He was distracted this afternoon but he should have been home by this time," Hope said as she finished the story and what transpired just today.

A few minutes later Broc was announced and the story repeated. The possible destinations were assigned and the men left.

"Well," Bliss said with a heavy sigh, "As usual the men are off doing something while we wait in terror of what news they will be bringing back to us."

"What do you think they will say if we venture out on our own? We can take Munroe and the men who are guarding the house." Chelsea said. "They would complain of course, but doing something would be so much better than sitting here."

"If we took the men as our body guards, they would have nothing to complain about," Bliss said.

"True enough and I don't have a man who would complain or lecture me about the dangers," Lacie said, grinning. "It will be just like old times when we used to do exactly what we wanted when we wanted."

"Flynt would order us to stay put and we would head off in whatever direction we thought would be the most fun in complete defiance of his wishes," Daryl said, laughing along with her younger sister.

Grams spent the evening with little to say, but she spoke up now, "I'm really glad Cook remembered the ginger cookies. I do my best thinking with the cookies and tea. You girls need to stay cautious and alert. Don't let the fact that Munroe and a few others are with you give you false comfort. Men can fail also."

"And what have you figured out, Catherine?" Hope asked. "If it's to stay in the house, you'll most likely have an argument on your hands."

"Don't be obtuse. That's not what I said. You should go in pairs." She waved her hand in the air. "Bliss and Chelsea as well will need to stop home and check on your babies. While you all were chatting, I made sure the stable boy and Cook's little boy were agreeable to going with you. They would love the coin they would earn, and that way you can get messages back to me. Don't know how to get in touch with the men though. Perhaps they have a plan of sorts."

"Most likely they've coordinated between themselves. I'm sure we'll hear something soon. When they find Flynt, I'll figure out some way to let you all know."

"We have to be back here before the men or there could be hell to pay," Bliss said.

"We can always use Hope's tactics to get them off kilter."

"What would that be?" Chelsea asked.

Daryl laughed, "Why, Hope stares at Flynt's mouth and it seems to leave him speechless."

"Yes, and if that doesn't work, I stare at his crotch. He calls it blatant seduction and that my lust for him is always getting the better of me."

Grams bit into a cookie, nearly choking from the direction of the conversation. "You girls are going to drive your poor men crazy. Perhaps you should try to be more biddable."

"Crazy with lust," Hope said with a laugh. "If he never figures out that I love him, I'll always have this lust thing to captivate him. Catherine, there is no fun in biddable."

"He won't get bored with you," Daryl said. "I do know how Donal will react if I use the same ploy."

"Better not," Bliss warned. "He'll have you on your back, your skirts tossed before you can say nay. If you mean to keep from marrying the poor man, it's best you don't get with child. He'll have an argument to hold over your head for the rest of your life. He won't want to...well he won't want to give up his child."

"You are playing with fire and a possible angry man. That is not wise," Chelsea warned.

"True enough, I need to take care. Not sure what exactly I want where Donal is concerned, except that I remain single."

"There will be time enough for you to reconsider all your options unless you become pregnant. Donal is wealthy and holds more power than you. He could force you to give up the baby. I seriously doubt if Flynt would step in, in your defense if you chose not to wed."

"Donal could do that and do you really believe Flynt would be so callused?" Daryl asked, seemingly startled by the revelation.

"Well yes, Donal could do that as well as make your life miserable if he resented what you're taking away from him. He's clearly smitten with you, and he's not a man who would allow a woman to rule his life. He would do what he pleased and what he deemed right."

A deathly quiet filled the room, the silence startling and obtrusive. Hope heard her heartbeat as well as what seemed like the rattling of everyone's breathing. Lights flickered all over the house and the candles that had been lit, the flames wavering. She inhaled a quick startled breath.

Hope felt as if a ghost walked across her soul, a sudden shivering encompassing her.

She recalled her mother talking of such things, omens of bad luck, the women of the harem also speaking of similar happenings.

She always thought the women superstitious but now... Now she realized there must be some psychic force involved. She knew Flynt was in trouble, hurt and even reaching out to her from some type of spiritual world.

What to do now?

When she closed her eyes, she saw the tiny room he lay in, his eyes wide open, giving her the first hint that he wasn't dead, that his spirit was alive and talking to her. The space was void of furniture, dark and she knew he searched for strength to move.

"He's hurt," she whispered.

"What is it?" It seemed everyone spoke in unison.

"I don't know, a premonition of sorts. I saw Flynt in a small dirty room, unable to move, yet conscious."

"Where?"

"I don't know. It's cold and he's bleeding. The furniture was old and ratty. He needs help but we can't do that until we figure out where he is."

Broc strode into the room, his face grim etched with lines of concern. "Didn't find him." His voice was gruff. "No one who I talked to has seen him." He seemed to notice the coats and scarves that had been set out. "You ladies weren't planning on searching for him, now were you?"

He looked at Bliss pointedly. "I recognize the guilty expression. Well it's a good thing I got here before you left."

"She and Chelsea were going to check up on the babes," Catherine said with a stern look pointed in Broc's direction. "You need not be getting high and mighty with your wife. She has hers and your best intentions at heart."

"You don't need to defend my wife. She's very good at doing that herself. That might be part of the truth but not all of it. In any case, without further information we don't have a clue where to search."

She sighed softly wishing things were different. "The room was in the seamier part of town. I think. It looked old and a bit dilapidated and filthy as well. We could start by looking in the slums," Hope said. "I want to come with you."

"You can't. It's no place for a woman or a man alone for that matter. I'll take Munroe with me."

"Can't do that, sir. Flynt told me to stay with the women folk and I intend to do just that."

"I'll go search by myself. Tell the others when I return where I..." he stopped, turning to see who was suddenly coming in the front door.

"Donal, Cam, thank goodness. We're heading to a different part of town. Perhaps the poorer neighborhoods. I'll fill you in on the way. We need to take a carriage. Flynt is hurt."

Once again, the women were left alone. Hope rose, walking from one room to the other until she was exhausted, needing to sit and do some serious thinking.

"He'll be fine," Catherine said, standing beside her, her hand on Hope's shoulder. "We all ken it."

"You don't know that. If only I could have seen where he was. It could take them forever to find him.

"He's going to be fine. You saw his eyes were open, keep remembering that," Bliss said.

"He's going to be fine. He's really going be fine."

~ * ~

"What are we going to do with him now? He's still breathing and look," the man pointed, "His eyes are open. He can see who we are."

"Boss told us to leave him for dead but to make sure we didn't kill him just that he won't survive. Seems to me that's the way he is now, near death and barely breathing. He'll be dead and on his way to hell within the hour."

"Don't like this one bit."

"No, neither do I. Don't want to be anywhere near here when his body is discovered. We need to get out of this place and not look back."

"You think he's bleeding out?" The man stepped closer to Flynt to get a better look. "His eyes are closed now."

"Won't be much longer. Grab his purse. Make it look like a robbery. We can keep whatever he's got."

"He's dead now. Right?" The man rubbed his jaw, staring at him.

~ * ~

Later the two men stood in front of Sean McGinnis with the news that Flynt MacTavish was a dead man. They'd personally seen to the crime and waited until he drew his last breath.

"You didn't leave until you were sure MacTavish was dead?" Sean reached into his pocket to pay the two men, unsure if they spoke the truth or not. "If I find out anything different, you'll come to regret lying to me and that's a promise."

"He's departed to the other world whatever that may be," one said with a dramatic flair.

"Half the coin today. You'll get the other half in a day or two when his death has been confirmed. I need to see it reported in the papers."

Sean wanted to go into the city and see for himself. He knew there would be men looking for MacTavish He wasn't about to risk being caught anywhere nearby.

Elated but still unable to resist, he walked outside and mounted his horse. Riding close to the old buildings, darkness seemed infinite. Few of the gaslights functioned in this part of town. He caught sight of Cam and Broc. Quickly, he turned his horse around but not soon enough.

The shout reverberated through the blackness of the night, sending a shiver of dread up his spine. He should have resisted the temptation that called to him.

"Stop him. Stop that man!"

Pushing his horse hard, he sped through the street. No one followed as he raced toward the outskirts of town, meaning to elude his pursuers in the countryside beyond.

This is what he feared and his curiosity brought him into the middle of the fray, putting his life at risk. He would be accused although he was sure no one could trace him to the murder. It would be their word against his. Yet if he were caught, he would be found guilty of the arson he committed, adding murder to his list of crimes would get him hung.

His sigh was resolute and complete. He turned his horse towards a brothel he knew, needing to find some pleasure this evening. Of course, he did have something to celebrate. Flynt was dead and without an heir. No one to claim the land he held as well as the land his father lost so many years ago. If he got away with this, his future was looking up.

It was fitting, he decided. Fitting to celebrate the years of tyranny he'd endured at the hands of the MacTavish's.

"Hold."

He turned hearing the words but disbelieving them. It was a woman who commanded him. "What do you want? Who are you?"

She held a gun on him and he found himself surrounded by four other women and Flynt's valet. "Where is my husband?"

"Bloody hell, how would I know and why would I care? The man has been the bane of my existence since I can remember."

In his chest, his heart thundered. What the devil did she think she was doing, acting like a man? Her husband should beat some sense into her. Too late, he chuckled to himself. Her man was dead.

166

"I'll shoot you in the stomach if you don't tell me."

Another shiver ran up his spine. From the sound of her voice he was sure she would do just as she said.

"Your husband doesn't speak with the likes of me. He won't have anything to do with a McGinnis. I'm sure I don't have any idea where he is off too, probably whoring."

"That's because you're too pretty," Hope said, raising the pistol. "Now tell me where he is and stop making things up."

"I'd do it if I were you," the valet said. "She's a damn fine shot."

"Don't miss what I shoot at," she said."

"In any case, if she missed, I wouldn't," Bliss said so very calm another shiver travelled up his spine.

"Nor would I."

"Or I," Lacie and Daryl finished. "Where is he?"

Sean decided on prudence not his more stubborn side. Four women bent on his destruction were not odds he wanted to challenge. "Back in town at the Blackmire Inn. Was told he's in room 203. Told, mind you. I didn't kill him."

"You know he's been hurt. You hired someone to kill him." Hope's voice was soft but menacing. "You won't get away with his murder or his abduction. My friend Arie has a way of dealing with people such as the likes of you."

Distraught beyond her patience, Hope cried out, "Nay," she shot, the bullet grazing his ear, blood sliding down his neck. "That's for what you had done to my husband. That was not a lucky shot. I could easily put the bullet in the middle of your forehead."

Chapter Seven

Flynt slowly rolled over, the groan rumbling forth, seeming distant and not from his body yet it was. His head was still throbbing, but the knife wound up his thigh was his main concern. Painfully, he drew himself to a sitting position, leaning against the wall and breathing hard. He set his head on the hard surface, content to rest for a few minutes then a few minutes longer.

Breathe slowly, inhale, exhale, he struggled for air. Do it again. He closed his eyes, concentrating on regaining his strength. With each rapid heartbeat he drew more courage and determination. His life depended on him saving himself. Even though they would search for him, it would take a miracle to find him in this hovel.

Minutes later, he opened his eyes. Checking his leg, it seemed the bleeding had slowed. He pulled his shirt from his pants, ripping off two strips of cloth. One he folded and pressed against the length of the tear. It was jagged and the edges of the slash were red, infection setting in.

With the second cloth, he wrapped it around his leg, tying it tight to keep pressure on the wound. Once again, he'd spent all his available energy but he felt confident he'd stopped the bleeding if not the infection that would take his life if not treated quickly.

Trying to rest, his thoughts wandered to Hope. He smiled. She would be worried about him and he wondered about the time, late he supposed. Dinner would have been served hours ago, and she would be speculating where he was, worrying. The girls would have gone to his townhouse after the shopping trip. That thought brought him back to the reasons why he was in this predicament.

He'd been distracted by the dressmaker's revelation about his youngest sibling and one of his best friends. Leslie had set his sights on Lacie, no doubt about it. He would have to trust the Duke not to take advantage of her. She was unknowing after all and Leslie was a man of the world. Despite the premature misgivings, he liked the idea of Leslie courting his youngest sister. He would be a good match for Lacie. He decided he would not let anyone else know his feelings anytime soon.

Hope, he sighed. If he'd paid attention to his surroundings, he'd be with his wife. She'd be staring at his mouth then his crotch. He couldn't say he'd always waited until they were in bed to make lust with her. There was the time on the dining room table. He didn't like the fact she didn't love him, didn't say the words anymore. Just lust, and he started that unholy arrangement by denying the existence of love. Perhaps when all this was over, he'd make lust with her against the wall. He didn't doubt the vertical would be just as good as the horizontal and the lusting would be even better. Might be a lot like having butter upon bacon.

Ah, if he hadn't been so stupid and arrogant.

Suddenly he woke, startled by a noise. He prayed the men hadn't come back to finish him off. In this condition, he'd be and easy mark. As quietly as possible, he pushed himself into a dark corner, even while knowing if someone was looking for him, they would still see his nearly lifeless form. Hell, even if a person wasn't searching for his body, his appearance here was obvious.

"Ah, what do we have here?" A man stumbled into the room, crumbling to the floor in a drunken stupor. "You're in worse condition than me if that's possible. What happened to you?"

His visitor was no help to him and thankfully he wasn't after his demise. Seemed just a drunk old man. Flynt wished he had a few coins in his pockets, but McGinnis' men took all the coin he carried with him, which wasn't much. He rarely had money with him, his credit being good wherever he went.

"You hurt?" The man looked at him, seemed to study him. "Maybe I can help you out?"

Flynt wanted to laugh. If anything, this man needed more help than he did. Perhaps not. Neither one of them seemed to have enough energy to stand let alone walk out of here by their own means.

"Was attacked a little while back. Need a walking stick if I'm going to get out of here and find my way home. If you can help me with that, I'll see you rewarded."

Flynt didn't think the man could get out of here on his own, at least not until he slept the liquor off. He would have to make do with this would be rescuer as well as his inadequacies as a houseguest for the time being. There were no others beating down the door to lend assistance.

The man seemed to perk up a toothy grin on his face. "Try to help. You say it'll be worth my while? What does that mean?"

"What would you like?" Flynt asked, expecting his answer to be a whore and a bottle of whiskey.

"What would I like? You really mean what you said?" The drunk rubbed his whiskered jaw, blood red eyes shining at him, his graying hair standing on end.

"Name it and I'll see if I can make it happen."

"Want a job and a roof over my head." The man glowered at him as if challenging him to make good on his word. "Can you do that? Was that just an empty promise?"

The request shocked Flynt, but he did intend to carry through with his agreement. Between he and his friends, someone should have something the man could do to make a living.

"What can you do? Be honest now. Do you have any skills?" He understood just because a man was down on his luck, it didn't mean if given a chance he couldn't prove himself.

The man seemed to perk up. "I used to train race horses. Did that until I made a costly error in judgment. Because of that mistake a real gem died. I mourned his loss more than most anyone I've ever known. The stallion was like a friend to me."

"Let me guess. You were let go. Seem to remember something like that. Happened about six years ago. Am I right? The horse was called Star Fire?"

If this was the man he was thinking, of his reputation had been sterile until this incident. Mayhap he did deserve a second chance and if he didn't, well, then he still meant to provide him with the opportunity to prove himself.

"You are right. Lost everything. No one would hire me after that. My wife left me. Ran off to America with some man looking for adventure and put down new roots, enticed by the promise of land."

"I'll see what I can do. You'll have to stay off the bottle otherwise the deals off. I've a friend who owns a few racehorses. Maybe he can put you to work doing something you love."

"Never was a drunk," he muttered. "Truth is, I just use it to drown my memories and wish for a miracle. Maybe I got that miracle tonight."

Flynt closed his eyes again. He supposed this might be the dream the man was looking for. The conversation drained his energy, but when he opened them again the man had vanished. Gone. He wondered if the vision of the drunken man was brought on by fever.

When he unwrapped the wound, the redness had grown and he felt as if he was burning up. Perhaps the man didn't exist. He closed his eyes again and the next time he woke, the darkness had begun to recede. Dim morning light slanted in through the one window in his tiny prison.

"See your awake now. Found you a walking stick and something to eat. You're going to need some water too."

"How?"

The man shrugged, his grin seeming to cover his face. "Promised you'd pay for it. Said you were a duke or something. Don't think the bartender would have given me the food, but he knew me before the incident." He held up a bottle of whiskey. "Got this too."

"You promised not to..."

"Not for me but for you. Drink up and I'll pour the rest on that slash in your leg. I'm a man who keeps his word."

Flynt broke off a chunk of bread, his stomach rolling a bit but he understood the need for food. He chewed slowly while the man unwrapped his leg. "Think I should know your name if I'm going to give you a job and trust you to patch me up. Mine's Flynt MacTavish." He tried to hold out his hand but didn't have the energy.

"Guessed as much. Before I got so drunk I couldn't think straight, I heard some gents asking for you." He held his hands up for a moment. "Before you start asking, they were gone when I went back to the bar."

"It's almost dawn now. Suppose I couldn't have expected

anything else."

"You couldn't have done anything if that's what you're thinking. Mr. MacTavish, I'm Kelly O'Brian. I've fixed my share of horses. Never one slashed with a knife but rocks and other debris on the tracks and training fields have cut some."

Flynt took another long swig of the whiskey then wiped his mouth with the back of his hand. "Nice to meet you, Kelly. Let's finish this and we can be on our way. I'm eager to get home. Need to do that before my wife comes looking for me."

"You're not going anywhere with my husband."

The voice came from in front of Flynt.

He grinned. "Too late. Don't mind her. She's my wife and she shouldn't be here. Guess we weren't fast enough seeing she's standing by the door brandishing a pistol at you. Finish with the whiskey." Flynt handed Kelly the bottle.

If he could have throttled her, he would have, so he put the thought to the back of his mind for a task he would have to do later. His sisters stepped into the room behind Hope, all with guns pointed toward Kelly.

"Unhand my brother, "Bliss said, the pistol in her hand. "I'll shoot you."

"He's helping me, Bliss, and I've promised Kelly a job. He's earned what I promised, so let him finish and put down the weapons."

"My gun is on him."

"As is mine," Lacie said.

"Mine as well," Daryl said.

"You've got some mighty fine women folk," Kelly chuckled, looking over the women and holding up his hands. "Don't mean your man any harm, but I can't finish this with my hands up."

Watching carefully, he slowly lowered them, continuing his work.

"Disobedient," Flynt mumbled.

"You should be proud of them. Wish I had somebody who cared enough about me to come looking for me when I didn't come home." Kelly poured the rest of the whiskey in the slash then rebound the wound. "Time to get you home. You ladies wouldn't have a spare carriage at your disposal? Know he can't walk and most likely would fall off the horse."

172

"Mighty fine women folk. Did you hear that Flynt?" Lacie repeated. Then, "No, no carriage at hand. I've a stable boy who'll race like the wind to get this message to Grams, and she will be sure to send what you need. In fact, I'll go with him since I don't have a man here who will lecture me on what I can and can't do." She then coked her head sideways and grinned at him.

"You still have me to account to," Flynt shot out, watching her retreating back.

At least it was light and the night's revelry had come to an end hours ago. Lacie would be fine.

"She needs to get help," Kelly told him. "She's plucky that one. Whoever has his sights set on her is going to have his hands full."

"As are we all," Hope said as she sat beside Flynt and pulled him into her arms before whispering, "Should I stare at your mouth now or when I get you home? Perhaps your crotch would be a better choice today."

"Best do it now. When we get home, I'm going to put you over my knee and thrash you soundly." His mutterings seemed to make her laugh.

"Liar, now you owe me a kiss." She touched his face, running her hands down his chest as if trying to make sure he was alive and well.

"You need not worry. I'm alive and it will take more than that ruffian who pulled his knife on me to kill me. Not when I've a wife who is in sore need of discipline. Have to stay well so I can make sure you understand my manly commands."

"If you try anything like that, I swear, Flynt MacTavish, I'll stare at your crotch and you'll forget whatever it is you're planning to do to my poor female body save make lust to me."

He groaned. There was nothing to it. She had him and he could do nothing to retaliate. Kelly was sitting nearby, chuckling, seemingly having overheard their conversation.

She was running her fingers through his hair and he swore if he didn't hurt so much, he'd be thoroughly prepared to toss her skirts and a satisfied man as well. "I'm not going to let anything happen to you."

"How much longer do you think it will be? I'm having a blessedly hard time keeping my eyes open."

"Ten more minutes perhaps," she said. "That depends on whether or not your friends will chastise Lacie for finding you and getting help before they actually come get you."

"Good thing Leslie isn't here then," Flynt mumbled, closing his eyes. "It might be tomorrow before I'm rescued. He's by far the more autocratic than any of us. I'd like to hear what he would have to say to her so I can commit his words to memory."

"It's the spy in him, I suppose. He has to be able to take charge," Bliss spoke up. "Now that we've found you, I'm not looking forward to Broc's temper or what he thinks to be his words of wisdom. Do believe I'll try out Hope's technique of diversion. It should work well."

"Me too," Chelsea said. "Waiting to find out what exactly Cam will do is harder than the actuality. My mind goes to places that he threatens but never does."

"Ach, your man's bark is louder than his bite." Kelly seemed to be enjoying himself and the conversation.

Bliss paced the tiny room, occasionally stopping to stare out the door. Flynt wanted to float off to oblivion and even while he recognized the fact if something happened that would threaten the ladies, he was helpless to do anything.

It seemed he did sleep. He woke suddenly. Broc, Donal and Cam stood over him, glaring at him as if he'd done something wrong.

"Where are the ladies?"

"All but Hope have been sent home a few minutes ago," Broc said. "Thought they should get out of harm's way as soon as possible."

He smiled. "They figured it all out and turned up here. How did you ever let them out of your sights? Someone should have been left at home to make sure they did what they were told."

"No one would be here to bring you home. If not for the ladies, you could have died here. While I'm sure Kelly would have done his best where you are concerned, he would have been hard pressed to carry you all the way to your townhouse," Hope said, indignant that what they'd done had diminished just so the men could strut their prowess.

"Would have just gone to the bar a few doors down." Kelly

shrugged. "Once the owner knew I would pay him back, he would have sent a message anywhere I asked. We had this all under control. Didn't we, Mr. MacTavish?"

"Yes, I'm sure you did but I didn't."

He wasn't about to admit that he might not have made it through this if not for his wife and sisters. That was the gall of it all. He'd lost all control and the ladies he was supposed to be protecting, rescued him. He couldn't take it, just couldn't figure it all out. Everything in his life seemed upside down.

Broc and Cam pulled him to standing before they put him between them, his arms wrapped across their shoulders. "Suppose I could haul you over my shoulder, but this has a bit more dignity," Cam said, seeming to hold back a laugh.

With a lot of grunting and groaning, Flynt and Kelly were in the carriage, Hope letting Broc help her inside and the vehicle was moving.

"You didn't tell your friends about me," Kelly said.

"Didn't need to. They assumed since the ladies allowed you to live, you didn't have nefarious purposes where I'm concerned. Hope would have shot you, you know. If she'd thought for a moment you harmed me or threatened to do just that."

"Don't doubt that for one second." Kelly laughed hard and long. "Whishing I'd done a better job of choosing the right lady for myself. Watching Hope and the others there is no doubt in my mind if things got tough for you, they'd stay by your side, not run off with the first man who waved a sizable purse in their direction. You're a lucky man even if you don' know it yet."

Flynt wasn't sure he wanted to listen to Kelly's lecturing all the way home and in the presence of his wife who would undoubtedly lord it over him every chance she found. Kelly was also right in his assessment. He was a very lucky man having found Hope.

He shivered, a sudden chill encompassing him. Hope seemed to notice and drawing a carriage blanket from beneath the seat, covered him with the rug.

"You're cold and your jacket is damp."

She looked to Kelly as if he might have an answer.

"It was rainin' last night and the mist didn't seem to want to leave. When I stumbled upon him, I didn't notice anythin' but I passed out shortly afterwards. When I came to, all I could think about was checkin' on his leg and taking care of him. Especially after he gave me an offer I couldn't refuse."

"I see, remind me of that promise, why don't you?" Hope asked, looking from her husband to Kelly. "Why would Flynt offer you something?"

"Guess we needed each other. I'm thinkin' he thought I wanted another bottle and maybe a whore to warm my bed for the night. Didn't ask for that though. The way I see it, I was getting a second chance to better my life. He was sent to me to find him."

"What did you ask for?"

Despite the exhaustion and the fever that seemed to be taking hold of his body, Flynt smiled at his wife. She was defending him, making sure no one hurt him. That was his job but the gesture was endearing. In any case, she pleased him. He'd keep her even if she was a bit headstrong and only lusted after him.

"Only for work and a roof over my head. Been tired of sleeping on the street and abandoned rooms when I can find them. Get chased out more than get to stay." He pulled on his shaggy beard.

"Did Flynt agree?"

"Seems so. I came back with whiskey for the wound and food for the stomach. Told him I'm good with horses, any kind but especially race horses."

"I see, Flynt doesn't own any race horses," Hope countered as they rode.

She touched his forehead. "You're hot, too hot. One minute you're freezing and the next you're burning up with fever."

"He needs to be cooled off," Kelly said. "Can't do that until we get you home."

"He's going to be alright, isn't he?" Hope asked.

"Thinkin' you should send for the Doc before you do anything else. He needs to take a look at him. We can cool off his body and help him fight the fever while we wait. He'll be getting hot then cold probably for the next few days. Looked at the wound before we left and I believe the whiskey did its job, but I'll have another look if it's okay with you."

"Munroe will help you. We're here now."

Even his teeth seemed to be burning up. He didn't know what was going on, his mind a blank. It seemed he was being tossed about this direction then that. Suddenly, he was naked and lying on his bed. When he opened his eyes, Hope stood over him, wringing her hands, tears sliding down her cheeks. Looking at her, she tried to brush them away with the backs of her hands.

He tried to reach out and speak to her but only managed a croak, his throat parched so badly he couldn't form words. She was sitting next to him, running a cool cloth across his forehead, bathing his body with the dampness. The sensation felt good. He breathed deeply, staring at the pitcher of water and hoping his sweet wife would figure out what he needed.

She continued stroking him with the dampness. "The doctor was here a little while ago. He says you'll be fine and that you're just pretending to be sick so you can get some sympathy from me and special favors as well. You understand, of course, that you don't have to pretend. I'll give you anything you want. You remember, your brain is not addled, that I'm in lust with you." She smiled and seemed to look at him one brow arched to perfection. "Ach, of course I ken what you want."

She reached for the pitcher beside the bed and poured him a glass. "Doc said just small sips at first." She held the glass to his lips, tipping it slightly, a few drops sliding down his throat. Suddenly, the water glass was on the bedside table.

"Remember, he said not too much at first. As soon as you cool down and feel up to food, Cook has made some chicken soup. Well, broth for you, but soon you'll be able to eat the chicken part."

He nodded, trying to assimilate all that she said.

"Do you think if I stare at your mouth, you'll get better faster because of course you are lusting for me?" she stared at his mouth. "I could stare at your crotch."

He groaned but didn't think she heard him. Unfortunately, nothing down there seemed to work at the moment. He closed his eyes for a few seconds, letting the cooling cloth work its miracles. Yet it seemed just as his temperature escalated, he was now shivering.

"No worries," she said smiling. "This is normal. Will most likely go on for another twenty-four hours or so. You've got to sleep when you can."

"So." He swallowed hard and she gave him another few sips of water. "Do...? he finished before trying to clear his throat.

"Of course I'll rest." She lifted the covers then, climbing in beside him, her arms wrapped around him. "Wake me if you need anything."

She was asleep. He would recognize the easy breathing any time. He needed to get better soon or Hope would be sick. It couldn't be easy for her taking care of him. He closed his eyes Once again the heat encompassed him. He didn't remember the time between or that Hope slept more than a few minutes. She was bathing him again. Unlike the last time he woke, the room was dark, only a few candles giving light.

"You've got to sleep." He heard Catherine talking to her. "I'll take over for a few hours. You've been at this for days now."

No, days? He'd been sick for that long? How many days? Yet he knew he was getting better. While his body seemed to be sweating, the heat was not nearly as intense as he remembered.

"Water," he managed to say.

"No, go on with you," Catherine said. "I'll give him the water."

"Can't. Not when it seems he is getting better. His eyes are no longer glazed over, and his temperature is not as high as even a few hours ago.

Hope brought the water to his lips. The coolness slid down his throat. "I believe I'd like something to eat now and I want you to sleep. You can join me in this bed after we eat."

She grinned, sensing the long-awaited recuperation. "I could kiss you."

"You should. Don't let my manly prowess stop you. For now, though," he remembered his early words, "we best keep our lust for each other on the horizontal. Don't think I could stand long enough to do the job."

She punched him on the shoulder before looking at Catherine, a blush painting her beautiful face. He was getting his wits back as well as his strength. All would be well. She would see. He would put her over his knee for her part in this, but it would all be for naught because he couldn't look at her naked without making lust.

"Well, I'm glad you're feeling better. Doc said I should tell you as soon as possible and now seems like the soonest since you are teasing me and testing my fortitude.

"What does doc say you must tell me?"

"While you were sick this week and because the infection in your leg spread, he had to amputate it."

His heart stopped and he reached beneath the covers spilling his water in the process. "Liar."

~ * ~

"Perhaps you weren't ready to hear that." She grinned shamelessly. "I do think you rather deserved something, maybe not that something after talking about the vertical, horizontal thing so shamelessly in front of your grandmother. Shall we consider ourselves even?"

"Never." His low growl told Hope this wouldn't be over anytime soon.

"That's what I thought. I'll have to put my feeble brain to work on that. I'll think of something. You will not best me." She smoothed her skirts, trying to think but at the moment nothing seemed to come to mind.

"I don't doubt that you will. Now are you going to rest? I would sleep better if you climbed into bed with me." His wide grin stole her breath.

She wanted nothing more than to do his bidding, but he did need to sleep and he was in no shape to make lust. "I would make sure you are well before I come to your bed. I'll sleep in the other room."

"You can try." His words were slow and lazy, sent out to challenge. It seemed he meant to have his way in this.

She wasn't going to let him hurt himself. "You're not strong enough for that even though your manly parts tell you that you are. You don't want to break open the stitches. You cried like a baby when the doctor stitched them in."

"So, you say. Since you're lying again, you owe me another kiss. That's two." He was casually sitting, his back against the headboard and his hands folded in his lap. Even injured he presented confidence and inbred arrogance.

She shrugged then, "Ask Catherine, she'll tell you the same story. You screamed and screamed just like a woman, and with every little poke of the needle the cries grew louder."

"It's not nice to hold something over a man's head that he can't remember. Besides, not for one second do I think what you're telling me is true."

"I will see you in a few hours. Your sisters want to make sure I haven't killed you during your convalescence. They don't even remember that you might have passed on for being so stupid as to get kidnapped then stabbed, and for the life of me I can't fathom why."

She stepped through the adjoining door and looking over her shoulder she grinned, giving herself one more win in this game they played.

He would come for her. She knew that for a fact. The only question was how long it would take him to get out of bed and walk to this room. She could have joined him, but he issued the challenge. A challenge she couldn't refute. To give in to him now would plague her the rest of their lives. She would stay strong. He would have to figure out if he could stand then walk this far. If she heard a loud bang, she would have to check on him.

He would do that on purpose just to watch her run through the door. A soft sigh, she knew he would do just that. She couldn't very well ignore him. Could she?

What to do?

He would wait until she was vulnerable. She counted the seconds pretending she was undressing. Nothing happened. Curiosity consumed her. Thoughts of peeking into the room to see what was going on nearly made her forget his ploys.

He must have fallen asleep. She inhaled a long deep breath trying to figure out what she should do next. So exhausted she couldn't think straight, she decided bed was the proper choice.

She was just slipping on her nightdress when an arm wrapped around her waist.

"Got you and you're not going to need this for what I've planned." The kiss on the back of her neck sent shivers of raw passion sweeping down her spine.

He won and she didn't care. She'd missed this even though it had only been a few days. "You should not be out of bed." She reprimanded him then found herself tossed over his shoulder as if he was a plundering pirate bent on ravishing his captive.

"You should be in mine. Don't ken what you were thinking." His hand rested possessively on her rear. "Don't ever forget that."

Well, that was where she wanted to be, but he wasn't in any shape to make lust with her. "Your leg must hurt."

"All of me will feel better when you're wrapped in my arms. Now that you're my wife, I don't like sleeping alone and don't intend to start tonight."

"Need I remind you that if you overstrain yourself, you'll have to have the stitches redone?"

"You're going to make lust to me tonight."

She was thinking that over, contemplating the possibilities when he set her on the bed, standing over her and grinning like a besotted fool.

"Did you figure it out or do I need to explain everything?"

"You look pale." His eyes were dark circles and his skin although tanned from the sun, was not a healthy color. The bandage wrapped around his leg was a stark white.

"We can't do this." Yet he was aroused and the thought of him inside her did the same to her.

"My health is improving by the second." He walked to the other side of the bed.

"This goes against my better judgment, Flynt MacTavish. It's only been four days since you nearly died. You are in no condition to do this." Her protests, she knew, would not be heard. If she persisted, he would say that he was a man and by rights was strong enough to do just as he pleased. It was not her place to refuse him.

"I've made up my mind. Now, do I have to do everything?"

"You've done nothing," she said, still staying away from his open arms.

Once she succumbed to him, he would have won.

He was going to win anyway.

She settled into his arms, closing her eyes. "I will sleep with you. That is all."

She tried to keep her breathing slow and unaffected by the feel of his fingers running up and down her spine. Tried to slow her heartbeat when those same fingers caressed her breasts. Attempted to stay so still he would think she was asleep.

In any case it seemed he didn't care. He would have her and it was what she wanted. "Flynt, please," she whispered quite by accident.

"That was what I was hoping you would say. Say it again, my sweet little lassie. I do like to hear you beg."

His hands and fingers found her most erotic places while his lips seemed to dance in other places.

He lifted her then so she sat astride him. It was what she thought, yet she wasn't about to comply so easily. It just would not do to give over to him without challenging the moment and his arrogance. No, she would make him wait.

Once again, he lifted her so she was open to him. She felt his rod touch her then he slowly let her down until he filled her.

"You are hot and wet, so ready for me. I cannot wait for this game you play to reach its proper conclusion."

She refused to move on him, though, not because she didn't want to but because she needed to feel him inside her, feel his length before there would be no choice but to give in to him. He was alive and for too many days she was afraid for him. She closed her eyes and looked to the heavens, thanking the god above who wasn't ready to claim him.

"Look at you," he paused, "and me, together."

She did, the tiny sound escaping her made him smile. "We are as one. Do you think we'll create a child this time, or have we already done that?"

She closed her eyes, imagining, letting him work his magic. She felt the spasms take over her body. She could no longer resist, no longer stop from moving on him. She heard his groan, the deep rumble from his chest. Their voices blended together as they cried out each other's name.

Spent, she fell on his chest, his hands possessively stroking her back, holding her close. He slowly calmed her.

"Thank you," he whispered, "even though I had to work damn hard to get it, and I'm still alive to talk about it."

"You better not talk about what we did unless it's with me." She pushed away and punched him on the chest. "Don't want Catherine hearing anymore of your tall tales."

He laughed and the sound was good to her ears. "We need to sleep and I promise you I won't force you again."

"You did no such thing. We both wanted the lusting." With his arms around, her he rolled them both to their sides.

"Glad to hear that."

It seemed he was asleep as soon as the words left his mouth. She lay in his arms finally understanding how close she'd come to losing this man she loved more than her own life. He would go after McGinnis with a vengeance now. He would seek his revenge.

Arie should play a more active role in this. He would take care of the man and make sure he never bothered them again. Perhaps there was an out of the way destination he could take him to or like the others who kidnapped Chelsea a harem where they could be sold as slaves.

~ * ~

She must have slept. Now she woke to sunlight and more advances from her aroused husband. "I want to make an heir if we haven't already." His teeth gently closed around her earlobe.

"Is that different than making lust?" She smiled when she heard his growl of displeasure. Then he was deep inside her and she forgot about everything but the pleasure and the love she felt for this man.

It seemed the seconds ticked by turning into an hour. She turned, gazing at him, at his beautiful sensuous lips. "I swear, woman, you have no shame."

"Sir, it's Munroe. You and the missus decent? Stupid question. I know you're not, but the siblings are downstairs wanting to see you. I've a bath, well two and food. Cook has prepared a huge breakfast for everyone in the dining room. Not telling you to hurry but if you don't want them beating down your door in an hour or so, best you get going. I believe they have little patience."

Munroe was going to be angry with her. He tried his best to stay with them. She would make sure Flynt didn't hear about the part where they gave him the slip. If it did come up, then she would figure out a way for Munroe to shine.

It was as much his friends' fault as it was Munroe's. They should have known what their wives were capable of, still capable of. She formed a plan. She smiled and rose. The bath was waiting in the other room. She meant to bathe and dress before meeting her husband and going downstairs to greet the siblings.

Finished, hand in hand they walked down the steps. Everyone stood, eager to see him.

"As you all can see I survived and the bigger question is what has happened to McGinnis?"

"Can't find him. He's disappeared, but he's bound to resurface sometime soon," Broc said. "We've people out looking for him. Not much he can do but leave the country or stay in hiding."

"Pray he's left the country," Lacie said. "Good riddance."

"Leslie, you're back. When did that happen?" Hope asked as she ushered Flynt to a chair. "You need to sit."

"The morning that Flynt was found." He was standing behind Lacie, and it seemed to Hope his hands tightened possessively on her shoulders.

"For how long?" Hope had been surprised to see him. He was usually away for longer periods of time.

"The rest of this week then I'll be sent to Paris and onto Bordeaux. I wanted to see Lacie's new gowns and make sure everything was in order."

"I take it you didn't trust my judgment." Flynt sounded defensive and the irritation he'd felt at Leslie seemed to surface.

"Someone had to make sure Lacie was properly covered. You were not stepping up to the job." Leslie grinned before focusing a possessive gaze on Lacie.

"It's not that. It was how you knew her measurements." Flynt had not thought before blurting that out.

Hope punched him. "Don't you dare keep embarrassing your sister."

Flynt had a moment of good manners when he looked a bit chagrin. Then, "Is this an official request to court Lacie? I must do my duty as her brother or make sure you stay far away from her."

"Hadn't thought that far ahead, but if Lacie is agreeable, let's make it official."

He turned to her. "Are you?"

She flushed a delicate color of rose. "I suppose. Don't really know but only if I don't have to attend any balls."

"If you'll sound a bit more enthusiastic, I'll promise no balls in the immediate future."

"That hardly makes me feel better. How long is the immediate future?" Lacie asked.

"I'll be gone for two to six months, possibly longer." He pulled her closer to him. "When we wed, as the Duchess of Southcliff, there will be a ball or two expected from you."

"I'll try. This is all so...scary, confusing, different. You confuse me and surprise me. I don't have any idea what you will do or say next. You've ushered me into a world I don't understand, never anticipated being part of."

She stiffened her back then. Something that surprised Hope. Good, she was retrieving her backbone. She would need it to stand up to all of Leslie's posturing as well as his manly demands.

"When you get to know me better, perhaps then I won't be so terrifying or confusing. I don't mean for you to feel anything but pleased when it comes to me and you."

Flynt rose then, his legs shaking slightly. "We should go into another room and discuss what is to be done with McGinnis and how we're going to go about finding the man. Another thing," he turned to

Leslie. "One of my benefactors the other day was a man by the name of Kelly O'Brian. The name mean anything to you?"

"He was a horse trainer if I'm thinking of the right man, a damn good one. Always wondered what happened to him."

"I promised him a job and a roof over his head. Think he would have helped me without the incentive, but there it is. If you don't want to use him to train your race horses, I'll hire him for my stables. His knowledge would go to waste though."

"Why did he disappear?" Leslie asked, seeming to wonder and perhaps piecing together what he recalled from the time.

"An accident, a horrible accident involving one of the most promising horses in Scotland. The owner let him go and after that no one would give him a chance. You willing to open a new door on his life?"

"If his talent is half as good as I've been told, then I'm more than willing. Have always believed a good man should get a second chance."

Hope watched them leave, relief that they were going to the other room. She leaned forward, smiling. "So, tell me, what happened to all of you? Flynt has merely told me he would put me over his knee and thrash me until I cried out for him to stop, which of course he wouldn't do. And if he had his hand on my bottom, his male mind would divert to something pleasing."

Bliss smiled, "Broc pretty much told me the same thing, so I stared at his mouth. He was so unnerved he forgot what he said he was going to do. We made love. He told me how much he loved me and that I was his. I wasn't to do anything like that again. A woman shouldn't ever stare at her husband's mouth."

Chelsea laughed, pretty much the same for me. "I told him if I had to rescue him, I would do it in a heartbeat and not worry about what he might say once his wife saved the day. A woman is as good as any man. He told me he was stronger and I should stay in my place. I quickly told him I was smarter than he was and that made up for his brawn."

Daryl looked away for a moment then back, color flooding her cheeks.

"You didn't?" They all spoke in unison.

She nodded, "But no one is supposed to know, but it's not entirely what you're thinking. More like that time at the beach house when he made me feel things I'd never thought of before. I told him I realized how life could just be taken away at a moment's notice and I didn't want to waste time. He was more than happy to oblige. We never got to the part where he would thrash me if I didn't obey him. He's so easy going I doubt if he would ever make those kinds of demands on me."

"Don't delude yourself. He will. After all he's a man and he has no other recourse than to act that way," Hope said.

"He asked you to marry him then," Bliss asked.

"Yes, but I told him no and I stand by that no. He told me he would keep asking until I responded correctly. I won't, you know, change my mind and tell him what he wants. I'll never let a man dictate what I can do and what I cannot."

"You know you could be pregnant right now," Bliss put it bluntly.

"No, I can't. We didn't. Well, he knows. We won't do it again. I told him that too," Daryl said.

Bliss turned to Lacie, "Please tell me Leslie didn't persuade you too."

"No, he was a perfect gentleman for a change. You know we could go find Sean McGinnis. We don't have to leave it to the men. I used to ride out there on what he thinks of as his property. There is an old cabin. We could confront him."

"We should do that today."

"We could take him to one of Arie's ships."

"Naked, he would have to walk there without a stitch of clothes on," Chelsea said. "We'd have to let him wear his shoes."

"We're not cruel," Lacie added.

"What will we tell them? They'll want to know, keep tabs on us," Daryl asked. "We have to come up with something they'll believe."

"We don't want them to be suspicious. That wouldn't do at all," Bliss said.

"We should say we're going to your bakery. I need to work on your books and from there we can figure something out," Lacie said.

"Yes, but we don't need to ride to the bakery. It's just down the street. We will need the horses if we're going to that cabin. It might take a few hours.”

“Suggestions?” Chelsea asked, shaking her head as she looked in the direction the men had gone. “The men don’t seem to be going anywhere. They probably don’t have a clue as to where to look.”

“We could behave ourselves and tell them what we know about the cabin,” Bliss said, lifting her shoulders a bit. “Just a thought.”

“Take the chance on the next knife or the next bullet doing its job and killing Flynt.”

“Or Broc.”

“Or Donal.”

“Or Cam.”

“Or Leslie.”

“Not a chance. We need to take care of Sean McGinnis ourselves. That way we know it will be done properly. The men have had several weeks and have done nothing positive. They are no closer to catching that man today than they were three weeks ago when all this happened.”

“Perhaps we should meet tomorrow. With all of them in the back room and Munroe prowling around the house, there is no way this will work out,” Hope said. “Unless perhaps we can enlist Kelly O’Brian’s help. Flynt gave him the room in the stables and hopes Leslie will hire him to train his racehorses. He seemed to like the fact we took matters into our hands.”

“He’s a man. He’ll side with Flynt and tell us no,” Chelsea said. “Worse, he’ll tell them what we’ve planned.”

“What is there to do? Just wait until they leave us alone?” Daryl asked. “They are in control, and that’s exactly what I don’t want to happen in my life. Donal will not control me. I won’t have it.”

“We’re still stuck here until they leave unless of course you can think of somewhere we can all go.”

Leslie strode into the room. Not wasting a moment, he pulled Lacie into his arms and kissed her, a long deep kiss. Pulling back, he touched her on the lips. “I will hurry back as quickly as possible. Don’t do anything foolish.” And he was gone.

“Don’t do anything foolish,” Lacie mumbled repeating Leslie’s words while she touched a finger to her lips. “He thinks he owns me now and all I've agreed to is for him to court me."

"He almost does," Daryl reminded her. "When he returns and weds you, he will own you. You should do as I've vowed. Not to marry, ever. That way he can't own you but you can still sleep with him."

Daryl thought she had everything figured out, but if she guessed right, Donal was dancing a merry jig with Daryl and he did own her now, ring on her finger or not.

"You slept with Donal. Did he take precautions?" Hope asked, knowing she needed to have another conversation with this sibling of Flynt's. "You know you could carry his babe as we speak."

"We spoke on that." Daryl tilted her head, chin going up.

"What did he say?" Hope couldn't let this go. It was far too important.

"That he would know his child, but in any case, we slept together but we didn't, you know sleep together."

"Thank God," was the collective words.

"Any man would want that," Broc appeared, bending down and kissing his wife. "I am leaving, have business at the shipyard to take care of. You ladies have a wonderful time. Don't do anything foolish," he warned as he left the house.

Two were gone. Maybe if they were lucky Cam and Donal would leave soon and Flynt would be so exhausted he would fall asleep. One could only hope. In any case, she could find a way to leave the house.

Sure enough a few minutes later Cam repeated the process, kissing his wife and telling her not to do something foolish. If she didn't know better, she would think the men overheard their conversation and planned on intercepting them.

Donal was right behind him, spouting the same nonsense.

What were they up to?

She held her breath when she watched Flynt walk to her. Then, "Are you going to tell me not to do something foolish?"

"No, my sweet little lassie. The words would be a waste of time. You will do what you will do despite my words of warning." He left, walking upstairs towards the master chamber.

~ * ~

Sean paced the tiny one room cabin muttering to himself. "How had this gone all so terribly wrong?" Yesterday he arrogantly rode into town believing Flynt MacTavish dead only to discover the miraculous life saving strategies of the ladies and Kelly O'Brian.

His men had assured him the man would die, perish in that slum of a building before anyone found him. The knife wound hadn't even become infected.

"We thought he'd die," The man sitting in the room with him said. "We should get out of here. I'm sure there's a ship headed to Port Rush or we could really start over and head for America."

"We could of course do all those things. How do you plan on paying for the trip?" Sean asked.

"I could work my way there. Ships always need crewmembers. Better than ending up in the Royal Navy or with a bullet in my heart. Not interested in fighting."

"Not interested in working either," Sean said. "I do have enough coin for my passage."

"Then it's done. We make our way to the docks and find a ship. You can buy a ticket and I'll find the captain. See if he's got anything for me to do."

"Best be careful not to run into Broc. He'll have us at the constables in a blink, and I know he has an office on or near the docks." Sean was trying to think of every possible scenario.

"You got anything to pack," the man asked.

"Just a few things in the other room. I'll grab my bag and be out in a minute." Sean strode into the back room, finally feeling a bit of encouragement. He wanted out of Scotland and now was his chance.

The day was bright and sunny just as his disposition. He stepped into the front room.

"Sean, we got trouble."

Chapter Eight

They, Broc, Cam, Donal, Leslie, and of course himself, met in the tack room of the stable waiting for the women to do something stupid. Flynt's heart seemed to beat in his throat and his nerves felt close to shattering, he was so terrified for Hope. He couldn't lose her, feared the worst if they would somehow lose track of the women.

"Hush, here they come," Flynt said looking over his shoulder to the men behind him. "We've got to give them a healthy head start and make sure they don't know we are following them."

Inside the stables the ladies talked about the sunshine and the possibility of rain as well. Their conversation gave no clue as to where they would be going. Flynt left the door partially ajar so he could hear but nothing, except the word bakery was indicated as a possible destination. They wouldn't ride there. The store was just a few blocks down the street.

"So, they're gone and we have no idea where they are off to," Leslie said, his tone harsh as well as demanding. "We need to try to follow them without being seen. I don't like this, any of this. While I'm new to the machinations of your wives, don't you think it would be prudent if you exercised some manner of control over them? It's not appealing to have any one gainsay my orders, especially my soon to be wife, and I don't care to run all over the countryside looking for her, knowing she is getting herself into trouble she might not be able to find a way out of."

"Easier said than done," Flynt muttered, knowing his words to be the truth.

"I might know where they are off to." Kelly walked into the room with a lively step seeming to enjoy this. "Thought I could help you gents out since the women have the upper hand in this one. Don't want to see them get hurt. I've noticed they are a determined confident lot and with good reason I might add."

"What do you know?" Cam asked. "The more time we waste here exchanging words the better the chance they'll find some way to get into trouble."

"Might have heard Miss Lacie talking about a small cottage on the old McGinnis land. Thought he might hide there until things cool off a bit. They could be headed that way, or not. Seems they want to take up where you folks left off. Impatient they are, to see an end to all of these troubles. More determined than you are, I suspect. They are a protective lot where their men are concerned."

"That's my worst fear coming true. We planned this in hopes we would be wrong, but now I don't think so," Flynt said roughing his hair with his hands, his stomach rolling.

"We should have hogtied them and gone after McGinnis ourselves," Broc muttered, pacing the tiny room, his exertions doing nothing to help the cause.

"If you recall, we've failed miserably as have the constables at finding the man. He's eluded everyone. His patience seems to outdo those who gave up looking for him. Still, there's nowhere for him to go. How did Lacie know about the cottage?" Flynt asked, pausing to think. "That's a fact I don't understand."

"Said she used to ride out there," Kelly said.

"As her big brother and caregiver, you should have had some idea what she was up to as a young girl," Leslie said still sounding angry with Flynt. "You gave her way too much leeway. She could have been hurt."

"She used to always be somewhere alone. I'm surprised you let her ride all over the countryside by herself," Broc said, looking to Leslie as if his sympathies were with him not Flynt. "Used to be out chopping wood, shirtless and I'd look up and she'd be sitting on the fence watching me. We talked about things no one her age should have been asking a man."

"Hope you put your shirt on as soon as you saw her," Leslie growled. "I'm the only shirtless man I want Lacie seeing even though it all happened in the past. You should have been more prudent. What the hell were you doing with your shirt off?"

"It better not be before the wedding," Flynt said before pausing. "That's a whole lot better than you seeing her."

Leslie grinned as if remembering something pleasant. "Agreed but as you well know, it's too late for that. The dressmaker can attest to that fact. The woman did blush when I described Lacie to her."

It seemed to Flynt the duke wanted to goad him further. Damn, but all this was his fault. He'd been remiss. "You don't need to laud it over me. I'm understand I'm negligent in my chaperone duties but to my defense, Grams was supposed to take over those responsibilities after my fiasco with Bliss."

"We all know what her rules are. The girls should be able to do as they please," Cam said, "I'm certainly delighted Chelsea did just that. "I couldn't have asked for something better. If she wasn't as forthcoming and courageous as she is, I would most likely still be courting her and trying to figure out how to be the perfect gentleman. She took courtship matters into her own hands and showed me what she wanted."

"Best we saddle up. Don't want them to get too big a lead," Flynt said, wishing the conversations about his sisters and their husband's love lives wasn't out for all to hear. "Kelly, you want to come with us?"

"Probably should to run interference between you gents and the women folk." He laughed. "Besides there isn't anything left to do here today. The duties you've assigned me can be accomplished by a lad, not that I don't appreciate this opportunity and roof over my head. It's a miracle for me, sure enough."

"What do you suppose they plan when they find him?" Cam asked, shaking his head in seeming confusion. "He's a man. They can't possibly think to overpower a man, can they?"

"Daryl informed me the other day she was smarter than me and that made the difference in my brawn. She really believes what she's saying and that she can best a man," Donal said as he looked toward the women riding so nonchalantly into trouble.

"That's what makes this all so dangerous. All of them believe this nonsense about being stronger and smarter than men," Leslie continued in seeming disbelief. "I've never encountered anything like this. I don't like the fear and I don't like Lacie being around Daryl. She's a bad influence. Daryl is putting notions in Lacie's head that don't belong there."

"You afraid she'll decide to go her sister's way and not marry. Mark my words, Daryl will marry me, maybe not sooner but definitely later. I like the idea they confide in each other. Perhaps Lacie will help convince Daryl marriage is not so bad. One can always hope," Donal let out a long slow breath of air, looking to the heavens as if searching for guidance. "Don't know how long it's going to take to change Daryl's mind, but I will do just that."

"Terrified she will do the opposite and Daryl's ideas will stick in her head. I'm going to be away so I will have no influence, no way to convince her she can't live without me. Afraid she's at a vulnerable and gullible place in her life." He stared hard at Flynt. "Before I leave, I need to find a way to bind her to me and I will if I get a chance. Even if it means bedding her before the wedding."

"You'll have to take your chances with seducing her. You should have resigned from that damn job years ago except you were bored. Good God, Leslie, you've a huge tobacco farm in Maryland as well as the business here that change the weed to something usable. You're a duke. Yet you put your life in danger just because of boredom."

Flynt didn't like the idea of Leslie seducing his little sister, but he was resigned to the fact there really was nothing he could do about it. Perhaps his Grams was right. The girls would do what they pleased in order to get what they wanted. At least he agreed with the end result of Leslie's plans.

"All true," Leslie said. "For some reason I crave excitement. My family as well as myself have decided I need to settle down and sire an heir. My younger brother has no interest in any of the family matters, although he is usually quite willing to visit Maryland. I often wonder about that. In any case, he has by last count a total of four bastards. That was two months ago. He could have more now. One of us needs to produce a legitimate heir."

"I thought you were the bad boy in the family," Flynt laughed, enjoying Leslie's vulnerability, something the man rarely showed. "Why compared to him you're a stuffy old man. He puts all of us to shame."

"Don't put me in the grave just yet. I've got a lot of plans and a lot of living to do before that happens," Leslie chuckled despite the gravity of their undertakings today. "All of them include Lacie. She has somehow stolen my jaded heart and I like the feeling."

Mounted, they headed out, watching the horizon, pleased with what they saw. They could just barely see the five girls in the distance. "Pray they don't mean to look behind them. Perhaps we should spread out."

"The distance is too far. They can't tell who we are just as we can't tell them apart from anyone else, except there are five of them and that's a dead giveaway," Leslie said. "Can't risk them thinking they are being followed by their husbands. If they were really smarter than us, they wouldn't have been so blatantly obvious as to what they were up to."

Donal and Leslie dropped behind and to the left, keeping Flynt in their view while Cam and Broc did the same to the right keeping Leslie and Donal in view. Kelly stayed with Flynt.

Flynt didn't feel like talking. At the moment he was left with just his thoughts that were simmering, his anger growing now that he didn't have the others to jest with. He tried concentrating on any number of things but his mind kept returning to Hope and the danger she was placing herself in as well as the possibility of their child. He couldn't handle it. All this new responsibility of looking out for a wife who thought she was a man. She was risking their baby. Hell, she shouldn't even be on a horse, needed to be in bed, doing nothing.

What was she doing?

What was he to do?

Kelly rode up beside him. "Decided I'd join you all in this endeavor even though my feelings side with the ladies. Another man on this quest wouldn't hurt. I always say, the more the merrier. A penny for your thoughts, sir?"

"You want to start earning that roof over your head." Kelly's easy banter was a godsend. He needed his rational voice in this. "I want my wife home and safe. She needs to be in bed."

"That I do. Want to earn my way. Leslie seems nice enough. Has he told you if he wants me to train any of his horses? Though I'm puzzled why you think she should be home in bed."

Flynt meant to ignore that question. It was too soon to be talking to others about Hope's possible pregnancy. "That he did. Said he was always willing to give a good man a second chance." Flynt was pleased to see Kelly's grin. "By all accounts you're a good man who was down on his luck and didn't know how to pull himself out of the quagmire he found himself in. You would have helped me despite my promise. I ken it."

"Glad of it. I won't let him down, but I plan on explaining to him exactly what happened with that horse. While I could have changed the circumstances if I had known a storm would come up out of nowhere and a tree would fall over then I would have. Couldn't predict that storm or the accident."

"Is that what happened? I don't remember much of the news but that's hardly reason for dismissal," Flynt said as he lost site of the girls.

They rode over the top of a hill then down. His breath caught in his throat. That was not something he would have ever bargained for. He needed to see them every second. His fear for Hope grew as his heart pounded against his chest.

"Most of it. The horse panicked and ran right straight into the trunk. Tried to jump over it. I did all I could to gain control of the terrified animal but to no avail. When all was said and done, I couldn't save him."

"Where were you?" Flynt asked hoping for a much-needed distraction from the fact he could no longer see his wife.

"On the training field. It was the only tree in the whole damn place, and the horse was there at the exact moment the lightning struck. Bad luck never followed me before but after that my life got worse."

Flynt looked back. Far in the distance, he saw Broc and Cam. There was no way the ladies would see them. They would see two men, that was all. He told himself they would never suspect but he was sure they did.

"Don't you think Hope will suspect it's you?" Kelly asked, clearly thinking the same way he did. "Maybe we should switch places with Broc and Cam. They would appear different from the two us."

"Less chance of suspicion," Flynt laughed, understanding they'd most likely been had. "Perhaps our wives are smarter than we give them credit for."

He wanted to believe in Hope's intelligence but that just wasn't the way he'd been brought up.

"Well, those girls found you when no one else could. They are wile little devils and I'm sure that in the back of their minds, they expect their men folk to follow. They'll take diversionary tactics and that's a fact. I'd be shocked if they didn't."

"Don't think they would quit their mission even if they knew we followed them," Flynt said, knowing that for the reality that was his wife and sisters. "We failed, truth of the matter is, we didn't take the time to discover what Lacie knew. A question, a simple question was all that stood between finding Sean McGinnis and the ladies trying to talk the man and his thugs down."

"Don't think they do know," Kelly said. "Ignoring you is not part of their nature. I think you understand what I'm trying to say."

"Perhaps, but Hope wouldn't risk her mission just to confront me. If she had her suspicions, she'd ride faster and somehow try to elude me. She'll confront me after the fact and not a moment before, simply because she knows I'll discipline her."

Discipline her, what a bunch of gall on his part. All he wanted was to keep her healthy and alive.

"Yes, well, I've heard enough to know your form of discipline is more like making love to your wife until she's so exhausted she can barely stand or think." Kelly belly laughed.

"Lust, we make lust not love," Flynt said, distasting the word more each time either he or Hope used it.

"Ah, so you're refusing to admit you love that wee bit of a lass and have to use other words to describe your feelings. Lust. Seems that if you lust after her so much, it's also love. Best you think about that a wee bit before you convince her you don't love her. Love is important to a woman, but what do I, a lonely old man who lost his wife to another, know about love?"

"Already done that. Now I have to convince Hope I love her. Not quite sure how to do that after I've told her so many times it's lust she is feeling not love, not even passion or desire which have a better sound to them."

"Just tell her. That is all you need do. Say the words then make love. She'll know the difference."

The men crested the hill and true to what Flynt had just said, the girls were no longer visible. He turned in his saddle, wishing for some clue as to the direction they would take.

"Didn't you say Lacie found the cottage on old McGinnis land? If I remember correctly it's behind us and to the right. Cam and Broc might be seeing the little gals right now. We certainly won't."

"So, you're saying they had their suspicions and took some defensive tactics to hide from us." Kelly laughed. "In my mind it was more than a suspicion. They were sure you would not lose track of them."

"From prying eyes, they surely did just that. We should have noticed a few miles back that they were going in the wrong direction if they were truly searching for Sean and not out for an afternoon ride."

"We should have. It's just that I didn't want to admit it, anyway I hoped they were up to nothing dangerous even though I knew better."

Denial was never good and could certainly cost a life.

"That they heeded your words? No, seems they are taking matters into their very own capable hands. Knowing them and having seen them in action, I've no doubt they'll succeed in their endeavors. Once again McGinnis will be shocked at what he unleashed by wanting his family land returned. One of them alone is formidable, but all those women together..."

"I'm sure you believe that. Hope doesn't. None of them is as strong as a man and they can't overcome strength with their brains even if that were true."

"Between them they've five guns, possibly more and as you said earlier, they believe they are smarter. Perhaps confidence is the key to winning against a man. They will catch him unawares and thinking he's got control when he truly doesn't."

"If anything, they'll terrify the man into surrender. I know she does that to me on a daily basis." Flynt smiled at his thoughts.

She did terrify him quiet often, but it was with her verbal tenacity not her strength or her intelligence. Hope had a way of putting their life together in a different light.

"Should we turn right then and head down the hill. We are bound to find something of interest if not our ladies."

They caught up to Cam and Broc. Flynt whistled which brought Donal and Leslie to their sides.

"You've lost them?" Donal asked. "I would feel better if I had Daryl in my sites. She can get into trouble just by overthinking something."

"And Lacie," Leslie sighed. "She might not be standing up to me like her sisters do to their men, but she's not a whit of common sense. Just as Broc watched her flying over the countryside with not a care to her well-being, so have I. It's part of what drew her to me in the first place, and I've had to wait a dastardly long time to do something about my feelings. Don't intend to lose her now."

"Kelly and I believe the cottage is to the right and perhaps over that hill. It's at the farthest edge of the old McGinnis property. That's where they are headed. I'm sure of it."

"They might be there as we speak," Broc said, his horse sidestepping seeming as eager to intercept the ladies as his master.

"They might. I say we go now and not waste another minute," Leslie said, his horse seeming just as eager, his forelegs prancing.

Flynt felt the grimness of the situation settle into his soul and seem to encapsulate him. He spurred his horse forward, listening to the sounds of the other horses behind him. His heart raced as fast as his mount. Rain threatened and even as they drew closer, drops of moisture began to hit the ground. Wind whistled through the trees. A storm was coming.

The distance seemed to inch closer, mile-by-mile. He closed his eyes for a moment trying to calm the splintering nerves in his body, trusting his horse. They crested the hill and far below them they saw a cottage and five horses tethered nearby. Blessed hell, but it was all true. All their worst fears and wildest imaginations were down there and now inside the cabin.

The ladies were confronting the man who tried to kill him. Now

Hope was in trouble and could be recipient of another bullet.

"What do you think?" He reigned in, his horse sidestepping.

"Proceed with caution. Don't want to spook anyone into doing something stupid. At the moment we don't have a choice except to trust in our women," Leslie said, his voice just audible over the rising storm, rain suddenly pummeling the ground even though blue sky appeared in the distance. The tempest wouldn't last long.

"What do you propose?" Flynt asked, waiting for a plausible plan. His first inclination was to do just what Leslie advised against.

"We'll ride half the distance and tether our horses. Then proceed cautiously and very quietly by foot." Leslie gave more directions. "We'll let the women decide what we'll do. Though we must be ready."

All Flynt wanted was to make sure she was healthy and whole, all body parts just the same as when she left then somehow make sure she didn't do anything like this again. He had no idea about how to go about that. Nothing he tried in the past worked, certainly not his threats of beating her. Taking away privileges might be a solution, but what did she do that would be considered a privilege? She never overspent and he knew for a fact she never used all the pin money he gave her weekly. Confining her to the house or even the bedroom would not be a punishment, and he could never keep her from seeing his sisters.

What to do?

He and Leslie were at the door and he could over hear the conversation. Hope was clearly in charge. Holding his breath, he listened.

"You cannot possibly think to overpower me and my man." McGinnis was speaking now. His words held a hint of disbelief.

"We can and we will," Hope said, her voice ringing with confidence. "We gained entrance with no problem. We are all good shots, perfect aim as you well know. I've been known to hit a coin at one hundred feet and as you can see, I'm only a few feet from you. If I wanted, I could maim you for life, which might be better punishment than killing you. You wouldn't be able to suffer if you were dead."

Flynt heard the laughter in her voice.

"Don't believe a word of it," McGinnis said. "I could walk out that door right now and you'd be afraid to use that pistol."

"I suppose your manly pride is mistakenly telling you those things. You can try to walk out that door, and while I don't want to kill you, I promise you I'll shoot you in the knee."

"You couldn't hit my knee." He started to walk, his voice filled with bravado.

Flynt held his breath. A shot was fired. Then he heard Lacie.

"I'm a better shot than my sister-in-law and I don't have any qualms about killing you although...the duke of Southcliff might not appreciate it if I were to end up in prison. That was a warning shot. By the way you're bleeding. I took a second knick out of your ear. If you keep this up, you might not have an ear at all."

Flynt was sure his littlest sister was grinning.

"That's my woman," Leslie said with a bit of wonder and pride in his voice. "Suppose she's listening to your sisters, but I'm not opposed to that. Believe I'm beginning to appreciate a woman who can think for herself and won't cave at the first sign of danger. Need that in a woman."

"You can say that now but wait until you are truly wed and left with the duty of protecting her. She will never give you a dull moment," Flynt told Leslie before turning his attention back to the conversation behind the door. "Perhaps you want to rethink your courtship."

"My other man will be here soon, then it will be three men against silly women who are aping men. Just you wait," McGinnis said.

Broc crept beside them. "Lacie shot at McGinnis. The bullet whizzed by his head. I'm sure it grazed his ear.

"Seems they do have everything under control. Want to see what they've planned next," Leslie said giving the women more credit than Flynt was willing to admit to.

"Go on back and keep an eye out for what they're doing. We might want to back off and give them some space," Leslie said, grinning and seeming to enjoy this moment.

"Not too soon. Need to hear more," Flynt cautioned, "and we need to keep an eye out for that third man."

"Start undressing," Hope said then, "Both of you."

Flynt heard the words, shocked to his core. It was what he'd thought of when punishment of this man came to mind. Believed Arie would instigate this. Perhaps he did. As one of Hope's dearest friends it was likely she sent a message to the man for help and advice when she knew her husband would lock her in the bedchamber.

"Did you hear what I think I heard?" Leslie asked, a silly grin on his face. "I know I said I didn't want Lacie looking at any naked man except me, but looking at McGinnis would make me appear very favorable."

Flynt was nodding his head, "I believe so. This should prove interesting."

"You heard her. We're going to take you and your man to a good friend of mine and he's going to find you employment of the type where there are no wages. Sent a message to him just last night and told him what I thought he should do. He's in complete agreement."

"Not going to undress."

"I think you will if you value your life." Another shot rang out. "Perfect, grazed your other ear this time. If I aim a little to the right my bullet will hit you in the middle of your forehead," Lacie said with a smugness Flynt recognized.

"I'll have to remember to keep all my guns locked up," Leslie mumbled.

"Don't' get her mad," Flynt agreed, thinking the same about his wife.

"Start now," Chelsea said. "Undress or we will have to resort to other measures. Your life or naked, two choices that don't seem so hard to make."

A few seconds passed then another shot and a scream. "My God man, take your bloody clothes off."

"You too," Hope said, laughing. "You don't think this is just meant for McGinnis, do you? After all, you're the one who actually attacked my husband."

"It's time, I believe, to retreat to a safe distance. Even if they see us, they'll ken we're not going to interfere. I'll get the others. You go on back to the horses and we'll watch what transpires next."

A few minutes later, the two men, stark naked except for their boots and with their hands tied behind their back walked slowly from the cottage.

Silently laughing, the men watched from behind a copse of trees. "By God, they did it," Leslie said, more than a touch of awe in his voice. "A few hours ago, I would have never thought it possible or believed it possible.

"Do you think they could do the same to us?" Donal asked.

"Not a chance," Leslie said. "I'd call her bluff."

"It's not done yet," Flynt reminded them all. "We're going to keep a comfortable distance between us and them. Nothing can go wrong."

Despite the seriousness of the situation, the men were hard pressed not to roar with laughter watching two men they despised walk naked down the road, five women on horseback pointing guns at them while rain drenched them.

"See, those ladies are indeed formidable. Wish I could find someone like that. Someone who would have my back through good times as well as bad, defend me even at the cost of their lives. Why should men have all that responsibility? Those wives of yours are proving just how smart and strong they are as well as how much they love you."

"Strength doesn't have to be measured in brawn I'm beginning to learn. Strength of character and mind are just as important," Leslie said seeming to understand the iron will of the ladies. "I've made a good choice for a wife."

~ * ~

"Don't understand for one second why they didn't barge in here and stop us," Hope said, wondering what had come over their husbands.

Obviously, they watched them leave and followed them. That fact had been a given from the moment they left the parlor telling them not to do something foolish. They must have met in the stable and she kicked herself for not checking the tack room or Kelly's room.

"Thought at first they were just giving us enough distance so we'd get in trouble and they could come to our rescue," Daryl said.

"We didn't get into trouble, now did we?" Lacie asked.

"How far are you going to take this?" McGinnis asked, clearly irritated. "We did your bidding, now let us go."

"Not a chance. There is a ship waiting for you down the Clyde a bit. You'll have passage to Istanbul. From there you'll be sold as slaves. Last man Arie sold was to a man who preferred men. Don't think he'll do that to the two of you though. The punishment, in this case, doesn't really fit the crime. I'm sure you will come to regret your greed as well as the thwarted attempt to kill Flynt. Too bad the third man didn't show up."

Hope looked over her shoulder and down the road, "Our husbands are still behind us."

"I'm surprised at their patience and can't for the life of me figure it all out," Chelsea said. "When we first spotted them, I was sure our endeavor would be over before it barely began."

"You know those two don't compare to my husband at all," Bliss mentioned. "They are really not that well-endowed. I doubt if they could give any woman pleasure."

"Suppose we were lucky in that," Chelsea said. "Cam is amazing, terrified me the first time I saw him fully aroused."

"Quite glad you tied their hands behind their backs. That way when they walk through town everyone will be able to see most all of them and what little men they are," Bliss said laughing.

"Do you think our husbands will admit we accomplished what they could not? They've been looking for McGinnis for a couple of weeks now, and we found him in less than twenty-four hours, thanks to Lacie," Hope mused thoughtfully once again looking over her shoulder. "He waved at me."

"Flynt had the audacity to wave at you?" Lacie turned around and was greeted with the same appalling gesture from Leslie. "As did the rest of them."

"I for one don't care," Darryl said laughing. "I want Donal back there and not here. The fact they are leaving us with the task of delivering McGinnis and his crony to Arie is not only astonishing but in good taste as well. I applaud them for their patience in this."

"They must trust us a little bit," Bliss said cautiously.

"Well, I should hope so," Daryl spoke up. "I know he's not my husband and I also ken that I've no life experiences with that man, but still a husband should trust his wife, don't you think?"

"Of course he should but that doesn't mean he will let you do whatever you want. He has to assert himself and make sure everything is done as he wants," Hope said, understanding that was just foolishness but unable to completely change her husband's brainwashing.

"I've come to realize he will allow me to win an argument or two," Bliss said.

"Only when he knows unequivocally you're right," Chelsea put in, "at least that is the way Cam is."

The mist let up, the clouds disappearing. Bright sun covered the land now as they were very near their final destination.

"Do you think they'll be getting sunburned? They've lily white skin," Lacie said, "Leslie must spend a lot of time in the sun. His skin is far from fair. I'd like to see him naked." She quickly peered over her shoulder, seemingly afraid Leslie might have heard. "Was that a shameful thought?"

"No, it was a perfectly normal thought. When I first met Flynt, I wanted to see him, all of him then I would blush shamelessly at the thought even if he was nowhere to be found."

"Well, now I'm really curious how he will look," Lacie said. "I don't think he has a paunch of a belly as these two have. I'm supposing he looks something like Broc. I have seen him half naked when he was chopping wood. Now I realize he was working so hard because of Bliss."

"He was, I suppose. He was frustrated and angry with me half the time although I did nothing wrong. He spoke about you, too, not by name and if I'd thought on it more, I would have known the truth." Lacie said. "You were the woman he was seeing and falling in love with despite the fact he thought you were below him in status. Status shouldn't really make a difference where love is concerned."

"Well you didn't figure it out and that's a good thing. You were innocent then, more than you are now but still... I would not have wanted you to ken it was me that caused him so much aggravation," Bliss said. "I never told him my last name because I was afraid he wouldn't want me then."

They reached a road. It was more like a wide path and headed the last part of the journey toward the Firth of Clyde and Arie's ship. The men still kept their distance for now, but Hope expected that before they reached the ship the men would at least be riding beside them.

What did she know? She had expected them to interfere at the cottage. As time passed, she became more and more nervous about tonight as well as the repercussions. They were showing unaccountable patience. She inhaled long and deep, maintaining at least in her mind she'd weather anything he might do. His threats never amounted to anything, but she'd never overstepped his wishes to this degree. He should be furious with her when she really thought about what they'd just done.

The closer they got to the ship, the more her stomach rolled. This would not do, she had to be stronger and wiser. She had to have quicker thoughts to outwit him. Their next verbal exchange promised to be a wealth of importance. If she was shaking so hard she could barely move, all would go his way. She just wouldn't allow that to happen.

Finally, they could see the rigging on the ship and suddenly the men rode adjacent to them. Not a word was said. She swallowed hard trying to keep her gaze focused on the ship and not her husband when all she wanted to do was read his expression.

When Arie rode out to greet them, she said a silent little prayer of relief. Arie would not challenge her as her husband would. As soon as she handed over these men, she would be alone with Flynt and at his mercy.

"I see you were successful," Arie greeted them his smile wide. "I was under the impression you were doing this yourselves."

"We did do it by ourselves," Hope said indignantly. "They materialized a few seconds ago. Suppose they want to take credit."

Flynt wisely kept his mouth closed and she was surprised.

"The ladies were remarkable. Thought out all of this by themselves," Kelly pointed to the men who were standing stark naked in front of Arie's crew who were jeering at them and making pointed comments not fit for a lady's hearing. She didn't care, she was proud of herself and the sisters as well.

"What do you have planned?" Broc asked. "They should know ahead of time so what they did can fester in their minds for the duration of the trip."

"You ladies didn't tell them what you were up to? Why doesn't that surprise me?" Arie asked laughing. "I would have thought you threatened them."

"Of course we told McGinnis. Didn't believe us at first. They did have a choice though, death or slavery. They chose the latter," Hope said, grinning then turned to stare at her husband, a challenge on her lips if he made even one comment, though she knew from experience he would do what he pleased, nothing less.

"We knew you paraded the two men who kidnapped Chelsea naked to your ships and we thought that was a fine touch," Lacie said with a tiny shrug then she looked at Leslie and smiled shamelessly. "Besides, I wanted to see a naked man. Needed something to compare with the man who is courting me."

Leslie let out a roar of laughter. "There is no comparison, as I'm sure you've figured out," he said looking pleased at her comment. "I will show you as soon as possible, perhaps when I get a chance in private to speak with you about today's adventure."

"Here it comes," Daryl muttered. "He's going to start controlling you and you have to figure out if that's what you want for the rest of your life. I know I don't."

"That's what you think now," Donal said, presenting an arrogant manly smile to her. "I intend to change your mind. Tonight possibly, above the bakery. By the way, who is minding the till while you play at men's games?"

"Good luck with that," she murmured, but it seemed she didn't have as much confidence as usual and it also appeared she meant to ignore Donal's question. Who was minding the till was not his business as she intended to point out at a later date?

"Thank you for the men. They will be a much-needed addition to the workers at my father's home. I assure you they will not be able to escape. And just for you, Hope, I will keep them naked for the remainder of the trip. Unfortunately, my father will insist on clothing once they are put to work. He would not want them to burn from the hot sun or be injured in some way. Maintaining their health will be important."

Hope shuddered, knowing first-hand how true Arie's words were.

"My trusted captain will see they are secured for their journey. They will be given the basics of life, nothing more. They won't be needing their shoes although that was nice of you since they were marching overland."

At that moment several of Arie's men divested them of their footwear and forced them aboard the ship. They watched as the sails were furled and the ship slowly made its way into the middle of the Firth of Clyde.

She stared at the ship, unwilling to confront Flynt even when the others left, paired off, each to their own destination and conversation about today's adventures. She closed her eyes, breathing deeply and waiting for Flynt to speak first.

"We should go home now. It will be getting dark, and I don't want us to be on the open road at night."

She had nothing to say. He would wait until they were alone and she would have to comply with that. The longer the upcoming conversation could be put off the better in her mind. Perhaps when they arrived home, she could use some of her tactics to take his mind off the chastisement surely awaiting her.

Of course it would give him longer to think of something to say, or do.

"You're strangely quiet," Flynt said as he rode along beside her, one brow arched to perfection.

"Don't have anything to say," she smiled at him, refusing to stare at his mouth even though she knew it was her best defense and knowing he expected her to do so.

He appeared confused and anxious as well. "So, you feel well? You're not acting yourself."

"I'm fine, just tired." She discovered suddenly that she was exhausted, wanted nothing more than to sleep for twenty-four hours.

What to say to him, she had not a clue.

"Is this another ploy to make me forget the conversation I intend as well as the reasons to convince you to never do something so foolish again?" he queried, suddenly seeming not quite as concerned as he'd been a few seconds ago.

"No, no ploy, Flynt. I'm hard pressed to keep my eyes open, that's all, and I really don't care to banter about the future conversations." She closed them then and didn't mean to.

"You're not going to fall off your horse, are you?"

She pushed hair from her eyes, "I don't know. I might." She knew that to be the truth.

He watched her closely as they rode. It was true. She might just fall off but not to get her way in anything. The past week then the slow days of recovery she was rarely able to sleep, tending to his fever and praying it would vanish. Last night, feeling more himself, he kept her up more hours than she slept.

He rode beside her and suddenly she sat in front of him, his arms around her. She was thankful for his strength and warmth as well. He pulled her close and she leaned into him.

"Now you can go to sleep and I promise you, you won't fall. Kelly is behind us. He'll take care of your horse. I'm going to miss that man when he goes to work for Leslie."

She did dose then woke. She blinked a few times, "How much longer?"

"Ach, you are eager for your punishment?" He laughed then and she knew he had something different in mind than threats.

She would have to think quickly or he would win but right now she remained helplessly exhausted. "No, not eager for anything except my bed and twenty-four hours of sleep. I should be doing fine tomorrow. At that time, you can dole out whatever it is you have planned and not a minute before."

"What ails you? Are you carrying my heir?"

"Nothing ails me and I..." she paused then, thinking about all the things the ladies in the harem had spoken of about pregnancy and bearing children. "I wouldn't want to bolster your male prowess, but I quite possibly could be."

"Well, you probably just won. I would never thrash or berate a woman carrying my child. I don't want to put you or my child in harm's way."

"A woman? Your wife!"

She turned enough so she could pound his chest. The effort taking too much energy she leaned into him again, closing her eyes thankful for him. "That was really not well done of you, getting me pregnant so soon. You could have waited a couple of months at least." She sighed softly and as much as possible on a horse, nestled into the solid wall of his chest.

"I beg to differ. The deed was very well done by me and thought out in its proper order. It's most likely a boy."

Against her, she felt him puff his chest. "No, it's a girl. Mothers can tell such things, intuition, you ken." She closed her eyes again and when she opened them, they were riding into the stables, Kelly waiting for them.

Flynt handed her down to the man and he held her until Flynt dismounted, claiming her again.

"I'm beginning to think that as a woman you will always have the upper hand. I'm going to have to use my very manly mind to figure out how to best you. You are pregnant with my child. Now I will have to wait the duration before I thrash your incredibly lovely buttocks." He gently placed a kiss on her forehead.

"I would never let you forget but you did have the upper hand last evening. If you recall, you got your manly way with me even though I protested."

She closed her eyes again, content to let him carry her upstairs. She didn't want to argue or play verbal games. Sleep was all she wanted.

"If I recall your protest was to plead for me to make lust with you."

Of course he was right.

He set her on the bed, coming down beside her. "Sleep, I just want to hold you and think about the male child growing in your womb."

His hand settled possessively on her belly.

"Would you be terribly disappointed if the wee one is a girl?" She hoped he would not. "I'm quite willing to try a second time for a boy if perchance you don't get your male heir the first time."

"All the fun is in the trying. I've heard babies are difficult in that they never let their mother's sleep."

"Just like you. You keep me up most every night. You would have to promise to help or at least find a good nanny if you wish to continue on in the same manner." She yawned then.

~ * ~

When she woke the sky was dark and it seemed, although he didn't admit to it, Flynt was exhausted also, as he lay snoring softly beside her. He'd been sick. At first, she feared for his life and as soon as he could, he defied all the rules invalids should adhere to.

She kissed him on the cheek, feeling refreshed and ready to get on with evening. One quick look at the clock told her it was a few hours past dinner. Cook would have left the meal in the warming oven.

When he woke, she was sure she would discover his plans for her. She smiled, murmuring softly, "I wouldn't have it any other way."

Indeed, there was food, more than either of them could eat. She piled a tray with something of everything, including the plates and glasses as well as silverware before carrying them upstairs.

Munroe caught her half way and took the tray from her. "Let me help."

She had left the door ajar, so pushing it open she walked inside and showed Munroe where she wanted him to set the tray on a table near the bed.

Sitting down beside Flint, she placed kisses over his face until he opened his eyes. "Are you ready to wake up? she asked. Accusingly, "You have slept the night away as well as the next day. Lazy bones. You told me you were well and you could be your manly self and make lust with me," she sighed dramatically. "You were wrong. Why you don't even have as much energy as a pregnant lady."

He groaned pulling her down and into his arms. "Good God woman, but you are lying again." He kissed her then, his tongue challenging her to open for him.

She obliged him, giving over to his wishes, but once she gave in, completely ready for him, he pulled away, grinning at her and staring at her mouth, his hand on a breast. "I'm hungry. Believe we should eat now."

She let out a tiny mew of displeasure. She had been sure he was going to make love to her. Perhaps this was her punishment. He meant to tease her, arouse her then deny her. That couldn't possibly be his ploy. If it was, it would be just as much punishment for him.

She decided she would play along with him. "I'd like wine. Are you serving, or should I?"

His scowl reinforced her earlier thoughts. She didn't smile or show him in any way she guessed what he was trying to do. He wanted her to beg. She wasn't about to do that. "I'll serve."

A few seconds later, they were seated at the table, gazing at each other over dinner. "What did you do today while I slept? Go to the dressmakers? Talk to your sisters in law? Perhaps take up needlepoint?"

"None of the above. I thought up different ways I could make lust with you." She smiled, staring at his lips. "Would you like me to tell you what they are?"

He choked, spewing a tiny bit of wine across the table. "You know I don't like it when you call what we do making lust. I don't want you to say that word any longer. I forbid it." He was clearly displeased with her. "It doesn't become you."

"What do you want me to call what we do? Nothing else sounds quite right." She paused, tapping a finger to her chin. "I suppose I could say making passion, or making desire or hungering for you." She was shaking her head. "It's either got to be lust or love. What should I say, Flynt? It's your choice. I'll comply to your very male wishes and superior mind. You know I always obey you."

He cleared his throat and in a low growl. "Maybe you shouldn't say anything at all. We'll just do it when the mood hits."

"Well, that wouldn't be any fun. So, I should say, Flynt let's do it and you'll toss my skirts. Until you come up with something better, I'm going to say making lust."

She saw his features change to an even deeper scowl, the crease line in his forehead deepening noticeably, and she hoped it was just a matter of time before he would admit to love.

Dear Lord, but she loved this man with all her heart.

"The meat is very good tonight, don't you think, not too tough or dry?" She graced him with a flirtatious smile, then lowering her lashes,

"If I wasn't already pregnant, we could try again tonight but since I am with child, we should most likely sleep in separate beds. Wouldn't want to hurt the baby."

His scowl suddenly changed to a grin. "Making lust does not hurt the child. I'm sure Gram's has said so. If not, we can ask her."

He was diverting, seeming unwilling to comment on her statement. "Not nearly so nice as the mashed potatoes. I do so like mashed potatoes with gravy. Do you like the wine?"

"It's passable. I'd like a pint of beer instead. Since you are with child you must eat more food. I'll make sure you are eating for two."

She dropped her fork, her mouth hanging open in shock, "You want me to become as big as a cow." She glanced at her belly. "One cannot even see that there might be a child inside my womb. That would hardly count as eating for two now would it? Even when the child is born, it will not be my size. No, I'm not going to eat more food, at least not yet." Retrieving her fork, she placed it beside her plate, telling him she didn't intend to eat another bite. He would see it as defiance. It wasn't, just practicality.

"I will check with the midwife tomorrow. I'm sure she'll have something to say about the amount of food needing to be consumed."

He continued to stare and she felt the brunt of his gaze, arousing and tempting her. If he was going to pull away every time they were close, then she wasn't going to give him the opportunity for her to want him.

She refused to meet his gaze. "Grams is a midwife. I don't need anyone else. I trust her. Besides I've delivered more children than I can even remember. She will tell you just as I will that I need to make sure I eat the right foods, not more. In any case, if you don't believe me, ask her."

"You will speak with her tomorrow and relay what you learn to me. I won't question anything that makes sense, however, you might be rather charming if you grew larger. I believe I will like it when your breasts and belly grow immense. You might even get bubbies as big as Lacie's."

"You don't like me the way I am?" A rage at his words simmered inside her making her need to toss her glass of wine at him, but she refrained. It would be a waste of good wine.

"I didn't say that. You will be very charming when you are very pregnant, beautiful at any size. I look forward to any changes that come to pass."

She needed to accept his words at face value. The pregnancy would be challenging for both of them. "Of course, but don't you think it's a little too soon to tell. I don't want to get my hopes up, even though you are eager. This will just not do to tell people then find out it was all a mistake."

He placed her hand in his, "I will say nothing until you feel it's the right time. Grams can know then."

"We'll wait at least one more month. By then we won't be guessing."

~ * ~

Kelly settled into the small cottage adjacent from the stables. He grinned, thrilled at his change of fortune. His loyalties now lie with both Flynt and his family and the Duke of Southcliff and his soon to be wife.

He would never make the same mistakes again. The duke even told him there was a woman he would introduce him to, one who was kind and would make him a wonderful wife if they got along.

That was the question though. He'd been told by his first wife he was difficult in the best times even though he'd tried to give her everything she wished for. Long ago, he decided she wished for more than was possible on a trainer's salary.

"Hello."

Caught by surprise, he dropped the hay he'd been shoveling to his horse. He turned, "Hello."

"Here. Lord Stewart said you might be hungry so I brought you some freshly baked cinnamon rolls and a cup of coffee. Where would you like them?"

"Why don't you join me? I'm Kelly O'Brian and you? Do you have time?" He sat on a pile of hay. "You can put the food here." He patted a spot beside him.

"I'm Sara, and I don't think the duke will mind if I spend a little time with you. If I'm right, he sent me out to meet you. He's trying to play matchmaker."

She laughed softly and he was intrigued by the sound.

"He did tell me there was a woman he'd like me to meet. Is that you?"

"It is." She looked at her hands in her lap. "You should eat. If you like, I'll bring you something every morning."

She was absolutely lovely. Her curly red hair intrigued him and he wondered if it was as soft as it looked. "I'd like that as long as you stay and keep me company while I eat."

"The duke will be away for a while and my duties are few when he's gone. I do tend to need something else to keep me occupied."

"I could do that, keep you company."

He watched as her tiny pink tongue swept across her lips. He'd like to kiss her too. Perhaps in time once they knew each other better. He assumed she wasn't a virgin. By the looks of her she was in her mid-thirties, about his age. Her sparkling green eyes seemed to be filled with amusement.

"Good, but don't let me keep you from your work." She started to stand.

He put out a hand to stop her. "I've finished everything for the day, and at the moment I'm just puttering around doing things I see that need to be done. By my mind, this stable needs a lot of refurbishing to make it one of the best in Scotland. I'll do everything that is just labor and make a list for when the duke is home again, of things that will cost money.

"I can sit here for a while?" She pulled off a strip of roll, eating it daintily before sipping the coffee. "You don't mind if we share the coffee? I only brought one cup."

"Don't mind at all." He liked the idea of sharing. Something his first wife detested.

Chapter Nine

"I should turn here," Lacie was eyeing the roads, a perplexed look on her face. Then back to Leslie, "Shouldn't I?"

He smiled, ulterior motives at the forefront of his mind. He needed her to make a decision today not tomorrow or sometime in the future. While he'd hopped to make love to her before he left, there might not be enough time to bind her to him in that manner. Instead he decided on something more permanent and lasting, something that would forever give her the protection of his name and perhaps if there turned out to be time, he would consummate their vows.

"I'd like you to be coming home with me right now. If you want too that is." Then, "We can speak of more pressing, life changing issues."

"Whatever for?" She started to turn the horse down the street heading for the MacTavish townhouse. Looking over her shoulder as she turned away from him, "These few weeks have been overwhelming. I need time to think."

"That's just the thing, Lacie, I don't have that luxury."

"You're expecting things of me I've no real comprehension of."

He needed to be blunt and to the point as well. "I want to marry you tonight. I'll call in a few favors. We will be man and wife. You will be the Duchess of Southcliff. That way..." He wasn't sure he wanted to tell her she would then be his. "That way, I can ensure your safety."

Her sharp inhale surprised him, but he waited as she seemed to freeze while he hoped she was thinking about all he said as well as repercussion for her life.

"That's absurd."

He chose to ignore her response. Then continued, "We can have a proper wedding when I return. Everything you've ever dreamed of and a plush reception if you'd like. We will of course at that time include your family and any friends you might want to invite. You can plan it while I'm away."

She waved a hand in the air, her lips pursed as if she was about to say no. "Don't want anything extravagant. It's just that this is a complete surprise to me. Why? You don't love me."

He supposed blunt and to the point could have unforeseen consequences. "I want you. I like everything about you. I need to make sure you are mine and cannot change your mind in the months I'll be away from you."

Lord but he understood from the beginning this would not be easy. He just could not think of words that would sway her. Everything he said was about himself and his wishes.

She pursed her lips and he was tempted to grin. "I..." she paused, looking a bit sideways at him, "well this is happening way too fast. Only a few hours ago I agreed to a courtship and now you want to wed. Isn't that a bit uncommon?"

"Perhaps this way should be common. It would be a waste of time to wait longer just to court when both parties ken what they want. Marriage, a life together and perhaps children, an heir."

"That's just it. I don't really know what it is that I want." She gazed at him for the longest time, her eyes focused on him. "I suppose we could. I know if there is anyone I'd like to wed it is you. There is nobody else."

"Good, then it's decided." He pointed down the street that would lead them to his home, "After you."

A huge weight had just been lifted off his shoulders, feeling suddenly content for the first time in months. It would have been nice though if she were a little more enthusiastic.

Good Lord, but he wanted to know what was in her head. He supposed he couldn't expect eagerness when the question shocked her. He would have to make do with a reluctant bride and carry on with the supposition she'd like to marry him. Trouble was he wouldn't have time to change those feelings before he left tomorrow morning and he was deathly afraid she might come to regret the impulsive decision. He wanted to introduce her to the pleasures of lovemaking but once again, time was a factor and he just didn't know if he had that precious commodity at his fingertips.

The rest of the trip was passed in silence. He was thinking of all he dared and that which he didn't. When they reached the stables, she'd dismounted and was leading the horse to a stall.

He grinned, understanding she would never expect someone else to take care of her horse. "I've Kelly and two other stable hands to do that." Yet when he looked around, no one appeared.

"Where are they? Don't like to keep the horse waiting for water, a bit of food and a brush of their coat to make them feel wanted and loved."

With little effort she found what she was looking for and began to give the love he fancied for himself to the mare.

Blessed hell, that was what he desired, simple things. He laughed out right. "A bit to eat, wine and a few loving strokes by your hand sounds heavenly to me. What more could a man crave? Lucky horse. Perhaps when we're inside you can pamper me just like that."

"I'd be happy to do what you request, but I'm not sure I've the necessary skills," she said from over her shoulder, smiling. "This is what I like more than anything. If I'm a duchess, can I come to the stables anytime I want or will you tell me it's not befitting my station?"

A stable lad heard them and appeared, taking the reins of his horse, "Sir, sorry I'm late?" He nodded in Lacie's direction. He appeared reluctant to interfere. "Should I take over?"

"Leave her be. It's what she wants. I, for one, will rarely tell her no, especially when it's something she loves."

He leaned on the stall, watching her, knowing full well this was the right woman to have in his life. She was young but she knew who she was and pretty much what she wanted. Convincing her she desired him, might prove challenging.

"You can come here, to the stables, anytime you like. Now, have you made up your mind about the wedding?" His gut tightened, praying for the right answer, for the one he sought.

"No unnecessary balls, you promised," she paused then, tapping her chin and looking as if she meant to tease him, "and I can ride anytime it suits my fancy. I suppose the answer is yes."

"I do have one request though."

"And?" She suddenly looked apprehensive and on the verge of changing her yes to a no.

"When I'm not at home, you ask Kelly to ride with you. When I am at home, you ask me. I don't believe the Duchess of Southcliff should always be prudent and abiding all society rules in everything she does but there will be times. Now mind you, I'm not making rules or setting limits, well I guess to some degree I am but..." He inhaled a long deep breath, understanding how this could change everything.

She stopped brushing the horse then smiled at him, a beautiful gentle smile one he meant to recall all the lonely nights when he was away from her.

"I can live with that." Then, "But what?"

"Then I need to set everything in motion. Kelly!"

"Sir?" He rounded a corner of the stable, pitchfork in hand.

The man was there even before he expected. "Thank you, put the pitchfork down. Would you run down the street to the church and bring the minister back quickly? Tell him it's an emergency of the gravest importance and cannot be put off until another day."

"So, you really are going to tie the knot right now right here. I'll be back as soon as possible." He grabbed a horse and set off, not bothering with a saddle.

"Shall we get ready?" Leslie held his arm out for Lacie, knowing his grin stretched from ear to ear, his happiness as well.

For a moment she looked down, then back to him. "I am ready, I think. It would have been nice if the trail dirt didn't cling to me as well as my riding habit. I'm sure my hair is a tangled mess."

"You are ravishing to me." Once again, he felt his grin stretch across his face. "No one more beautiful."

"That certainly isn't the truth, but I will accept the compliment, graciously, in the guise of a woman who is very nearly a duchess. By the way I never coveted a title. Only you." She blushed as if she suddenly realized what she said. "Is there somewhere I can clean up a little?"

"I can order a bath for you. Fortunately, I've several gowns I commissioned a few weeks ago when Flynt bought you the ones you are now wearing."

He shrugged, staring at her, realizing the seamstress must have misread her measurement when she fashioned this riding habit. The corsage was extremely snug.

"Thank you, a quick bath, and something clean to wear as well will be greatly appreciated."

They strode to the house, and once inside Leslie bellowed orders. His servants scurried quickly about, doing as he asked.

He led her up the steps and into the master chamber. "While I'm away, I'd like you to sleep here, but if the bed seems too large without me, the adjoining room is yours."

Servants came in with hot water and towels. "The bath is ready, Sir."

He smiled, pointing to the adjoining room. Then he turned on his boot heel, striding to another room. Undressing, he slipped into the hot water brought for him, enjoying the heat and trying to decide which one of the dresses he purchased for her should he give her.

Deciding he would give her the gown that most resembled a wedding gown, he hurried. His valet set out clean clothes for him, suitable for a nice evening. Her new gowns he'd put in his armoire in anticipation of this night. He picked out an ivory colored gown with Belgium lace adorning the bodice as well as the hemline, one that would enhance her sky-blue eyes. He shook it out, pleased with his selection then knocked on the door. No one answered.

He placed it on the bed, telling a servant that she was to help her with the gown and to tell Lacie it was a gift It should fit since he commissioned it before he left town in hopes she would wear it soon. "Also tell her to come downstairs to the parlor when she is ready."

He whistled as he walked down the steps, seeing his home in a new light. This would be Lacie's home soon. It pleased him greatly. All he wanted now was coming to fruition.

"I see you spruced up a bit." Kelly walked in with the minister behind him.

The two embraced, "Never thought you'd do this. Can't wait to hear you say your vows."

"In truth neither did I. Never thought I would find someone who made me laugh and want to embrace each day to the fullest. She challenges me."

Lacie did that for him, had made him laugh since she was a young lady of fifteen. He yearned for a lifetime with her, of smiles and sunshine of knowing he could accomplish all he set out to do. He would have her support and gentle love. He paused at that thought. Love, he'd never believed in its existence before now.

"You be needing a best man?" Kelly asked, appearing hopeful he'd be given the position in light of the fact there was no family here nor had he summoned any. "If you do, I'm ready for the job. Promise if she tries to run, I'll find her."

"For this wedding, I can use you. Don't have time to send for Flynt or any of the others for that matter. Don't want to either. They might protest the wedding, and I truly don't need any interference."

"Probably not what the lass be wishin' for," Kelly said. "Her sisters might protest the rush but they'd never be saying no."

"I promised her the real thing as soon as my mission is over, a real wedding and reception. They can all attend then. By the way, I promised her she could ride any time she wants but also told her you would go with her. Don't have time to give you other duties, but I'm sure you'll find something to keep you busy." He paused again. "On the other hand, I want you to make sure Flynt gets the message I leave about our wedding. If he doesn't, he might ride over here and haul her home."

"I'd love to ride with her and keep a fatherly eye out for any danger. It will be fun and I'll make sure Flynt gets the missive. I'm sure she'd like her things as well."

"Sarah is my cook. I think you'll like her. Her husband passed on a few years back and I think she's lonely. Spend as much time as you like with her. Without me in residence she doesn't have much to do, no one to cook for you know. Maybe she'll bake her famous cinnamon rolls."

"Sarah, you say. Think I'd like to get to know her better. Saw her the other day." He was running his fingers through his long beard. "Maybe I'll even trim this ragged monster a bit."

"She's a bonny lass. No hard feelings if for some reason the two of you don't like each other," Leslie said.

"I'm ready," Lacie said, standing at the foot of the steps.

He didn't even hear her walk into the room she'd been so quiet. "You're quite fetching. The gown is lovely on you."

Again, he was struck by the snugness of the bosom and how she seemed to be close to popping out of it. Perhaps, he thought again, when he recalled her size to the dressmaker he'd not remembered accurately.

"Thank you, I didn't know you would have a gown for me. It's beautiful but..."

He intended to ignore the "but" as well as the uncertainty of her voice. What she was thinking was quite true, and the realization made his brows draw together, concentrating on the why. No question about it, the bodice was too tight. He wasn't going to mention the fact and put a damper on this evening, "There are more gowns and they will be placed in your wardrobe. Kelly will help you retrieve your other things and help explain what we are doing here. He's already promised to relay the message that we are wed to Flynt."

The minister cleared his throat, staring at him. "We should begin since you told me there was no time to waste. I've important business myself."

Kelly turned to Leslie, "He does. I interrupted him from his dinner."

"Ah, important things," Leslie was slowly nodding his head. "I see you like your meals more than you used to."

"Of course, some of us like to pursue danger and there are others who wish to remain content and happy," the minister said, laughing at Leslie. "My meals are important to me. Shall we get on with this?"

"Yes, yes, we should. There are only a few hours left of my day and I'd like to use some of them up with Lacie as my wife. I won't be around for a few months after this as you all know."

"So, you're wanting the fast version of the ceremony?" the minister asked, grinning at Leslie then his soon to be bride. "I'll do away with anything that is frivolous or unimportant."

Leslie nodded and it seemed before he could take a second breath, the minister pronounced them wed and told him he could kiss his bride.

He did, his lips found hers, lightly touched and explored for a moment, then, "You are my duchess, and evn in our haste, I did not forgot your ring." He brought a beautiful diamond sapphire ring from his pocket then slipped it on her finger. "It was my mother's wedding ring. It is now yours and perhaps, god willing, someday it will go to a son or daughter to be presented to their fiancé."

She closed her eyes for a moment, including a long deep breath of air. Then, "I think I like the sound of that. What now?"

"We toast the bride and groom," Kelly poured champagne. "In their case not on a honeymoon but to the bedchamber."

"Cut the cake, don't anyone forget the cutting of the cake. Don't care how impatient the duke is to get his bride alone. The cake must be cut and the pieces eaten." Sarah placed a small cake on the table in the parlor.

They did and it was over, Kelly and Sarah leaving them alone as they watched the couple leave arm in arm.

"Will you come to the master chamber with me?" he asked, pulling her close to him, his hands cupping her derrière, hoping she felt his hard arousal against her belly also hoping it didn't frighten her.

While he fondled her the other night, touched her in places she'd never been touched, he'd kept most of his clothes on, only unbuttoning his shirt so she could run her hands along his chest. Everything they did tonight would be uncharted territory for her.

"I suppose it's expected. Are you going to create all those wonderful feelings inside me again?" She placed a hand on his arm. "I liked what you did. It was very manly and very nice." Her small pink tongue swept across her lips and she seemed to be staring at his mouth.

"I certainly intend to do just that." He groaned then smiled at her, trying for encouragement, not fear. "Are you nervous lass? There is no need."

"I am. I've never been wed before or so vulnerable. I don't know what you are going to do, and I'm anxious to learn even though Hope has told me it will hurt the first time. While some think I'm adventurous, I've never liked pain and I'm always cautious."

"What else has Hope told you, lass?" he growled displeased to hear the words. "Not sure I appreciate her telling you things that will frighten you. I will take every care possible to make this night perfect for you."

"She didn't mean to scare us just teach us about our bodies. Don't you think it's my right to know what will happen in the wedding bed?" Her back stiffened and she looked at him as if there was an argument brewing.

He'd never thought about what a woman should and should not know before the marriage bed or anything else including pregnancy. He supposed mothers always spoke to their daughters but Lacie didn't have a mother. Where sex was concerned, Hope might be the closest person to a mother she would have. "Suppose it's your right. I would have liked to teach you though."

"I'm sure there are things Hope left out. She was only repeating what she heard from the ladies in the harem."

He thought over what Lacie said and supposed what she said was true. "We're here."

He opened the door for her. Even to him, the bed seemed huge and he had reservations about how he meant to proceed. Slowly at first, he decided. They'd shared so little, just one evening of cuddling and foreplay, hardly enough for her to understand what would happen between them. Well, there was that first kiss in the stable a few years ago.

"Can we have a glass of wine?" Her hand shook within his. "Truth be told I am nervous, more than just a little. I would like to be perfect for you."

"You are perfect, don't worry. Anything you want is yours for the asking. A glass or two will calm you, and I'm sure the tray of food will be good. We haven't eaten since this morning. You must be starving. I know I am."

He was starving for her. He could wait to eat. After all, they had all night. He wasn't supposed to be leaving until early morning. He would make love to her throughout the evening and she could sleep as long as she wished in the morning. He would give his staff the directive.

He poured the wine before sitting beside her in front of the fireplace. "You like to ride. What else makes you happy?"

"Singing, but everyone tells me I'm off key. So, I only do it when I'm alone. No one else can hear me then."

"I'd like to hear you. Sing for me."

He tipped the wine to his lips, drinking a goodly portion. It seemed he was also nervous. He'd never made love to a virgin before and never intended to again.

"Never," she laughed. "Don't want you making fun of me too."

She stared at his mouth over the rim of her glass, her eyes seeming to shimmer with desire.

Blessed hell, that tiny gesture had him hard and in need even before the first kiss. He gritted out, "Where did you learn to do that?"

"Do what?"

She sipped then continued in the same vein only this time the direction of her gaze was at his crotch.

He'd been with practiced courtesan in his time and none had ever been so blatant. She was not only obvious but she aroused him as no other possibly could. "You bloody well know what I'm talking about."

"I shouldn't give away my secrets, but I guess it didn't have the same effect as when Hope does the same to Flynt. You sound angry. Are you? I promise to never do it again." she said, setting the glass down waiting for him to say something.

"Staring at me, at my lips, at my privates has the very same effect on me as Flynt. You're playing with fire when you do that. Come here and I'll show you what happens when wives give out the message that they desperately want their husbands."

She was too slow. He wrapped an arm around her and drew her to him. He placed her hand on his heavy arousal, his breath catching in his throat at the erotic sensation. "This is what you do to me. Can you feel me?"

Moistening her lips, "I feel you but I don't really ken what I've done to you, or what it means."

He closed his eyes, begging himself for the restraint he needed, reminding himself she was innocent. Of course, she didn't understand what it was she did. She would find out soon enough. "I'll give you that. You can stare at any part of me anytime you like, but be assured you should be prepared for the result."

"What would that be, the result?" she asked, her head a bet sideways as her lashes fluttered delicately against her cheeks.

"You will find out soon, tonight." He settled his mouth on hers. Then, "You should open for me as you did the other night and we'll explore all the possibilities."

She did as he slipped his tongue into her mouth then managed to unfasten and slip her dress from her body. She was very nearly naked. Her breasts would overflow his large hands. They were different from what he remembered though, larger, and he couldn't quite figure out how that could be in such a short amount of time.

"I want to see you, Leslie. It's only fair you're looking at all of me. My chemise hides nothing."

"Very well," He let his shirt and cravat drop to the floor. "Is this what you want?"

"Almost," Once more she stared at his chest then his crotch. "I want to see what a man looks like beneath his pants. Not those other men, but you. Only you."

His groan rumbled deep in his chest. "Not yet but soon."

His lips molded over a veiled nipple, sucking and worrying it and he was delighted with the tiny mew of pleasure she gifted him with. Moving his hands along her legs then the bottom of her chemise, he lifted it over her head, his body hardening with need for her.

This was his most cherished moment as he looked upon her, his duchess. She was the most beautiful woman he'd ever seen or known, inside and out.

She ran her fingers into his hair, pulling him to her. "Are you going to make love to me now? I need you, need something. I don't know what it is but you have to give it to me. Please."

"Soon, don't be in such a hurry. Things such as these are best to savor to remember." He touched and explored every part, coming between her legs as her hips arched to meet him. Temped to come inside her, he held back knowing she wasn't ready and putting the pain off until he could hold back no longer.

The knock on the door didn't register in his mind at first as he was so absorbed in Lacie's pleasure.

"Sir, this is urgent. You need to open the door." His valet, Liam's voice came through.

"Bloody hell, nothing is as urgent as what I'm about right now." Leslie tried to keep the anger and desperation from his voice. He had known all along this might happen but prayed it would not. Understanding he would be called away before he had the chance to consummate the marriage, he placed a chaste kiss on Lacie's lips.

"What is it?" Her voice shaky from the arousal he successfully built in her. "Don't leave me."

"My valet, I fear he has bad news for us. Nothing I can put off or stop."

He stood then covered her, disappointed that this short bout of lovemaking was all he would get before he left. He'd meant to leave his seed inside her. A possible heir before he disappeared on his last mission would have been nice but it wasn't going to happen.

She sat, holding the covers to her marvelous breasts. "Then do what you must."

He opened the door to Liam who held a sealed note in his hand. "Here, I understand this is not a good time, but it is the way of things."

"You know what is written inside?" Leslie asked as he tore the message open and read.

"The gist but not everything. Sorry to interrupt." Liam waited, stiff backed, hands behind him.

He strode to Lacie, "I'm so sorry. I have to leave now, not in the morning as I had wanted. Take care of yourself and when I come back, I promise I will make this up to you."

~ * ~

Daryl puttered around the bakery, tidying up and putting off ascending to the second floor where she lived. She was pretty sure Donal would be waiting for her, expecting the same lovemaking as a few nights ago. Now that she realized there could be repercussions if she became more impulsive and allowed him more liberties. She wasn't about to allow him to coax her into doing things she knew she shouldn't.

It just wouldn't do. She did not want to be unwed and pregnant. Of course, he had a solution for that predicament, but his solution was untenable.

With everything done downstairs, she untied the apron she wore. Neatly folding it and placing it on the table, she apprehensively looked up the steps leading to her home. Inhaling a long deep breath for courage, she started up the narrow stairs.

She was hungry and exhausted from her day. Unlike the others she'd been up at four o'clock making pastries for the early morning crowd who came to buy for their families and to sit and enjoy in the small café. She had trekked cross-country in order to bring Sean McGinnis to justice. It would have just been nice if the bad boys did their jobs as they were supposed to do. Women shouldn't have men's work to accomplish along with their own. In the women's defense, the men did nothing so it was up to them to take care of matters. Unless women did the chore, nothing was ever accomplished.

When she stepped into her small sitting room, Donal was not there. She sighed a moment, relieved she wouldn't have to fend off his advances so she wouldn't succumb to his ever-roaming hands and lips. Good Lord, when he kissed her, she couldn't think straight or even in a roundabout manner. It seemed he always found new places to caress her with his mouth.

She took off her shoes then unbuttoning her blouse she walked into the bedroom. Her hair was already falling from the tight bun she fastened earlier this morning so she shook it out letting it fall around her shoulders.

"Think I'll cut it all off," she murmured.

"Don't you dare."

Startled, she gasped as she looked up to see Donal sitting on a huge bed that wasn't hers, his back against the headboard and his hands clasped behind his head a smug smile adorned his handsome face.

"Arrogant rogue," she mumbled, inhaling deeply as she tried to make up for the air she just lost. "How did you get in? What are doing here and why is that bed in this room? It's not mine."

Grinning from ear to ear, he patted the mattress beside him. "You should relax and I'll answer each comment and question one at a time. Come here and we'll discuss this matter."

"Very well." She plopped down on a chair there was now barely room for. Clasping her hands in her lap before meeting his attentive gaze, "I'm waiting."

"Not until you sit on the bed with me." He appeared perfectly relaxed and at ease.

She wanted him to look as nervous as she felt.

She tried for a prim voice, one that would set limits from the very beginning of this conversation. He needed to understand her feelings here. It was much too risky for her to comply with his bidding. "I don't dare," her voice very nearly a whisper.

"Then your questions go unanswered, and I don't plan on feeding you until you sit beside me."

Once more his masculine grin reached from ear to ear, his eyes simmering, seeming to understand how much she needed food right now.

"That's alright with me." She lifted her shoulders in a gesture that should tell him she really didn't care. Now that he mentioned it though, the scent of the food was tantalizing her senses. Her stomach growled and she was sure it was loud enough for him to hear.

"Ah, my *petite cherie*, food, relaxation, a scintillating conversation, what more could you ask for?" Still ginning he once more patted the bed beside him. "Come here and you can have all that and more."

"It's the more I'm afraid of. I don't want to give you what you're asking, and I'm afraid I can't say no. When you touch me..."

Still she didn't move, determined to let him know she wasn't as easy as he thought.

"You should not be afraid of me, Lass." His brows drew together, seeming to concentrate on her. "But I see no fear in your eyes. You wouldn't lie to me, would you?"

She gave a resigned sigh and did as he asked, determined though to not give in to his manly requests as well as the eloquence of his seductions. Where women were concerned, he knew what he was about, but she was smarter and more determined. She would best him in this...if she chose. "First, the questions are to be answered then I want the food."

"I had my French cook serve the food she loves most. Should I get you a plate and some fine Bordeaux? After we eat, I will answer every question to the best of my ability."

He served her, still grinning from ear to ear as if he knew he'd won already. He seemed a man well pleased.

"Can we sit at the table?"

She needed distance between them and sitting side by side on his bed would not do the job.

"*Non, mademoiselle*, the fair will be better enjoyed in a leisurely fashion if we stay right here."

He proceeded to heap his plate, giving himself almost as much as he dished up for her.

"You really expect me to eat all this?"

She bit into the *Beef Bourguignon* then rolled her eyes. "Oh my, this is good. French cook you say?"

"You might want to eat everything since you've eaten little to nothing today unless of course you snacked downstairs on your delightful pastries. She agreed to make *pain au chocolat* for your breakfast, plain croissants if you prefer and she also said she'd help you out in the bakery since that is where I will be."

That would be heaven.

She just might clean her plate but she wasn't going to admit anything to him. Eating and drinking wine, the conversation stalled. When he set his fork down and looked at her, she knew it was time for the questions, and she wasn't at all sure she would like the answers or even if she wanted to know anymore. If she didn't ask the questions, he would inevitably move on to something else, the something else she was afraid of.

She began anyway, deciding to put off the advances she knew were sure to come. "First question, how did you get in my home?

Everything was locked, just like you expounded to me in more words than I care to remember," she told him indignantly casting him a wary glance. "You shouldn't be here, on my bed, like you belong here."

"Ah, I was proud of you to see that you followed my advice. I really didn't expect such easy compliance from you. Last time I walked right inside, unlocked door no barrier to keep me out or anyone else. So, you want to know how I got inside." With a very masculine shrug, "I had a key made. What did you think? I certainly wouldn't break the door down and while I could pick the lock, those nefarious activities are better left to Leslie."

"Without my permission?" She was incredulous at his audacity. "You had no right without my approval. You should have asked me instead of frightening me half to death when I walked into my bedroom."

"I never meant to frighten you. I assumed since I plan on eating with you every evening, you would give me consent to have a key of my own made. After a hard day of work, how can you turn down this delicious food and you don't have to prepare any of it? I would be willing to bet that this evening and most evenings you would have gone to bed hungry."

"There is an apple on the counter as well as a slice of bread."

"As I said, gone to bed hungry. I wouldn't like you to waste away in front of my very eyes."

"Charity is not something I will accept. While it's very nice and thoughtful of you, I'm going to support myself and do it with no one's help. You cannot coerce me. I won't allow it."

Ignoring her, he took the plate and silverware from her. "Cook will see to the dishes." He left the room for a few seconds returning with the bottle of wine then holding it up. "More?"

She held out her glass realizing suddenly his ploy was working. Well, one more tiny glass couldn't possibly get her tipsy and unable to think or say no to him, could it? He was ignoring her wishes though. She didn't want his charity, his money or his cook.

Well, perhaps his cook.

She didn't want to think about that any longer. "Second question, what are you doing here? Well, that is somewhat obvious but I know feeding me is not the only reason I found you nonchalantly sitting on my bed, on someone's bed, but it certainly is not mine. What did you do with mine?" she sighed then, "I'm sure you have other motives."

He slowly sipped his wine. "I would tell you that you wound my tender manly sensibilities, but I won't lie. I do have other reasons but they don't all revolve around sex with you. I need more from you than just a romp on this big bed of yours."

"Yours. What is it you want then?"

She meant to put the man on the spot even though she knew from past experiences he was adept at diverting and not answering anything he didn't want to answer.

He tapped her glass with his, "Cheers to us, a relationship with you, a long term one, one that involves marriage and children. A lifetime commitment is always preferable to one-night frolics with a beautiful endearing woman, one who holds my thoughts in the palm of her hands."

He took liberties, placing his hand on her belly as if he intended for her to remember their shared intimacy.

Admitting it to herself was one thing, but admitting it to him something entirely different. She liked the feelings he elicited in her when he touched her and kissed her. At the moment, his hand on her stomach felt right as she also knew his kisses would also feel right.

"I will remain single."

The protest was weak and by the expression on his face she understood he knew her thoughts or at least guessed them. Without much effort he could wear her down. Just like her sister's husbands did with them, he would then control her every move.

"That is what you believe today, but I am the man to change your mind. Don't know how long it will take, but I intend to do just that no matter."

Unable to do anything but ignore him, she cleared her throat. She saw his very real manly grin recognizing he won this round. "Third question, why is this bed here, in my bedroom?"

For a very brief moment he looked chagrin and that surprised her. She would accept this rare moment into her brain and keep it there for future reference. "Why?" she asked when he hesitated.

"Because I plan on spending a great deal of time in it with you." The sheepishness was gone if it ever was on his face. Perhaps the image etched behind her eyes was her imagination. "I had the bed custom made so now my feet won't hang over the end."

"When pigs fly," she mumbled beneath her breath, knowing if he chose to sleep in this bed, he would. The words to make him leave when she wanted him in her bed would never materialize.

What to do now?

"A kiss for goodnight?" he asked as he slipped his arms from his shirt, baring his well-muscled chest.

She tried to swallow the lump in her throat that emerged unbidden when she was greeted with the sight of his naked chest. "You cannot mean to take your clothes off," she said, surprised yet not so surprised. What had she thought he would do, go to bed with all his clothes on?

"You cannot expect me to sleep in what I was wearing today?" He sounded incredulous.

"Well no, but..."

She truly had no words to describe what she was feeling; excitement, anticipation, a headiness she truly didn't understand. Why, she'd already encountered him with no shirt on. But she really hadn't seen him, looked at him. Now she stared at his naked chest unable to remove her gaze. Terrified but eager, she inhaled a long deep breath. "If you must but then I'll keep my clothes on my person, thank you very much."

He shrugged as if he didn't care, watching her as his hands lingered on the fastenings of his pants. He didn't turn his back but removed both his pants and his boots. Now, he stood in front of her wearing only his drawers.

For a moment she was sure she was drooling. My God he was gorgeous, every manly part of him. She wished he would take everything off. He didn't say anything but pulled back the covers and got into bed. "I promise you I won't ravish you unless of course you ask or agree to marriage." His hands behind his head, he watched her, seeming to wait for her to make a decision.

Thinking sleep was needed and comfort was essential, she pulled a nightdress from her amour and stepped through the door into the sitting room. "I'll dress out here," she told him.

"Need I remind you that I've touched and kissed nearly every inch of you?" he called out.

"No, please don't. That was a one-time happenstance. You won't' again."

"Twice. It's happened twice."

She closed the door, leaning against it with her eyes closed for a few seconds, understanding how difficult the evening would be.

Why wouldn't he just go away?

Because you know he's determined and he wants you. He's single minded in his purpose. He could take the bed and she would sleep on the sofa. She smiled, understanding he would be angry and that he might not allow it, but she would have made her point.

A few minutes later she was cuddled beneath the afghan that usually decorated the sofa. Even with her eyes closed though she found sleep elusive. Her body thrummed with heat, aching in places Donal had touched. She couldn't get the sight of Donal's nearly naked body from her feeble women's brain. She'd never felt this way before, aroused and needy and knowing why. A week ago, she wouldn't even understand what she was feeling and know what she so desperately wanted.

The ticking of the clock told her she needed her rest. Tense from expecting him to stride from the room and physically take her to the bed, his bed now, she counted the ticks. He didn't come for her though and she finally dozed, the clock waking her from time to time.

She supposed it was a good thing because she might not wake up early enough for work, needing to be rested and ready to spend the morning in the kitchen downstairs. The chime on the clock rang four times. Jerking awake, her breath stopping, Donal was leaning over her.

"Time to wake up, sweet lassie. You could have had a much better rest with me on the bed but I respected your choice," he told her. "Maybe tonight you will make a better decision."

She pushed hair from her eyes blinking a few times in an attempt to regain her equilibrium, a few moments to allow his words to sink in.

"Work."

She pushed the covers away. My God but he was now naked. She inhaled swiftly, the sight of him stealing her breath.

"I'll go in your place if you like. While I don't know the first thing about baking, my French cook is already at work in the kitchen. When you dress and go downstairs, you can either enjoy her croissants and a cup of tea or you can do whatever it is that you do." He grinned.

She wanted to reach up and touch his beard, trace the line of his mouth with a fingertip. "You didn't haul me to bed with you."

"No, that is your decision, although I must confess, I was enticed. For a few minutes I watched you toss and turn, nearly beat the small pillow to death, but I resisted the temptation even though we both knew it would have been for your personal gain." He stepped back, giving her room to rise.

"Thank you, I guess I didn't expect you to act the gentleman in this case."

She stood a bit too fast, wavering. He steadied her and she felt the length of his body against hers.

"I assure you it was no act. I am a gentleman and as such I would never force you or coerce you if I sensed you didn't want the same things I did."

"Just coax me into bed and do things, things I..." She couldn't finish the words.

"Not unless you wanted me to make love to you. I must admit you presented me with a devilishly difficult challenge last night. One I'm proud to say I mastered."

He left her then, retreating to the bedroom. A few minutes later he returned fully dressed. "I'll see you downstairs."

She watched, amazed and relieved as he strode from the room. Had she really wanted him to take her to his bed? Perhaps she had. She would have the day to analyze her motives as well as his and what she truly wanted.

Analyzing anything wasn't at all necessary. She wanted Donal and she wanted him to make love to her. He planted the seed fully inside her head. The sensations were not something she wanted to live without.

No, she thought of her sisters as well as Hope. Their advice had been sound, but she was going to have a difficult time admitting anything of the sort to Donal. His reaction if she did was something that eluded her.

When she walked into the bakery, new aromas filled the air. She didn't think she'd ever smelled anything so divine. It was the croissants she concluded.

"Sit please," Donal's cook said.

"Do you have a name?" She decided to play along with this strange game he played. "I'd like to call you something besides Cook or Donal's cook."

"*Je m'appelle* Justine," she smiled. "Donal has not asked in all these years. *Merci.*"

"You know I'm Daryl. *Enchante.*" Daryl said.

"Since it appears you have been here for a while, what can I do?" She thought she should feel resentment at the intrusion into her life, but she didn't. "The meal you made for us last night was amazing by the way."

"*Merci beaucoup*, I've started the bread rising. That is all. You should bake whatever your specialties are. Your customers will want them first. They come every morning to buy your baked goods."

"Ah, but I doubt that. Once the scent of your croissants reaches their noses, especially the chocolate ones, it will have them drooling."

"It is just as I thought, you and Donal are right for each other. You should wed him before some other lass gets him." Justine hummed a merry tune not seeming to realize the impact of what she just told her.

Before another lass gets him.

Her stomach rolled. Those words gave her reason to think. At the thought a slow simmering grew inside her. Donal wanted a family and to be wed, a lifetime commitment. He didn't want someone to give him illegitimate children, ones to whom he couldn't pass on his wealth and holdings.

So, was she just stubborn and stupid as well? Had ideas of being controlled by a man set into her head to a point where the notion was detrimental to what she really wanted from life? Perhaps they had.

What to do now?

"Where is Donal?"

She suddenly missed him, and was almost too eager to tell him of her change in plans.

"He had someplace to be. Said he'd stop by later for coffee and a bite to eat," Justine told her. "Not to worry."

"I thought he'd be down here." She paused, her hands in the bread dough she was kneading.

"He had work."

"I don't even know what he does," she said, her mind swirling with different intriguing possibilities. He certainly didn't lack for funds although some of it might be from inheritance.

An heir, that was what she was denying him. It wasn't right of her and as Justine pointed out, he would look elsewhere if she continued in this manner.

"He owns land in Maryland, a tobacco plantation and several ships. A few years ago, he and Leslie invested in land."

"I see. Isn't tobacco supposed to be good for you? I've heard it cures all kinds of ailments."

"I've heard that too. What I do know is that the smoke makes my throat sore and I cough a lot when someone is smoking nearby. Hate to be around anyone who is smoking and it is banned from my kitchen," Justine said.

"I don't like it either. Never seen Donal smoke. Do you know if he does?" she queried, realizing there was little she knew about the man except that every time she saw him, she couldn't breathe and her pulse raced. If she was seriously considering his proposals, she should really find out as much as she could about the man he truly was.

"He has a cigar on occasion."

"But not in your kitchen." Daryl laughed softly, wanting to talk to him about this property in America as well as the tobacco.

"He doesn't set foot in my kitchen anymore. Used to come in and try out the dishes I was preparing and get in the way. He was always underfoot. Don't let him do that now. He respects my wishes because he knows I can seek revenge with the food if he doesn't."

"You wouldn't." Daryl poured over some ideas in her head.

"You're right, I wouldn't and he knows it. While it took me a while to convince him he was driving me crazy, he obeys my wishes now."

"It seems he obeys mine too. I'll have to find a way to convince him otherwise." She was thinking about last night when she chose to sleep in the other room instead of the bed with him. He obeyed her unspoken wish and left her to sleep by herself.

"He's a good man, that one. Mind my words, don't let him get away. If you do, you'll rue the day."

Hands at the small of her back, she stretched, a smile on her face thinking of the night to come and the amazing things he'd do to her body. She nearly groaned.

"What has you grinning, lass?" Donal stepped through the door.

"Thoughts of you and the possibilities of things we might share."

~ * ~

Two weeks later the girls sat in the MacTavish parlor in Glasgow. Hope was thrilled to have all her sisters-in-law visiting. They came together to help Lacie get over the loneliness she seemed to be feeling at Leslie's departure.

The afternoon was dreary and without sunshine. Rain pummeled the ground while the wind blew incessantly.

Lacie gave a heavy sigh. "I don't even remember what Leslie said about our endeavor that day. All I can recall is that he kissed me a few times before he received a message and vanished."

"He does write you every day," Daryl said.

"Yes, but what he says is pretty much the same. I suppose he can't tell me what he is doing, and the funny thing is that I miss him as if we'd been together as man and wife for years. Strange, isn't it?"

"I know I can't possibly understand your feelings, but if Broc left for a week let alone months, I'd feel so empty inside I'd want to scream."

"Was Broc angry with you that night? All of you were so afraid of what they would do when you got home." Lacie sipped the tea and tried one of Gram's ginger cookies.

"Well, I for one am glad you had the good sense not to sleep with him before marriage and having his child. Life is so much easier for everyone when things are done in the proper order."

"Since he's gone somewhere in this world, I won't have that problem," Lacie said.

"Well, consider that a godsend," Bliss said. "It certainly wasn't easy for me when Broc vanished without a word and I was pregnant."

"I felt so sorry for you, my dear. When you were about to go into labor he shows up and wants to marry you." Grams sipped her tea. "That wasn't supposed to happen quite that way."

"No, no it wasn't," Bliss seemed to be reminiscing about the night she gave birth to the twins and married Broc."

"Broc is with the babies?" Grams asked with a little chuckle.

"He is and by the time I get home, I will have to spend the remainder of the evening calming them down." She placed her hands on her belly. "I truly hope this is not another set of twins. Four children under the age of three are far too many. Even though Broc has offered to hire a nanny numerous times."

"So, what did he say when he got you home?" Hope asked, wondering if all the men had been so agreeable and not just Flynt.

"He said he was proud of me, but if I ever put my life in danger that way again, he would put me over his knee and thrash my backside." Bliss grinned. "I told him what a liar he was and he begrudgingly acknowledged the fact."

"Why do they all bluster with threats when they never mean to carry them out?" Chelsea asked. "Cam was the same way and pretty much said the same things."

"What about you, Daryl?" Lacie asked. "You seem different less opinionated perhaps. I can't seem to figure out what exactly is going on with you. Quiet, I think is the word."

"I suppose I should tell all of you. Donal never really mentioned what he thought about that day. He made himself a key to my apartment, bought a huge bed so his feet wouldn't hang out when he slept with me."

"Things went wrong when you told him you'd never marry him?" Grams asked. "Can't say that I'm surprised."

"No, but Justine, his cook, said the words that opened up my eyes. That very day I decided I would tell him I'd changed my mind," Daryl said, her long face apparent to everyone. " I didn't get a chance that afternoon. Now I haven't seen or heard from him in two weeks."

"That doesn't sound like a terribly long time," Lacie whispered.

"We should speak of things that put a smile on our faces and not tears in our eyes," Hope said, looking around the room. "Finding love is never easy. So," she retrieved a bottle of whisky and poured everyone a drink before pouring herself a cup of tea, "here's to figuring out exactly how men think," she sipped the contents then poured everyone another glass. "Here's to the safe return of Leslie and Donal no matter where they are or what they are doing." They all drank then she poured another. "Here is to our two sisters, Lacie and Daryl, finding the happiness they deserve."

Daryl set her glass on the table. "The thing is, wherever he is or what he is doing, his man always follows me. See he is here now telling me it is time for me to go home."

"You don't have to comply," Hope laughed. "What has happened to your backbone?"

"The thing is, I'm always thinking Donal might be home and perhaps lying on top of our bed waiting to give me a second chance."

"You must go. Perhaps this time he will be there."

Hope wished the best for Daryl, but she was afraid that perhaps she had disavowed a relationship far too many times.

"One last drink," Hope said, lifting her cup. "We should meet again every week. It is good for us to share."

Chapter Ten

"We need to talk."

Flynt was watching his wife puttering around the dining room. She seemed to be rearranging all the glassware in the cabinets then putting everything back to the way it was in the first place. He understood she was putting off the discussion they needed to have a few nights ago. The conversation was past due.

"About what?" She smiled prettily at him before going back to work.

He studied her carefully. One month, perhaps, and her body so far changed very little. Possibly imagining things, he was sure he felt a baby bump last night when he held her. "I know what you are about and it won't work. You are obviously no longer exhausted. You've put that glass away three times, but really I'm not counting." Good Lord, but he didn't want to get her angry.

She sat down, folding her hands on top of the table then with a slight lift to her shoulders then her hands on the base of her spine, she was stretching. "No, I'm not tired at the moment but who knows how I will feel in a few minutes. My disposition as well as my stomach change quickly."

He cleared his throat wondering what if anything she was thinking. This had to be done now, today, before something else happened that needed his attention. He always had control. After all he was the oldest and only male child in the MacTavish clan. "You do know what you and my sisters did the other day was irresponsible and reckless."

"Wait."

He watched, baffled as she suddenly raced from the room. He

followed at a slower pace to find her bent over a basin while losing the contents of her stomach. The smile he felt growing needed to be tamped down. She certainly wouldn't appreciate his happiness. This was a positive sign she carried a child.

"Come back to the dining room when you are finished. I'll ask cook to bring you some toast and hot tea. Perhaps you can keep that down."

He sauntered back to the dining room, pleased with himself. Hope was with child, a possible heir. Ready to spread the word, he understood she would still want to wait to say anything, always a possibility of a miscarriage.

When she didn't return, he went looking for her, finding her sitting in the parlor. He sat down opposite her.

"I'm not finished," she told him wearily. "In fact, I'd like to return to my bed if you don't mind."

"Our bed," he quickly corrected her, thinking of the right words to use in such a situation. "We will have our discussion then you can go to bed. I'm feeling as if this is a ploy to put off the inevitable."

"I didn't just pretend to throw up." She glared at him, not his mouth. "This is all your fault and don't you dare puff up your chest with that so-called manly pride of yours. This is no fun for me and if you believe it is, you better keep thinking about it. I am miserable." She raced to the basin again.

"Whether you are in bed or not, you would still be sprinting to the basin. Sitting in the living room has no bearing on your stomach."

He wasn't about to argue with her that this predicament was just as much her fault as his. After all, she stared at his mouth and wanted to make lust with him just as often as he did. "Since you are feeling wretched, this seems as good a time as any to talk about the adventure you set in motion the other day."

"You would think that." She rinsed her mouth with some water before sitting down again. "Men can pretend they know but they don't." She held up her hands when he began to speak. "No, don't. I don't want your false sympathies no matter how you try to hide it. You're grinning inside and pleased as a peacock with all your colorful feathers spread out around you."

"I'll get that toast for you. I'm sure cook has it on the dining room table. Unless of course you would like to return to the dining room to eat."

He stood and feeling properly chastised, he strode into the dining area. Blessed hell, he was supposed to deliver the lecture and once again Hope turned it back on him.

"I'd like to go to bed now," she said to his back.

He heard her but he wasn't going to give permission, not that she would wait for it. If she truly wanted to retire right now, she would. She was definitely in a bit of a snit, and he concluded once more this would be the best time to confront her. Turning, he stopped in the doorway. "Not until—"

"You will proceed to tell me how a mere woman should not have approached a man with a gun, made him strip naked and sent him on his way to becoming a slave. How dare you?" Her voice rose and it seemed she shook with emotion. "You and your fellow bad boys did nothing. Someone had to save you from that man so we could get on with a normal life."

Defense mechanisms kicked in and his reply was nothing like he rehearsed earlier this morning. "You're absolutely right, and I will dare anything when it comes to the life of the woman I love...lust after." He grinned trying to correct the mood yet quickly realizing what he just told her. "Now, how often do I tell you that you are correct in your words? You should mark this day down on your calendar so you can remember it. I know I will." He left then and returned with the food and drink he promised.

"Not often enough." She bit into the toast, smiling, seeming to have heard what he just admitted. "I'm most likely going to lose this food also. Not sure why I'm eating now. Something tasty and edible for me is much more suited for the end of the day versus the beginning."

"At this rate you are going to have trouble eating for two let alone yourself."

He did begin to worry about her. When everything was said and done, he needed and wanted Hope more than an heir. He reminded himself her sickness was normal and it would go away soon. Perhaps they should have that talk later but if it was put off for now, well then, what he had to say would lose its impact.

She rested her head on the small table in front of her. "Please, can we put this off until the afternoon. This condition seems to go away later in the day. I will feel better and you can speak about all the different manly things you believe to be true and irrefutable."

"It is almost afternoon now." His voice was quiet. He rested his hand on her back, attempting to soothe yet realizing she was angry with him and his high handedness as well, but he didn't want his wife making a habit of fighting his battles. "You're right. The sickness should pass. Can I get you some more tea?"

She looked up, creases lining her forehead. "Yes, more tea would be nice, thank you so much. Perhaps you could put a little lemon and some milk in it. A teaspoon of honey would be nice also."

He rumbled around in the kitchen for a few minutes. It seemed cook left hot water on the stove. Took him a while to find the tea and tea ball. When he finally returned to the dining room, she was gone.

When he eventually found her, she was curled up on the sofa, her hands beneath her head, sleeping. His heart wrenched. It was so unlike Hope to nap in the morning let alone any part of the day. He would have to take better care of her and their child. Covering her with a quilt, he stepped back, gazing at his wife.

The woman he loved.

Ah, but he would have to figure out a way to take the words back. She wouldn't let him and he knew she'd heard, the expression on her beautiful face changing to shock when he spoke them.

The woman he loved. He had fallen for Hope. It was true and he hoped she had fallen for him.

But did she love him?

In the stables he discovered Kelly was no longer there. Evidently, Leslie didn't waste any time transferring him to his home. He would miss the man.

His business in town would wait. A few minutes later he was out of the city and riding hard. Days ago, his fear for Hope had been real and overpowering until he discovered the ladies did indeed have everything under control.

That fact didn't matter to him. It couldn't happen again and he hoped Broc and Cam made it perfectly clear to their wives that what they chose to put into action had been foolish. They could have died. He slowed his horse to a trot, taking in the view and trying to release the tension that had plagued him for too many days. She was truly sick and it wouldn't do well for him to make things worse for her. He had no choice.

What to do?

He rode until the sun was beginning its descent. She would be awake now, wondering where he had gone and probably relieved he wasn't just sitting in front of her waiting for her to open her eyes.

Turning the horse, he headed back to the city. A crisp wind stirred the leaves on the road as they swirled around his horse's hooves. When he looked to the west, thunderheads rose high into the sky. They would most likely have a storm tonight, and he prayed it would not carry over into his home. Although he didn't know how it wouldn't. The storm had been brewing for days now. He should have confronted her when the deed was still fresh in his mind instead of making lust with her.

He left the horse with the stable lad, striding to the house. She was sitting on the porch swing wrapped in the same quilt he covered her with earlier in the day. Her face was pale, her eyes huge. When she looked at him, he thought he saw tears. His heart melted.

"I didn't know where you went," she said, her voice whisper-thin in the cooling afternoon air.

"Just a ride. I had a lot to think about." He sat down beside her and wrapping an arm around her, he pulled her close.

"I understand what you've been trying so hard to tell me. Perhaps I don't have your strength, but I've more than enough tenacity as well as intelligence to put together a workable plan. We took few risks. There were five of us each with a gun as you recall, and we all know how to use the weapon." She brushed strands of hair from her face, ones that had come lose when she slept.

"Taking risks with your life is not something I can tolerate or even learn to accept." The truth was really simple. "You cannot do anything like that again." There he said the words, gave her the order he'd been rehearsing and now he waited for her rebuttal.

"It is alright if you risk your life? You don't think I was terrified to find you with your leg slashed open? You don't think that while you lay shivering in our bed one moment then burning with fever, I wasn't frightened?"

"There was no risk taken by me. I was attacked and left for dead. I grew sick with the fever from being left in the cold and dampness of the night. Yes, I'm grateful you found me, but Kelly had everything in hand. He would have brought me home with no risk to you or my sisters."

"Well, I am hungry now. While I can keep food in my stomach I should eat, don't you think?" She started to stand but he pulled her onto his lap.

"I need a promise, that is all."

"A promise of obedience?" she asked, with a note of annoyance in her voice then she stiffened her back. "You won't get it."

"No, I'm not sure what I want you to promise, but you've become so very special to me. The thought of losing you..." He stopped speaking, very unsure of what he meant to say.

"I plan on staying around for a very long time. You cannot get rid of me so easily, Flynt MacTavish." She tried to struggle off his lap but he held her tight, grinning.

His lips found hers in a long kiss meant to show her how he felt since he couldn't seem to find the words to tell her. Heat exploded inside and he was rewarded with the tiny sounds of pleasure that always rippled through her when he made love to his wife.

Not lust.

It was good to finally know how he really felt about Hope, his wife.

Close to her ear, whispering so his breath would caress her and arouse her. "I would like to make love to my wife right now."

"Make lust," she corrected him, but the smile on her face told him she heard exactly what he'd said and what he meant.

"No, my darling wife, I want to make love to you. Do you want to make love to me?" He rose with her in his arms then strode up the stairs to their room.

"Yes," she told him, and it didn't seem she wanted to dwell on the difference in words. "It seems I've been waiting forever for you to say the words. I supposed you've decided what to call what we do whenever the mood hits."

"Whenever you stare at my lips or my crotch," he murmured between kisses. "I think there is a true measure of lust on those occasions."

"Yes, there is that."

"I haven't heard you say it." He kicked open the door, striding into the room and gently placing her on their bed. Standing over her, challenging her," Say the words, my sweet lassie."

"Is that what my husband wants to call it now. Love not lust or hunger or passion. You've made up your mind? I don't want to misconstrue your dictates."

"I have and I don't want to hear anything about lust, never again." He came down on top of her, bracing his weight with his forearms, but he understood she would most likely tease him from time to time with the notion of lust.

"I don't know." She hesitated for a few seconds. "I've always liked the sound of 'make lust.'"

"Say the words. I want you to understand how I feel."

"I'll have to think about it." She closed her eyes then when she opened them, "What made you change your mind?"

Becoming even more vulnerable was not going to happen. He couldn't reveal everything he felt all at once. Slipping the sleeves of her gown from her shoulders, his hands found her breasts. Reverently, he kissed each one through the fabric of her chemise. Her tiny shiver of pleasure delighted him.

"I do believe they are larger today." He kissed her again and again. "Much, much larger."

She pounded his chest. "They couldn't be. It's too soon."

"Anything is possible. I felt the baby bump too." He rose to his knees, removing his shirt before doing the same to her chemise. "We really should have taken all of our clothes off before we started making love."

"What would be the fun in that? I've always wondered if you were ever so eager you would rip my clothing." Her hands rested on the fastening of his britches. "May I?"

"You certainly don't need to ask."

"What if I go too far? Do something you disapprove of?" She sucked her bottom lip between her teeth, her eyes wide and questioning but there was a devilish shimmer he'd never seen before.

He found the gesture endearing, but her words disconcerting. "I don't know what you mean? Go too far?"

She touched his face gently. "I don't suppose I know either. It wasn't long ago when I did whatever I pleased. You didn't care about me or say the love word. This is new and hard for me to understand. No one has given me orders now for a couple of years. That all ended when I escaped the harem."

"Your happiness as well as your safety are what is most important to me. You can't imagine how anxious I was to know you were out confronting a dangerous man, one who had my demise at the forefront of his brain."

"That's just it, Flynt. You were the one he wanted dead, not me. I was never in any danger." She lovingly held his face in her hands. "You should know I would do the same again."

"If he knew me just a little bit, he would have known your death would have sent a debilitating blow straight to my heart." He kissed her softly, held her close, realizing this was more perfect than anything he'd ever felt with anyone.

She sighed, pulling his face closer to hers, whispering softly. "I will promise to you if you do the same for me. Losing you would be just as devastating. When you went missing and no one could find you, I thought my life would end. I had to search for you. For me there was no other choice. Would you have wanted me to sit on my hands, crying huge sorrowful tears or go looking for you?"

He started to speak, "Hope," but she put a finger to his lips.

"No, I had no choice. I would have looked the rest of my life. There is nothing you can do or say that would change those feeling I have. I cannot and will not make that promise you seek."

"Our child," he paused, "You will have to change somewhat as will I. Do you want the baby to grow up with no mother or father?" He understood not just the mother but the father, as well, needed to reevaluate their lives.

"Of course not," she told him, sighing softly as his hands expertly roamed her body, lingering on the most carnal and sensual parts, "but I would never change what I did to find you and correct the wrong doing."

"As I will never threaten you with physical punishment." He paused then, "Well, I might threaten but as you well know I could never carry through with it." He'd turned her over, kissing her tenderly along her spine. "I could never thrash you. I pray you know that." As his hands tenderly caressed her bottom, his teeth and lips sipping also.

"It's your manly pride spouting nonsense. I've always understood that about you." She sighed again as his lips found even more tender and so very evocative spots on her body. "I don't know how you know where you can touch me to..." Her voice changed to a whisper thin sigh of pleasure.

He turned her over again, smiling, "Like here," he kissed, "And here," he bit gently, watching as her hips rose to meet him. But he was going to draw this out, prolong the sensual pleasure until she begged for him. He had the rest of the evening. When he finished this first time, they would eat then proceed to making love again and again throughout the night before traveling into the morning until they could no longer keep their eyes open.

"Yes, are you going to leave me now like you did the other night?" Beneath his hands her body tensed as if suspecting he would do just that. "That was very unkind of you, rude among other words."

"I apologize. It was not well done of me. I was angry and frustrated with the jeopardy you put yourself in, never mind the wee baron growing inside your womb, but if it's any consolation to you, my actions were as much punishment for me as they were for you."

"I thought so but I want you to leave right now if you intend to carry on in the same manner."

"Never again." He began to caress her again, exploring every part of her, kissing every place after his fingers touched. She cried out, nearly spinning away from him and climaxing before he wanted her to. He stopped then to watch her and slow this down so the lovemaking would last a very long time. "What I did was as much a punishment to me as to you," he told her again. "I never realized how much you mean to me than I have in the last few days."

"What do I mean to you?" she asked.

"Ach, my sweet, sweet lassie, you challenge me to admit feelings I'm not sure of." He lied now because he was very sure of how he felt about her after knowing he could have lost her. For some reason he couldn't explain to himself, he still couldn't say the words she was looking for.

Well, he did say a few. That would have to be enough for tonight. She did not reciprocate, still insisted what they felt for each other and the sex between them was only lust, nothing more. He meant to change that thought tonight.

"I'm sure that you as a man with only mistresses to make lust with never realized you might have feelings other than that."

"You would know so much about a man and his feelings." His brogue kicked in as he began to fall further under her spell.

"No, however I've a woman's intuition. That is good enough for me. Touch my breasts, hold them in your hand. I want to know if they are as large as Lacie's."

He choked and if he'd been sipping wine, it would have spewed all over her. "You want me to do what?" He remembered the earlier conversations. "I wouldn't know because I've never held Lacie's breasts in my hands, only yours."

"Your countless mistresses," she reminded him.

"I've only had one mistress not countless. I'm apologizing for saying what I did earlier. I like you just the way you are today and how you will be tomorrow, whatever that is. I never meant to offend you."

Blessed hell but he didn't like to spend so much time trying to make up for things he said before. He'd never felt so obligated to tread lightly on her sensibilities. She did after all carry his child.

"I'm glad to hear that, now kiss me again or I might think you mean to leave me aroused and needing you in the most primal and provocative ways imaginable."

~ * ~

Hope woke to an empty bed. The night had been wonderful and revealing in so many ways, too many to count. She realized he took a giant step forward in telling her he wanted to make love not lust to her. Grinning, she touched her belly. It was a tiny bit larger. His seed must have taken root the first or second day of their marriage, during their honeymoon at the beach.

A pot of tea sat beside the bed as well as dry toast. He was always thoughtful even when he was displeased with her. She poured a cup and leaning against the headboard she drank slowly and indulged in a bite of the toast, hoping it would stay down. According to the women in the harem, the sickness usually lasted three months, sometimes less and sometimes more. Well, she had this to look forward to for a while.

Dressed now she wandered through the house looking for her husband. Instead, she encountered Munroe.

"Believe he's outside on the porch swing waiting for you." He pointed in the direction of the door.

"For me?"

Her gut tightened as she wondered if the magic of last night was about to be whisked away from her. Suddenly she wasn't so eager to see him.

"I believe that is what he told me," Munroe smiled, nodding his head. "For your convenience there is a basin now in every room. My wife, bless her soul, used to get horribly sick when she was with child."

"He didn't tell you, did he? We talked about not doing that."

She would punch him if he was already bragging about his manly prowess.

"No, ma'am. No need to get upset with him just yet even though I'll wager he'll give you plenty of opportunities. I just recognize the signs. You were either sick or pregnant. Enjoy your day."

"Thank you. That was very sweet of you, although it is rather embarrassing to always be running to a basin."

"No need to be embarrassed. You aren't the first woman and you won't be the last to experience morning sickness. There is even one on the porch for your expediency. I will leave the two of you alone," he said then walked away.

She wanted to turnaround and leave by the back door. Instead, she inhaled a long deep breath before venturing outside. Somehow, she needed courage this morning. The night had been eventful, and she had no idea what he would say to her now.

"Flynt?" she queried as she stepped through the big door and onto the porch.

"Come sit down. I was waiting for you. Were you able to keep the toast and tea in your stomach?" He waved his hand in the air. "By the way it's a beautiful day. Would you like to go for a walk or perchance a ride?"

"Possibly this afternoon when I know I won't get sick. You are acting rather strange."

She had never seen him this solicitous or sweet. Not that she didn't like this side of him, but it was odd.

He was up to something and she meant to find out exactly what it was.

"How so?" he asked, wrapping a quilt around her shoulders. "Are you comfortable? Can I get you more tea?"

"I'm not cold or thirsty not hungry either for that matter," she said but she didn't take the covering off. She supposed she would indulge him today. "I don't need to be coddled. I'm pregnant, not dying or sick."

"Let me do just that," he laughed, pulling her close before placing a gentle kiss on her forehead then one on the tip of her nose. "For today at least, I want to do everything for you."

"Alright then, today, but this can't go on when it is unnecessary. All you will manage is to make me crazy." She did enjoy his attentions though, but she also knew she would grow tired of them if he continued in this manner. "Shouldn't you be at work?"

"You trying to get rid of me? I'm wounded." With his hand on his heart he sighed heavily.

"No, I don't know why I said that. It's Saturday and it seems you make your own hours."

"Sir, ma'am," Munroe stood at the door a smile on his face. "I've the basket and blanket for you. There's a bottle of wine too. My wife used to take a sip or two to calm her stomach. She always said a little wine was the best cure for morning sickness."

"Set it on the floor, please. We won't go for a little while. We are still discussing the pros and the cons of our adventures," Flynt said, adjusting the quilt around he shoulders. "The breeze is brisk, don't you think?"

She watched everything, feeling a bit jaded. She didn't trust him, not one little bit. "What are you up to, Flynt MacTavish? I need to know."

"So suspicious. Honestly, I'm up to nothing. You are a breath of fresh air, and I just want to enjoy the morning with you," he laughed, "Perhaps I should just take you to bed and we can spend a pleasant day there."

She punched him then. "I don't like this, not knowing why you are grinning and acting so solicitous. I don't trust you right now, Flynt MacTavish. What is going on with you?" She raced for the basin, silently thanking Munroe for his considerations. She would not have made it into the house.

He was beside her, rubbing her back. "I would do that for you if I could. Don't like it when you are sick." Then he paused. "Is there anything I can get you? Do for you?

"At least it's not a permanent condition. I'm hoping this part will be over in a month or two. No need to feel bad, I'd let you do this for me if I could. Since it really is all your fault."

"Are you still blaming me for your condition?" he asked. "I thought you enjoy what we do together."

"Making lust?" One eyebrow rose a smidgeon, "It is all your fault. I would have never thought to do all those things to me or you if you didn't make suggestions, if you didn't teach me. Therefore, I would not be pregnant and constantly running to a basin to lose my breakfast."

"Delightful things and you like what I do. We could practice right now, here on the porch."

She rose from her spot over the basin. "I'd like a small glass of that wine or you could fetch me the tea. Tell me really why you have the basket of food and blanket." He wanted to go for a walk or so he said, but he wouldn't need the food or the blanket for that.

"Would you like to go back to our estate in the countryside? I know winter will be here soon, but it really is more comfortable. I'll bring Grams to the house in about seven months in case you have the child early as Bliss did."

"You would do that?" She liked the country better than the city, liked the fresh air and the breezes that blew from the ocean. They were a day away from the ocean, a fast carriage ride, no more. "Yes, and perhaps we could go to the house on the Firth of Clyde. Bring back some memories. I'm sure Cam wouldn't mind."

"Anything you want, my sweet lassie. The world is at our disposal. Just ask and you will receive."

"Anything?"

She laughed as his brows drew together trying to figure out what it was she was going to ask for. She sipped the wine he poured earlier. It cleansed her mouth and settled her stomach just as Munroe had said it would do. She sipped again, thinking some of that dry toast might be good right now.

"Within reason," he informed her.

"Now, do you really believe I would ask for something unreasonable? I would not wound your manly pride that way." She watched the ever-changing expressions on his face.

"I do."

He smiled at her though and she really didn't know what it was he thought.

"Well, not today. Today I would like to go home. I suppose you've packed everything we need." She wondered when he had time to do all that. Of course they would not take everything, just the essentials at first. He and Munroe might make a couple more trips into the city to close the house for the duration.

"Your clothing and mine are on their way as are Munroe and Cook. All we need now is to climb into the carriage and enjoy the ride. I am truly looking forward to going home. That of course is the reason for the basket of food and the warm blanket. We want to be comfortable on our ride."

"You knew I would say yes."

She wondered at that just as she was not surprised that he wanted to leave the city.

"I suspected and hoped. If you told me you wanted to stay here, I would have simply recalled everyone." He held out his arm to her as the carriage rounded the house as if the driver had been listening to their conversation. "How did you do that? Let the driver know we were ready."

He shrugged his broad masculine shoulders before winking at her. "It is just a talent of mine."

He helped her inside after the vehicle stopped in front of the house. "What about the horses?" She asked as he wrapped an arm around her. "Are they already at the country house or are they coming later?"

"Kelly has agreed that he will help transfer them, for a handsome price now that his services are wanted," Flynt said. "He is a wonderful man, and I'm saddened to know he fell on hard times for such a petty reason, something that could happen to anyone."

"Leslie is away and Lacie must be horribly lonely." She now had second and third thoughts about leaving the city.

"She is working for Daryl in the interim. We all know how bad Daryl is with figures, and Lacie can make sense of numbers with her eyes closed. She will not be overly lonely or lacking for companionship."

"I'm glad she has someone. What must it be like to agree to be courted one day and abandoned the next?"

It seemed Flynt didn't want to talk about his sisters. In the carriage, he asked, "Comfortable?" A basin sat on the floor opposite her. Lord, but she hoped she would not throw up again. So far it had only been once today but the morning was turning into the afternoon and that was always a good sign. Perhaps the sickness was ending before it barely started.

"I am." She let out a long breath she seemed to be holding. Her stomach rumbled. "Shall we eat?"

"I'm famished," he told her, staring at her mouth.

She punched him hard and he obligingly grunted. "That is not well done of you, teasing me when I'm in such a fragile womanly state, one you caused. We can't possibly make lust in the carriage. There is not enough room and I'm not a contortionist, although some of the women in the harem could do some amazing things with their bodies."

"Like what?" His eyes simmered with passion and yes, lust. "I'd like to learn all about those astounding things they can do with their legs and arms. Perhaps if you practiced you could learn."

"That light shining in your eyes is pure lust not love. It's hunger and desires and raw passion all wrapped into one carnal bundle, and I've a pretty strong feeling you know what I'm talking about. Most likely you could explain everything to me and my mouth would fall open in astonishment."

"You do not have to be a contortionist to make love or lust with me in this carriage. You could merely sit on my lap then straddle me, and I'd let you keep all of your clothing on your person. All you would have to do is open your legs for me, and both of us would be happy and content for the rest of the trip."

She mulled that over in her head for a few seconds. "Would it be as good for you as it is for me? I know you said content but is that the same as good or more than satisfied? I should inform you now that I would make you wait for your pleasure. You would have to wait a verra long time, maybe until just before we get home. The timing would be left solely up to me or I won't do it. Not even for you, my dearest husband."

"Just as good, maybe even better if you do it right." His grin stretched from ear to ear. "Do you feel good enough to try? Will you open your legs for me then sit on my most manly part? Can you do it right?"

"Well." She laughed, loving the way he put things, "If we do this, it would be you I threw up on. We should eat first so I have food in my stomach."

"You wouldn't dare something so despicable. Perhaps we could reconsider. I could hold the basin in front of you. While you have your way with me." He was still staring at her mouth then his gaze dropped to her bosom.

Heat swept through her and she knew she'd be slick for him, more ready for anything he wanted. "No, I would be much more comfortable if we waited. We can do it another time. Sometime when I'm not pregnant and throwing up every few hours." She opened the basket of food. "Let's see what is in here."

"Nothing I'm hungering for." His brows drew together as he drew a line down her jaw. "That's where I want my lips. Right there, he touched her with one finger, and there."

"Behave yourself," She tried to swat his hands away but nothing seemed to deter him. In truth though none of the food appealed to her at the moment. He was not letting his need for her go. In a few minutes she knew she would be melting for him. She already was.

What to do? Give in to him and this wonderful persuasion to his way of thinking he seemed to be initiating?

Lifting her skirts, his hand found its way to her underclothing. Within seconds there was no cloth between her and his exploring hands and his man parts. He was an expert at coaxing her to melt in his arms. While his fingers continued to arouse and heat her, his lips did the same, discovering bare skin and more intimate places than ever before.

He was lifting her. She settled on him. He was deep inside and she was moving. She heard his manly groan of pleasure and she realized in this position she did have all the control. She would proceed just as he had last night and make this joining last for as long as possible.

She grinned at him. His mouth was moist just as she was slick with the moisture his fingers created.

Holding his head with both hands, she kissed him, opening his mouth with her tongue but when she knew he wanted her to move, she held still, teasing and arousing in a way she'd never been able to do before.

He wanted her in the most primal and enchanting ways and she meant to keep him aroused and needing her desiring her in the most elemental and magical ways.

"Does this please you?" she asked then moved on him just a tiny bit, the smallest amount to entice him even further. There was so much more to this lovemaking they could explore. Maybe not now in this carriage, but later over the days and nights to come.

"Ach, my sweet, sweet lassie, more than you could ever know." His hands on her waist once again told her he wanted her to move on him.

She obliged, ever so slightly, prolonging this just as he did last evening. She kissed him again and again, slowly moving but not enough to bring him to his climax. She liked this, felt more aroused than ever before. She wanted him to touch her in that spot that made her spiral out of control, yet wanted him to wait until she could hold back no longer.

He must have decided it was enough, that she would not control the love play between them. He massaged the tiny bud that gave her so much pleasure she would spin away from him as well as herself. Yet the pleasure would be so great it would leave her barely able to move, breathless and weak as a newborn kitten as well.

Her head back, she gave in to the heat and sweetly painful pleasure he created. "That's it, lassie. Just relax. Let it come. I want you to enjoy this. Come for me, cry out my name and I will be a man well pleased."

She did as the tremors took over her body. "Flynt." She cried out his name but he covered her mouth with his own taking the scream into his mouth.

When they were finished, she rested against him, her head on his chest. "I cannot survive much more of this, you ken. You will certainly be the death of me."

"Hope," he murmured, placing light and very gentle kisses on her face, "You are a treasure, one I am so verra glad I found. I've wondered often enough why it took me so long."

"Was that making love or lust?" she asked, gazing at him, her voice so quiet he needed to bend close to hear her.

"Both, I believe." He chuckled at her puzzled look.

"How?"

"I ken the lust makes for good sex, but there is no meaning in the act if there is no love between the two people. I've never loved another person, but now that I care for you so much, the sex between us is so verra different."

"What are you saying?"

She wanted to hear the words even though he insinuated them before and skirted around them now. Care was not love.

"I'm saying that I love you, Hope MacTavish, and I'm very glad you came to me even with the loss of your memories. My life has forever been changed for the better when I met you."

He waited then gazing at her and she wanted to go over in her head what he told her before she reciprocated the feelings. He loved her.

"Well?" he prompted, no grin on his face now. It seemed he might fear what she would say.

"Well, so as not to wound your manly pride. I love you, Flynt MacTavish, but unlike you, I've known for a long time, even before you married me, I knew I loved you. I think the first time I saw you it was love I felt. Always love, well perhaps there have been times when my feelings slanted toward lust."

"My God, but I must be a stupid fool. In my defense, I did know I was falling for you. Falling for Hope." His strained expression turned to a smile.

"I have fallen for you and have been doing that these few years. Falling for Flynt. I do like the sound of that." She breathed deeply, finally hearing the words she longed for so long.

"Falling for Hope," he murmured.

"No, Falling for Flynt," she corrected.

"I love you, Hope MacTavish."

Epilogue

Flynt set down his cards, standing while he looked to the door. "I'm done."

"You tired of losing all your money?" Broc laughed as he pulled the coins from the center of the table.

"Can't concentrate." He walked to the door of the third-story room, whiskey in hand and gazed into the hallway. The scream from below set his nerves on edge and left him grimacing. He felt nauseous, his gut twisting in fear.

"Really, everything is going to be fine. The first one takes longer, I've been told. Although my boys didn't want to wait at all." Broc was still chuckling seeming to enjoy his friend's distress.

The scream piercing through the floor nearly sent Flynt to his knees.

"Screams are absolutely normal," Cam said, "although worrisome to say the least or the most, whichever you choose to define them."

"Come back and have another drink. This could take hours more." Broc was striding back to the table. He picked up the cards, shuffling them a few times before putting them back in their holder.

"Suppose we're done here." Donal sat back, tipping precariously on two legs, his hands folded across his stomach. "Don't understand what has you so worried. Isn't this normal?"

"Just wait until it's your wife screaming."

"Dinna have a wife yet." Donal was grinning from ear to ear, clearly enjoying the evening as were all of the bad boys, except Leslie who was still somewhere unaccounted for. This was not something he wanted to repeat, yet Flynt knew Hope wanted more children. He just didn't know how he could go through this another time.

He was sweating, moisture beading on his forehead, his pulse racing.

"It's twice as bad for Hope than you, you know. Best you stay strong," Broc said. "Don't be feeling sorry for yourself."

"I'm beginning to understand why they don't like to wait for us when we're out and about. Sitting and doing nothing is impossible." He started for the stairs only to be held back by Broc.

"They don't want you down there. They will tell you that you'll just get in the way. Women's work," Broc told him from first-hand knowledge.

"They intimated I'd faint," Cam said striding to stand beside them. "I wouldn't have done that, faint."

"Perhaps a walk outside will help," Donal said. "We could all go for a ride and return when it'd dark."

"A long hard ride sounds appealing to me," Broc slapped him on the back. "Let's go."

"It's dark now," Flynt wiped the moisture from his forehead with a handkerchief. "I'm going to find out what's happening."

"I tell you they won't let you in the room and if you try, they'll remove you fast. The door most likely will close on your nose," Cam said, seeming to remember the ordeal he went through when Chelsea miscarried and later when she gave birth to their little boy.

"My choice so I'll take my chances," he grumbled, stepping into the hallway and towards the stairs.

"Your life, I suppose."

Flynt was very nearly bowled over by Broc's twins who raced past him and into the arms of their father.

"Da," they both cried together as they managed to reach Broc and wrap their tiny arms around his legs. With a grunt he lifted them so he held both in his arms.

"What brings the two of you here?" He kissed each on the cheek before noticing Bliss framed in the doorway.

"While we all wanted to be here when the baby was born, the twins need to sleep and you need to take them home." Bliss walked in, holding her arms out to take one of the boys from him.

"You don't want to stay?"

"I'm staying. Everyone else is going to retire for the night and come back in the morning. If all the sisters as well as their husbands barge in to see the little one, it will be overwhelming for Hope. She deserves better."

"Why are you staying, why not—?"

Bliss cut him off, placing her fingertip on his lips. "Because I can help more than the others and while Chelsea could also, Cam can't feed their three-month-old. They will be going home soon. Lacie will stay here in her room, and Daryl is also going home to her apartment over the bakery."

"Everyone is coming back in the morning?"

Flynt stepped forward. "Thank you, everyone is welcome then the little one, with any luck, will be ready to meet its aunts and uncles and cousins."

He cringed when another scream from below hit him in the gut.

Chelsea and Cam said their goodbyes as did Daryl, Donal as well. When Flynt wandered downstairs, it seemed Lacie had already retired for the night. He poured a drink before sitting on the sofa in the parlor.

Restless, he gulped the whiskey then walked outside. The evening was crisp and a bit chilly for early June. The air was clear and so much cleaner than in the city. Leaning against the railing he watched the shadowed vehicles leaving for Glasgow. They should not be traveling at night but they were all together.

They would come again in the morning. The baby he hoped would be born before then. He turned to look at the light shining from the window upstairs. From time to time he saw movement, gliding smoothly from one place to another in the room. Once he was sure it was Hope he saw walking but pushed that thought to the back of his head. She would be in the bed.

He thought of all the reasons he loved her. All the reasons it took him so long to admit to the fact thinking of his lust for her, which was very true, just as true as his love for her. Every time she screamed; he was afraid of losing her. This is what his lust got him, worry about her life. He heaved in a huge and very ragged breath of air. One child would have to be enough for them if she made it through this birth.

Holding the drink in both hands, he gazed into the night. A screech of an owl, the slow chirp of crickets, all were normal sounds to be heard. Frogs croaked somewhere near the gazebo. From above there was only silence.

Flynt's heart stopped beating for a moment while his breath caught in his throat. He didn't know how long he'd spent on the porch staring at the night sky and listening to all the sounds. Trying to steady his restless nerves, he drew in a long slow breath.

Suddenly, the cries from above were different. A thin wail of a baby sipping its first breath of air. His pulse raced. He turned inside, racing up the steps two at a time then coming to a halt in front of the door to the master chamber, his fist raised to knock.

The door opened before his knuckles could connect with the wood. "Bliss." He tried to look around her and see inside the room.

"You have a boy. As soon as Grams cleans up the baby and Hope as well, you can come in."

The door was shut in his face and just as Cam related, it hit his nose. He leaned his back against the wall and slid downward to sit on the floor. His head was in his hands, terrified for Hope. Nothing had been said about their state, either one of them.

Waiting was intolerable but it seemed he had no choice. The seconds ticked by on the grandfather clock downstairs just as it seemed his life was ticking away. The chimes sounded three times. She must be exhausted. He ran his hands through his hair several times.

"You can come in now."

It was Bliss speaking but Grams stood behind her. They both had dark circles under their eyes and drooping shoulders. "What, oh?"

"We're leaving for our rooms," Grams said. "Wake me if there is need, otherwise I intend on sleeping until noon tomorrow."

"The others will be here early. If neither one of us is up, don't let them in until Hope gives her consent. Obviously, she is exhausted and if they have any common sense, they will stay away until at least the afternoon. After that I'm sure Hope will be ready to see all the well-wishers."

Flynt did not wait. He slipped inside the door closing behind him. She was feeding the baby. Tears welled in his eyes, sliding down his cheeks in wavering ribbons of moisture. His emotions swirled inside in a fevered pitch.

Her smile was exhausted and hesitant. She stroked the infant's cheek as he suckled at her breast. "You will never let me live this one down but you were right. It's a boy, a beautiful boy. Your manly lust created a boy."

He didn't even care if she used the word lust. He sat down on bed beside her so he could see the child more thoroughly. She pulled him away from her breast as his tiny lips continued sucking.

Flynt held out his arms. "May I?"

Hope handed the boy over to him. "Are you happy?"

"Now that he has come into the world and you are safe, yes. I couldn't have bore it if anything happened to you."

"Or him."

"Or Struan." His voice was strong yet soft. "We haven't spoken of a name, but I would like to call him Struan Alexander MacTavish."

"It's a good name," she said, smiling at him even while her lashes seemed to be drooping.

He'd opened the blanket, counting his fingers and toes, so proud of his wife and son he could barely contain himself. "I love you," he whispered."

"As I love you. You well ken I fell for you the first time I set my eyes on your handsome face. Falling for Flynt," she murmured as she seemed to be falling asleep right before his eyes.

"No, falling for Hope," he corrected as he set Struan in the crib that was set up in the room before disrobing and climbing into bed with his wife. Pulling her into his arms, he listened to her breathing and the steady beat of her heart.

His life would never be the same and he would never change anything.

Coming Soon
by
Christine Young
at
Rogue Phoenix Press

Dancing for Donal

Chapter One

Fall 1825
Glasgow, Scotland

"Well, I see nothing if anything has changed in these parts. It's still raining and the wind whistles through the trees. I'm chilled to the bone." Graham Chamberlin, known as Gray to his friends, Donal's little brother walked into the front door, taking off his hat and the raincoat he wore before striding into the downstairs office.

"What are you doing back from Maryland? Didn't expect to see you this soon. Why did you come home? You weren't due back until next month." Donal sat as his desk, a pen in hand, finishing correspondence to be sent to his brother who was supposed to be in the States overseeing the tobacco plantation.

"Came home to look for a wife. Seems there are not many women in the states, only married and blacks. While the nights aren't as cold there, it's still nice to have a woman to welcome into my bed and warm me. A wife is what I'm needing these days, a good Scottish wife."

"Daryl MacTavish is off limits to you." Blessed hell that's just what he needed, his brother chasing after all the eligible skirts in Glasgow.

"I suppose everyone else is too. Fine by me. Knowing you, she is most likely uptight and a prude as well. Prim and proper is not what I like in my women. I want wild and unrestrained passion in my nights."

His brother had never met Daryl, thank god, and he truly didn't have one clue as to what he yearned for in a relationship. What he did know was that Daryl was far from uptight and a prude. "Where do you ken you'll find a suitable mate? Not at the balls and recitals, I doubt. I ken, debutants don't seem to be your sort of woman."

"Don't know yet, perhaps the markets. A lass who is not afraid to get her hands dirty with a solid day of work and one who will be warm and passionate in bed. One of us has to give this family an heir. You certainly are not accomplishing the job. What has you digging in your heels, if you ken who it is you want?"

"Yes, well, I've given that a great deal of thought and it won't be long before we have an heir." Donal scribbled a few more lines to the message he was working on before sealing it and setting the letter aside. Even though Graham would not be on the receiving end of the missive, someone needed to see to the information written here.

"Has the little MacTavish lass agreed to go along with your proposal? She's a tiny slip of a woman and you're a great brute of a man. Do you ken if you'll fit? You might just rip her apart." Graham belly laughed, seeming to enjoy the cruder side of his comments.

"Are they all so uncivilized in Maryland or do you have a first priority in that department." Donal handed the letter over to his valet. He stared at his little brother, wishing he knew the real reason Graham was in Scotland. Nothing was obvious where Graham was concerned. While he had the reputation of a bad boy, Graham was the real bad boy in the family. He sensed something was wrong though.

"I'm the first," he laughed, helping himself to the brandy. "The premier. Like to say I just tell it as it is."

"How many bastards do you have?" Donal confronted him, a grim look on his face. "Hope you are taking care of them yourself and not with Chamberlin funds. It's likely you'll go broke if you don't learn to keep your sizable man parts in your pants."

Graham grinned from ear to ear, "You jealous, big brother? He sobered. "I've no bastards. While I lived with the Cherokee, I almost had a child. The boy died in childbirth as did his mother. You don't have to worry about anyone soaking up the money."

"I'm sorry about your son, the woman as well." He paused momentarily, thinking there was more to this story than Gray was willing to tell. "Our business is doing better than ever, but I will admit to you the largest part of our strength comes from the production of the tobacco here in Scotland and the change into usable forms. Our factories out shine the money we take in from the crops. So, how many blacks do we have who are still slaves?"

"At last count fifty. Their quarters have been updated and the ones who have learned to speak English have relayed to the others that they are earning a wage and as soon as they have earned enough to pay off the price we paid for them, they will be free men and women. Whatever children they have will gain their freedom along with their parents. After that they are given their papers and they can decide what it is they want to do with the rest of their lives."

"And how many stay?" Donal asked, concerned they would have to continue to buy workers. Buying people for slave labor was abhorrent to him, but in order to keep the plantation a working one, he needed farmers. "Are we still offering a plot of land to those who stay?"

"Most remain on the plantation. They don't have much choice. There is nowhere for them to go except north to Canada and that is a risk most don't want to take. The journey is long and hard, fraught with untold dangers. If they can keep their families and earn an honest day's living as a free man or woman, they are happy. I am constantly on the lookout for more land, but I have to keep traveling west. Don't know how long we'll be able to keep up the practice."

"Good, good, let's keep doing what works for us. I do understand we won't make as much money, but I don't believe in slavery. I want our plantation to run smoothly with working people earning an honest day's living."

"There are those who resent what we are doing. Their slaves grumble about the fairness of it all then point to us as a symbol of bad luck and anarchy. The plantations owners don't want to see their way of life interrupted and that's what they fear we are doing." Graham sat down, sipping his brandy and seeming to enjoy the comforts of home.

"Good, good, I suppose you plan on staying until you find a mate who wants to follow you to Maryland." Donal had always wondered how long Graham would want to remain in a foreign country. Now he knew. Graham had tied all the knots in the states that needed tying and was most likely back to stay. He had mixed feelings about Graham's return and understood he would have to find someone he could trust to replace him, "You're not going back are you?"

"Don't plan on it. We've an amazing overseer. He is a remarkable and intelligent man who will make sure all goes as we have intended. He thinks as us about slavery, that is. I don't believe it will be too many years before slavery is abolished all together. There are growing trends to do just that, especially in the north."

"Then what will you do here? He paused a moment. "Ah, you say you want a wife. I wish you all the luck in that endeavor. We are not getting any younger."

"No, I only stopped here to say hello and perhaps let you feed me for a day or two. I'm off to my inheritance. The land grandmother left me in her will. As you well know, I was gifted with land in the highlands just north of Edinburgh. A crumbling estate if I recall near Linlithgow. One that is large enough to keep me busy. Perhaps I'll find a suitable lass there."

"Then it is settled. Dinner and in the morning you will be off to new and inspiring adventures." Donal was pleased with his brother. He seemed to be growing up and taking on more responsibilities.

"You will be left in these vast spaces to woo your darling Daryl. I really do believe she is too tiny for you. You should look for someone who will match you muscle for muscle, height for height." Graham laughed, pouring himself a second glass of brandy. "I'm going to miss all this. Suppose I'll have to make sure there are all the necessities where I'm going put down roots."

"My brawn or her lack of it is not the point. She is the woman I want and will wed whether you think we will fit well together or not." His words had never been spoken more true. Something about the little lass with the bright and unruly red hair had always intrigued him.

He rose from the desk where he'd been sitting, thinking of Daryl and wishing he could see her this very moment. Striding to the window and trying to forget his brother was intruding on his solitude when he wanted someone else to be doing the same thing, he stared at the countryside. The rain must have stopped, but the wind still did more than rustle the leaves on the trees.

He smiled, his grin widening as his brother rambled on about something, he wasn't sure. In any case he didn't care. He now had plans for this afternoon. It was high time he said hello to his future wife and begin to initiate her into the ways of a man and a woman. It seemed to have been eons since that night he kissed her. What age had she been? Possibly sixteen, but the kiss made a lasting impact then the second time at Cam McEwan's beach house.

"Do you mind if I leave? Make yourself at home as I'm sure you planned. It seems I've an important errand to run." His heart raced at the idea of an encounter with the little spitfire as well as in anticipation of the kiss he envisioned.

He cleared his throat, turning then to speak to Graham. "I don't plan on returning until later this evening. Close up the house and I'll let myself inside. Enjoy your evening."

Donal strode from the room with single-minded purpose and a primitive need he'd never felt before. He'd seen Daryl and he assumed Lacie racing across the grounds toward the tiny pond and waterfall Daryl often visited. He was looking forward to a spirited and passionate confrontation, but first he had to get rid of the youngest sister.

There were so many possibilities.

The afternoon was before them in all it's glory. He couldn't have asked for anything better.

In the stable he mounted his favorite stallion, Achilles, and urged him to run. They rode toward the MacTavish estate, hoping to see Daryl. In any case he would begin his pursuit of her today. He pulled Achilles to a stop, staring at the apparition in front of him.

Blessed hell, but even from this distance she was beautiful, strands of her wild red hair flying around her face and behind her, catching the sunlight, her small torso moving in perfect rhythm with her horse. His body tightened with need, thinking how well they would move together in bed. Good god admit it, sexual need was at the forefront of his mind.

If she wasn't a virgin and innocent, he would ride after her and take her wherever they ended up. He would pull her from her horse and onto his lap. Lord but he imagined what it might feel like if she straddled him and they made love while they rode. That fantasy, he supposed, would be nearly impossible. Still, it was a thought worth pursing one day if he dared.

He couldn't remember the last time he felt this way; eager, enthusiastic and full of lust.

Lord, he had to retrieve at least a small amount of the control he was famous for. He had plans and he wanted to stick to them. Frightening her today with his thirst was not part of the plan.

He grinned. Unexpectedly Daryl MacTavish had fallen into his plans. He would have to be careful here, not too much persuasion, just enough of a taste for an innocent lass such as the young MacTavish girl to follow him willingly into marriage. This could turn out to be one of the best days of his life. From this moment on, he would diligently pursue Daryl in the guise of courting.

She was on his land. Trespassing. The thought gave him reason to smile, perhaps a favor in return for allowing her to enjoy the property.

His smile grew as his heart felt lighter for the first time in months. He'd been waiting for just this type of opportunity. She had been harder than the devil to get alone. It seemed she worked day and night in her bakery. He'd stopped by a few times, had coffee and a pastry of some sort. He never really knew what he was eating because he couldn't stop watching her.

Ah, this was indeed Saturday afternoon. She was taking a much-needed day and a half of rest. He knew first hand the shop was closed on Sundays. Perhaps he could spend some time with her tomorrow, too, continue the courtship, the wooing of Daryl.

When they married, he'd remedy that. She didn't need to work six days a week. Lord knows Flynt should have made sure his sisters were better taken care of. None of them should have the need to work. When they wed, he would give her everything she needed or wanted.

Having seen the direction she rode, he followed the path to one of the most beautiful scenes on his property, a place perfect for the first stages he planned, a kiss, a taste of Daryl. Again, all he needed now was to figure out how to get rid of the little sister, prompt her to leave of her own accord. Yet somehow he felt she would oblige him. There was something amazingly astute about the littlest MacTavish. Only one year younger than Daryl, she would make some man a wonderful wife.

The ground flew beneath the horse's hooves. He tried to formulate a plan in his head as he raced forward. He had followed her here numerous times and watched from afar as she would wade in the pond on hot summer days, showing her delicate slender feet and ankles. Today was not one of those.

He was ready for this encounter, more than ready.

When he finally reached her, she was sitting by herself on a rock, watching the waterfall that fed the small creek. Sunlight filtered through the budding trees. The light was meager but it danced and played on the ground as well as on her vibrant red hair, creating a myriad of colors. He was sure the strands would burn his fingers if he touched them.

He stopped for a few seconds and watched, trying to commit the scene to his memory. Lacie was nowhere to be found. He delighted in that fact. Daryl would be alone with him for the first time since that unusual encounter a couple of years ago and the one at the beach house that sent his blood boiling. Lord, both were so long ago he couldn't recount exactly, but he remembered the moments as if they happened yesterday.

The chase, the catch then the kiss.

The bad boys, Flynt, Broc, Cam, Leslie and himself had been in Flynt's house on the third floor drinking and playing cards. Flynt's sisters were hiding in the room spying on them. Each man gave chase to one of the sisters. He didn't know about the others, but he caught Daryl and kissed her. It seemed Leslie must have chased after Lacie.

He would remember that kiss forever.

She was too young then, but the kiss haunted him over the years. Daryl MacTavish was no longer too young to pursue and conquer, to chase, catch and kiss. He was the man to do just that. He would court her in his own manner, taking his time with her. There would be no way he would give her a chance to say no to any of his proposals, including marriage.

She turned to look at him then, her eyes wide with surprise he hoped and not fear. He had been quiet. "Hello, Daryl. Mind if I join you? Nice day, don't you think?" he asked, stepping forward, not waiting for an answer. He stood beside her. She rose, pressing her hands down her skirts.

The smile on her face brightened, and he couldn't help but think she might be pleased to see him although it appeared a tiny bit nervous. He couldn't help but wonder if she also remembered the kiss as well as the beach house confrontation.

"I didn't invite you here." Her voice held a nervous ripple as she spoke.

"It's my land," he told her, cocking an eyebrow while he took her measure. She was wearing a light green riding habit, a bit of lace showing at the neckline. The hat she wore was tossed on the ground beside the boulder she'd been sitting on and the green plume appeared to have wilted in the sun.

"No, well, of course you're right. So, I was just thinking it might be time to leave." As if undecided, she stood then sat down again smoothing her riding habit then she stood again. For a few seconds she gazed at the waterfall before turning her attention back to him.

"Don't ken what you want to do?" He laughed, keeping the sound behind his teeth.

"No."

"I wouldn't want to be the cause of your departure. You are always welcome to come and go on Chamberlin land." Once more he moved closer and as he did, she stepped back, bumping her legs against the large rock she'd been sitting on. She moved one step forward.

"Of course not, it's just that..." She swallowed then he watched as her breasts rose with the deep breath she inhaled.

"There is no need to be nervous. I thought I was your friend." At this moment he was a man well pleased, her expressive blue green eyes lending good reason for the quick impression. He stepped closer and it seemed with each step he took she stepped back then she turned away from the rock.

"I'm not," she moistened her lips before sucking the bottom one into her mouth. "Nervous."

Liar. Her lips were moist now, ready to be tasted. He grinned at the notion. "I watched you fly by on your horse. You were a bit reckless. I assume you don't ride that way every day." He needed to put an immediate halt on all her careless behavior.

Now and with little effort on his part, her back was against a tree and there was nowhere for her to go. "I ride that way when the mood hits." She closed her eyes for a few seconds, her breaths tiny and ragged. "Flynt doesn't care so I do whatever I please."

Now he stood in front of her, so close he could feel her tiny and very rapid breaths as they whispered across his face. He wanted to see if her heartbeat matched his.

That, the racing of her horse, would end with their marriage.

"You remember that day I kissed you?" Lord, but he hoped she remembered as clearly as he did.

She nodded her head, more strands of hair coming lose from the pins, spilling around her shoulders. He picked up a strand, holding it between his fingers. "Silken fire," he murmured, hoping some day the length would touch him with fire and she would respond to him with passion.

"I don't ken what you are talking about." Slowly, and unbeknownst to her provocatively, she swept her tongue across her mouth, her eyes shining with raw hunger that someday he meant to unleash.

"Chase, catch then kiss, that is what I did that evening and if I recall, you wanted my lips to caress yours just as much as I did. Would you like that today?"

Once more she moistened her lips, gazing at his mouth and he had the most disconcerting feeling she knew what she was about then suddenly she looked away, breathing thinly again, her breast rising and falling.

"You did chase me when I ran from the room." She agreed with him.

"And you wanted me to catch you." His grin, he was sure, reached from ear to ear. "I ken the fact as do you."

"I would never admit to such a thing. I ran because I wanted to get away." Her body quivered slightly and he hoped the trembling was the thirst for his kiss rising within her slight frame.

"Whether you admit to it or not, the fact remains I caught you. Just as I've caught you now. You do recall what comes next."

"Don't ken why you say that," she murmured. Once more, her tiny pink tongue swept across her lips. "I've no idea what you are talking about."

"If I'm not interpreting all the signs wrong, you're wanting me to kiss you again, just as you did that night." He bracketed her head between his hands, smiling, waiting for her to acknowledge the truth of her feelings. His mouth was close, her erratic breathing as well as the fluttering pulse and the base of her neck told him all he needed to know.

"You would be wrong." Her breasts rose and fell again then again with the blatant lie.

"Sweet little liar, but I will not kiss a lass who says no." With his thumbs he created tiny circles on her neck. "Do you want to say yes or no to me? Don't think too long as the opportunity to kiss me could pass."

She closed her eyes, her breath quivering as she waited. Then finally, "Yes, please." She opened her eyes then, her gaze focused on his mouth then her question shook him to his core. "Are they as soft as I remember?"

She unmanned him with those words. Soft?

This was what he sought, her compliance and willingness to kiss him, but he meant to prolong this as long as he was physically able. His voice shook now with his need, "Please what? You must say the words if you want that kiss and Daryl, I don't think there is any part of me that is soft."

"Your lips are," she said steadfastly, trying to make her point. "I wouldn't say so if it wasn't true."

He bent close to her ear, shaking off her comment. "Say the words, lass. Tell me how much you hunger, no yearn for my kiss." Next to him he felt the slight shuddering of her body, her breasts now pushed against his chest, there rounded firmness enticing him to take more than he intended today.

"What?" she looked startled, confused yet she still focused on his mouth.

He felt her fingertip on his lips. "Ach, lass, you cannot tease a man this way. It is not well done of you."

"They are soft and wet, just like I remember."

He groaned, the gist of her words going straight to his groin yet still waiting for her to say the words that would allow him to kiss her. "Chase, catch, now I'm still waiting for the last part. Tell me you want me to kiss you or we will be like this forever."

"Please," she sighed, his lips nearly touching hers. He felt her breath and nearly kissed her.

"Please what?" he continued knowing she wanted but seemed afraid to give permission. "Why do you hesitate so? What is it you are afraid of?"

"I cannot say." Her hands ran through his beard. "Your beard is soft too. I like the way it feels on my hands."

He groaned. He was sure she was remembering another time when she granted him more than a kiss. He'd been hell bent to teach her a much needed lesson and had gone too far.

"You must," he said, wishing he had not started this game. He knew she wanted the kiss, the caress of his mouth against hers.

"Donal, I do want you to kiss me more than anything."

He heard enough, his mouth fashioned itself across hers. He forgot everything but the sensations the kiss evoked within him. The tiny sounds undulating from her told him she enjoyed the kiss even while her fingers sifted nearly frantic through his short beard and hair. He kissed her again and again, his tongue sweeping across her mouth. He needed to find a way inside her.

He pulled away, slowly, one by one withdrawing all the pins from her hair until it's massive unruly length curled around her shoulders and down her long slender back. He ran his finger through the strands. She was so beautiful he could barely inhale a breath. "Open for me, open your mouth and let me inside."

Staring at him again, ignoring his words, "Your lips are soft and so is your beard. You didn't have a beard two years ago."

"Or the last time I kissed you and held you in my arms." He meant to remind her of other intimacies they could share if she was willing and would agree to be his wife.

She inhaled a sharp gasp, her eyes widening with the

comprehension of that day and what she allowed him. "That is not well done of you. In any case, there are parts of you that are soft. Even if you are unwilling to admit to the fact." Her words whispered from her lips.

So affected by her sweet words, he could barely contain the passion and hunger warming his body. He needed more from her, "Part you lips, lass. I need to feel the warmth and taste the sweetness only you can offer. I need to be inside you in more ways than one, but I'll settle for this right now."

"You didn't do that last time." She sounded confused but when he set his lips on her, she parted for him.

And before he took advantage he whispered, "You were too young and I really had no business kissing you. The time after that..." He didn't finish simply because he didn't wish to remind her of the events at the beach house. If he did, she might run from him.

"But you did."

"So true." He was inside her now, touching her teasing and exploring every sweet part of her. This was a heaven made in hell to provoke him and tempt him to toss her skirts right where they stood.

When she responded with a passion and hunger as primal as his own, he knew waiting for her had been right and positive. They would do well together as man and wife. Together they would share passion and sensual delights. He would give her whatever leeway she desired, and he would pamper her even let her run the bakery if that was what she still wanted. Still he needed to hold back. This was uncharted territory for her.

It seemed he could not help himself. His hands cupped her breasts. The tips hardened beneath his caress. Her head fell back, instinctively giving him more access to her body. She was untried, inexperienced yet it seemed she knew what to do.

"Should you be touching me there?"

Surprised, he smiled at her, "Should you be allowing it?"

He didn't wait for an answer, understanding he needed to claim her. She was a prize men would covet, and it might be some time before she would agree to a marriage or Flynt would agree for that matter.

He partially unbuttoned the shirt she wore so he would have access to her neck and perhaps steal a look at the valley between her breasts. Sucking and licking, teasing with his teeth, he slowly put a mark at the base of her throat. It was his claim to her and he decided he would make sure it remained until he could put a ring on her finger making their path together official.

Pressed against her now, his sex was hard and throbbing against her belly. Never before had he stopped when his rod felt as if it might burst. Everything with this woman was a first. He wanted her to feel him. If he guided her hand to him, he wouldn't be able to stop.

Chase, catch, and kiss.

He drew away having accomplished that as well as a bit more. When she opened her eyes, they were glazed, stunned, simmering with the sexual pleasure he introduced her to.

"Is that all?" she asked, fumbling with a button on her shirt and to his delight managing to undo one more.

The soft curve of her unveiled breast called to him. Taken with a brief moment of chivalry, he buttoned her shirt. "You need to keep your garments closed all the way to the top."

The shimmer in her eyes changed to fire and he was sure it was anger, her tiny hands fisted as her sides, "I will button and unbutton my clothes the way I want them, when I want."

Stepping back, his arms crossed in front of him, "Very well, what is it you want? Unbuttoned or buttoned?"

With his calculated words her eyes seemed to cross as she stiffened. "Unbuttoned of course."

"Then please allow me. How many, two three or all of them? You must tell me when to stop." He felt as if someone else took over his mind. He was a besotted fool for egging her on this way. If she continued in this vein, he'd be hard pressed to keep his promise to himself, but he would enjoy the view as long as she presented it to him.

~ * ~

She unbuttoned the three that he'd undone then the fourth she'd nervously fumbled with. "I won't allow a man to dictate to me. I will do as I please." She understood she was stubborn to a fault and this could have serious problems if she continued on this path. She wanted those kisses and more but he stopped, grinning at her.

"So," he began eyeing her open blouse with a soft chuckle that both enticed and irritated her, "If I tell you to do one thing then you will immediately do the opposite?"

"No, I will weigh the consequences of both choices." In this case she didn't, she just reacted to him. Her head was muddled. She had dust for brains.

"Ah, I see what you're about, good thing I'm a gentleman. The result of your actions just now could have me tossing your skirts and coming inside you with my sex not just my tongue, although my tongue would be nice too. I would like to taste you. Is that a consequence you've considered? I suppose it would also be an invitation to any man you might run across."

She pursed her lips together, her gaze focusing on his mouth and the irritating grin. She was thinking about what he said and not understanding most of it except the part about him coming inside her since she liked what he did with his tongue, what he did at the beach house as well. Her expectations wouldn't go any farther than that, "I might like you tasting me. You, not any man, she amended, smiling at his lips, "tossing my skirts. You did something like that before and..."

His scowl and the deep breath he inhaled led to him saying, "Do you have any idea what you just suggested?"

"No, not really. Maybe you could explain." What she did know was that she felt things in certain parts of her she'd only felt twice before. Those sensations were at his hand. Also, she remembered, Hope, one of her friends, had tried to explain things to her but she still didn't understand all of it, all Hope tried to tell her. Most of what Hope said came from the women she'd known in the Turkish harem that Hope's mother had been taken to when she was captured.

"I'd rather show you." He moved closer to her, his hands clenching and unclenching at his sides. Yet the grim expression on his face told her he wasn't pleased. His silver blue eyes were drawn together. They looked like smoldering steel.

"But you won't because I'm too naïve and inexperienced to understand. I ken it but I was hoping you would be the man to change that circumstance." She wanted him to deny her words. More than ready to find out what having her skirts toss would be like with this man, she wanted to challenge him to the point where he would indeed show her. Being told as well as threatened about the things he was going to do was no longer enough.

"Not until we are wed." His words were gritted out in a husky voice she'd never heard from him before. "When the vows between us are said..."

"Well then," she paused, a fingertip pressed against her lips, "I will never have the experience of you inside me except of course your tongue. Is that what you want?" she tried to take a different route.

For a moment, he seemed puzzled. "Why is that? And of course I want more than my tongue inside you, but..."

"Because I'm never marrying. As I think I said before, I'm never marrying you or anyone else. If you want to have me, it will be only with me remaining in control of myself. You, or any man, will never own me. I'm not chattel to be bought and sold to the highest bidder."

"I've no intention of owning you or buying you. The last thing I would ever want to do is sell you. That notion is absurd. I will change your mind concerning marriage, but obviously not this afternoon." He extended his hand. "Come, it's getting late. I'll take you home."

She understood she was defensive, but she needed to make her point before time went on and he wouldn't believe her. "I can get home by myself. No need to waste your time on me."

"Of course you can. If I believed otherwise, I wouldn't have chased, caught and kissed you. A woman who cannot take care of herself, I wouldn't be interested in, if they could not find their own way home." He still extended his hand, expecting her to take hold. "Now, I would love to hold your hand in mine while we walk to our horses. If you don't want to then..." He seemed to be waiting for an answer.

She was too astounded by his words to think clearly. When he cleared his throat, his arm still outstretched and waiting for her to take his hand in hers, she accepted. His hand circling hers was big and warm. She felt overwhelmed as if he consumed her yet the feelings were good and right for her.

The feminine part of her was pleased.

In silence they walked to the horses. He gave her a boost up and she waited for him to mount, watching the play of his muscles as they stretched his shirt as well as his pants. Touching her lips with a fingertip then looking his way, she wondered if he felt the same as she did.

It seemed he read her mind, "Yes, the kiss was good for me too, so good I'd like to try again after I see you home. Would you like that? Another kiss? Perhaps in the stables or maybe in the kitchen, or we could take a glass of wine to the parlor and kiss on the sofa."

"I'd like that. Any place would be nice. Your lips are soft," she spoke slowly, watching him as he pulled up beside her. It was difficult to remove her gaze from his luxuriously soft moist lips as she recalled how they caressed her, but she would try.

It seemed he needed to change the subject though, "Would you like to race to that tree down the road. It's far enough to challenge your mare, but not so far my stallion would have the advantage of his great strength and size."

He was referring to himself comparing them in a way she didn't want to acknowledge. Yet a strange exhilaration filled her. She would race and win, showing him she was faster, more than equal despite his great size. Nodding, she nudged her horse forward, knowing she would need a fast start to even have a chance of beating his stallion in this short bout.

"Cheater."

His words were loud and as was his laughter. She bent over her mare, close to her neck as she urged her forward and faster. "Go fast. Don't let that brute beat us. You can do it." But she heard the pounding of the hooves behind her, closing the distance.

The tree passed her by just as Donal did. She didn't know if he staged the tie or if they really did finish dead even. In any case, she didn't care, pulling her horse to a slow walk.

"Did you plan that or was the race a tie?" she asked, smiling sweetly as she flirtatiously tilted her head to one side, understanding by the look in his eyes she would never know the truth.

"I beat you fair and square even after you started too soon." He laughed and the sound filled the air. "You had to cheat to even come close to a tie. If you did not start early, I would have passed you sooner."

"I like the way you laugh," she sighed softly, wondering if all men were so obtuse. "You won't tell me the truth and we both know you didn't win."

A cool evening breeze caressed her flushed skin. Donal challenged her. She liked the way the challenge felt. He baited and teased but still he never laughed at her or the conditions she was beginning to set for their relationship. It seemed to her he let every demand she made go by the wayside, giving her her way in everything. Then, she reminded herself, he was a man set in his manly ways. He'd never let her have her life as her own or tolerate her disobedience when the stakes were different. This was just a game to him. It was too bad, because he was exceptional to look at and his kisses left her mind reeling.

Lifting his manly and very broad shoulders he continued to say, "I'm a man, of course I won. It goes without saying." The sound of his warm chuckle sent a little thrill down her spine. His words were another challenge he was sending her way.

He captivated her, enchanted her and aroused her to such a degree she couldn't think straight. If he wanted, he could do anything, caress her anywhere and she would not say no to him.

What to do, because he understood the power he possessed.

"Men don't win everything just because they are a man. Women are just as smart or smarter than men. We are quick and strong, strong enough to give birth. Could a man do that?" She grinned, believing she held the best argument. He could not refute childbirth or deny a woman's strength in that matter.

"Perhaps some are as smart. I'll give that to you but as to decision-making, they are sorely lacking in said skill. If you recall, you were riding hell bent across the field, not a wise choice when there was no reason."

"Nothing untoward happened and it never has."

"Call it luck," he said as he arched one perfectly shaped eyebrow.

"Why?" She was shocked by his comment.

"Women usually think with their heart not with the logic that comes from rational decision making. You were lucky your horse did not step in a hole and throw you. Worse, your mare could have broken a leg and you would have been forced to put her down."

She chose to ignore the latter part of his words in favor of her strength. "And if they didn't, no woman would have more than one child except those like my sister Bliss who had twins." She would not let down her argument, knowing she was right.

"As long as the man gives his woman a choice. There are those who don't wait, holding their breath for the woman they are courting to give them permission to kiss them. And there are some who take that which is not freely given."

"Some men take. I ken it." Once again she was thinking about Donal and his strange behavior today. He did wait for permission. She longed for him to do so much more than kiss. While she had ideas, she just didn't know exactly how they would actually play out. So, she could not tell him what she wanted. When she used his words to say she would like him to do something wicked, he said no and that he would wait until they were wed.

"As to men giving birth," he paused as if searching for the right answer. "Maybe, maybe not. But that does not make a woman stronger."

"When you hear your wife's screams when your first child is born, then you will understand what I'm saying. When you watch her lose her food for the first few months, then you will ken how strong she is. There is so much more. I don't care to elaborate." She pointed, "Look, we are almost home. You have my permission to kiss me again."

"Are you truly ready for another kiss or do I need to chase and catch you first? There is something nostalgic about the chase as well as the kiss."

"I believe you've already caught me, at least for today. My body thrums with a need I don't' understand. I want things you plan to deny me unless we wed. It's not fair, you know."

"Tell me..."

She looked down for a moment unable to explain the sensations to him, didn't know what she should say and what she shouldn't. Then she was shaking her head, "I cannot." Embarrassment consumed her as heat rushed to her cheeks.

"Why?" He persisted, a silly grin on his face.

"Do you always pursue things so tenaciously? I cannot. That should be good enough for you."

He sighed deeply while his eyes narrowed suspiciously, "Sadly, it is not enough. Why can't you explain to me how you feel?"

She glared at him, understanding he would not let up until he had the answers from her he sought. "Because I don't have the words and because even if I did, it would embarrass me."

"I will help you with the words," he told her as he brought his horse closer to hers.

She nudged her horse forward, wishing the conversation into oblivion. Heading into the stables she dismounted, ignoring him the best she could. A stable lad approached but she waved him away, wishing to take care of her horse and hoping he would forget the conversation in the ensuing moments.

Before she could even give the horse water and food, he was leaning nonchalantly against a wall watching her with his hooded eyes, seeming to study and evaluate everything she did. When she looked at him, he smiled, a masculine all-knowing grin.

He didn't say a word, just waited, his expression unchanging while she brushed her horse. There was nothing more she could do, nothing to take up time. "You can go home now that you've seen me to mine."

"I would be remiss if I did not accompany you into the house. Perhaps your cook left food warming and we could share a meal. I do understand you've not invited me inside or to share food, but I would accept if you did."

"I'm sure there is food. What I'm not sure of is if I can eat anything." She knew she could not. Nothing would sit well. The butterflies in her stomach just would not settle.

"I assure you that you would be able to eat if you explained yourself. The omission is lying heavy on your breasts, rattling your nerves and making you irritable. Your stomach is now taking the brunt of all your confusing emotions. I like all sides of you though."

"Perhaps you would like something to drink," she murmured, latching the stall door and heading for the main house, still trying to ignore his presence so close to her.

"Only if you imbibe as well. A little alcohol would ease your mind and you would be able to divulge those feminine secrets that I would love to learn about. Wine will help you relax."

She didn't look back. Her pace quickened. She'd never been so embarrassed. Heat flooded her cheeks at just the thought of explaining anything feminine to him.

"I'd prefer brandy."

"Whatever you wish."

She could not walk fast enough to distance herself from him. His footsteps echoed behind her. He was allowing her escape for now. Well, she decided he commanded and would expect anything he wanted, but she didn't have to comply with his wishes. Wasn't it after all her wish to have the control of her body, mind and thoughts?

Inside the kitchen, she sat down at the table, letting him decide whatever it was he was trying to decide. She wasn't going to eat because she simply wasn't hungry. He poked around, finally finding the meal cook had left.

"Bangers and mash, perfect for a cold spring evening, don't you think?" He dished up two plates. "Since you didn't send me packing. I assume you would like to eat with me. Or is it the next kiss that has you in anticipation unwilling to send me away?"

He poured glasses of wine instead of searching for the brandy before setting the bottle on the table.

"I don't want to explain anything to you."

"Eat up." He waved his fork in the air a manly grin stretching across his face. "You will need your strength for the good night kiss I've planned." Then he paused again, "If you be tellin' me yes when I ask." He was enjoying every moment.

"You no longer want me to explain?" she felt a moment of relief.

"I didn't say that now did I? I will have my explanation before I leave tonight." He sat back, washing his food down with his glass of wine then pouring another and topping off hers. "A man my size has big needs. Eventually you will learn that and in time you will fill mine just as I will take care of yours."

"I don't think so." Slowly, she sipped her wine, gazing at him over the rim of her glass. Automatically her gaze slipped to his lips as she recalled how soft and warm they were. She couldn't stop the tiny mew of pleasure that sighed softly from her, nor could she hold back the manly grin on his lips as he realized she was thinking about that kiss and the ones to come.

"We shall see." He lounged in his chair, tilting it back so it was settled on just two of its legs. "Should we continue this conversation in the parlor, perhaps a more fitting place for two adults to have intimate discussions about feminine things as well as another kiss."

"I'm quite happy here." She wanted to put off said discussion, hoping the ensuing darkness would prompt his departure.

"Your very feminine ploy is obvious and it won't work tonight. If I have to stay all night, I will hear you out and teach you that you don't need to feel embarrassment with me. You can say anything you want. I'll never judge. You will learn that you can talk about feminine conditions and I will listen with grave interest." His words were softly spoken but to Daryl very believable.

"It's no ploy." She was adamant and meant to stand her ground.

"No kiss then." He challenged further. By the way, your sweetly tasting pink tongue moistening your lips tell me you are anticipating my mouth over yours. You want to be inside me. Am I right or wrong? Be honest now, lass, or I might never trust you again."

"Right, of course you are correct." She rose then and walked to the parlor. Give him what he wants and embarrass him, she wanted to say.

He followed her, so close behind her she was sure she felt his manly warmth penetrating through her clothing. She waved a hand in front of her in a feeble attempt to cool her body and not beg him for that kiss.

"Are you hot?" he asked.

She felt his breath on her neck where he pulled her hair back. "No, no, never that. It's just..." He turned her then and his lips and teeth caressed her throat, teasing and creating a wild havoc the same sensations he wanted her to explain, exploding inside her.

"Little liar, don't' you know you must always tell me the truth. Your face is flushed and it is your thoughts about me, us that cause the unusual brightening of your cheeks."

"I don't mean to lie, it's just that I can't think when you look at me that way. At times I'm not at all sure I even know my name. You do things to me. Don't you think you should leave?"

While he was studying her, she sat down in a wing chair, folding her hands in her lap to keep them from fumbling with her buttons. What she needed was to sit on them, but that would prompt another discussion she didn't want to have.

"Another glass of wine?" He filled hers before she could tell him yes or no, before she could even figure out if she wanted one.

"I..."

"I've left you tongue tied again? Did you want to unfasten another button? I didn't request for you to fasten them. At least I can't remember such a demand when I'm enjoying the lovely view you are giving me. Your breasts are quite beautiful. I believe they would fill my hands and I've large hands. Also, I believe you would like the way your breasts will feel when I hold them."

She looked down then and saw what he was seeing. Her gaze went to his, her eyes she knew were wide with surprise. Yet she didn't move to fasten them or cover herself. "I..."

"Again nothing or very little to say?" He chuckled softly and it was an easy laughter one that exuded confidence and male comfort.

Unlike herself he was at ease with this banter that had her scrambling for words her mind in a coil. She could not help but wonder at the lack of gray matter in her head. At the moment her brain must be filled with dust or cobwebs, perchance both.

When she looked up and noticed his silver blue eyes seem to darken, she couldn't help the words tumbling out. "You do things to me, things..." She inhaled long and deep searching her mind for the words and came back to the explanation she didn't want to give him in the first place. "Things I don't know how to explain."

"You have unfastened so many of the buttons I can almost see the dusky pink circles surrounding your nipples. I like it that you are not wearing a corset. Oh dear, but if I say that, will it mean every day in the future you will wear one of those horrible contraptions?" He paused, a fingertip to his chin. "I tell you honestly, you have to wear a corset. There is nothing more to it. Yes, a corset it is. They are so much fun to take off a lady, the right lady anyway."

She nearly laughed at his posturing and wondered if she was indeed the right lady. "I will don a corset when it pleases me. And you may have all the fun you wish to have taking it off, when it pleases me and not a moment before."

"Ah, lassie, feminine wiles. I'm surprised you are not tilting your head a bit sideways and demurely lowering your splendidly dark lashes. I so dearly love to render them useless. I will make sure the notion of unlacing your corset pleases you when it pleases me."

She stiffened, feeling the imaginary brunt of his hand against her face. He needed to go home as she was near total exhaustion, which was the reason why she could not stay a step ahead of this conversation.

"I would like that kiss now then you can leave." She turned prim and proper, needed a night of sleep so she could think clearly tomorrow not that she needed to because she probably wouldn't see him. The breath she inhaled was not enough as she choked on the sip of wine caught in her throat.

"I believe your words were, and I quote, 'My body thrums with a need I don't understand.' You still need to explain that to me so I can stop doing those things to you if that is what you desire. My manly sensibilities need to know the truth as I only mean to please you."

"You can't really expect me to say what I'm feeling. You're a man and you would never understand anything about a lady." She held her breath, praying for him to say she didn't need to expound but knowing he would never give in. He would either get what he wanted or he would stay."

"Ah, but I do want to know about feminine things only a lady knows. I'm always curious and eager to learn. How will I discover these truths if you don't enlighten me? One cannot expect to learn without a teacher."

"Can't I just have that kiss and say goodnight? We really don't know each other so well as to say the things I'm thinking. I know you don't really mean everything you are saying. Do you?"

"Every day we are going to know each other better. Now, perhaps I can help with this difficulty you are having. What part of your body thrums with need?" He folded his hands in front of him, appearing to be waiting patiently as one roguish brow arched skyward.

Her fingers went to the buttons on her shirt as she tried desperately to calm herself. For a moment she looked down then back to his eyes. "Parts, where I shouldn't talk to a man about. Lady parts. Things men aren't supposed to know about."

He smiled, "We've made progress. Now how do they thrum?"

She moistened her lips before looking to the sky for Devine intervention. "They pulse and I'm hot, swollen. I need to..." she looked at him afraid she might die from mortification. "I want you to touch me, I think, and perhaps wet. I dinna ken anything else, but I believe you can fix my problem or make it worse. I'm not too sure."

"Very good, you have earned your kiss. What you have told me is that your most beautiful feminine folds, the soft petals that will embrace me after we are wed," he paused, "once we are wed, are ready for me to come inside you. Do you want that? Do you wish for me to come inside you?"

He drew her onto his lap. Once again the kiss was long and sweet, so very deep that she was swept away on the magical enchantment he created. "Donal..." she sighed into his mouth.

"Are you hot and wet, ready for me?" he asked as one hand cupped her breast and the other her waist drawing her closer.

She nodded, her hips seeming to move of their own accord, desperately trying to get closer to him, begging him to explore and plunder her most private feminine parts. She arched her back as she seemed to lose what little control she had from the beginning. "Yes, will you give me relief?"

"Not until you become my bride." He kissed her again and again, his lips finding the mark he made earlier, enhancing so it would stay there until he had another chance to sip in that beautiful spot. His spot. "Your feminine folds are swollen and hot your body is slick with your cream. If you were not a virgin, I would delve inside your sheath, but you are and I want more than that from our relationship."

"Please." She wanted more than that too. "I will never be your bride," she whispered with no conviction, "So you can show me what it is I need. You can come inside me now. You can have me whatever way you want to have me, you can have it with me."

Abruptly, he pulled away, gazing at her, studying her. "Will you meet me tomorrow at noon by the waterfall? We can kiss again and perhaps I'll introduce you to another part of lovemaking then we can go into town together. I would once again like to see you safely to your home above the bakery, but if you'd rather go by yourself and have no one to talk to, I would not consider interfering in your peace and quiet. You would also risk the dangers of the road."

With that said, he set her on the couch. For a moment he stood by the door then with a nod he left.

Daryl leaned on the windowsill and watched him leave. Her knees were so weak she could barely stand. He left her confused, disoriented to be sure. If she wasn't mistaken, aroused significantly to be uncomfortable. Hope told her kisses would do that to a woman and that is why men kissed them. She touched her breast as he had. It was a light caress and all he did was hold them in his hands.

When she touched herself intimately, she was wet, slick with moisture just as he told her she would be. She wondered what it was he would do, how he would caress her to take away this strange ache. Hope told her things but not nearly enough. What he did at the beach house came to mind. She wanted him to do those things again.

Tomorrow she would tell him what she did.

~ * ~

The night before he left, Graham slept fitfully. He'd not wanted to tell his brother about the real and very threatening activities in the states and the talk that could set families against families. Leslie advised him against saying anything prematurely and told him he would look into the problem. He had emissaries he would send, but all that would take time. Leslie told him his brother Link would take care of everything.

No need to worry Donal.

"Well," he murmured. Then I'm on my way to the Highlands, his manor near Linlithgow. He had no idea what he would find there or if there would be a wife for him. He would just have to see what developed. The crumbling estate, he mused, rubbing his chin thoughtfully, didn't exactly sound like a place where one could make a home and raise children, but he was going to try.

Graham Chamberlin pulled Draco to a halt just as the large drive to the Chamberlin manor began. He'd spent too long in Edinburgh. With luck on his side he made it to his ancestral estate, gifted to him by his grandmother, just before the first snows of winter would start. What he discovered in the city was that the life of leisure and balls he was invited to didn't suit and neither did any of the debutants he met there.

As he studied the lane and the row of trees leading to the front steps, he noticed three different heads poking out from three trees along with spindly arms and legs waving at him. He laughed outright, remembering days long past. Times when he and Donal played in the same trees, usually not in the dead of winter though.

After watching for a few minutes, he nudged Draco forward, keeping his attention on the lads and wondering just how old the boys were and who they belonged to. Clearly, they appeared to be at home in his trees. He pulled up beneath the first trees.

"Come down, lad. All of you present yourselves. Front and center," he called out in his sternest voice, hoping they would obey but not having any illusions.

They seemed to take his order to heart, all three dropping to the ground in almost perfect unison. Urchins to be sure landed sure-footed on the grass beside the lane. They all needed to be scrubbed from head to toe, possibly twice but they would clean up well. He needed to laugh but didn't want the laughter to come at their expense.

The threesome lined up in front of him, straight faced and stiff as boards.

The tallest and he assumed the oldest of the trio spoke. "We were told to watch out for you and welcome you home. Heard you were coming just last month." He inhaled a deep breath, obviously meaning to say more but was interrupted.

"No one told us we'd have to be here on the lane for two weeks. Did you know it's cold out here?"

"I was never informed I had a deadline." Graham's laughter was unchecked this time.

"Well, someone should have done just that or you could have sent a message." The tallest said indignantly. "Not like it's summer."

He'd just been properly chastised by the boy and meant to proceed with further introductions lest they think it okay to reprimand an elder. "Do you have names? I'm Graham Chamberlin." He waited for acknowledgement and perhaps some information if they were agreeable.

"I'm Dodge," the tallest said as he cleared his throat. "Been called that for a long time now. Don't have a last name, far as I know. None of us do."

Graham reckoned he must be nearing nine or ten years. He directed his attention to the next in line.

"I'm Ollie." The lad nodded, his hair falling in front of his face before he looked up and pushed it away with his hands. It was hard to tell Ollie's age, but he was pretty sure the boy was younger than Dodge, perhaps eight or nine.

"And you?" This lad was small and seemed to need at least three good meals in his belly. The others must have helped into the tree because he wasn't tall enough to reach the lowest limbs.

"Midget," he grinned, "Please to meet you, sir. We're supposed to make sure you have everything you need and show you to the house."

"Who sent you?" From what Graham heard about the estate, he didn't think anyone here would care if he was greeted or not.

The boys looked at each other, sharing glances several times before they seemed to come to a silent agreement.

"Ria sent us."

Graham found himself nodding his head and rolling all the names around in the cobwebs that made up his brains right now, and could not come up with one person on his list of employees who was named Ria.

He dismounted, intending to walk with the boys to the stables and discover a little bit more about their truths and how much more they would be willing to tell him. "Who is Ria?"

As he walked past them, he wondered if they intended to stay on the lane. Looking over his shoulder, Ollie was drawing circles in the dirt and Dodge, was tugging on Midget's hand. Once again, seeming to reach some form of silent agreement all three started walking.

"Ria's no concern of yours," Dodge said, his voice gruff and taking on a prickly edge. "We protect her so you don't have to worry about her or go near her."

Protect her? Bloody hell who or why would she need protection from. For a moment he thought to ask them for more information. By the slant of their lips he didn't think any more material about this mysterious Ria would be forthcoming. Instead, he decided to let them lead the way to the stables and give them time to become accustomed to him. Clearly, they had trust issues.

A few minutes later, Graham stopped in front of the stable doors. "Do you know how to take care of a horse? Draco needs a brushing down then food and water. Any of you want to do that?"

"Don't know nothing about horses," Dodge said, looking at him as he had mush for brains. "Don't know how to ride."

"I'm afraid of the huge beasts," Ollie said, once again his gaze directed to the ground below and what he was doing with his foot.

"I'm not," Midget volunteered. "Don't think I'm big enough to brush him."

"Then perhaps at least one of you should learn. What do the three of you do around the house besides wallow in the dirt?" The words were uttered harsher than he'd intended but nonetheless he meant what he said. Everyone would have to do something in his household if they expected to be fed and clothed.

Once again Dodge, the apparent spokesperson for the trio, said, "I'd like to learn how to take care of your horse. It's the only one in the stable now but don't have the time. There are a few more out to pasture. Have to protect Ria and right now she could be in trouble. We've been away too long watching for you." His words were said defensively and to make a point of telling him he was at fault if anything happened to the mystery lady.

The boys looked at each other for a few seconds. Once again it seemed the silent conversation between them was understood. They took off at a run, and Graham watched them speed around the back of the house where the servant's staircase would be found emptying into the scullery.

If there were no horses in the stable, would it figure there was no stable boy? Graham led his horse around the house, resigned to the care of Draco. Entering the outbuilding he searched for anyone who could help him.

"What can I do?" A man strode from a room at the far end of the building.

"Draco needs to be brushed down then fed and given water. Is that your job?" Graham asked, handing the reins over to the man, impatient now to discover what was going on in the main house and establish himself as the owner. Apparently, there were things that needed tending.

"I'll take care of anything, sir. Nice to have you back in residence, sir. You staying this time?" the man asked.

Graham stared hard, his eyes narrowing. "Shamus, is that you?" He held out his hand in greeting. As lads Shamus played with him as well as his brother Donal.

"It is and you're a sight for sore eyes, I tell you. It's about time someone arrived here to right the wrongs going on in this place."

Graham clapped his old friend on the back, thinking he might have to take a few minutes more to find out a few things. "Got some questions if you're up to answering them."

Shamus looked over his shoulder as he rid Draco of his saddle and blanket. He took a few seconds to start brushing the stallion. "What do you want to know?"

Graham positioned himself against the stall, crossing his arms in front of him. "Let's start with the lads. Who are they and why are they here?"

Shamus grinned as he stroked the horse several times. "The lads, so you met them. Not surprised that Ria sent them to greet you. What did they tell you?"

"Not much, just that their job is to protect this woman, Ria." He waited then, studying the man.

Shamus hauled out a bucket of water and once Draco had his fill gave him his food.

"Dodge do the talking?" Shamus laughed.

Graham nodded, his brows drawing together as he waited impatiently for Shamus to be a bit more forthcoming.

"He's the oldest and if you were looking closely without assuming anything, Ollie is a little girl and Midget, of course, is the youngest. They came with Ria one day about a week ago and they've stayed, although Ria keeps herself scarce with good reason. Not really sure why they stayed, but the house is shelter for them."

"Where did they come from?"

"If Dodge can be trusted the worst streets in Edinburgh. Had to do things, if you get my drift, just to eat. I'm surprised they let on that Ria is a woman."

"I'm beginning to understand a few things. Why does Ria have reason to keep herself scarce?" He didn't like the direction of his thoughts, although there were a myriad of reasons why the lady might not want to be found. A week ago, he mulled that over in his head. Dodge had said a month. Obviously he lied.

"Around these parts the main reason is well known and I'd be hopin' that your first order of business would be to get rid of Leod, your manager of the estate. Don't recall his last name, whether or not I was ever told I can't be remembering. Think the lady is hiding from something that happened to her in the city, but that's just my gut telling me things. There's no evidence I could be right or wrong."

"And why would I want to get rid of this man?" He didn't like the fact the questioning and answers began with Ria and ended with Leod. Again, his mind travelled in a direction Graham didn't appreciate nor would he allow.

"He's turned Granville Manor into a whorehouse. Pretty simple. Don't think it's what you would want for your home. Now, is there anything else I can do for you?"

"Answer more questions when I have them."

"Whatever you like."

"Millie still here?" he asked as he pushed away from his position, meaning to see for himself at the main house.

"Only because she keeps praying either you or Donal will show up and set this mess to rights. Suppose her prayers have been answered."

"Suppose they have." Determined, Graham strode to the manor, walking up the broad front porch steps. When he stepped inside, a man stumbled drunkenly down the stairway from above. His pants were unfastened and his shirt hung loosely from his shoulders.

This must be the man Shamus was alluding to a few minutes before. He spread his legs, his hand at his side. "Who are you?"

"I believe the better question is who are you. I'm the owner and didn't realize anyone was living here. The home, I was told, is empty."

"Leod is the name. I took up residency here when it seemed no one was going to claim the land and the crumbling home. Didn't ken why it should go to waste. So many in these parts are homeless."

"I see, well, you'll have to move out."

"How do I know you're tellin' the truth and you are who you say you are?" He stumbled a bit then hanging on to the back of the chair, the man stared at him, his eyes narrowing in seeming concentration.

"You don't, except for my word as a Chamberlin. Graham couldn't imagine anyone living here unless they were desperate. "You haven't seen fit to make improvements?"

The man shrugged, his body seeming to relax. "No funds. If you'd sent money, I would have done something."

"Most likely drink it away," Graham mumbled.

A woman ran down the steps naked but holding a dress in front of her.

"You use my home as a whore house?" Anger began to simmer inside as he perused the rapid flight as well as the woman's backside.

"She wanted it. I was just obliging her wishes." The man's grin was nearly toothless, and what Graham could see of teeth they were yellowed and brown.

"That's why she was naked and racing away. Get out." With a shaking hand, he pointed to the door.

"My things..." the man started up the steps.

"I'll have them put on the front lawn. You can have them picked up when you please." Arms crossed in front of him, both impatient and angry, he waited for the man to leave.

When Leod finally exited the house, he let a long sigh of relief from his lungs. Striding through his new home, he examined every part of it, every nook and cranny. He was just about finished on the third and last floor when he noticed a movement, a tiny shadow push back against the wall and the softest whimper.

He reached the spot in two quick strides then hunkering down, he peered behind a lose wallboard. What he saw surprised him. Two huge blue eyes peered at him from behind a set of knees drawn to her chest.

"Who are you?"

She pushed back farther. From beneath her ragged skirts two sets of dirty, bare toes caught his attention. She pushed grimy and disheveled hair from her face, but the terror he saw in her eyes lingered.

"Cat got your tongue? He almost laughed but held it not believing for a second she was seeing anything humorous in this situation.

She was shaking her head, clearly terrified of him. In all his life he couldn't recall any woman every being frightened let alone terrified when he was present. His thoughts travelled back to the man.

"Did Leod hurt you?" He would have the man tarred and feathered if he hurt this tiny delicate woman.

She was shaking her head no.

"Good then. Come on out and tell me your name." He held out a hand to her.

She pushed back farther.

"I promise I won't hurt you," he paused, realizing he wasn't getting anywhere with her. "At least tell me your name."

"Ria."

"That's a fine name, Ria. Now tell me why you are hiding here on the third floor?"

"Leod." Tears slipped from her eyes.

"Blessed hell," he muttered. One look at the man and he knew trouble surrounded him. "You told me he didn't hurt you."

"Aye, but he wanted to rape me."

Other Books by Christine Young
Available at Rogue Phoenix Press

My Sweet Broc
Bad Boys Book One

He's a bad bad boy...

Broc Wallace is a fun-loving rake who never thought any beautiful woman could melt his heart. He lives life in the present enjoying the camaraderie of his friends and the pleasures of his mistress. When Bliss races into his life, he is ill prepared to deal with her secrets or give up the tenor of his life. When the truth is revealed, he finds himself unable to forgive and forget the betrayal.

...but she's sweet for him

Bliss MacTavish knows she's playing with fire when she refuses to tell this bad boy her name. He tempts her with sweet whispers of seduction knowing her innocent nature will be unable to refuse all he yearns to give her. Deciding to follow her heart, she finds the repercussions more than she bargains for when she gives herself to this bad boy.

Crazy for Cam
Bad Boys Book Two

He's a bad bad boy...

Lord Cam MacEwen, Viscount of Rosehill, tries his best to be proper and court the lady of his dreams in the acceptable way. The feat proves impossible when the lady in question uses every means at her disposal to tempt him. He fights his jealousy for another man as well as the need to make her his own, finally giving in to her irresistible passion.

...but she's crazy for him.

Chelsea MacTavish wants the bad boy she fell in love with and kissed just before her eighteenth birthday. With feminine wiles and irresistible allure, the sensuous lady plans to best Cam at his game of hearts and make him forget his need to court her properly.

Foolish for Piper

The pickpocket...

Piper has spent her life surviving the streets of St. Giles Parish in London, a den of iniquity and crime. Masquerading as a boy she escapes the whorehouses the young girls are sent to as they come of age. The day she encounters Brett MacLachlan begins the same as every other one. When she picks his pocket, she has no idea her life is going to change irreversibly.

...and the mark

Handsome aristocrat Brett MacLachlan has come to London for his amusement only to find his world turned upside down by a thief and her dog. From the moment he spots her, Brett knows there is something intrinsically wrong. In his arms, Piper discovers passion and joy. Yet secrets of her past haunt her, and a scar will tell the true tale as well as her identity.

Taylor's Destiny

She traveled to another time and place to change destiny...

Enjoying a day of sailing, Taylor Maxwell never expected after a suffering a concussion she would wake up in another century. A resilient independent woman in the twenty-first century, the blond beauty is ill prepared for life in the 1800s. Her first sight of the naval captain who rescues her makes her heart stop, giving her hope for her future.

His life is transformed by a woman who appears from nowhere...

Born to a life of ease, Reid Stewart defies the dictates of those born to aristocracy and chooses a life of adventure in the navy and as a spy for the crown. When he discovers a nearly naked woman on the bow of small sailing ship, his heart warms. His love for Taylor and his need to protect her from a man who pursues her might cost him his life as well as hers.

Caitlin's Duke

She played a fiddle in an Irish pub....

Caitlin O'Shea Is the most beautiful woman Roc Leighton has ever seen. With her blue violet eyes and long black hair she captivates him. In turn he mesmerizes Caitlin. Caught in the power of his gaze as he watches her, she is wise enough to know he desires her but will never give his heart to her. Caitlin has vowed to never be any man's mistress.

And fell in love with an English Lord...

Roc knows the first time he watches her play the fiddle and dance around the pub, she will be his next mistress. Despite her protest, he will find a way to convince her that her place is with him. While Caitlin's determination to keep her vows, fate takes a cruel turn and she is forced to seek refuge with Roc.

Catching Meara
Book One in the McKenna Clan Series

Meara Thorton was a feisty, world-class computer hacker—cornered by the FBI and shockingly given the chance to be their newly acquired technical analyst. Brilliant and intuitive, yet aching with the loss of everyone she has cared about, her restless heart led her to discover a love she fought and a world she didn't know could possibly exist.

Sweet Sexy Sadie
Book Two in the McKenna Clan Series

From the first time Sadie's eyes met those of Brody McKenna in the hot Sierra Madre Mountains, theirs was a potent attraction—not gentle, slow, and easy, but hot, hard, and all-consuming. The daughter of a dysfunctional family, Sadie had dreams no man could wrench from her with hot sex and an all-consuming passion. She'd challenge this alpha male with all the strength she possessed. But her red hair, fiery temperament, and indomitable spirit obsessed Brody...and he knew he had to find a way to show her he was more than he appeared and convince her to make a life with him.

Sweet Misbehavin'
Book Three in the McKenna Clan Series

Cast adrift after fleeing the home of Jokul, the ice demon, Atantsi, a firestarter, grew to womanhood as she moved through time to keep the demon from finding her. Though stubborn and courageous, she was ill prepared to use powers she had not been taught. Her first sight of the intoxicating Carr McKenna left her breathless, and her second encounter gave her hope for a future she never thought she had.

A playboy, a second son and a shifter, a man who thought his life would be carefree, Carr McKenna was shocked to discover the woman he'd paid as an escort is a firestarter who is running for her life. He is the leader of all the McKennas around the world and that he has multiple powers. His passion for Margo and the need to defend her might cost him his life as well as hers.

Sweet Talkin' Sugar
Book Four in the McKenna Clan Series

Lyonesse McKenna, was dreaming or was she? From the instant Lyn saw Deacon McClain across a black jack table in a crowed Las Vegas casino the unmistakable attraction sent Lyn's senses flying into overdrive. Her family of shapeshifters believed in soul mates. She'd always been skeptical yet she couldn't help but question the way her heart sped when he looked at her.

When Deacon appeared in Las Vegas he knew his first job was to save Lyn from a Sea Demon, but the next order of business was to convince her he would someday mean more to her than she'd ever expected. But her stubborn nature and unbendable spirit consumed Deacon...and he had to chase away all the demons real and imagined in order to win her heart.

Sweet Surrender
Book Five in the McKenna Clan Series

Ripped from her family at the top of Infinity Cliff, Kimi McKenna finds herself thrust somewhere into the future. Dark elements threaten to destroy the earth unless Kimi can work together with the white witch to stop the destruction. Confused by her mate's role in the conspiracy, she refuses to acknowledge the connection. But amidst raging fire and attacks on the people she is coming to hold dear, she allows Maska O'keefe into her heart.

Maska O'keefe has loved the beautiful shapeshifter for years. Unable to save her life years ago, he vows to watch over her as he is given a second chance to convince her that even though he is a witch and not a shifter, they are indeed soul mates. Kimi's divided loyalties between her family and the cause she is now a part of will determine their relationship. Only the part she plays as the messiah can bring this to a conclusion in the final battle.

Dakota's Bride
The first book in the Lakota/Pinkerton Series

When Emma St. John received her brother's letter imploring her to escape her stepfather's vengeful scheme and to trust Dakota Barringer with her life, she was willing to chance it. But the handsome, brooding riverboat owner Emma found in Natchez a danger of another kind. For Emma soon found herself surrendering to an unrelenting desire.

Raised by the Sioux when his parents were killed, Dakota had been betrayed once before by a white woman. He wasn't about to trust another, especially one claiming that her stepfather, a powerful U.S. senator, had framed her as a murderess. But he couldn't let Emma's intoxicating effect on him. Now Dakota would risk his very life to protect the innocent beauty who had seduced him with her tender love.

My Angel
The second book in the Lakota/Pinkerton Series

A BEAUTY IN BUCKSKINS
When her father decided to send her to a finishing school back East, Angela Chamberlain refused to be confined to stuffy drawing rooms. Instead, the daring spitfire who could shoot like a man and ride like the wind longed for a life of adventure and romance—and she knew exactly who could give it to her. Devil Blackmoor was a hired gun with a dangerous reputation. But Angela was willing to go to the ends of the

earth to capture the handsome devil's heart.

A DEVIL IN DISGUISE

He'd come to America looking for excitement, but Devil Blackmoor got more than he bargained for when he encountered a beautiful rebel who answered his kisses with a wild innocence that touched his very soul. Yet standing between them were more obstacles than either ever dreamed. For Devil had strapped on a gun for the wrong man. And that made Angela his enemy. Now he'll have to choose between his duty and the woman he loves more than life.

The Locket
The third book in the Lakota/Pinkerton Series

The year is 1894. Seeking revenge for crimes against his family, Misha Petrovich follows a path that leads straight to Ariel Cameron's boarding house in Mist Harbor, Oregon. A family heirloom in Ariel's possession leads Misha to believe she is guilty. The locket has been handed down to the oldest girl in the Petrovich family for generations. Ariel is innocent of wrong doing, but her father is not. Misha is torn by his feelings for Ariel and his need for restitution against her father. Knowing that the relationship between them is fragile, Misha does everything in his power to protect Ariel's father. His efforts are to no avail when her father is shot. Ariel comes to realize Misha's steadfast courage and determination to protect her and her father despite what has happened to his family. Ariel's love and devotion heals Misha's heart.

The Talisman
The fourth book in the Lakota/Pinkerton Series

Running from a marriage that lasted one night, Dr. Moriah McKeown discovers the land she has settled on is coveted by determined and lawless men. Yet the proud young woman who once vowed never to abandon her home has second thoughts when her adopted children are threatened. Her only recourse is to enlist the aid of a dark, dangerous gun for hire.

Haunted by the past and a betrayal he will never forgive, Ian Civanovich uses his fast gun and his reckless courage to forget the faithlessness of a woman in his past. He will trust no female—nor will he rest until the threat hovering over Moriah McKeown is put to rest.

Forever His
The fifth book in the Lakota/Pinkerton Series

Struggling to come to terms with the part she played in Jacob St. John's death, Etta Barringer resigns from Pinkerton Agency and seeks peace and solace in a Rocky Mountain Cabin.
Jacob has vowed to discover the reason Etta has betrayed him, sold him out to his enemy and left him for dead.

Isolated in their cabin, they discover their love for each other and learn to trust. But the trust is shattered when Jacob learns she is married to his sworn enemy; the man who left him in the desert to die.

Allura's Secret
Twelve Dancing Princesses Book One

Allura McClellan is horrified by her father's decision to take out an ad in the Times awarding her to the man strong enough and smart enough to win her hand and uncover her secrets. She's an intelligent young woman who takes great delight in the freedom allotted to her by her father. She's well aware that marriage would effectively curtail the adventures she's shared with her sisters and cousins.

Hunter Gray is nothing like the other men who've arrived to vie for Allura's hand in marriage and everything that goes along with it. However, he is the first to refuse to concede defeat and pursue her despite her attempts to disguise her true appearance. It's her temperament that is of more concern to him than her looks. Hunter has worked all his life with the hope of someday owning his own land. Now that it looks like there's a very real possibility that everything he's ever wanted is within reach nothing is going to deter him – including Miss Allura's disagreeable disposition.

Amorica's Wager
Twelve Dancing Princesses Book Two

Amorica Hepburn was sent to London to find a husband. Finding a man was the last item on her agenda. With her two cousins, Amorica wagers she can dissuade her suitor before the others. Despite her efforts she discovers a chemistry that cannot be denied. Suddenly she is the arrogant man's wife, pledged to a marriage neither desire. But swept off to his ancestral home above the Dover cliffs and into his strong embrace, Amorica is soon possessed by a raging passion for the husband she had vowed to despise…

Damian Andrews couldn't afford to trust the emerald-eyed spitfire who happened upon his secret. Amorica's hatred of all men of his kind only inflames the war that rages between them. Still, he can not control the intense desire his stubborn bride inspires, or make her surrender to his will until he has conquered the headstrong beauty on the battlefield of love…

Ravyn's Marriage of Inconvenience
Twelve Dancing Princesses Book Three

A REGAL BEAUTY
When the duchess decides to wed her to a wastrel and a fop, Ravyn Grahm takes matters into her own hands and declares her engagement to another man. Instead of fessing up and telling her great aunt what she has done, she goes through with the pretense. Ariec Lakeland is the bastard son of

an earl and has a dangerous reputation. But Ravyn is willing to do most anything to keep the duchess from discovering the lie.

A DEVIL-MAY-CARE SMUGGLER
He'd bought land in America, looking to put down roots and end his life of adventure, but Ariec Lakeland got more than he bargained for when he encountered a beautiful heiress who made a promise she didn't want to keep. But the promise could not be undone and standing between them were more obstacles than either ever dreamed. Ariec had made plans to spend the rest of his life in America and that was at odds with Ravyn's plan of living in England and running her father's estate. Now, he'll have to choose between his dreams and the woman he loves more than life.

Christel's Sunrise
Twelve Dancing Princesses Book Four

He Made Her An Offer...

Life has thrown Christel McClellan some experiences that could have devastated a less determined woman. Beautiful, self-assured and fiercely independent, she is trying to forget the loss of her stillborn child. But is the child alive?

She Couldn't Deny...

Life is carefree for Ryder MacLaren who loves to see what is on the other side of the sunrise. Laird of Clan MacLaren, he is wealthy, handsome and happily unencumbered...until stunning Christel McClellan enters his life. When he hears her story, he believes the child she thought dead has been sold to a wealthy buyer.

Storm's Passion
Twelve Dancing Princesses Book Five

SHE MADE A PROPOSAL...

Life strikes Storm Graham a shattering blow when she learns her father has bartered her to a man she detests. Storm is beautiful, self–assured and fiercely independent, and refuses to be a pawn in her father's schemes, yet she can find no way out of this bargain made in hell. Going on the offensive she asks the wealthiest man on the eastern coast of England to marry her, never believing she might fall in love.

HE TRIED TO REFUSE...

For Hadden Johnston life has provided everything he ever wanted, including a sanctuary for homeless children. He is wealthy, handsome and happily unencumbered...until stunning Storm Graham marches into his life and proposes a marriage of convenience. Yet this type of marriage to a woman who inflames his senses is far from acceptable. If he's going to be tied down, he will move heaven and earth to have this woman warming his bed.

Gotta Have Fayth
Twelve Dancing Princesses Book Six

A regal beauty with raven hair and piercing blue eyes, Fayth Graham is unwilling to parade herself in front of the wealthy Lords of England during the season. Seeking a means to dissuade any man wishing to wed her, she seeks a way to ruin herself for marriage. When she unexpectedly meets a man with sparkling gray eyes and an infectious grin, she decides this is the man who will keep her from agreeing to obey.

He returned from six months at sea, looking for a few nights of pleasure with a willing lass, but Jarret Kinsley got more than he bargained for when he met a beautiful debutant who responded to his kisses with a wild innocence that touched his heart. Yet the obstacles looming between them might rip them apart. Both had vowed never to marry, so when consequences of their dalliances got in the way, Jarret would have to choose between the life he's always desired and the woman he loves more than life.

Ella's Pleasure
Twelve Dancing Princesses Book Seven

A WHISPER OF PLEASURE

Ella Hepburn was an auburn haired debutant from the harsh Scottish coastline—a wild innocent to be seduced and tamed. A spirited beauty, she captivated Drake Montgomerie's jaded heart—while succumbing to the smoldering desire she felt for her unyielding suitor.

A WHISPER OF DANGER

In Drake Montgomerie's glittering world of money and privilege, young Ella discovered passion and desire could overcome everything she'd been taught to resist—entangling Drake, the heir apparent, in a lethal coil of aristocratic family intrigue. But grave peril would only nurse the sparks of a love that knew no limits and a magnificent ecstasy that would not be denied.

Eveleen's Seduction
Twelve Dancing Princesses Book Eight

A WHISPER OF SEDUCTION

A brutal attack on Eveleen Hepburn's cherished island off the Scottish coastline leaves her shattered and bewildered. Learning a man she once trusted can kill as easily as he can breathe even though the deed saves her life, creates questions that need answers. An innocent beauty, she enchants Logan Maxwell's cynical heart—giving in to the raging passion she feels for her mysterious suitor.

A WHISPER OF INTRIGUE

In Logan's Maxwell's world of espionage and privilege, young Eveleen discovers truths about herself she never expected, and a need for passion and love can overcome all her fears if she learns to accept certain truths. She finds herself entangled in a lethal battle for land that was once owned by French nobility, taken from them during the revolution and sold to Maxwell. But grave peril would unleash the flames of love that simmers, creating a magical union that cannot be refuted.

Tavia's Deception
Twelve Dancing Princesses Book Nine

WHISPERS OF DECEPTION

When her father decides to send her to London for her season, Tavia Hepburn resolves to see the world instead. The raven haired beauty decides to disguise herself as a lad and find employment on a ship bound for Barcelona as a cabin boy. But she never bargains on finding passion and love to a red haired sea captain who rescues her from certain death.

WHISPERS OF MURDER

For James Macmurra, the world is black and white until he meets a young debutante, who turns his world upside down. He's unable to deny Tavia's intoxicating effect on him. In a match tense with obstacles, unwillingness to divulge secrets, and unforeseen peril, irresistible desire and passion grows into undeniable love. James would risk his life to shelter and protect the innocent debutante who seduces him with her sweet love.

Larena's Fascination
Twelve Dancing Princesses Book Ten

WHISPERS OF FASCINATION

Fiery, free spirited Larena Graham never wanted to marry a duke. She is thrilled to be in love with the fourth son of an aristocrat, Gavin Broon. But when it seems Gavin ignores her, she set her sights on politics and bettering human life. Unsuspecting intrigue and a plot against her, she continues her dangerous plans despite Gavin's wishes.

WHISPERS OF TRUST

Gavin has every intention of properly courting the beautiful Larena until he must leave the city in order to put his affairs in order. Returning to London, he finds the woman he means to make his own is embroiled in political protests that could lead to a prison ship. Larena must learn to trust the handsome Scotsman whose most pressing mission is to protect her and keep her from harm.

Tira's Education
Twelve Dancing Princesses Book Eleven

WHISPERS OF EDUCATION

Learning how to build ships is Tira Hepburn's only dream until she meets Jamie Lundin and her world is turned upside down. With her raven black hair and vivid green eyes, she tempts Jamie and pushes him to defy his vows. She never bargains on finding an irrevocable love and a passion to a man who cannot fulfill her dreams despite his burning desire for her.

WHISPERS OF A BARGAIN

Arrogant and self-assured Jamie is brought up short when Tira captures his heart. All his carefully made plans are put to the test when he decides to teach her the art of ship building if she will spend a week with him alone on his ship. He is unable to deny Tira's intoxicating effect on him. When Tira leaves him behind unwilling to live with him without the benefit of marriage, he races after her. Jamie will risk everything to shelter and protect the innocent debutante who seduces him with her sweet love.

Aidan's Love
Twelve Dancing Princesses Book Twelve
Whispers of Love

Aidan McLellan has loved since she first set eyes on him as a young girl. Spontaneous, wild and eager to grow up, Aidan haunts his waking thoughts day and night, insinuating herself into his life. With her fiery red hair and sparkling sapphire eyes, she seizes Blade's heart even while he tries to resist the innocent child until she becomes a woman.

Whispers of Courage

Blade has waited what seems a lifetime to claim the woman who captures his heart as a little girl. Claiming his inheritance before his younger brother takes what is rightfully his, Blade must convince Aidan of his sincerity after years of avoidance and wed her before his father dies so he can return home, securing his rightful place. Everything is put to the test when his life as well as Aidan's is threatened by the man who once called him brother.

Twelve Days to Love

When Archer Steele shows up at Calanthe Durand's failing plantation with an alligator over his shoulder, Cali thinks she's never seen a more handsome man. During the war she had to defend herself and her servants from both union and confederate soldiers. Independent and self-sufficient, she vows to never marry.

But Archer Steele has different ideas. The first time Archer sees Cali in town, he feels an instant attraction. He decides he will do everything and anything to convince the beautiful Miss Durand he is worthy of her love. During the weeks leading up to Christmas, he gives her twelve gifts in hopes she will fall in love with him. Yet they are faced with challenges they must overcome before Cali can commit to a marriage.

Door to Heaven

Jessica Lawrence is the stepdaughter of a woman born in the twentieth century transported back in time to the year 1868. An acclaimed suffragette, she raises Jessica to believe in the equality of women. Jess Law believes everything she was taught, and when the time is right she becomes a private investigator. Courageous and impetuous, Jess finds danger in her quest to save all women from white slavery. Her passionate mission results in a wedding to Roc Newman, a man she knows can steal her heart...

Roc can't trust the sapphire-eyed spitfire who invades his home in search of secret papers and knocks him flat with her karate moves. Jessica's refusal to obey his wishes serves to inflame the war between them. Still, he cannot control the intense desire his reluctant bride inspires, or make her surrender her independence, until he has conquered the headstrong beauty on the battlefield of love...

Rebel Heart

HER REBEL SPIRIT DEFIED HIS OUTSIDERS SOUL... She was velvet and silk, eyes the color of a summer storm and amber hair. Victoria DeMontville, because of a promise and a codicil to her father's will, was forced to marry one man to protect her from another. She hated Cameron Savage with a fierce passion. But to hold on to her genetic research and find a cure for the deadly Signe virus, she must pretend to love the enemy at her door, come with weapons of fire to melt her icy heart...

HIS OUTSIDERS TOUCH IGNITED RAGING PASSIONS...He wore a mask, disguised as the Phantom, a true legend come to life. Even as war and debate over new genetic research engulfed them all, he would find his greatest adversary in the beauty who'd branded him an outsider and barbarian, the woman he was born to possess, his soul mate.

Safari Moon

Solo St. John, a wildlife photographer, is preparing for a trip to Alaska. Suddenly, Solo finds women of all sorts invading his privacy, his home and his office, all cooing nonsense words and blatantly throwing themselves at him. Solo doesn't know why, and he has no idea how to rid himself of the persistent women. He finally decides to beg a favor of his best buddy Nyssa Harrington.

In love with Solo for the past ten years and knowing he doesn't return her feelings Nyssa doesn't want to talk to Solo. She knows if she accepts his phone call, she will not be able to resist the temptation to hope again.

Straight to Heaven

Running from demons, Alexandra McMurdie stumbles into Forbidden Ground where up is down and elements of nature are contested. Though a strong independent woman in the twenty-first century' she is unprepared for life in the 1800s. Her first site of the formidable James Lawrence makes her heart skip a beat, giving her cause to reconsider her desperate need to find a way home.
Born with a silver spoon, James' life was torn apart during the War Between the States. Moving west he vows to put the life he once knew in the past. When he discovers a half-frozen woman near Gold Hill, his heart begins to thaw. His love for Alexandra and his need to keep her from a man who has pursued her through time might cost him his life as well as hers.

A Valentine's Anthology

The Lending Library-a fantasy by Christie L. Kraemer

Faeries try to fit into the human world when the forest where they make their home is destroyed by a mysterious enemy.

Chasing Rainbows-a contemporary romance by Genene Valleau

An eccentric aunt, an inventive uncle, a mother who wears poodle skirts, and a brother who wears pearls provide a hilarious backdrop for the courtship of a young woman who yearns for a "normal" family.

The Gift-an historical romance by Christine Young

A man and a woman on opposite sides of the Civil War get a second chance at love after one final battle returns soldiers to their war-torn homes to rebuild their lives.

A St. Patrick's Day Tale

Christine Young, C. L. Kraemer, Genene Valleau

Tumble through time…

…to Ireland in 1817, when tensions are high between Protestants and Catholics and fae people guide the fate of villagers. A lovely Catholic lass stumbles upon the weakly ritual fisticuffing between Irish lads. She falls into the lap of a handsome young Protestant. Family ties, grudges, and two conniving faeries threaten their budding love. But the faeries outsmart themselves when they hijack a time machine that has mysteriously appeared in their forest and are whisked to…

…Eugene, Oregon in the 20th century, amid a property feud between the local faeries and night elves. The conniving faeries from Olde Ireland try to stir up more mischief. However, a warrior gnome convinces the magic folk to control their own destiny, and forces the intruding faeries to take refuge in the time machine again, spinning their way toward…

…A modern day castle in western Oregon. An eccentric inventor is determined to reclaim his wayward time machine and save his beloved wife from her latest misadventure. If only they can travel safely past the black hole…

a May Day Anthology

Christine Young, C. L. Kraemer, Rosemary Indra, Genene Valleau

Highland Miracle — Christine Young

HURTLED THROUGH TIME, Sean Michael Sterling, landed in the midst of a May Day celebration he didn't understand, assuming the role of Laird Sterling.
ILLIGITAMATE CHILD OF NOBILITY, Reagan Douglas searches for a way out of her half brother's house.

Defying the Odds — C.L. Kraemer

The night elves on the hill aren't happy without their magic. They concoct a plan to punish those who were involved in the act that rendered them almost human. Meanwhile, Uther, the rogue night elf, has returned to woo the Librarian to be his eternal mate.

Love in Bloom — Rosemary Indra

When childhood friends reunite it takes two fairies and a matchmaking daughter to help them admit their true love for each other.

No More Poodle Skirts — Genie Gabriel

After drifting for years in the innocent age of the 1950s, a woman struggles to join today's world by finding a career and a new love, with some help from her zany family.

Once Upon a Christmas Moon

Christine Young, C. L. Kraemer, Genene Valleau

TWELVE DAYS TO LOVE

When Archer Steele shows up at Calanthe Durand's failing plantation with an alligator over his shoulder, Cali thinks she's never seen a more handsome man. During the war she had to defend herself and her servants from both union and confederate soldiers. Independent and self-sufficient, she vows to never marry. But Archer Steele has different ideas. The first time Archer sees Cali in town, he feels an instant attraction. He decides he will do everything and anything to convince the beautiful Miss Durand he is worthy of her love. During the weeks leading up to Christmas, he gives her twelve gifts in hopes she will fall in love with him.

BOOTS AND BLADES

An ancient evil from the old country has arrived in the high desert of Oregon. Gnome children are vanishing then re-appearing, showing various stages of traumatization. Tiamoon, warrior gnome, will put her skills to use alongside Killian, a handsome warrior, also in need of a cause.

CHRISTMAS PAWSIBILITIES

With their world destroyed and their space ship malfunctioning, the dogizens of Planet Canid have little choice but to crash land on Earth. They face tortuous experiments at the hands of the Geeks in Green...or they can trust an eccentric inventor and his zany family to deliver the Canine Queen's puppies and help them celebrate new lives.

www.ingramcontent.com/pod-product-compliance
Lightning Source LLC
Chambersburg PA
CBHW061936170626
46813CB00006B/2416